FATAL LAST WORDS

Quintin Jardine

FATAL LAST WORDS

headline

Copyright © 2009 Portador Ltd

The right of Quintin Jardine to be identified as the Author
of the Work has been asserted by him in accordance with the
Copyright, Designs and Patents Act 1988.

First published in 2009 by
HEADLINE PUBLISHING GROUP

1

Cataloguing in Publication Data is available from the British Library

978 0 7553 2915 1 (Hardback)
978 0 7553 2916 8 (Trade paperback)

Typeset in Electra by Avon DataSet Ltd,
Bidford-on-Avon, Warwickshire

Printed in the UK by CPI Mackays, Chatham, ME5 8TD

Headline's policy is to use papers that are natural, renewable and
recyclable products and made from wood grown in sustainable forests.
The logging and manufacturing processes are expected to conform
to the environmental regulations of the country of origin.

HEADLINE PUBLISHING GROUP
An Hachette UK Company
338 Euston Road
London NW1 3BH

www.headline.co.uk
www.hachette.co.uk

This book is dedicated to my daughter Susie,
without whom the sun would not shine.

Acknowledgements

My heartfelt thanks go to

Andrew Smith, who helped me kill someone in my world, but who is dedicated to preserving lives in his.

Catherine Lockerbie, and her predecessor, Faith Liddell, who have brought their outstanding ability and their grace to the role of director of the Edinburgh International Book Festival, and have made it into the phenomenon that it is.

Mira Kolar Brown, for minding my language.

My colleagues in the craft, all of whom I respect and admire; no names taken in vain.

One

'Up with the bloody lark?' she murmured. 'I don't hear the little bastard among that lot. He's still sat on the nest, sensible bird that he is.'

She was on the move so early that the dawn chorus was still singing at full volume; robins, blackbirds, wrens, pigeons and even the occasional seagull, all doing their best to wake the elegant old grey city from its slumbers.

Not that Randall Mosley relied on nature for her morning call; like much of the developed world, she set the alarm on her mobile phone to haul her back to life. Back home in Murrayfield, Denzel would be making the most of her absence, grabbing an extra couple of hours' sleep before switching on his computer and starting work on his project.

The morning was bright and the sky was a very pale blue, promising one of the dry, warm days for which she and her staff had prayed during the second half of August, those seventeen days around which her world had become focused, in what was the first year of her new role. She pressed the button to lock her car. If she had taken the direct route into Charlotte Square, through her basement office at Number 5a, it would have meant cancelling and resetting the alarm system, so instead she headed out of the park, shielding her eyes against the low sun as she turned into St Colme Street, and until she could turn out of its glare into North Charlotte Street. She saw not a single moving vehicle as she walked, only those in the residents' bays, and the overnighters hoping to stay where they were for free throughout Sunday.

She was breathing heavily as she reached the top of the steep pavement alongside Number 1 Charlotte Square, and cursing the few spare kilos that made all the difference. Weight-watching had become a constant in her life, and it was made none the easier by the round of receptions and parties at which her attendance was an unspoken obligation. She liked to believe that she was a strong-willed woman, but she had discovered that her resistance was low when it came to the trays of canapés that seemed to pass constantly before her during the summer months. They had culminated in her own launch event, from which she and Denzel had escaped just after midnight . . . six and a half hours earlier . . . once the last trio of her journalist guests had headed off along Young Street, in the hope that the Oxford Bar would still be open.

The main entrance to Charlotte Square Gardens was still closed and under guard, but she used her key to open the small, squeaking gate in the north-east corner of the iron retaining fence. As she stepped inside, one of the night security staff, alerted by the sound, appeared from a small igloo-shaped tent; it served as the press pod during opening hours, and was pitched on the left of the wooden walkway on which she stood.

'Morning, Randy,' the man greeted her, with a Welsh lilt, as she approached him. He was clean-shaven, and his uniform was military sharp, but his spectacles failed to mask the dark circles under his eyes.

'Hi, Gwyn,' she replied, her accent flat and cosmopolitan. 'All quiet during the night?'

'Eventually,' he told her. 'Things never really settle down from the Saturday frenzy until about two in the morning, given all the pubs there are around here. We had no bother, though, unless you count a couple of drunks taking a piss through the railings on the far side of the site.'

Mosley frowned. 'I count them; the smell tends to linger, unless it rains. Mind you,' she conceded, 'I suppose I'd rather have a mild smell of urine than the quagmire that I'm told my predecessor had for the last couple of years.'

'So far so good then,' said the senior guard. 'Have you checked the long-range weather forecast?'

She smiled. 'Every day, Mr Richards, every single day. Currently they're promising warm and sunny for the first half of this week, with a good chance of it continuing through the month.'

'Pray to God,' he muttered.

The director of the Edinburgh International Book Festival did not believe in God, but she allowed herself a small compromise. 'Amen,' she muttered, as she moved on, towards the big rectangular module that served as her on-site office.

She knew that it would be empty; at that hour of the morning some of her people would be struggling into wakefulness, many would still be asleep, and one or two of the younger brigade might have just made it home from a night in the clubs. Still, she let herself in, moving methodically from desk to desk, checking that nobody had left without putting everything in place for the day to come. Everything was as it should have been; she knew that her fussiness was unnecessary, and that her morning ritual would upset her more senior staff had they known of it, but it was something she had to do if she was not to spend much of the day fretting about things that might go wrong.

When she had finished her round, she moved across to her own desk, took her laptop from her rucksack and pressed the 'on' button. When it had booted up, she logged on to the internet through the wireless network, and opened her mailbox. As usual it was stacked with incoming. She had banned the Festival staff from communicating with her by email, reminding them that the vocal method was still best, but that had only removed a small percentage of the total. Of the survivors, most came from authors, their publicists, their agents and, in a couple of cases, from the family members who managed their diaries. She worked her way through them as quickly as she could, forwarding the majority to the people who could deal with them best, until all she was left with were four, one from her chairman congratulating her on the success of the opening day and offering a far too belated apology for his absence from the Welcome Party, two others from people she felt were too important (or, in one case, who felt himself too important) to be delegated, and another that had caught her eye.

She opened the first and swore, yelling, 'Now he tells me!' loud enough to draw a quick glance from Gwyn Richards, as he passed by the window.

The message was from Micah Sodje, an African novelist who had won the previous year's Man Booker and who was rumoured to be a hot tip for the Nobel Prize, soon to be announced. He was her top attraction for the following Sunday and his event had sold out within hours. 'Dear Mrs Mosley,' it began inaccurately, ignoring her doctorate, 'I am afraid that I find that progress on my next work has been slower than anticipated, owing to the effect of my success last year. If I am to meet my delivery date and keep my editor happy, something has to go, and I fear that it has to be Edinburgh. Please accept my withdrawal, with regret.'

'Son-of-a-bitch!' she shouted, wondering whether she knew enough members of the Swedish Academy to turn the Nobel vote against the defaulting author. 'Now I've got three hundred and fifty tickets to be refunded and event sponsors to be smoothed! Who the hell does he think he is?'

Fuming, she searched through her contacts list until she found the address of Sodje's publicist, then forwarded the cancellation with no message other than a long black line of exclamation marks.

Controlling herself with an effort, she moved on to the next item.

The screen name *adma* was showing. It gave little away, but she knew whose it was, and that it was personal rather than business. Aileen de Marco was Scotland's First Minister, and a neighbour, as her official residence, Bute House, stood next door to the Book Festival's more modest office. Not long after she had taken office, she had invited the equally newly appointed director for coffee, to canvass her opinion on the way the arts had been handled by the administration of her own inglorious predecessor. Mosley had been struck by the politician's frankness, and de Marco by her guest's global knowledge and evident enthusiasm for her subject; the two women had become regular correspondents. She opened the message.

'Hi Randy' it began. 'Bob and I are finally holding that informal dinner party for four that I asked you about. You said you might manage an evening off next Thursday; 7:30 for 8, ambulances at midnight. We hope that you and Denzel will be able to join us. Nothing fancy on the table, nobody posh around it, just the four of us. Cheers, Aileen.'

Mosley's normally even temper was restored immediately. She had been anticipating the invitation since de Marco had mentioned it a few days before. She was looking forward also to meeting 'Bob', the First Minister's partner. Deputy Chief Constable Robert Skinner was something of a legend in Edinburgh. Aileen had never said much about him, but Mosley had heard stories of him from others; 'formidable' was the most cautious adjective that had been used to describe the man. The others had ranged from 'charismatic' to 'ruthless'. She had been told that the relationship had taken the city by surprise when whispers of it had begun to circulate, since Skinner's past had included several confrontations with politicians. But she had learned by her own experience that the First Minister was a one-off, and she suspected that he was also. She typed a one-word acceptance, 'Absolutely,' and sent it off into cyberspace, then moved on to the last remaining item in the mailbox.

5

She was puzzled by it, not least by its timing; the display on her screen showed that it had been received at the very start of that very day. But Ainsley Glover had been at the party to the bitter end; she had met him when he arrived, and had spoken to him later, just before he had been commandeered by that boozy Glasgow journalist, Ryan McCool, and she could not recall his carrying anything as conspicuous as a laptop bag. She pondered and eventually decided that his internet service provider was one of those that was guilty of delays in forwarding messages to recipients, but that left the unanswered, nagging question. Why should he have sent her an email, knowing that he would be seeing her at the reception?

Trust a crime writer, she told herself, to come up with a mystery; and trust Ainsley, in particular. He was one of those guys who, everyone assumed, saw himself as the main character in one of his own books, and he made no attempt to dissuade them of that notion; his sleuth was a rough-cut Glaswegian detective inspector called Walter Strachan, and Glover had a terrible habit of adopting an appropriate accent when reading from his work on public platforms, even though he had been born in Edinburgh and educated at Loretto School, among the privileged. Still, she frowned, murmuring, 'What the hell could this be?' as she clicked the 'Read' icon.

The message was as short as it was to the point. Three words: 'randy yurt dying'. Followed by a few more, informative, explanatory: 'Sent from my BlackBerry wireless device.' The mystery solved.

Mosley's mouth set in a tight line as she considered the message. She checked the sender address: *Allyg@wattiestrachan.com*. No mistake; it was him. She pushed back her chair, spun it and rose to her feet in a single flowing movement, then headed for the door. Gwyn Richards was standing a few yards away, on the walkway in front of the signing tent, in conversation with one of his night staff. She called to him, and waved him towards her as he looked round. He frowned at her peremptory summons, but headed in her direction.

'Do you have a key for the author tent on you?' she asked him.

He reached into his trouser pocket and produced a ring, attached by a cord to a loop on his belt. 'I've got all the bloody keys,' he replied. 'You know that.'

'Yes, of course. Sorry, Gwyn. I need you to open it.'

'What's the rush?' he grumbled. 'The caterers won't be here for an hour and a half yet.'

'I know, but I need to get in there now.'

'No worries. Come on.' He led the way past the office and round a corner to an area that was fenced off from the rest of the site, containing and giving privacy to a tented complex, centred on a large round tent, with smaller circles to the left, right and front. The director stood back as he unlocked the padlock that secured the double doors, then stepped past him as he threw them wide open.

The interior was neat and tidy: the people who staffed the hospitality centre at which Festival guests were greeted all knew that their last duty of each day was to leave the place set up for the following morning. The reception desk was clear, apart from the boxes that held complimentary tickets requested by participants, notepads, and several pens in a tin. At the further point of the central tent a glass-fronted drinks fridge stood, empty but for a couple of bottles, ready to be re-stocked for the day. The only relics of the day before were the inevitable curly sandwiches, and the last few plates and glasses, left for washing up.

'What is it?' the guard asked Mosley as she stared ahead of her.

'I don't know,' she murmured, letting him step past her and move beyond the desk, into the main area. She watched him as he peered around, first to his left, then to his right. Suddenly he seemed to freeze. His knees seemed to buckle slightly, but he recovered himself in an instant.

She moved alongside him, her gaze following his . . . and saw what had made him react. In the side pod, with the sign at its entrance that read 'Quiet area for event preparation', a man was sprawled on his back along a cushioned bench. A small splash of vomit lay on the floor beside him, and there was more on his shirt and on his suit. His head was pressed forward by a wooden support, chin digging into his chest, so that he seemed to be staring directly at them.

But Gwyn Richards had served in the first Gulf War, in the First Armoured Division during the uncompromising advance into Kuwait. He had seen the strange postures that death can contrive, and he knew full well that those milky eyes were seeing nothing. He stepped closer, and as he did came recognition. 'Is that who I . . .' he began.

'Yes,' said Randall Mosley, 'it is. It surely is.' She began to move forward as if to help, but the security chief put out a hand to restrain her.

'No point,' he told her. 'You'd better call the police.'

TWO

In common with most uniformed officers, if he had to work on Sundays, Sergeant Ian McCall preferred the early shift. OK, maybe it did curtail Saturday night, but he and his wife were no carousers, so that was a burden that could be borne. The upside was that the best part of the afternoon and all the evening was his; that meant he could catch the football on telly . . . if there was a game that took his fancy.

He was in Lothian Road when the call came in, in the passenger seat with his rookie partner at the wheel. 'Police attendance required at a sudden death at Charlotte Square Gardens.'

'Got it,' he radioed back to the communications centre. 'Sergeant McCall and PC Knight are in the area, will respond. We should be there in two minutes.' He paused. 'Isn't that the Book Festival site?' he asked.

'No idea,' the operator replied.

'Yes it is, Sarge,' said Kylie Knight. ('You know you're getting old,' McCall, who was forty-three, had declared to a colleague, 'when we start to recruit coppers called Kylie.') 'I was at an event there last night. The speaker was Bruce Anderson; remember that politician who was Secretary of State for Scotland a few years back, the one whose wife was murdered?'

'Big audience, was it?' asked McCall, the question heavily layered with sarcasm. He was not a man with time in his life for politics and he had little understanding of those who had.

9

'The tent was full,' she told him. 'I know,' she added, seeing his reaction. 'I was surprised myself. It was quite lively, though.'

'Forgive me, Kylie, but you don't seem the sort to give up a Saturday night to listen to a guy like that.'

'I'm not, but my boyfriend's a politics student, and he wanted to go. He says that Anderson's interesting. Apparently he's been threatening to switch to the Nationalists, and he's written a book, attacking the government that he was a part of.'

'Did you enjoy it?'

'Not much, but Byron did; he was on his feet at the end, and afterwards he couldn't stop talking about the way the man's reinvented himself . . . like Al Gore, he said, whoever he is.'

'American footballer, I think,' McCall ventured. 'What did you think of him?'

'I can't honestly say I took to him. He struck me as an angry man. Byron says that he is; he says that he feels the Labour Party didn't give him the support he should have had after he lost his wife, that they used it as an excuse to shove him on to the sidelines, and to keep him out there.'

'Was the DCC there?'

Knight frowned. 'Mr Skinner? Not that I saw. Why should he have been?'

'Because if you go far enough back, you'll find that he was Anderson's security adviser, when he was Secretary of State.'

The young constable shrugged. 'His name wasn't mentioned. Aileen de Marco's was, though. Anderson said that she was . . . How did he put it? He was so pumped up when he said it that he made me laugh . . . a Westminster poodle at the head of a government with no authority, and that she had sold her soul to her coalition partners to stay in power after the last election.'

'The DCC will not like that,' the sergeant grunted. 'All the same . . .'

He took out his mobile and called his base at Gayfield Square. 'Put me through to Inspector Varley,' he said as he was answered. 'Jock,' Knight heard him say. 'It's Ian here; we've just taken a shout for a sudden death at the Book Festival site. No idea who, but it's a pretty high-profile venue, so I thought you'd best know about it.' Pause. 'Yes, OK, see you there.'

As he spoke, Knight swung the car from Princes Street into South Charlotte Street. 'Where do I park?' she asked. 'At the entrance?'

'No, because there are traffic lights there. Take a left turn into the square.'

'Can I do that, Sarge? Isn't it one-way?'

McCall sighed. 'Kylie, this is a police car. You can do pretty much what you like, short of blocking the chief constable's driveway. Go round the square and park on the far side. It's no through road there, apart from taxis . . . and us.'

The constable followed his direction; there were several empty bays on the far side of the square and she pulled into the one closest to the entrance, and in front of the side gate. It was being held open by a middle-aged man in a security uniform, with thinning red hair and a goatee beard. The older police officer recognised him from previous meetings. 'Hello, Mr Richards,' he called out as he climbed from the patrol vehicle.

As he did so, he was aware of a tall, tanned figure, with close-cropped, steel-grey hair, his muscles sharply defined in a red T-shirt and tight black shorts. He saw him run along the pavement to McCall's left, then down the ramp that provided wheelchair passage between the roadway and the Festival site, heading towards North Charlotte Street. As the man's eye took in the scene, his stride seemed to falter momentarily; but if he had considered stopping, he put the idea to one side and carried on, loping across the roadway, down the slope and out of sight.

'He's up early,' Knight exclaimed. 'Shouldn't we have stopped him?'
The sergeant smiled as he shook his head. 'We'll hear from him soon enough, I'll bet.'

Three

The top hinge of the bedroom door creaked as he eased it open. Bob Skinner winced. That's the trouble with historic buildings, he thought. They can never quite keep up with the maintenance. He held his breath in the hope that the sleeper would not wake, but after a few seconds she stirred, and peered out from under the covering sheet.

'Thanks,' Aileen de Marco mumbled. 'I might as well have come out with you. What time is it?'

'About ten to seven,' he replied, as he peeled off his T-shirt and tossed it into the furthest corner of the bedroom.

'Bob!'

'Sorry, babe. I couldn't sleep, so . . .'

'So you went out for a run. This is becoming a habit. You should take something to help: pills, or even alcohol.'

He shook his head as he stepped out of his shorts. 'Pills, I never will; as for alcohol, if I did that at my age I'd be up in the middle of the bloody night anyway.'

She propped herself up on her elbows and gazed at him. 'At your age? Is that what this is about? You've got a big birthday creeping up on you and it's getting to you?' She smiled. 'Bob, my love, you don't have to prove anything, you know; not to me, not to anyone else, and certainly not to yourself. You don't have to get up at six and go running round the streets, or along the beach like you do when we're in Gullane.'

'It doesn't do me any harm,' he said, his tone unusually defensive. 'I like to keep in shape.'

' 'You're already in terrific shape, for . . .' She paused, and he grinned.

'For a man of my age, you were going to say?'

'No, I wasn't,' she protested, lying. 'But it's true. Look at those scars on your body. You have a stab wound there,' she pointed to his side, 'you've been shot in the leg. Then there's the pacemaker in your chest, for . . . what's the name again of the condition you have? I can never remember.'

'Sinus bradycardia.'

'Sounds like a runny nose.'

He tapped his left pectoral muscle, just below the collarbone, where the pacemaker was located. 'With this thing it's less of a problem than a runny nose.'

'Then why are you trying to use up the battery?'

'I'm not. It doesn't work like that anyway. The device is insurance against a recurrence, no more than that.'

'Fine, but it's there, and you've come through the experience like you came through the others, because you're so damn fit.'

'And I have to work to stay that way,' he countered, turning and walking naked into the en-suite bathroom, twisting the shower's mixer tap to reach the customary temperature, and stepping under the power spray.

Aileen slipped out of bed and followed him. 'But not that hard. I think it's got to the stage where you aren't going running because you can't sleep, you're making yourself wake up so you can get out there and flog yourself.'

'That's what you reckon, is it?' he said, raising his voice above the water sound. As she nodded, he reached out, took her arm, gently, and drew her into the cubicle and under the shower head, pulling the glass door closed after her. 'Then you're wrong,' he told her. 'I'm not sleeping very well just now because I've got a lot on my mind, and I run because I do some of my best thinking on the move.'

She picked a bar of soap from its dish and began to rub it over his body. 'And what are you thinking about?' she asked. 'Not about going back on our deal, I hope.'

He chuckled. 'No danger, my love. You and I will be married. I was thinking about asking our friend Jim Gainer if he'd perform the ceremony. I know you say you're an atheist, but you're baptised, so . . .'

'The Archbishop?' she exclaimed. 'Friend or not, he'd have difficulty with that, Bob; you're not a Catholic, and even if you were, you're divorced, remember.'

'But I wasn't married in his church.'

'I don't think that would make any difference. Besides, you're an atheist too.'

'I'm not so sure about that any more,' he said.

She grinned. 'In that case you're an agnostic.'

'I'm not even sure if I'm one of them. But going back to Jim, I do realise that a full-blown nuptial Mass would be a non-runner, for both those reasons. However . . .' he paused, with a small intake of breath as she reached a sensitive area, '. . . I have spoken to him, and if we have a civil wedding, he'd be prepared to bless it afterwards at a small private ceremony, families only, that sort of thing; if you'd like it, that is.'

She frowned. 'Bob, I'd love that, if you're prepared to go through with it. For my parents' sake if nothing else; they go to church still.' He took the soap, and reached behind her. 'But when I mentioned our deal, I wasn't talking about the wedding. I meant you putting your name forward for the chief's job.' She wriggled. 'And don't think you can distract me that way either.'

'I promised you that I'd apply, didn't I?' She nodded. 'Well, I've also promised my daughter, Archbishop Gainer, and the chief himself. So even if you'd changed your mind about your end of our bargain, I'd have some job backing out now. My form has gone in, all duly signed, it's been acknowledged and I'll take my chances with the interview board.'

'Which is absolutely apolitical, and will judge you on your record. So you're a certainty.'

'I wouldn't go that far. I've no idea who the other candidates will be; all I know is who won't be contenders, and they include Andy Martin, Willie Haggerty, Brian Mackie and most other chief officers in Scotland. I'm the bookies' favourite, I concede that much, but the job should be open to applicants from England, so I'm taking nothing for granted. But going back to your original question, I've got two things on my mind. One is the immediacy of Jimmy's departure. In two days' time he goes off on pre-retirement leave; that means that when I go into the office on Wednesday, it'll be as acting chief constable. You'll concede that's worth thinking about.'

'Granted,' she said. 'Now what's the other thing?'

'You.'

'Me? Why me?'

He put the soap back on the dish, and picked up a tube of shampoo. 'I'm worried about you,' he told her, as he began to massage it into his hair.

'Why, in God's name?'

'I'm concerned about the effect your job's having on you.'

'I'm fine, Bob. Do you think I can't handle it?'

'Far from it. In the circumstances, I can't think of anyone else who could handle it half as well as you do, not even our worthy Prime Minister, or his sainted predecessor. But it's those very circumstances I'm talking about. Your crowd squeezed back into office by the skin of its teeth; in truth, every political journalist I know tells me it was you that won the election, in spite of your party rather than because of it. As a result you're spending the bulk of your working day watching your back; much of what you do is a compromise. It's not, "What do I believe we should do?" It's got to be, "What do I believe my coalition partners will go along with?" You're not that sort of operator, Aileen. Although you never use the phrase, you're a conviction politician, with a clear moral compass, far more so than those people who proclaim out loud that's what they are. It's getting to you; I can see that.'

She watched him as he rinsed foam from his scalp. 'We all have to live in the real world, love.' If he had been defensive earlier, now it was her turn. 'I have to do what I can with the mandate the people gave me. The coalition has a majority of one, and we as a party have one seat more than the Nationalists. My convictions, or most of them, were expressed in our manifesto, but the voters didn't exactly endorse them. Yes, I'll grant you, I find the present circumstances difficult, but there's nothing I can do about them. The Scottish Parliament is elected for a fixed four-year term, other than in exceptional circumstances. Even if I wanted to I can't go bleating to the electorate and ask it to take my handcuffs off.'

Bob stepped from the shower, leaving her under the spray, and picked up a big white towel. 'No,' he agreed, 'but you do have another option.'

She stared at him. 'What? Are you saying that I should resign as First Minister?'

'If that's what you wanted to do, I would support you. Hell, whatever you want to do, I'll support you. But that's not what I'm saying. I'm suggesting that you could wash your hands of those vacillating wankers you're in coalition with. The way the numbers lie, they've only got a few seats in the Parliament, yet they're puffed up with their own importance, and they're treating you like . . . They're treating you in a way I don't like. So maybe you should tell them that their services are no longer required.'

'Bob, that's the only possible coalition out there.' She turned off the shower and he tossed her the second towel from the rail.

'I know that.'

'Are you saying we should go it alone?' she asked. 'Form a minority executive?'

'I'm saying you could. But please, call it a government, love. That's one thing the Nats have got right. You could boot out all the coalition ministers, appoint your own people, then put your manifesto before the Parliament and say you're going to look to implement it, point by point. You'll lose on some issues, but you'll win some too. What do you have at the moment? The policy equivalent of orange squash . . . diluted to taste by the ball and fucking chain you've got fastened around your ankle.'

She looked up at him as she began to dry herself. 'I couldn't do that off my own bat, even if I wanted to. I'd have to get party approval before I did it.'

'Your parliamentary party will back you, and you know it. The anti-Aileen movement, the old Tommy Murtagh sympathisers, they were pretty much wiped out at the election.'

A slow smile spread across her face. 'Maybe you should keep on with your running after all,' she chuckled. 'You've given me something to think about this morning, and that's for sure.'

'So you will think about it?'

'Oh yes, you can be sure of that. I'll think about it, and I'll even talk to a couple of close colleagues. For example, Gavin Johnson, the Lord Advocate: I'll need his opinion on the constitutional position, whether I have a right to form a government . . . as you'll have me call it . . . as the head of the largest single party. I'd look pretty daft if I sacked all the hangers-on and they trotted off and formed a coalition with the Nats.'

'That's not going to happen. The Nationalists will only get into bed with people who're as committed to independence as they are.'

'Don't be so sure. There are opportunists in every political party.'

'Not their leader, though, and he's as much in control of his lot as you are of yours. As you said, your coalition is the only possible one out there. But that doesn't mean it's desirable. Our country's had enough of coalitions, Aileen, for a while at least. That's what I'm trying to say to you; that's my gut feeling.'

'Point made and taken.' She wrapped the towel around herself. 'Now, since we're up, will we get back to Gullane? Or, since Trish and the kids are due back from Sarah's at midday, and you've got to be at the airport to meet them, do you want to wait, and go from here?'

'No,' he said. 'I'll take you back home. We'll have breakfast there and then I'll go; otherwise, it'll be a hell of a crowd in the car. Besides, I don't really like hanging about in the official residence; it's all right for crashing out after we've been to a function, but I don't feel comfortable here. However . . .' he paused, 'before we go I want to nip across the road. I saw one of our patrol cars pull up outside the Book Festival when I was out. I think I'll go across and check it out, just in case your pal Randy's had a bit of bother overnight.'

'Can't keep your hands off, can you?' She smiled at him again. 'You see?' she challenged. 'You're going to be no ordinary chief constable.'

Four

Sergeant Ian McCall winced as the mortuary attendants twisted the dead man's head, violently, to straighten the neck, as they eased the body's bulk into the plastic coffin.

One of them noticed his expression. 'Another few hours and we'd have had to shove a bloody sight harder than that,' he said. 'This one's only been dead for a few hours, so rigor's only just setting in. We had a body once, a guy that gassed himself in his garage in a wee sports car wi' a hard top. Wasnae found for a day. Fuckin' job we had getting him out, then the two of us had tae sit on his knees and his chest tae straighten him out. We could hear the joints crackin' like. Then there was—'

'Save it for your memoirs, pal,' said Inspector John 'Jock' Varley tersely. He turned to the medical officer who had just certified that Ainsley Glover was indeed far more dead than any of the characters that he had killed off during his fourteen-year, twenty-book career. 'You're sure about your diagnosis?' he asked.

The doctor stared at him, frostily. 'I'm as sure as I can be,' she said. 'It looks like a massive coronary. The man was significantly overweight and, from what Dr Mosley tells me, had a history of cardiac problems.'

The inspector looked at the director. 'Is that so?'

She nodded. 'I didn't know him then, but I believe Ainsley had a mild heart attack a couple of years ago. A warning, he called it, when he told me about it. And he was diabetic; last night he asked me if I could find him a quiet place to inject himself.'

'So how did he get in here, and how come he wasn't found until this morning?'

'The yurt isn't usually locked until the site closes,' said Gwyn Richards.

'The what?' McCall exclaimed.

'The tent,' Mosley told him. 'It's a Mongolian nomadic design, and yurt is their name for it. The Book Festival has used it as the author centre since long before my time; it's become a tradition.'

'And is it traditional to lock it for the night without checking that it's empty?'

The voice that came from behind them was friendly, but there was something about it that commanded attention.

'And you are?' the director asked as she turned to face its owner, tall, with close-cut but lustrous, freshly washed grey hair, dressed in jeans and a pale blue check shirt. Then her face fell. 'Not the bloody press,' she moaned, glowering at Sergeant McCall. 'I thought you told that young PC not to let anyone in here.'

'Don't blame the officers,' the stranger said. 'They'd have had trouble keeping me out.' He extended his hand. 'Bob Skinner, deputy chief constable. I passed by earlier, just as Ian was arriving; I thought I'd better check it out.'

Mosley was dark-skinned, but she felt a hot flush come to her cheeks. 'God, I'm so sorry. I should have known.'

Skinner shrugged. 'Why? You and Aileen may be friends, but we've never met.' He looked at Gwyn Richards. 'Security, yes?'

'Yes, sir,' the Welshman replied. 'And to answer your question, my boys are supposed to check that all the buildings and venues are empty before they're locked up for the night, but the yurt's not that big, so to be honest they often just glance in then switch the lights out, without checking every inch.'

'How many do you have on site?'

'Me and two others, one of whom's going to have a bit of explaining to do.'

'Unless he did check, and the place was indeed empty.' The big DCC grinned. 'But let's not over-complicate matters. You found the dead man when you opened up this morning?'

'Yes, but—'

'I asked Gwyn to open the yurt,' said Randall Mosley. 'I found an email from Ainsley—'

'Ainsley?'

'The dead man is, sorry, was Ainsley Glover. He's one of Scotland's top-selling crime novelists. He's more than that, really,' she added. 'He's quite a public figure.'

Skinner nodded, his face suddenly sombre. 'I know.' He stepped forward and looked at the body. 'As of a few weeks back, he's been an MSP, directly elected to a constituency, not one of those who're taken from a party list.'

'That's right,' the director confirmed. 'He stood as an independent anti-Trident candidate through in the west of Scotland; his election was quite a surprise.'

The big police officer looked towards the coffin as the attendants strained to lift it from the floor. 'Not as big a surprise as this, though,' he murmured. 'Just leave that for a bit, gentlemen, if you don't mind.' The pair looked puzzled, yet at the same time relieved to lay their burden down.

He turned back to Mosley. 'An email, you said?'

'Yes. It was very short. It said that he was here, and . . . well, it was pretty clear he was in trouble.'

'Was it timed?'

'It hit my mailbox at twelve minutes past twelve.'

'How did he send it?'

She pointed to the discarded device, which still lay on the floor. 'He seems to have used that.'

'But that's a phone as well. Why didn't he call you, call anyone, or even send a text?'

'The man was dying,' the medical officer said, sharply. 'He'd have been in pain, afraid and probably very confused. What he did might seem illogical to you, but in the circumstances I wouldn't really expect him to act normally.'

'How old are you, doctor?' Skinner asked. 'I'm sorry, we haven't been introduced.'

'Dr Rina Brookmyre, and I'm twenty-five . . . if that has anything to do with it.'

'Your experience has. I've been a cop for longer than you've been alive, and I'm here to tell you that the prospect of imminent death usually gets your attention. If Mr Glover was able to type an email, then find Dr Mosley's address in his directory and send it, he was surely capable of pressing the "nine" key three times, then the "call" button.' He turned to Varley. 'Jock, what brought you along here? Is the Gayfield Square office so bad that the duty inspector has to attend every sudden death?'

The inspector scratched his moustache as he returned his gaze. 'Ian thought fit to call me, sir. Given the venue, and the fact that it's going to be crawling with people in an hour or two, I felt that I should come along.'

Skinner nodded. 'That was my thinking too, when I saw the car arrive.' He looked down at the director. 'Randall, I don't want to make life difficult for you, but I need this area cordoned off for a while. I want nobody else in here until my CID people have checked the scene thoroughly. Thing is, I know this place is crawling with crime writers, but I really don't like locked-room mysteries.'

Five

'Why have we caught this one?' Detective Inspector Sammy Pye asked quietly. 'It's a bit off our patch.'

Neil McIlhenney nodded agreement, as the two men stood in the centre of the yurt. 'That's true,' the detective superintendent conceded, 'but Gayfield Square don't have the staff to handle this at the moment. Some clown . . .' he said, jabbing himself in the chest with his right index finger, 'who calls himself CID commander in Edinburgh inadvertently approved a holiday rota that left a DS in charge there for the second half of August. We've got a dead MSP in that plastic box on the floor; no way am I lumbering a detective sergeant with the investigation. You're almost at full strength, apart from DC Montell, so you've got it. Besides, it's the head of CID's policy to put expertise and efficiency before territorial layout. If he was here, and not on bloody leave himself, he'd say that your diplomatic skills might be required.' He paused. 'Speaking of Montell, who's he on holiday with?'

'His sister, or so he told me; they've gone back to see their folks in Cape Town. Why?'

'Oh, nothing.' He was silent for a few seconds, as if he was weighing up whether to say more. Then he went on. 'I'm never quite sure how things are between him and Alex Skinner, that's all.'

'What does the DCC say? He talks to you, doesn't he?'

'Not about his daughter's love life, he doesn't; not that he'd know anyway. He told me a while back that Alex had laid things on the line for him: he doesn't ask her, and she doesn't ask him. I suspect that my daughter will be taking the same line with me one of these days.'

'What age is Lauren now?'

'Still short of fourteen. She's a great kid, though; she's a big help to my wife with the baby. Wee Louis' turning into a handful, and his mum's finding out that having your first when you're in your forties is a hell of a thing. Not just your first; in my case he's number three, and it's still quite an upheaval.' Suddenly he smiled broadly. 'Speaking of babies, I dropped in on Maggie Steele the other day. Her Stephanie's a right little cracker, and Mags is looking great too. She's finished all her chemo, she's got the colour back in her cheeks, she's looking fit, and her hair's growing back in. She's got a pageboy style; never seen her like that before.'

'That's great to hear,' said Pye. 'As for Montell and Alex, if there ever was anything, I reckon now they're just good friends and next-door neighbours, and that's how it's going to stay. I thought I caught Alice Cowan giving Griff the eye a week or so back, and I didn't see him look away.' Pye glanced around the yurt. 'Has the DCC gone?' he asked.

'Yes. He left just after I got here; and I'm off myself in a minute. I don't see anything to keep me here. The young doctor's adamant that Glover died of a heart attack, but the boss wants all bases covered. He's not saying that it's a suspicious death, but there are one or two questions that need to be asked and answered before we can wrap it up and report to the fiscal.'

'There'll be a post mortem, won't there?'

'Of course, as soon as you can dig up two pathologists to carry it out. You'd better see if Professor Hutchinson's available, since the deceased is a public figure . . . it's sad but true, you don't stop being a celebrity just because you're dead. If old Joe can do it, he'll bring in his own assistant.'

'What about the scientific team? Should we call them?'

'What's your view?' McIlhenney countered.

Pye frowned. 'Dr Mosley?' he called to the director, who was standing alone at the entrance to the yurt, looking harassed, and possibly impatient also. 'Has this place been cleaned since yesterday?'

'No,' she replied as she stepped towards them. She glanced at her watch, which told her that it was twenty minutes before eight. 'The contractors are due on site in about five minutes.'

'Since the Festival began,' the DI continued, 'how many people have been in here?'

'We only started yesterday, but even at that . . . my staff, authors, their publicists, editors, sales people, media, caterers . . . there must have been well over a hundred.'

Pye glanced at the superintendent. 'Then it's a forensic haystack. If we were looking for something specific, maybe, but we're not, so it would be a waste of time and money.'

'Then don't bother,' said McIlhenney. 'Just get on with interviews. Do you have enough people? If you feel you haven't, and you ask me nicely, I will stay and help.'

'No, boss, I can manage. We both know this is a formality anyway.'

'Then get it done as quickly as you can. Move the body to the morgue, and let Dr Mosley's cleaners in so she can be ready to start the day's programme.' The director looked up at him gratefully. 'Give me a call once the autopsy confirms the cause of death,' he told Pye, a parting shot as he headed for the side exit, beyond which the black mortuary van was parked, ready for its sad cargo.

Six

'You know what I'd like to see on your government's agenda?' Bob asked as he took the right turn on to the dual carriageway that headed out of Edinburgh, to the east and the south. 'You should make this road motorway right down to the border. Perhaps that would shame the English into upgrading their side, and go some way into cutting the number of deaths on the damn thing.'

Aileen had heard the complaint before, not only from him but from opposition MSPs. 'Give me the money,' she replied, 'and I'll do it.'

'Raise your own taxes and you'll be able to,' he countered.

She stared at him. 'You know, your politics bend with the wind. Most people think you're right-wing; eventually I pin you down as left of centre, now you're turning bloody nationalist on me.'

'No, I'm not,' he protested. 'I'll always support you. But there's a compelling argument for cutting ourselves free —'

She laughed. '. . . from the oppressive yolk of Westminster, were you going to say? Are you sure you're not writing speeches for my opposite number in the Parliament?'

In spite of himself, he grinned. More and more he was finding it difficult to maintain a serious discussion with her; whenever she wanted she seemed able to deflate him, and to steer them back on to comfortable ground.

'That'll be the day. Did you enjoy last night's event?' he asked, changing the subject with no pretence of subtlety.

'Very much,' she said. 'Sir James Proud's last occasion as host at an ACPOS dinner; it was an honour to be invited.'

'Yours and ours, my dear. Mind you, I've a confession to make: Jimmy engineered it. The rest of us insisted that Chrissie should be there. Although we have women members, he wanted another female guest, and who better for the Association of Chief Police Officers Scotland to invite along than the First Minister?'

She wrinkled her pert nose; it was a trademark gesture. 'I'm not fussed. I'll turn up for a decent dinner even if I am window dressing. It was good to see Andy Martin there too. Why didn't he take up your offer of a bed at the residence, do you think?'

'By the time I asked him, he'd booked his hotel. Also, I suspect he knew that we'd be up and off at the crack of dawn.'

'He knew that you would, you mean. It's a pity he wasn't there this morning. You could both have gone across to the square. That would really have made Randy Mosley's day.' She paused, and took a sip from the water bottle that Skinner always carried in a holder in the central console of his car. 'Why were the police there, by the way? You never did tell me; just rushed me off when you got back.'

Bob's eyebrows came together in a frown. 'I've been saving that one. If I'd told you straight away, you might have insisted on going across there to see for yourself, and they're going to be busy enough.'

She twisted in the passenger seat, to look at him directly. 'What do you mean?'

'There was a sudden death,' he told her. 'One of the guests at the opening party went off into the green room and turned purple. He seems to have taken a heart attack and died, at least that's what the doctor says. He was locked in through someone's mistake, and wasn't found until this morning, when Randall turned up to open the site.'

'That's terrible. But what makes you think I'd have wanted to see? It's not how I'd choose to begin a Sunday, or any other day for that matter.'

'Maybe not, but this is going to break into your day. The dead man's known to you.'

Her mouth hung open for a second or two. 'Who is it . . . or who was it?' she asked. Her eyes widened. 'Bruce Anderson was speaking there last night. It isn't him, is it?'

'Hmm,' Skinner grunted. 'Not him, or I'd have been grinning all over my face when I got back. No, it was Ainsley Glover, best-selling crime writer turned populist Member of the Scottish Parliament.'

'Oh no,' she sighed.

'I'm afraid so.'

'There's no mistake?'

'My darling, when I said he'd turned purple in the hospitality room I was speaking the truth. He couldn't have got any deader if he tried.'

'What a pity. I didn't have much of a chance to get to know him, but he seemed a nice man.' She fossicked in her bag for her phone. 'I must call the duty press officer and tell him to put out a statement of regret, expressing sympathy to the family.' She sighed. 'Oh, what a shame; I was really looking forward to seeing him perform in Parliament. You know, I was even thinking of offering him a job in the administration. He got in on his anti-Trident ticket, but he seemed to be shaping up as an ally of ours.'

'I'd have marked him out as the opposite, given his views.'

'Not necessarily; in fact, the Parliament's pretty solidly anti-Trident. Most of my people are, all the Nats and even one or two Tories, in private. No, Ainsley was quietly socialist. The truth is, he used to be a member of our Edinburgh Pentlands constituency party. We found that out during the election, but I made our campaign managers keep quiet about it. It was pretty clear that the seat he was fighting was going to be between him and the Nationalists, and sure as hell we didn't want them to win.' She gasped, then let out a low moan. 'Oh Jesus! That's just what I do not need.'

29

'What?'

'There'll have to be a by-election. And if the Nats win this time, they'll have the same number of seats as us. Remember your interesting suggestion earlier on, that I should run a minority government? If Glover's seat goes to them, they'll have just as much right to do that as we will. You might just find yourself marrying the Leader of the Opposition, not the First Minister.'

He reached out his left hand and ruffled her hair. 'In case you haven't noticed, I'm marrying you, not either of those.'

Seven

'What we need to do, Dr Mosley, DS Wilding and I,' said Sammy Pye, 'is to establish who were the last people to speak to Mr Glover before his death.'

'Why?' the director asked. 'The doctor says he had a heart attack. He was fat and he was diabetic. I'm sorry he's gone; he was a nice man, a very talented author and it's tragic, but I've got a Book Festival to run. As we're sitting here my staff are coming on site, and we're due to open to the public in twenty minutes.'

'We appreciate that,' Ray Wilding told her, 'and yes, all the indications are that it was a sudden death, no more, but it was unattended, no witnesses, and so procedure says it's a police matter. Plus, there's another issue. We need to get in touch with Mr Glover's next of kin. We always prefer if formal identification can be made before the post-mortem. The information will be on file in the Parliament, I'm sure, with him being an MSP and all, but it would save time if you could help us.'

Mosley seemed to soften. 'OK,' she sighed. 'Next of kin: it's my understanding that Ainsley was widowed a few years ago, and that he's lived alone ever since, in a big house out in Barnton. I believe also that he has two children, a son and a daughter.' She paused for a second, then nodded. 'Yes. In fact I've met the daughter: Ainsley brought her to the programme launch party in June. She's in her mid-twenties, and I'm pretty sure . . . that's right, he said she was a dentist.'

31

'Can you remember her name?' asked Pye.

'Carol. Now I think about it, when I saw him last night, I asked after her. He said she was fine and that she'd just joined a new practice, somewhere down in Inverleith. And he mentioned that she'd just got engaged, as well.'

'That's good,' Wilding murmured. 'It means she'll still be using her dad's name.' He glanced at Pye. 'I'll get on to that now, boss, OK?'

'Yes, do that, Ray,' the inspector agreed. 'See if you can track her down through the list of practices. When you find out where she lives, go straight there. Take PC Knight with you.' Wilding made to rise from his folding chair, until Pye raised a hand to stop him. 'Hold on a minute,' he exclaimed. 'My brain's still in Sunday-morning mode.' He reached into his pocket and produced Glover's wireless device, which he had encased, as a matter of police routine, in an evidence envelope. It was still switched on. 'My wife has something similar to this; she keeps her whole bloody life on it, so maybe Mr Glover did the same.'

Wilding held out his right hand. 'Let me see it,' he said. 'Becky has one of these things; I know how to access the data.' Pye passed the device to him and watched as he thumbed his way through the menu, without taking it out of the envelope. In less than half a minute, a broad smile of triumph lit up his face. 'There you are,' he declared, showing the screen to the detective inspector. 'Carol Glover, 7 Skopes Street, Corstorphine. I'm on my way,' he announced.

'Have PC Knight drive you in the patrol car,' Pye told him. 'If Miss Glover's there, call me to confirm, and let the mortuary know, to make sure that he isn't opened up before she's seen him. But give her all the time she needs to compose herself before you take her there.'

The sergeant looked at the young DI for just long enough to convey that some things need not be spelled out to an experienced officer, then nodded and left.

Pye gazed after him. 'That's me in Ray's bad books. I'm new in the rank,' he explained to the director. 'I still give orders that aren't needed.'

'The art of delegation is more complex than is often thought,' she replied. 'It's not just what, or to whom, but how as well.' She smiled, as if a memory had returned. 'If you really know what you're doing, sometimes you can delegate up the chain, as well as down. Now, can we get on, please?'

'Sorry. I asked you about people to whom Mr Glover may have spoken last night during your party in the Speigeltent.'

'It would probably be easier if I gave you the guest list; Ainsley was a pretty gregarious chap for a writer. They can be rather solitary as a species, but he seemed to be able to work a room with the best of them. I suppose that's what led him to stand for the Holyrood Parliament.'

'I'll take a copy of the list anyway,' Pye told her, 'but for now let's just stick to your own knowledge; those people you actually saw him speaking to at your party.'

'As far as I can recall . . .'

'Yes.'

'Well, there was Henry Mount, and Fred Noble, of course; they and Ainsley are usually described as the ruling triumvirate of Scottish crime writers. The three of them went into a huddle early on, before going their own separate ways. Then there was Sandy Rankin, the *Sunday Herald* reviewer . . . most authors find it politic to be nice to her. They were both with another journalist, Xavi Aislado.' She looked at Pye. 'Do you know him? A very tall man, very serious; he's the editor of the *Saltire* newspaper.'

'Yes, I know him,' said the inspector. 'I didn't have him down as a party-goer.'

'He doesn't look as if he is, I agree, but his paper is one of our major sponsors, so I suppose he felt obliged to come along. Anyway, Ainsley spent a few minutes with him and Sandy. It was then that he sought me out and asked me if I could find him a private place to inject his insulin. I told him that it would be all right to use the yurt, since it wouldn't be locked until everyone had left. After that, I saw him talking to Bruce Anderson: you know, the former Secretary of State for Scotland.'

'One politician to another?'

'I suppose you might say so. From what I could make out, although I wasn't close enough to hear specifics, but judging by their rising voices, and by the expression on Bruce's face, they seemed to be having something of a debate, and it was becoming heated.'

'I thought you said that Mr Glover was an amiable man.'

'Oh, he was, absolutely, but he never shrank from speaking his mind. From what I've been told, Bruce's politics have been broadly confrontational since he came back into public life, whereas Ainsley was a single-issue man who was out to create a consensus against nuclear weapons.'

'How did their discussion end?'

'I have no idea what was said, but I know that it ended acrimoniously. The last time I saw Ainsley he wasn't with Bruce, but with another journo, a guy called Ryan McCool, who has a column in the Glasgow evening paper.'

'They were still in the Speigeltent?'

'No. The party was starting to break up by then. Ainsley and McCool were heading towards the yurt.'

'It was still generally open to authors?'

'Not for business or refreshments, no. But some people had left things there; that's why it couldn't be locked at that point.'

'So you saw Mr Glover and this man McCool heading towards it, and the next time you saw Mr Glover was next morning, and he was inside and he was dead.'

'That's it.' She looked at him. 'Sums it up perfectly, in fact.'

'I don't suppose you have a contact number for McCool,' said Pye, poker-faced.

Mosley smiled. 'Oh yes, Detective Inspector. I have contact numbers for just about everyone.'

Eight

She drew her brush through her thick unruly hair, still damp from the shower, drawing it behind her head and gathering it in her free hand until she was able to slip a band over it and secure it in a ponytail. It was a style she never wore outdoors, but it was a part of her ritual as she prepared for the day.

Turning, she took her blue floral kimono from the hook on the bathroom door and slipped it on, tying it in a bow. On another day she might not have bothered; her apartment building sat right on the bank of the Water of Leith, Edinburgh's river, and was not overlooked by any nearby buildings, and so she often stayed naked, or in her underwear, until she was ready to commit to a choice of clothing for the day. But not that Sunday; not that morning.

She stepped out of the en-suite and walked through her bedroom, without pausing to shake out the tangled summer-weight duvet, then out into the living area and through to the kitchen. He was there, his back to her as he took two mugs from a stand on the work surface and opened the cupboards above, searching. He wore blue jeans, but no shirt, and he was barefoot. In the light of day, his waist seemed thicker than she remembered it, and his blond hair seemed to have acquired silver streaks . . . unless she had never noticed before.

'Far right,' she said. 'Open the furthest door on the right; that's where I keep the coffee . . . or the tea bags, in case your breakfast habits have changed.'

'No,' he told her. 'I still need a shot of caffeine to kick-start my day.'

'Make a pot for two, in that case; you'll find some ground Italian in the fridge, and a filter machine in the cupboard at your feet.'

'Black?'

'Did I ever take black coffee?'

'No, but it's been a while.'

'You can say that again, Andy Martin,' she concurred. 'You know, I really do find it strange that you're here, but thanks for coming nonetheless. Was my spare bed OK?'

'Yes, it was fine, thanks,' he replied, perhaps a shade too casually. 'I'm sorry, Alex; I should have gone back to my hotel last night.'

'Sure you should, and been remembered by the taxi driver, or the night porter when he let you in. You're still a pretty recognisable face in Edinburgh. Maybe I shouldn't have suggested that you come here. Christ, maybe I shouldn't have called you in the first place! I don't know what the hell got into me.'

He turned, and she saw to her surprise that he was wearing glasses, rather than his customary contact lenses. 'Unresolved issues,' he reminded her quietly, 'that was how you put it. After we met up at your dad's a couple of months ago, you felt that there were things left unsaid between us. I'd have met this morning for breakfast, but it was you who didn't want the two of us to be seen in public. That's how it went, wasn't it?'

'Yes,' she agreed, 'and too bloody right I didn't want us to be seen. I went out with the guy next door a couple of times, and the next thing I knew I was getting nudges and winks at work. If you and I were spotted together in a Stockbridge café I'd be getting more than that, and your wife would be getting phone calls.'

'Karen would handle them, especially if I told her the truth.'

'What, that your ex-fiancée wanted to prove to herself that she could discuss the circumstances of our break-up without running off in floods of tears?'

'Is that how it was?' he asked, as he found the coffee-maker and filled it with water from the sink's single tap. 'You wanted to repeat all those things you yelled at me in Bob's garden a few weeks back, but in a quieter voice?'

She smiled at his jibe. 'No. And be fair, last night I didn't; I behaved much better. No, it went deeper than that. I wanted to see whether you and I can ever have a normal relationship in the future, as two old friends.'

'And can we?'

Alex opened another cupboard and retrieved a brown paper bag containing four croissants. She twisted the control knob of her eye-level oven, setting the temperature to a hundred and fifty Celsius, then placed the curved French rolls on the centre grid.

'Honestly?' she asked, her back to him.

'There's no other way, kid.'

She turned and gazed at him; he had taken off the spectacles and hung them on his gold neck chain. She held his green eyes for a few seconds, then looked away. 'I don't know yet,' she confessed. 'We got a lot of stuff off our chests last night, that's for sure. I'm sorry I did what I did, Andy. I dumped all the blame for me getting pregnant on to you, and that wasn't fair. When I had the termination, I was angry with you. As I said last night, as I saw it you'd nagged me about starting a family as soon as we could, nagged me into coming off the pill.'

'As I suppose I did,' he conceded. 'Not constantly, but yes, I suggested that you put your career on hold to have kids. And that was selfish of me. Alex, I'm sorry about my reaction when I found out about it all. I hope that was the last immature thing I'll ever do in my life. You hurt me, so I had to hurt you. If I had taken just a few minutes to try to see your point of view . . . But I didn't.'

'No, you didn't.'

'And that's why you're not sure we can ever be friends again?'

'No, that's not why. We're square on what happened. We were both responsible for it, and we both handled it badly. That's behind us, I hope.'

'So what's your problem?'

'My problem is that every time I see you I'm confronted by the truth about the true level of my moral integrity, and by my lack of proper self-discipline. And isn't that a fancy phrase for a Sunday morning?'

'Yes. So what does it mean?'

'It means that . . . that, no, I don't think we can ever be "just friends". Because if I'm honest with myself, I have to admit that there's an obstacle in the way.'

'A big obstacle?' he murmured.

'The biggest, I'm afraid. I still love you.' She was aware that the sash of her kimono had worked loose. It was accidental, unplanned, but she did nothing about it as the ends slipped apart and the garment fell open. 'You know, Andy, I'm seen as this strong modern woman, but in some ways I'm just plain weak.' She looked at him again, and this time she held his gaze. 'You see how weak I am?'

He took a step towards her, reaching for the blue gown and pulling her close. 'What makes you think I'm any stronger?' he whispered.

Nine

'I hope this is serious, mate,' Ryan McCool growled as he settled into a chair at a small coffee table in the lobby of the Caledonian Hotel, the great red sandstone edifice that looks eastward along Princes Street, its facade angled as if it is trying not to notice the Balmoral, its grey rival at the other end of the famous thoroughfare. 'I crashed out at two thirty this morning, and I don't appreciate being hauled out of bed at this hour.' His lined face was pale, his hair was tousled and he was dressed in cargo pants and a white T-shirt which claimed that Prestwick Airport was 'Pure dead brilliant'. Little encouragement to the traveller, Sammy Pye thought, the middle word especially.

The journalist looked up at the waiter who had appeared at his side, without a summons. 'You better bring us coffee,' he said, then glanced at his companion. 'That all right for you?'

'I could use some, thanks,' the inspector conceded. 'I was up at half five.' He waited until they were alone. 'Yes, it is serious, I'm afraid. I've got some bad news for you.'

Instantly, McCool appeared much more awake. 'What? News as in real news, the business I'm in?'

'Yes, I suppose it is.' The detective had given no thought to the question of a public announcement. It appeared that the situation was domestic in essence, but the police were involved, and it was an issue which he would probably need to discuss with McIlhenney. 'But,' he continued firmly, 'this conversation has to

40

remain confidential for a while. There's next of kin involved.'

'That means somebody's dead?' Pye nodded. 'So why are you talking to me?' the journalist asked. 'You said you're a DI. Are you on a criminal investigation?'

'No, no, I'm not. It's something we've been asked to deal with, and it's a death, yes, but there's no reason to suppose that there was anyone else involved. I've got to make a formal report to the fiscal, so I need to talk to witnesses.'

'Witnesses? What am I supposed to have seen?'

'Who, not what. Last night you were at the Book Festival opening party, yes?'

'That's right, me and a couple of hundred others.'

'It wasn't as many as that, but never mind. Late in the evening, you were seen talking to Ainsley Glover, the author.'

'Inspector Walter Strachan's daddy, the MSP; that's right. I bumped into him late on, just as the thing was starting to wind down. He was in good form; he told me he'd just had a barney with that arrogant shite Bruce Anderson.'

Recalling Dr Mosley's comments, Pye was interested in McCool's confirmation that there had been an argument. Given Glover's medical history, such as he knew of it, excitement might not have been good for him. 'Did he say what they had rowed about?'

'I'm just repeating what he told me, mind, but it was about Trident. Anderson's in the "anti" camp now, but Ainsley said he couldn't help reminding him that as a member of the UK cabinet he'd been four-square behind it, and behind the nuclear submarine base at Faslane. You might remember, Bruce took part in a demo there a few weeks back, and got himself carried off the road by your lot. Last night Ainsley told him that was one of the most cynical things he'd ever seen. He reminded him that when he was Secretary of State, Bruce went out of his way to condemn an identical protest, and to praise the cops who put the boot in when they were breaking it up.'

'What did Anderson say to that?'

'As accurately as I can quote Ainsley off the top of my head, Bruce told him that he was an opportunist who didn't even know how to organise a street meeting, far less understand the complexities of global politics, and that he had only stood for the Holyrood Parliament to sell his fucking books. He also described Ainsley's Inspector Wattie as a stereotypical character without a shred of originality and wound up by calling him a fat, predatory hack. Ainsley thought that was great. He laughed out loud . . . Bruce is famous for having no sense of humour, and he doesn't like people laughing at him . . . and asked him if he could put that on his next book jacket. At which point Bruce told him what he could do with it when it was printed, turned on his heel and strode off to bore our High Commissioner to Australia.'

'It sounds like quite an exchange,' Pye commented.

'It was, but there's history between them. I didn't know this until last night, but according to Ainsley, a few years ago, one of his books . . . he mentioned the title, but I can't remember it now . . . had a character in it who was a fictional Secretary of State for Scotland. In the book he was a nasty bastard who got what was coming to him. Bruce decided that it was based on him, although Ainsley denies it to this day. After it was published, Anderson cut him dead at a Scottish Arts Council function. Later on he let it be known around town that Ainsley's name had gone forward for an OBE, and that he'd blocked it because he didn't believe he was worthy of it.'

'Nice man.'

'Not,' the journalist grunted, 'and that I can confirm at first hand. Nobody I know in politics would call Bruce nice, not since he lost his wife, at any rate. I knew him before; he wasn't to be trusted even then, but afterwards he became one hundred per cent bitter and twisted.'

As he spoke the waiter arrived with a tray, laden with a coffee pot, two cups, a sugar bowl and milk jug. He poured for the two men, then handed McCool a slip of paper. Pye waited until he had signed it.

'And Mr Glover,' he asked, as he added a little milk to his cup, 'what sort of man was he?'

'Ainsley's fine, in his crusty academic way. He can get your back up if he chooses, but there's no badness in him, only mischief.' He stopped abruptly. 'Hold on. You used a past tense there. Is that why . . .'

The inspector nodded. 'I'm afraid so. Mr Glover was found dead this morning, in the hospitality tent at the Book Festival.'

McCool's face went from pale to ashen. 'Bloody hell! What was it?'

'Our medical examiner's saying heart attack. We'll know for sure once they've done an autopsy.'

'When did it happen?'

'I was hoping you might help us with that, Mr McCool,' said Pye. 'The Festival director told me that the last time she saw Mr Glover, you and he were heading off together. Is that so?'

'It is, and it isn't. I was going to the yurt to pick up my bag; you can leave stuff safely there. The security people keep a pretty good eye on it. Ainsley was on the same mission, but he had something to take care of there. He told me he needed a place to inject insulin for his diabetes, and that Randy Mosley had suggested he do it there, for privacy.'

'So the two of you went into the tent?'

'That's right. Ainsley collected a wee pouch thing from a drawer behind the reception desk, then headed for the quiet area, round the corner. I didn't hang around; I picked up my bag and got out of there. One or two of us had agreed to meet up in the Oxford, along in Young Street. It all got a bit hazy after that.'

'Was there anyone else in the yurt when you got there?'

'No, just Ainsley and me, some curly sandwiches from earlier in the evening, and a tray full of dirty glasses, waiting for the caterers to replace this morning.'

'And you're sure you saw Mr Glover disappear out of sight?'

'Certain. I called after him as he went off to do his thing. Told him to be careful where he stuck his syringe. He laughed, and said he didn't use one. He said he was a writer so he used a pen injector.'

Pye looked at him. 'Think carefully, now. When you were with Mr Glover, did he seem in any distress? Did he complain of anything? Shortness of breath, for example.'

'Did he hell, as like. He was at full volume, triumphant after his run-in with Anderson. He must have had a fair bit to drink in the course of the evening, maybe more than he should have. He was slurring his words, and maybe he was a wee bit unsteady on his pins.' McCool frowned. 'Now that I think about it, when he told me where he was going, he did say that it wasn't before time, as he was starting to feel a bit hyper. Poor guy. The confrontation with Anderson must have got to him more than he knew, aye, and maybe the drink too. What a bastard, eh?'

'Are you speaking of Anderson?'

'Not this time, Inspector, not specifically. I meant life in general. We're on a high, and then it kicks the feet from under us. Tough on Ainsley: this time he didn't survive the fall. I suppose it's a lesson to all us middle-aged guys.' He exhaled heavily; then his expression changed, subtly. 'All that said, this is something I have to be interested in, professionally.'

'I appreciate that,' Pye told him. 'Give me a minute.' He took out his mobile and called Wilding's number. 'Ray, where are you?' he asked as the detective sergeant answered.

'We've just got to the mortuary.' he replied quietly. 'Miss Glover's just about to make the formal identification.'

'OK, thanks. When I'm done here, I'll join you there. We'd better both witness the post-mortem for form's sake.' He turned back to the reporter. 'What are you going to do with this?'

'For myself, nothing,' McCool told him. 'I work for an evening paper and today's Sunday, so I don't have an edition. But I should let the news desk on our sister daily know about it.'

'Ten minutes,' said the detective. 'Call them in ten minutes. By that time I'll have rung my boss and been in touch with our press officer.'

'You know anything about next of kin? Ainsley had two kids, hadn't he?'

'Yes, but that's as much as I'm telling you. I know you have to contact them, but you're on your own with that.'

'Give me something else, man, some sort of edge on the rest. Who found the body?'

Pye considered the question; eventually he decided that he had no reason not to answer it. 'Randy Mosley did, when she and the security manager unlocked the yurt.'

McCool's supplementary was instant. 'Are you saying somebody locked him in, after he was dead?'

'No, I'm not, and I'm not answering your next question either.'

'What's that?'

'You're not as sharp as I thought, Mr McCool. I was assuming you'd ask me whether somebody locked him in while he was still alive.'

Ten

'What is it between you and Bruce Anderson?' Aileen asked as she cracked eggs into a bowl in the kitchen of their home in Gullane, the East Lothian coastal village where Bob had lived for more than half his life.

He shook his head. 'It's nothing; ancient history.'

'Don't give me that. Whenever his name's mentioned, there's a look comes into your eyes. Not so much someone walking on your grave, more the other way round. You were his security adviser, and then you quit. I know you told me you decided that you couldn't do justice to both jobs, but what really happened?'

He leaned back against the door frame and gazed ahead, not at her, but at the wall opposite. 'Let's just say that I found out what sort of a man Dr Anderson really is.'

'What sort is he?' she teased.

'You should know; he used to be a member of your party. In fact when you were a fast-rising young Glasgow councillor, he was its leader in Scotland.'

'Yes, but I was very young then, I never got to meet him . . . not to talk to at any rate; I got to shake his hand at our annual conference once, as if he was a visiting head of state.'

'So what was the word, within your circles? There must have been talk about him. I know he wasn't the expected choice for that job when Labour took power in Scotland.'

'We didn't trust him,' she admitted. 'I don't know why. Maybe it was his background: he was a GP in Barlanark before he was an MP and some of us thought that a truly committed socialist might have felt that he could have done more good there than trampling on his colleagues' fingers as he climbed the ladder. But then he wasn't a truly committed socialist, as it turned out.'

'As he's proved since then, by staying in your party but more or less aligning himself with the other team.'

'And becoming one of my administration's most vitriolic opponents.'

Bob smiled softly. 'When I was a kid in Motherwell, I heard someone say, "The turned ones are the worst." I was innocent then; I didn't know a thing about sectarian bigotry, for I'd never been exposed to it. So I asked my dad what it meant; he looked at me, not angry but dead serious, and he said, "Son, I'd be obliged if you never use that phrase again." So I never did. But I still found out what it meant. From my experience it's only ever been true of politicians; present company very much excepted, of course,' he added quickly.

'Come on,' Aileen protested. 'Zealots are zealots, wherever they're found.'

'Ah, but Bruce isn't a zealot,' Bob countered. 'Those old Judean boys had a powerful belief that drove them on. Anderson doesn't; he's motivated by his own ambition, and his own arrogance. OK, plenty of people are, whether they know it or not, but most of them have redeeming features to offset it. Anderson doesn't; as far as I'm concerned, the man has no core values at all, he has no concept of loyalty and he's a fucking liar.'

'Mmmm.' The start of a grin tickled the corners of his partner's mouth, as she started to whisk the eggs. 'But apart from that, he's a decent guy . . . isn't he?'

Skinner's nostrils flared. 'He's the man who walked away from power when his wife died; to care for his young daughter, or so he said. What he also did was collect a fucking enormous insurance policy, another packet from the criminal injuries compensation fund, and a fat advance for a book about his tragedy. Less than a year after she lost her mother, the kid was packed off to boarding school; next thing anyone knew, Bruce had a new high-Tory girlfriend, and half a dozen directorships including a seat on the board of a political consultancy.'

'That doesn't make him a liar, though. He still practises medicine, you know. He probably meant what he said when he resigned as Secretary of State, but people change with time.'

'That wasn't what I was talking about. As for his medical practice, it's in a private clinic, giving health check-ups to punters who can afford it. No, Anderson betrayed me for reasons of sheer political expediency, and more than that, he lied about me to further his own ends.'

'What? When?' Aileen demanded, shocked.

'When he was in office. He inherited me from the previous administration as his security adviser. At first it was fine; we had regular meetings and he acted upon every suggestion that I made. Then my personal life went pear-shaped, Sarah and I split up for a while . . .' He stopped in mid-sentence. 'No, I've got to give up dressing that in soft colours. The black and white truth is that I left her, for reasons that didn't stand scrutiny then, and of which I'm ashamed now. She went back to the States with James Andrew, who was then a toddler, and I got involved with someone else. We wound up in a particularly nasty tabloid newspaper that thankfully no longer exists. Come on, you probably remember it; the story went everywhere.'

She nodded, looking at the floor. 'Yes,' she admitted. 'I do. But you got yourselves sorted out, though, you and Sarah.'

'For a while, but really, it was the beginning of the end for us. The truth was we'd fallen out of love, if we were ever truly in it.' He took a deep breath, and continued. 'Anyway, that's what happened in the interim. As you said, Anderson wasn't popular in your party. He had opponents on the left, and one of them, the thoroughly nasty Councillor Agnes Maley, was an arch-enemy of mine. So Bruce threw me to her as an offering, simple as that. As I saw it, and I still do, I was the victim of an invasion of privacy. If the situation had been the outer way around, him in the tabloids and not me, I'd have gone out of my way to put the guy who did it out of business. But not Bruce; he's a stranger to loyalty, as he's consistently proved since then. He's a fucking coward too. I had a big investigation under way in Edinburgh at the time, high-profile. He began by suggesting that maybe I needed to devote myself to it full time. I didn't buy that. Then he said that he really needed a full-time security adviser. I thanked him very much and said I'd be honoured to accept. That threw him. Finally I called his bluff; I said that if he wanted me to resign, I wouldn't, because I didn't believe that grounds existed, and I made him fire me. If he'd the balls he'd have done that in the first place, instead of all that prevaricating and manoeuvring.'

'No,' Aileen murmured, as she threw some chopped bacon and mushrooms into the bowl, then poured the mix into a hot frying pan on the hob. 'Not someone you'd like to watch your back, is he?'

'It got worse than that, though. Remember Jock Govan?'

'Sir John, of course; the old Strathclyde chief constable. He followed you into the adviser role, didn't he?'

'That's right; before I had left it, at that. In our big confrontation, Anderson told me that Jock had already agreed to succeed me. I went back to my office and I called him, to rip him off a strip. He went ballistic; he said that the Right Honourable Secretary of State had spun him a yarn to the effect that I was insisting on resigning because of the publicity. Jock told Anderson that he thought I was mad, and he refused to accept the job until he had made one last attempt to persuade me to stay on. When I phoned him, he'd just had a call from Bruce, assuring him that he'd tried his best, but that I was adamant. He even added that

I'd insisted it should be presented as a sacking, to get the lefties off his back.'

The First Minister whistled. 'Talk about standards in public life,' she exploded. 'Next time that man attacks me or my administration I will nail his sorry arse to the wall.'

Bob held up a hand. 'No. Please don't do that. It would just dig up a lot of stuff that I'd prefer stayed buried, for your sake, more than mine. Muck thrown at me will splash you too. I won't have that, as Anderson had better realise.' He smiled suddenly, shattering the grimness that had invaded the kitchen. 'Now let's forget about the bastard. Are you going to let that omelette cook itself?'

'No,' Aileen replied, 'I'm not, I'm just mixing it. I'm lousy at omelettes.' She smiled up at him cheerfully. 'You're much better at them than I am, big fella, so you get on with it while I juice some oranges.'

She stepped away from the cooker and handed him a long spatula as he moved in to take her place. At first he was focused entirely on his task, and over a minute went past before he raised his eyes to look out of the kitchen window.

'Bloody hell!' he barked. 'They're here now!'

'Oh,' said Aileen quietly. 'I wondered how you'd react when you saw them.'

Bob's eyes were fixed on the scene below. The car park that served Gullane's broad, sandy beach seemed to have been turned into a holiday camp overnight. He did a quick count and determined that twenty-one caravans, some approaching the maximum length that could be towed legally, were parked there. Each had at least one car alongside, and several vans and pick-ups were lined up beyond.

'Just what I need,' he moaned. 'Tinkers.'

'Bob,' she reproved him gently, 'you're being politically incorrect You're supposed to call them travelling people; they've got the status of an ethnic group, even though technically our courts have never recognised them as one.'

'They're recognised everywhere as a fucking nuisance,' he fumed, 'and that's for sure. I've got no objection to them camping on authorised public caravan sites for travellers, but that down there is not one of those. It's a car park for families who want to enjoy a day on the beach. You know as well as I do what's going to happen: parents and kids will be scared off. Look at them: half of them have got dog kennels outside their vans, and those will not be for wee dogs. These characters don't keep pets, they keep bodyguards. Christ, I can see three Alsatians tethered down there . . . and a bloody Rottweiler.' He flipped the omelette over in the pan, cursing quietly as he broke it in the process. 'As soon as we're done here, I'm going to give them the message.'

'No, you're not,' said Aileen quietly.

'I bloody am,' he insisted.

She shook her head and took the pan from him. 'Think about this,' she told him as she divided its contents into unequal portions and laid them on two plates, then carried them over to the breakfast bar, where cutlery and two stools waited. 'Where have they come from? Do you know?'

'I've been hearing stories about them from Brian Mackie for the last few months,' he told her. 'Assuming it's the same group, they've come from the beach park at Dunbar. It took three weeks to move them out of there. The council had to get an interdict from the Sheriff Court before we could act. Before that they were at Longniddry, same story, and before that Yellowcraigs.'

'Why did it take three weeks?' she asked. 'And why the need for an interdict in the first place?'

'You must know as well as I do,' Bob replied, 'that the law on the subject's completely upside down. There's an Act that says they can't do things like that down there, but we can't just enforce it, in case we infringe their human bloody rights, or we subject them to racially aggravated harassment. It's bollocks, a ridiculous situation. You should give priority in Parliament to sorting it out and giving us the power to act quickly against them.'

'I'll do that after I make the A1 a motorway,' she chuckled. 'But seriously, if ACPOS ask us, we'll look at it. But that's as may be. When they were at Yellowcraigs, or Longniddry or Dunbar, did the deputy chief constable turn up in person and tell them to move on?'

'No,' he sighed.

'And if you do it now, do you imagine these people are so other-worldly that none of them will think of getting on the phone to the tabloids and complaining that Bob Skinner's threatened them because they're spoiling the view from his kitchen window? Then how long will it be before there are stories that you did it because I told you to?'

'OK.' He held up a hand, and a forkful of omelette. 'I hear what you're saying, but I'm still not having it, not for our sake, but for the sake of the kids who're going to be put off using the beach and for the local dog-walkers who're going to be scared off by that pack of wolves tethered down there. I can sort them out in other ways.'

'Such as?'

'Vehicle inspections. I can send officers to check the tax, MOT and insurance status of every one of their cars.'

'Big deal.'

'One at a time. On the hour every hour. Starting at two in the morning.'

Aileen gasped. 'Bob, these folk have children.'

'So they won't hang around long.'

'And if someone happens to tell them who lives up the hill? No, you're going to have to do this by the book.'

He bolted down the last of his breakfast and swung himself off his stool. 'In that case, the book says that the first thing we do is ask them, nicely, to move to a designated traveller site. You don't mind if I do that myself, do you?'

'You think you're capable of nicely?'

A broad smile creased his face. 'When I put my mind to it, I am. I'll be so polite they'll bend over backwards to please me.'

'And if they don't?'

'Then they'll wish they had.'

Eleven

'What would you be doing if you weren't here right now?' Sammy Pye asked Ray Wilding.

'That's a bit personal, is it not?' the detective sergeant replied. 'Same as you, maybe.'

'And then again maybe not. Ruth's away at her mother's; she often does that when I'm on this shift. She'll be back by the time I knock off, though. We'll probably go out for something to eat later on.'

'Us too. The sad truth is, if I wasn't on duty I'd be stuck up a ladder with a roller in my hand. Becky's in a redecoration frenzy at the moment, and I'm the painter.'

'Is that right? When she moved up from London, I thought she was talking about getting a place of her own.'

Wilding smiled, sheepishly. 'She was, but we're . . . we're getting on fine together, so what's the point?'

Pye whistled. 'Is this Ray Wilding I'm hearing? The man with more notches on his headboard than Billy the Kid had on his gun.'

'I'm afraid it is. And I always swore blind I'd never marry a cop.'

'Marry? Did you say marry?'

'Well, in a manner of speaking,' the sergeant admitted. 'We're going to see how it goes.'

'And DI Stallings isn't missing the Met? She doesn't regard this as a backwater?'

'Hell no. On that last investigation she had the best result of her career. The DCC might have been involved in the arrest, with big Montell and me, but he faded right into the background afterwards, as is his way. Becky's on the record as the senior investigating officer. She'd never have got near something that size in London.'

'Excuse me, gentlemen.' The voice came from the speaker above their heads, breaking into their conversation. 'You're supposed to be witnessing this, aren't you?'

Both detectives looked through the glass screen that separated them from the autopsy room. In truth they had been trying to ignore, as best they could, the little old man in the green gown, while he and his assistant delved into the remains of the late Ainsley Glover as he lay naked on the stainless-steel table. 'Sorry, Prof,' said Pye, leaning forward to speak into the microphone that was set into a console beneath the window. 'I didn't realise we were getting to the exciting part.'

'You think you jest, young Detective Inspector,' said Professor Joe Hutchinson, Scotland's pre-eminent pathologist. 'Let me wipe the smile off your face. I have a cause of death for you. Would you like to step into my office?' He stretched out a hand in a gesture of invitation. 'It's OK, we've put all the bits away, or back.'

Reluctantly, Pye and Wilding opened a door to the left of the window and stepped into the examination room, just as the old man stripped off his surgical gloves and threw them in the general direction of a bin in the corner. They tried not to look at his assistant, who was busy sewing the subject back together.

'Heart failure,' Professor Hutchinson declared, looking up almost belligerently at the officers; he stood no more than five feet four and they towered over him.

'As the doctor on the scene told us,' said Wilding.

'Of course she did. In the end the heart always fails. Young Dr Brookmyre can't be faulted for that. Also, I gather that she was made aware of the subject's medical history. Is that correct?'

'Yes,' Pye confirmed. 'I wasn't there, but my colleague told me that Dr Mosley, the Book Festival director, said that he'd had a recent heart attack.'

'He had, although the indications are that it was fairly minor, as these things go. Even so, that would have led my young colleague to her diagnosis. If only ...' The tiny pathologist's eyes twinkled, he paused, and suddenly the detectives were on edge, knowing that their morning was about to change, and guessing that it would not be for the better. 'If only that young colleague had taken a closer look, then she might not have induced such complacency in you two flatfeet. Mr Glover died of heart failure,' he went on, 'but that always has an underlying cause.'

'And in this case?' asked Pye.

'In this case, if she'd bothered to smell his breath, a fairly routine piece of procedure, I have to say, she might have been less presumptuous.' He pointed to the body. 'Even now the scent is there. Go on, gentlemen, have a sniff. Go on, I insist.'

Wilding shrugged his shoulders, stepped up to the table and leaned over the body.

'What do you detect, detective?' the professor challenged.

'It's sort of sweet, isn't it?' the DS offered.

'Fruity, would be my description, but you get the picture. A classic sign.'

'Of what?' asked Pye.

'Of hyperglycaemia.'

'Low blood sugar?'

'No, my son, the opposite. We'll need some more detailed lab work than I've been able to do here, but it's already clear to me that the man's glucose levels were fatally high, absolutely off the bloody clock.'

'But he was seen going off to inject himself with insulin.'

'Well, he didn't. I've only been able to find minimal levels in his bloodstream. This poor chap developed ketoacidosis. That means he went into a diabetic coma . . . and died. When was he last seen alive?'

'Around about midnight.'

'And how was he?'

'Fine. He was lucid, in good form, although he did tell someone that he felt a bit hyper and needed to inject.'

'Well, he didn't. I put the time of death at about one thirty, without much room for error. If he appeared normal at midnight and died that quickly, he didn't dose himself with his insulin. More like he ate three or four giant-sized bars of chocolate . . . only there's none in his stomach, just some white wine and a melange of partly digested canapés. The only conclusion I can come to is that he died as a result of a catastrophic pharmaceutical error or, to use the vernacular, that he chose to top himself, by injecting himself with a massive dose of glucose. Either way, gentlemen, I wish you an enjoyable Sunday.'

Twelve

'Are you sure you should do this?' Aileen asked, as Bob slipped his warrant card into the pocket of the light cotton jacket that he had taken from his wardrobe.

'I've just been asked to do it,' he pointed out. 'In the last fifteen minutes I've had two phone calls from concerned neighbours, people who know me well enough to have our ex-directory number. One of them you know quite well, Colonel Rendell up the road. He's a crusty old boy, ex-military, and he was quite annoyed when he told me that his wife is afraid to take their dogs for their usual morning walk because of what's down there. He demanded, point-blank, that I go down there and sort them out. Yes, I could delegate the task; I could pick up that phone and have a van-load down there inside half an hour, doing those vehicle checks I talked about earlier. I could probably have some of their dogs taken away for examination by a vet . . . the bastards are noisy enough, that's for sure. But I don't feel inclined to. All I'm going to do just now is take the old colonel's wife's spaniels for a walk, as a favour to him, and maybe have a chat with our visitors along the way. What's wrong with that?'

'For a start,' she replied, with a smile, 'you'll look daft walking two spaniels. You'll keep your temper, promise me.'

'Of course I will. I won't lay a finger on them. I'll ask them nicely, like I promised you. I might even offer them a police escort to the designated site.'

She frowned, unconvinced. 'I think I'll come with you.'

'No,' he told her firmly. 'This is a police matter. I won't let you get involved.'

'Think you could stop me if I insisted?' Her tone was light but the challenge was serious.

'Don't let's go there, please,' he said, deflecting it. 'Let me do this, and see what comes of it.'

She yielded to him. 'If you must. Go on then, but step carefully.'

'Carefully and light as a feather, babe.' He turned and headed for the door, but before he had taken his third step, the phone rang. He turned and picked up the receiver from the table on his side of the new king-size bed that he had bought when Aileen had moved in with him. 'Skinner,' he said.

He had been expecting another outraged citizen; instead, Detective Superintendent Neil McIlhenney spoke into his ear. 'Sorry to break into your Sunday again, boss,' he began.

'Don't worry, chum,' he replied. 'It's well broken already. What's up? Nothing trivial, I take it?'

'I fear it isn't. I've just had a call from young Sammy Pye; he's at the mortuary. The sudden death at the Book Festival that you looked in on this morning: just as suddenly, it's got complicated.' Skinner frowned, but said nothing. 'Do I take it you're not totally surprised?' McIlhenney asked him.

'I don't really know why, but I'm not,' Skinner admitted. 'You know how you can walk in on an event and somehow it just doesn't feel the way it looks?'

'You mean when everybody else is seeing what they expect to see, a run-of-the-mill event, but you're looking at a crime scene? That's happened to me maybe three or four times in my career, that's all.'

'But not this morning?'

'I can't say it did, but I got there after you'd gone, remember. I didn't see the same as you, literally.'

'True. So what's happened to confirm my special insight?' He listened as the superintendent passed on Pye's news. 'Mmm,' he murmured, when the story was complete. 'Have you ever heard of that method of doing yourself in?'

'No, I haven't. But if I was diabetic, of a mind to end it all and I was looking for a method that was quick and painless, I can see that might be a reasonable proposition. Instead of balancing your sugar levels, shove them over the top, then slip into a coma, and die quietly and painlessly.'

'So why would he send Randy Mosley a message asking for help? Are you going to tell me he changed his mind after he'd done it?'

'I'm not going to tell you anything, gaffer, but that would make sense. Plus it's much more likely than the old prof's other explanation, an error by Glover's pharmacist.'

'I'll give you that,' Skinner conceded, 'but let's put an end to the speculation and do what needs to be done.'

'I'm already doing it. Sammy and Ray Wilding are on their way back to Charlotte Square. By now they'll have asked Dr Mosley to close off the hospitality centre and the author's quiet room . . . That's what they call the bit where he died. Appropriate, yes? . . . and not to let her cleaners take any of yesterday's rubbish off the site. Earlier on we had no reason to look for the syringe, or the pen, whatever the guy used. Now we do. More than that, we'll need to interview everyone Glover was seen with last night, including your old friend Bruce Anderson.'

Skinner made a low growling sound at the back of his throat. 'I'm tempted to sit in on that one, Neil. In fact I would if I didn't have to sort something out here, then pick up the kids. You keep close to it, and give Sammy a message from me: tell him to rule nothing out as far as Anderson's concerned.'

Thirteen

'Am I going to see you again?' Alex asked. They were lying naked on her uncovered bed, the duvet on the floor beside them. 'Or is that it? A quick shag for old time's sake and so long for another few years.'

'Jesus, kid, I don't know,' Andy Martin replied plaintively. 'I should, though. Right now I should be saying, like you did earlier, if you recall, that we're out of our minds to have let this happen. I've got a lovely wife and daughter, and another on the way. I don't need to tell you what they mean to me.' He stopped and his forehead creased into a frown as he raised himself on an elbow and looked at her, a question in his eyes.

She stopped him from putting it into words. 'Yes, Andy,' she said, 'I'm on the pill. I haven't been sitting here pining for you . . . not all the time. There have been a few guys since we split, but . . . never anybody who's given me a sense of permanence, never anybody I've even considered giving a key to the front door.' She looked up at him. 'You can't say that, though, can you? It didn't take you long to wash me out of your hair and settle down with Karen. What's with her? What does she have that I don't? Bigger tits, that's obvious, from what I remember of her, but what else ties you to her?'

He bridled at her sudden aggression. 'I love her. Will that do?'

'You're just after telling me that you still love me. Was that just bullshit?'

'No, it wasn't. I love you, in a different way. Karen's safe; she's comfortable; she makes me feel peaceful. You're different, Alex. You're

61

exciting; you're dangerous; you unsettle me. You turn me into a guy I barely know.'

'Do you like him?'

'What?'

'Do you like this guy?'

'That's the problem, I do.'

'Are you sure you don't know him? He sounds to me like the Andy you used to be. All those things you called me; you were the same. Now? If I'm honest, do you know what I thought when we met up at my dad's place? I thought, "My God, Andy's really done it. He's turned into a boring old fart!" Mind you, you always had that tendency.' She grinned. 'A tendency to be boring, that is, not flatulence.'

He held his hand, flat, above her left breast, touching the nipple lightly with his palm as he began to move it slowly in a circle. 'And do you still think so?' he asked her.

She shivered, and pouted her lips. 'Oww! I'll give you a couple of minutes to stop that. Let's just say you've proved that you haven't become irredeemably tedious. I've seen the old Andy again, and yes, I still love him.' She slapped his hand away, and pulled herself up into a sitting position. 'Which brings me back to the question you still haven't answered: what happens now?'

'What do you want?' he shot back. 'You're in the pound seats now. The minute I walk out of here you could pick up the phone and call Karen, tell her what's happened.'

She frowned, and poked him in the chest, hard, with her right index finger. 'The only reason you're in my bed right now is because you know I'd never do that. Not because I'd be afraid to, mind you. No, because the day I become the sort of woman who'd do that, I'm lost. What do I want? It's not something I've ever thought about until right now, but I know well enough. I want my career to go on as it has; I'm on course to become one of the youngest partners in my firm's history, and I don't plan to give that up. I want to stay childless for the fore-seeable future. If that means for ever, I can deal with that. And I want you, on any reasonable terms. I'll never demand that you leave Karen and the kids. I doubt if I could bear you moping around, perpetually guilt-ridden, and anyway, I'm not sure I'd want my weekends taken up with custodial visits. Selfish, eh?'

'No,' he replied. 'You're being honest, that's all. But what if I decide that I've got to be honest too? What if I decide I have to tell Karen about this? What if she kicks me out? Or what if I decide that I have to leave?'

'That honour demands it, you mean?'

'Something like that.'

She drew her knees up to her chest, hugging them to her and gazing straight ahead at her reflection in her wardrobe's mirrored doors. 'Then don't expect to move in here. I'm not sure I could handle that. You asked me what I want, and I told you, but there are other considerations too, Karen first and foremost. I don't want to be seen to have ripped her life apart. And then there's my dad. I'm not saying he would disown me. God knows, his own relationship history isn't unblemished. But at this stage in his life it would be a complication he doesn't need. Andy, I didn't plan any of this. What started in the kitchen and ended up in here, as far as I'm concerned it was completely spontaneous. Maybe you came here with visions of getting your end away, but it wasn't on my agenda, however I might feel about you.' She caught his eye in the mirror. 'But you're not going to leave Karen, are you? Because you love her too, and couldn't bear to hurt her. That's how it is, isn't it?'

He nodded. 'I'd need to think long and hard about it.'

'It's thinking long and hard that's got us into this mess, buddy,' she murmured, with a brief, wicked grin. 'Go back to Perth, Andy,' she told him. 'Go to church and tell your priest about this.'

'I don't think so. I haven't been to confession in a while. Alex, I—'

She put a hand on his mouth as if to stop it. 'Bottom line, do what you can live with. If you want to see me again, I'm here for you. If you want an occasional bit on the side, no strings, fine. That would suit me too. If you want this morning to be a one-off . . . I'd hate that, but don't worry, wee Danielle's pet rabbit will be safe from me.' She slid down beside him once more. 'Now, before you have to go back to check out of your hotel . . .'

Fourteen

'What have we got, Sammy?' Neil McIlhenney asked as they stood in the centre of the yurt.

'Nothing yet, sir,' the DI replied. 'By the time I sent the word back, the cleaners had bagged all of yesterday's rubbish, from all the venues . . . this place, the office, the two bars, the bookshop and the toilets, public and private. But at least they hadn't taken it off site. If Glover put his capsule in a bin after he'd used it, it'll still be there.'

'Capsule?'

'Yes. Glover told Ryan McCool, the journalist who was the last man to see him alive, that he used a pen device to inject himself, and that's how you load those things.'

'Where is it now, this pen?'

'Ray gave his personal effects to his daughter, after she did the formal identification.'

'Everything?'

'Not quite. She asked us to destroy his clothing; remember, he'd puked on his suit. She took away his wallet, watch, a Mont Blanc ballpoint and a pouch that I guess was the one McCool saw him collect from the author tent. The device should be in there.'

'What about the thing he used to send the email?'

'I've still got that; I thought the fiscal might want to see the original message.'

'Yes,' the superintendent agreed. 'We need to get the pouch back too.

65

Mind you, it's not going to tell us anything, is it? It's that used capsule we need. Who's doing the rummaging through the refuse?'

'Nobody yet. Ray's going to bring back all of Glover's unused stock of the things. Once we've actually seen one we'll know what we're looking for. Ian McCall and young PC Knight have drawn the short straw.'

'What are we looking at here, Sammy? The DCC's convinced that this one's iffy. What does your gut say?'

Pye smiled, and raised an eyebrow. 'D'you think I'm going to disagree with Mr Skinner?'

'It's allowed.'

'Maybe, but I'm not going to. One problem I've got relates to something else Prof Hutchinson told us. He said he was surprised that to get that amount of glucose into his bloodstream the man only had to inject himself with a single capsule.'

'Maybe he didn't inject himself at all. For all you know he might have taken it orally, swallowed the stuff in liquid form.'

'The prof's having the stomach contents analysed to check that out. But even if you're right, and he ingested glucose, he injected himself as well; that's not in doubt. Old Joe found a fresh prick in his left thumb, from one of the six-millimetre disposable micro-needles that these pen things use. He's taken some tissue from the area for analysis. Even if we never find the capsule or the needle, that should tell us about its contents, for example how concentrated the dose was. Leaving that aside, though, from McCool's description, although he was slurring, and a bit unsteady, Glover was in high good humour, laughing and joking with him. That's my big concern. It doesn't square with a man who's about to take his own life.'

'Who knows what people think at a time like that? Maybe he was on a high because of it?'

Pye shook his head. 'No, there's more; from something he said to

McCool, I've got no reason to believe that he thought he was injecting anything other than insulin.'

'So? What are you saying?'

'That I don't buy this as a bizarre suicide. Plus, subject to interviewing the chemist who supplied the dead guy, I don't see how this can have been a pharmaceutical accident. These capsules are factory-filled with insulin. If a mistake was made on the production line, or if there was sabotage, for that matter, if would surely have affected a whole batch, not just a few. We'd have had comatose diabetics all across the country by now. But the thing is, going by what I've been told, it's unlikely that they'd be dead, even given a high concentration. The quantity required to kill, at least to cause death as quickly as it occurred in this case, would be more than the maximum dose of insulin that any diabetic would be likely to inject. Maybe Glover had been careless, with the drink and the snacks at the party; maybe he'd allowed his level to get critical and one dose was indeed enough to push him into ketoacidosis, but that's not what Professor Hutchinson would have expected to find.'

'And even the Pope's no less fallible than he is.'

'So they say.'

'All of which leaves you with?'

'Deliberate and very specific intervention by another person. I believe that we have a murder inquiry on our hands, sir, and that's why I've asked the prof to go over the body again, inch by inch, to determine, if he can, the precise means by which this guy got enough glucose into his system to kill him.'

McIlhenney sucked his teeth. 'How did I know you were going to say that?' he muttered. 'I only wish I could argue with you. Fuck me, the biggest book festival in the whole damn world, with two whole weeks to run, and it looks like we've got a homicide right in the middle of it.'

Fifteen

He looked at the two cocker spaniels as they ran before him on the end of their extended leads. 'Joe and Jarvis,' he laughed, quietly. He had wondered how their classically military owner had come to name his dogs after two rock stars, until Colonel Rendell had volunteered the information, unprompted. The idea had been his daughter's. That woman, Skinner reckoned, had a wicked sense of humour.

'Dogs,' he murmured. 'Imagine, me walking dogs. What would you have thought about that, Mum?'

Robert Morgan Skinner had never been what his mother had called a 'doggie sort of person'. There had been a time in his childhood when he had wanted a pup, a golden retriever like his friend John, the teacher's son. He had been seven years old, he recalled, when he had put 'Puppy like Toe-rag' at the top of his Christmas list. John's father, a veteran of the North Africa campaign, had christened the animal 'Tuareg', but in Motherwell, a hard-edged town built around vast steel mills, that name was never going to stick. But his mother's frown, her dismissive use of the phrase, and the open contempt of his older brother Michael had planted in his young mind the notion that 'doggie people' were another race, incomplete personalities who were alien to the world that the family Skinner occupied.

At the same age, Alex had made the same plea, and he, too, had refused, one of the few occasions during her childhood when he had denied her anything. His reasoning had been legitimate, that as a busy single parent with unpredictable working hours, he simply could not fit a dog into his routine. She had accepted that, and had settled for a kitten; when it was flattened by a passing car, the pet phase had come to an end. Still, he had wondered, subsequently, whether he might have tried a little harder to make the canine work had it not been for the underlying prejudice instilled by his mother.

In middle age, Skinner rarely thought of his childhood family unit. He had been brought up in comfortable, even privileged circumstances; his solicitor father had been one of the most respected men in the community, and Bob had idolised him. His mother, though, had always been distant and, he had thought, unloving towards him. Of course he had been too young to have heard of closet alcoholism, far less to spot the secret that she had kept hidden from her husband for years, until after the seeds of her early death had been sown. Then there was his brother Michael, who had done his best to make his early years a nightmare, and who had returned to trigger a brief crisis in his middle age. Life was a coin, he sometimes thought, spinning in mid-air, with no logic or physical law determining which side finished on top. He did not regard himself as anything like the man his father had been, yet he had inherited his strengths and built a career upon them. Michael, on the other hand, had inherited their mother's weakness, and had blended it with an innate cruelty that had often spilled into sadism. And if that spinning coin had landed with the other side up . . .

His mind's eye looked back at the family in which he had grown up, and at those he had raised himself. 'What a record, eh, Bob?' he mused. 'If you've any honour you'll spell out to Aileen the history she's marrying into; give the girl fair warning . . . and the chance to change her mind?' Then he considered how he would feel if she did, and decided that instead he would do his best to learn from experience.

His musing was interrupted by a snarl, followed by a burst of furious barking from two German shepherd dogs, tethered to stakes in the ground outside a caravan, parked on the left of the road down which he was walking. Far from hiding behind him, Joe and Jarvis strained at their leashes, their feathered ears flapping as they tried to launch what in his eyes would have been a suicide mission.

As Skinner pulled them back towards him, winding in the retractable leads a couple of feet at a time, the caravan door opened and two men stepped out. The first was tall and lank-haired, clad in washed-out jeans and an Ozzy Osborne T-shirt. His companion was shorter, and lightly built; he wore a vest and tracksuit bottoms, and seemed all bones and angles. 'Sorry,' Ozzy called across, cuffing each Alsatian round the ears, silencing them instantly. 'They're bitches, and they're both on heat. They wouldn't hurt a fly, mister, honest.'

'I'll take your word for it.' He stopped, and looked along the line of mobile homes. The traveller seemed to interpret this as a signal, since he walked towards him. Skinner eyed him up and down; around forty, he reckoned, fit, air of authority about him. The other man could have been anywhere between early thirties and forty-five, his eyes narrow and much less confident.

'Are you the neighbours?' the tall man asked. The accent was predominantly Scottish, but with a faint touch of the Northern Irish.

'You'll forgive me if I say I hope not.' The police officer glanced back over his shoulder. 'My house is on the hill, yes.'

'I didn't think it would take long. Have the vigilantes gathered already, and are you the scouting party?'

Skinner shook his head. 'No, I'm just walking a neighbour lady's dogs, because she didn't fancy coming down here this morning. Their names are Joe and Jarvis . . . the dogs, that is.'

'Same as half the cockers in Britain,' the traveller chuckled. 'And my name's Baillie, Derek Baillie.' He glanced down at the other man. 'This is Asmir Mustafic; from the European side of the family, you might say.

70

So, they aren't hiding round the corner armed to the teeth, but it would be fair to say that the natives are restless, yes?'

'Only a few so far, but word hasn't really got around yet. And the people who use this beach on a fine Sunday in August, they haven't started to arrive yet either. They will, though, soon, and a lot of them are going to be upset, just like they were at Dunbar, and at Longniddry and at Yellowcraigs.'

'Upset to see a bunch of smelly, thieving pikeys sharing their space?' the man challenged. 'Just like you and your friends are upset by us spoiling your view?'

Skinner listened for aggression in Baillie's tone, but heard none, only a hint of resignation. 'To be frank,' he admitted, 'you don't improve it. There are other places you could park, even in this village. Why here?'

'We can get the vans in and out easily.'

'I like the sound of "out", I have to say.'

'In good time. But look now, are you a golfing man, sir?'

'I play, yes.'

'Well, it would have been just as easy for us to park right in the middle of your course, but we didn't do that.'

'That's private land.'

'You try telling that to the Rights of Way Society,' Baillie suggested.

'We do. So tell me, how long do you plan to stay here?'

The man scratched his stubble. 'It'll be about three weeks,' he replied. 'That's the way it usually pans out. Isn't that right, Az?' His companion nodded, and grunted assent. 'The police will be here soon, and they'll ask us to move. They might even pitch up mob-handed, but they won't actually do anything. They'll make it uncomfortable for us, but they won't find us breaking any laws, for we don't.'

'Camping here is breaking the law.'

'It's for the court to say that, my friend, and that's what will happen.

The council will go to the Sheriff, and ask for an interdict against us. Eventually they'll get it, and when we see it we'll move.'

'Where?'

'Somewhere else.' Baillie chuckled, and in spite of himself, Skinner grinned.

'You've got it planned all right. I'll tell you what—'

'I'll bet you will!' As the two had conversed, a few travellers had emerged from the caravans, observing the scene with casual interest. From the steps that led to the third along, a man jumped, heading for them as he shouted. He wore shorts, a checked shirt, and Timberland boots over thick green socks. He was short but thick-chested, red-haired, with a full beard that seemed to bristle. 'I know who you are!' he announced, speaking to the crowd, rather than to Skinner. 'Be careful, Derek, this man isn't who he seems.'

'And who do I seem to be?' the policeman retorted. 'Just another local idiot?' He turned to Baillie. 'For the record, my name's Bob Skinner, and my day job is deputy chief constable, but that isn't relevant to our conversation, unless you choose to make it so.'

'Don't talk to him,' the newcomer barked.

'Let the man make that choice for himself,' the DCC said lightly. 'Who would you be anyway, the shop steward?'

'My name's Hugo Playfair. I travel with the group, and I represent their interests.'

'Those sound like well-chosen words, Mr Playfair. You travel with the group? "Their" interest, not "ours"? Does that mean you don't see yourself as one of them? Without getting into stereotypes, your accent more than hints at that. Tell me, go on. Public school educated?' The man's right eye twitched. 'Good guess, Bob. How about university? Oxbridge or red-brick? Degree in sociology? Want me to keep going?'

'If you must know,' he said, his voice fallen to normal level, 'I'm attached to a voluntary body called REG, an acronym for Right for

72

Ethnic Groups. We defend people like Derek, Asmir, and groups like theirs from people like you.'

Skinner glared at him. 'You're going to annoy me in a minute, chum. I promise you, you've never met anybody like me.' He realised that his fuse had been lit; mentally, he stamped on it to extinguish it. 'If you'll grant me a few seconds' silence, I'll finish what I was going to say to Derek. A few hundred yards along from here there's a flat area that's kept as an overflow car park. It isn't in anyone's line of sight to the coastline; it's used very rarely, and never in August. As a gesture of goodwill on your part, Mr Baillie, I'd like you and your group to move along there. As a gesture of goodwill on my part, I will ensure that the chemical toilets that I see alongside your vans are emptied by the council and I'll have screens erected, to minimise friction between you and the local community, and to give you a bit of privacy.'

'You're going to get us out of sight?' Playfair snapped.

'You got it in one,' said Skinner. 'Does that bother you? Do you like being a public spectacle?' He turned back to the travellers' leader. 'As I say, this would be co-operation between parties, no more, and doesn't imply acceptance by me or anyone else of your being here. You will still be formally warned and asked to move; the council will still go for its interdict, and I'll take a personal interest in seeing that it's made as effective as possible. But my job is keeping the peace, and in the short term you'll help me do that if you accept my suggestion.'

'Be very careful . . .' Playfair began.

'Shut up, Hugo,' said Baillie sharply. He looked the policeman in the eye and nodded. 'Az and I will talk to the group about it. That's how we do things.'

'How will I know what you decide?'

The traveller smiled. 'Just look out your window in a couple of hours.'

Sixteen

'This job can be really glamorous at times, Sarge,' said Kylie Knight, as she surveyed the contents of the first rubbish bag that Ian McCall had opened and spread on a table in a storeroom behind the Speigeltent Bar, commandeered for the purpose.

'It's not the movies, Constable,' he conceded, 'that's for sure. Now, before we start, are you happy that you know what we're looking for?'

'Yes.' She held up a tiny hypodermic needle, enclosed by a safety cap. 'One of these.' She put it back on a corner of the table and picked up a full insulin capsule. 'And one of these, only empty.'

'Where did you get them, Ray?' McCall asked DS Wilding, who stood beside him.

'The insulin, if that's what it is, came from Glover's fridge. His daughter took me to his house. He carried a supply of the wee needles in the pouch that held the injecting pen. There were ten of the capsules, in sealed packs. The others have gone to the lab.'

'What for?'

'So we can determine whether they really do contain insulin. Did Sammy not tell you?'

'No. He's been keeping things close to his chest. All he said was that we needed to recover the things that Glover used last night, and that since they weren't found near the body, the assumption was he'd chucked them in the bin; hence Kylie and me up to our oxters in all this crap. You are going to help us, Ray, aren't you?' he added, as an

74

aside. 'Are you telling me that the guy shot himself with the wrong stuff? What? Was he doing heroin? Was the diabetes just a cover?'

'No, nothing like that; he was diabetic all right. Look, Sammy will brief you when we've got the whole story to tell, at least a bit more than we have now. Meantime, I'm sorry, but get digging. I'd love to help, but this shirt was a birthday present from Becky, and it's straight out the wrapper.'

'Christ, Wilding,' McCall sighed, 'you're as quick as ever with an excuse for getting out of the dirty jobs.'

'If you like, I'll see if I can bring in another couple of uniforms. It'll be difficult, mind, with the Hearts game at Tynecastle this afternoon, but if you reckon you can't handle this on your own . . .'

'Fuck off.'

The DS smiled and left them to their malodorous task, and walked back to the yurt. It had become their headquarters, Randall Mosley having moved the author facilities to the sponsors' hospitality pavilion on the west side of the site. He took a seat at the small reception desk, which he and Pye had commandeered. As he settled into the chair facing the double door, half of it opened, and the inspector stepped inside. 'We're out of here,' he said. 'Professor Joe wants to see us again, over at the morgue.'

'What for? I've had enough of that place for today.'

'He says he's got something to show us. He says he knows exactly how Glover died, and that we've been barking up the wrong tree. Not that I'm surprised.' He paused. 'Have those two started the sift?'

'Yes, just.'

'Good, for we really need to find what's in there. We're also going to need help later on. I know it's Alice Cowan's day off, but I hope she doesn't have any fancy plans for it.'

Seventeen

'Well,' she asked, as he stepped inside, 'are we getting a dog?'

He looked at her in amused surprise. 'Why the hell should you say that?'

'It's that strange smile on your face. I've been watching you all the way up the drive. You look as though you and the cocker twins have become firm friends.'

'Them? Margot Rendell has them spoiled rotten. They're crazy . . . and please don't mention the word "dog" to James Andrew, and especially not to Seonaid. No, if I looked moderately pleased with myself, it's because I am. I wouldn't say I've made a new friend, but we're on reasonably good terms.'

'You spoke to them?'

'Yup.'

'And you're all still in one piece? I can see you are . . . so they came through it unscathed?'

'We had a very civilised discussion, me and Derek. He's their leader, I think. He didn't describe himself that way, but I could tell by the way the rest looked at him.'

'Very civilised? That's more than I expected, the way you reacted when you saw them. But are they moving?'

'Take a look and see.' He led her into the garden room, as he liked to call the conservatory that overlooked the bay, and watched as she looked down into the car park.

'My God,' she exclaimed, 'they're packing up. What did you threaten them with? The SAS?'

'No threats, honest, and they're not going far, but the gesture might appease the locals.' He explained the suggestion that he had made to Derek Baillie, and his undertakings if they accepted it. 'He called his people together while I was on the beach with Joe and Jarvis. I'm sure their resident do-gooder argued against it . . .'

'Who's he?'

'An objectionable wee bastard called Hugo Playfair. He's their self-appointed spokesman; says he belongs to a pressure group called RON . . . no, sorry, wrong Kray twin . . . REG. He told Baillie, more or less, to have nothing to do with me.'

'I've heard of them,' Aileen declared. 'The group, that is. They brought a deputation to Holyrood when I was Justice Minister, demanding recognition of travellers' right to roam and to set up camp without hindrance wherever they please. I didn't see them, though; I was busy so my deputy dealt with it.'

'What did he tell them?'

'More or less what you'd have told him, but more politely; he pointed out that what he was suggesting had to be balanced against the rights of the rest of the community.'

'The demand sounds like Playfair's position. He doesn't seem to cut too much ice with Derek Baillie, though. When I came back up the path, he approached me and said they would do what I asked. Now I've got to keep my part of the bargain, but that won't be difficult. I can arrange for the screens myself; as for the other, I'll call the chief executive of the council when I get back from the airport with the kids. They've got a vehicle that pumps out septic tanks; that'll do the necessary.'

'What if he refuses? I can't fix it with the councillors any more; my party's in the minority in East Lothian, remember.'

'He won't refuse.'

'He might if he thinks you're standing on his toes.'

'If he does, then never mind his toes, I'll jump on his fucking head.' He paused. 'But seriously, babe, I know the man, and he won't be a problem. In fact he'll probably bollock his staff for not suggesting this themselves. The main complaint you hear about travellers is about the mess they leave behind. But what are they going to do? Dump their crap in the sea?'

'You are amazing,' she told him. 'You go down there a firebrand and you come back a convert.'

'I'm by no means a convert. I'm not even a sympathiser. I won't be doing anything specifically for these people. I'll have done it for the public good, and that's my job.'

'Do you know, you're sounding like a chief constable already, taking the broad view.'

'If I am, it's mostly down to you.'

'I'll take the credit if you choose to bestow it.'

'In that case,' Bob began, 'you won't mind if I go out for a beer later on, once the kids are fed and watered.'

She frowned. 'Why should I? We often do that on a Sunday, after the beach visitors have gone home.'

'I didn't mean us. I meant me. I've arranged to meet Derek Baillie and his mate Asmir at around half six, down in the Mallard. It occurred to me while I was sorting this thing out that I'm no different from the rest of the mainstream herd, in that I don't approve of the traveller lifestyle. But equally, I don't really know anything about it, least of all why they choose to do it. So I'm going to take this opportunity to find out.'

He was interrupted by the buzzing of the entry phone. He stepped into the kitchen and picked up the receiver. 'Bob,' a crusty voice crackled, 'Donald Rendell. I wonder if I might come in?'

'Of course, Donald.' He pressed the button to open the gate, then walked back into the hall and opened the front door, to greet his visitor, who was marching up the path towards him, his back ramrod straight as always. In his big right hand he held his customary walking stick, which as far as Skinner could see was more of a fashion accessory than a necessity.

As the ex-soldier approached, Skinner noticed that he was carrying a bottle of red wine in his free hand. 'A small gift,' the veteran said jovially, 'for walking the wife's bloody dogs.'

'Donald,' the policeman exclaimed, as he ushered the visitor indoors, 'I can't accept that.'

'Then it's not for you, it's for your good lady; and a refusal will offend.'

'In that case . . . Come on and have a seat. I have to go to the airport soon, but I have time for a chat.' He led the way through to the garden room.

The old man gazed out of the window, down at the car park. 'I'm sorry I was out when you brought the little buggers back. You seem to have been successful, from what I can see out there. Laid down the law, did you?'

'Limited success, I'm afraid.' He explained the compromise that he had reached with Derek Baillie. As he spoke, some of the good humour left Colonel Rendell's face.

'I see,' he said. 'It's something, I suppose, and I'm grateful for it. I have to tell you, though, Bob, that these people infuriate me. I spent my career in a disciplined service, and I cannot abide those who deliberately excuse themselves from society then use its namby-pamby laws to frustrate those whose rights they're infringing. If I could, I'd call in my old regiment and drive them into the sea, caravans, bloody dogs and all.'

'And children?' said Aileen, who had joined them, unnoticed.

'Maybe not them; it's their misfortune that their parents are brigands. They're victims, poor little sods. Maybe they should all be taken into care, until their parents see sense and agree to live a normal life.'

'It is normal to most of them, Colonel.'

'It's still bloody wrong, though.' He paused. 'I'm sorry, my dear, please excuse my language.'

Aileen smiled. 'I'm a politician from Glasgow,' she said, then nodded at Bob. 'Plus, I live with him. I hear what you're saying about those people's children, and I know quite a few people who share your views, but if the parents can demonstrate an acceptable standard of home schooling . . . and as I understand it, that's usually the case . . . there would have to be other grounds for intervention.'

'Their very lifestyle offers grounds,' the Colonel grunted. 'Look, I really must be off; I've promised Margot lunch at the Golf Inn.' He looked at Skinner. 'Thanks for your efforts, Bob, and for the dog-walking. You've made things better, I concede, but mark my words, there will still be some angry people in this village.'

Eighteen

Things had changed since his previous visit to the mortuary; Sammy Pye could tell that as soon as he walked through the swinging doors and into the examination room. He and Wilding had made good time through the quiet Sunday streets, and so he was surprised to see that Neil McIlhenney was there before them . . . doubly surprised since the pathologist had not mentioned that he would be joining them.

Professor Hutchinson read this in his unguarded glance. 'I thought it best,' he explained to the two newcomers, 'to call Neil. This incident has taken on a new dimension, and it's going to generate some big headlines around you gentlemen. After all, this isn't any wee backstreet junkie we're dealing with. This chap won't be hidden away on page three. He was a minor literary god, a colleague of yours, you could say, given what he wrote about. I confess to having quite a few of his Walter Strachan novels on my own shelves. And then of course there's his other life as an MSP. The bizarre killing of a parliamentarian is bound to stir the media into a frenzy.'

'Killing?' Ray Wilding repeated. 'Does that mean you've ruled out suicide?'

'Oh yes, Sergeant, and accident, too. I know for sure what happened to him and I will show you how it was done.' He glanced at McIlhenney. 'Is this death in the public domain yet?'

'It should be,' the detective superintendent replied. 'Our press

81

officer was authorised to make a statement as soon as formal identification was made.'

'That's right,' Pye confirmed. 'He was told to describe it simply as a sudden death, and not to imply that there was anything suspicious about it.'

'Hah!' the little professor chortled. 'He'd better backtrack on that one; there's plenty suspicious about it. Come here, and I'll show you what I should have spotted at the first time of asking.' He turned and, beckoning them to follow, walked towards the naked bulk of Glover's body which still lay on the autopsy table.

'Do we need to gown up?' asked Wilding, who preferred the view from the other side of the glass screen.

'Don't be daft, Sergeant,' Hutchinson replied. 'You won't catch anything from him, and whatever you might give to him won't make any difference now. Come on, all of you; I need to show you this. I headed up the wrong path, I'm afraid. I won't say I misled you but I didn't consider all the possibilities. He was full of glucose, as I said earlier, but . . .' He hesitated. 'My initial assumption was that somehow or other he had injected himself with the stuff, deliberately, by accident or through sabotage.' He took the dead man's left hand, still stiff with rigor, and twisted it so they could see the thumb, from which a section of tissue had been removed. 'D'you see? That's where the injection site was; the tiny needles that the pen devices use don't leave much of a mark, but I found one. But the thing is, the thing is . . .' suddenly he seemed embarrassed, 'when I considered the pathology of the thing, the process that leads to ketoacidosis and then death, I realised that injecting himself with that quantity of glucose even in high concentration simply wouldn't have done the job, especially subcutaneously, as that jab was. So I asked myself,' he continued, 'was he topping up what was already there? Echo answered "no" and damn quickly. If he'd had that amount of the stuff in his system before he injected himself with what he undoubtedly assumed was insulin, well, he couldn't have bloody well injected himself because he'd have been unconscious. Finally, that led me to ask myself, later than it should have, "What if he injected himself with something else?" So I began to check the tissue from the injection site for traces of other substances, and with commendable speed I came up with Pavulon.'

Pye looked at him blankly. 'What's that?'

'It's the American trade name of a paralysing drug used in anaesthesia, so that tubes can be put down the patient's throat without reflex resistance. What I'm saying to you is that someone must have switched the ampoule in Glover's pen thing. The effect would have been to incapacitate him, very quickly. And when he was under, that's when he was murdered.' He looked at each of the three detectives as if inviting a question; when none came, he continued. 'Someone . . . and for the record, the angle of injection precludes self-administration . . . took advantage of his condition to ram a needle into the muscle of his upper arm, through his jacket and shirt, and to inject him with a really massive dose of glucose, enough to render him comatose in a very short time. Look here,' he bent over the body, 'for this is what I wanted you to see. Mr Glover was pretty hairy, or it would have been immediately obvious.' He pointed to an area of the arm that had been shaved; in its centre was a red puncture mark. 'It's fresh,' Hutchinson confirmed, 'and when you take a really close look, magnified, you can see that fibres from his clothing have been punched in there. That's how your man died, chaps. He was murdered. I apologise that it took me longer than it should have to work it out.'

There was silence for a few seconds, until McIlhenney broke it. 'Joe,' he asked, 'once that fatal dose of glucose was given, would he have been unconscious at once?'

'Not unless his attacker hit him, and there's no sign of that. He'd have grown more and more dazed and confused, until finally he blacked out. The effect of the Pavulon would have been wearing off as the glucose took hold of him.'

'Could he have called out? Shouted for help?'

'I doubt it. He'd have been virtually helpless.'

'Would he have been able,' Pye queried, 'to send a message, say a text or an email?'

'That might have been possible, but he wouldn't have had much time to do it. Plus, it probably wouldn't have made much sense.' The old pathologist beamed. 'Gentlemen, I am pleased to tell you, albeit at the second attempt, that you have a murder on your hands, as cunning and premeditated a homicide as I have seen in my long and distinguished career. I wish you luck in trying to solve it.'

Nineteen

In his younger, single, days, when he was lower down the ranking structure, Andy Martin had been known to break the occasional speed limit, until marriage and fatherhood, accompanied by his appointment as assistant chief constable of the Tayside Force, had lightened his touch on the accelerator. But he drove northwards slowly, even by his newer, moderate standards, on his way back home to Perth.

Martin was troubled, more troubled than he could ever remember. He had been in dangerous situations during his police service and had handled them calmly, even ruthlessly when required, without suffering any significant psychological after-effects. He had known difficult times in his personal life too, but none of them had ever left him feeling as he did as he eased his family saloon across the Forth Road Bridge and on to the M90.

He was struck by the contrast with his mood on the previous evening, as he had driven down the same road, bound for the ACPOS dinner. He had been downright happy. The half-yearly statistical report had shown that crime in his area was down, and clear-up rates continued the upward trend they had shown since his appointment. On the home front, Karen's pregnancy had been declared completely normal, and they were looking forward to taking Danielle to Puerto Pollensa on what would probably be their last holiday as a family threesome.

The phone call from Alex had not come until he was almost in

85

Edinburgh. It had taken him by surprise, but in truth he had felt a surge of pleasure at the sound of her voice. They had not spoken since their accidental meeting at her father's house a few weeks before, their first since their break-up, yet she had been on his mind. When she suggested that he come to see her after the dinner ended at ten o'clock, he had agreed with barely a second's hesitation. Less than a day later, he found himself wishing that his phone had been switched off.

'Oh Jesus, Andy,' he murmured to himself. 'Couldn't you have seen this coming? Did she? Was it a set-up?' He thought back to the night before. He had arrived at Alex's flat at ten thirty, having taken a taxi from the Merchants' Hall to his hotel to change out of his evening dress. She had been busy herself earlier in the evening, attending the first night of a Festival show sponsored by Curle Anthony and Jarvis, her law firm, and the inevitable reception which had followed, and the early part of their conversation had been taken up with descriptions of their respective events. She had told him how bad the performance had been, and he had described Sir James Proud's valedictory speech to his colleagues, a mixture of recollection and humour, which he had ended with a toast 'to those who fell in battle', a tribute to Detective Inspector Stevie Steele, who had been killed on duty a few months before.

They had shared a bottle of Drostdy-Hof, a decent South African Sauvignon Blanc, to which, Alex said, she had been introduced by Griff Montell, and she had asked him how he was enjoying command rank, and marriage. He had spent the best part of an hour talking about his work, his wife and his daughter, and she had responded by telling him of the development of her career. In short, they had talked of the present, not of their past, time going by unnoticed until Alex had glanced at her watch and seen that it was five minutes short of 2 a.m. He had offered to call a taxi, but she had countered with the offer of her spare bed.

And then morning had come.

'Oh hell,' he murmured as he drove. 'What am I going to do?'

He considered the options open to him. He could be a man of principle, and confess everything to Karen as soon as he stepped through the front door. But what would he confess? That he had slept with his ex-fiancée, that it had been a terrible mistake? And if he did, what would be the result? His marriage might be over there and then. Would it? Maybe so; Karen was a strong woman and would not be afraid to throw him out. But maybe not; she loved him and she loved Danielle. Maybe she wouldn't break up a previously happy home because of one mistake. But that home might never be quite the same, he feared. His indiscretion might have been a one-off, and totally out of the blue, but even if she forgave him, the fact of it would hang over them like a cloud for a long time, and maybe for ever.

But then again, what if she asked him whether it would ever happen again? Could he promise that it would not?

'Do you want it to happen again, Andy?' he asked himself aloud as he swung round a long curve, and saw the blue water of Loch Leven on his right, and the castle where Mary, Queen of Scots, was imprisoned after her fall from power. For an instant he thought of her, and saw her with Alex's face.

She had said, in so many words, that she would be his mistress. He considered such a relationship, secret meetings, stolen time spent together . . . Queen Mary and the Earl of Bothwell. And he knew it would not work, for the very reason that Alex had cited for not letting him call a taxi in the middle of the night: Edinburgh was at heart a village, with a gossip mill so efficient that most secrets were not kept for long.

And anyway, would he want it?

'No,' he declared, shaking his head. Whoever had been to blame for Alex and him breaking up, it had happened, and he had moved on, to build a life that was happy if not completely fulfilled. He had gone to

Karen because she made him feel secure and gave him stability. No, not the old Andy, not the one who had fathered Alex's aborted child, but when he considered it, he did not want to be that man again. A small grin crossed his face. If that made him a boring old fart, then so be it.

So what would he say to Karen? Nothing at all, he decided. She managed the household and she would see the hotel charge on the credit card statement when it came in, and verify it against the bill, which he would give her, as he always did . . . and note, instinctive cop that she still was, that he had not had breakfast.

As that realisation crossed his mind, he saw a sign ahead for a motorway service area. He flicked his indicator stalk and took the exit.

He slipped right off the roundabout at the top of the ramp and into the car park. He had trouble finding a space, for it was almost full, a side effect of a music festival that was occupying many of his officers that weekend. He had paid a call on the site twenty-four hours earlier, then had left the district commander to get on with it.

A look into the cafeteria convinced him that he would be more comfortable in his car. He bought a bacon roll and a coffee to go . . . as a cover story rather than because he was hungry. He shoved the till receipt into his wallet and carried them back outside.

He put the coffee beaker in the dashboard holder, and switched on the radio as he began to attack the second stage of his breakfast. While he had been in Edinburgh, he had been tuned to the local station Talk 107, but the signal strength had deteriorated. He switched wavebands, and tuned to Tay AM. The volume had been set high, and suddenly the cockpit was filled by a powerful, uncompromising guitar sound, which Martin thought he recognised but struggled to place. By the time he had rifled through his formidable mental musical catalogue and identified it as that of George Thorogood and the Destroyers, the track was fading, to be replaced by successive ads, for a furniture warehouse, a double glazing company, and a car sales company.

He blanked out as the sales pitches progressed, his mind going back to Alex and what had happened between them. When the news jingle blared, he barely noticed it, and the first two items failed to reach him. It took a sudden change in the newsreader's intonation to recapture his attention.

'This just in,' the woman said, her smooth accent-free voice suddenly urgent and grave. 'Half an hour ago we reported that Ainsley Glover, the independent MSP and one of Scotland's leading authors, was found dead this morning on the site of the Edinburgh International Book Festival. After his press office initially stated that there were no untoward circumstances, Detective Superintendent Neil McIlhenney, the capital city's CID co-ordinator, is about to make a further statement. We're going live now to the Book Festival site; our reporter is Rhiannon Purvey, from our sister station, Radio Forth.' She paused.

Martin was bolt upright in his seat, his bacon roll forgotten and gripped only loosely. 'In the light of new information which led to a renewed examination of Mr Glover's body,' he heard his former colleague declare over a buzz of background noise, 'his death is now being regarded as suspicious and a full-scale investigation into the circumstances is under way.'

'Do you mean a murder investigation, Superintendent?' a female reporter called out.

'That's the way it looks, Rhiannon,' McIlhenney confirmed.

'Are you following a specific line of inquiry?'

'At this stage, no, we aren't. We were advised by the pathologist of this new development only twenty minutes ago. Our first priority is to interview everyone who was in Mr Glover's company at the Book Festival's launch party last night. Once we've done that, we'll go forward from there.'

'Could you tell us how he was killed?'

'Yes, but I'm not going to.'

'Neil,' another voice broke in; Martin thought he recognised it as that of Jock Fisher, chief reporter of the *Saltire* newspaper, someone who'd been around long enough to be allowed familiarity. 'Ainsley had a barney with Bruce Anderson at the party last night. I know that for sure because I was right next to them. Does that mean you'll be interviewing the former Secretary of State for Scotland?'

'Have I not just said so?'

'Will you be interviewing him as a suspect?'

Martin could picture the gleam in McIlhenney's eyes. 'Jock,' he said heavily, 'you and I are both too old for you to be trying to put words in my mouth. If you were as near Mr Glover as you say you were, then we'll be interviewing you as well. If you'd prefer that to be under caution we'll oblige you, otherwise it'll be as no more than a witness, just like Dr Anderson.'

The journalist chuckled. 'You can keep your handcuffs in your pocket. Do you have any idea of a motive?'

'At this stage no, but that's one of the reasons why we're interviewing everybody. That's all I can say for now, ladies and gentlemen. DI Samuel Pye is the lead investigator. Any further information will come from him.'

'Do you expect an early arrest, Superintendent?' Rhiannon Purvey asked.

'I don't have any expectations at this stage, only hopes. It remains to be seen how quickly they're fulfilled. Now, if you'll excuse me . . .'

Andy Martin reached out to switch off the radio, whistling softly as he did so, then took his phone from its hands-free socket and trawled through his contacts list for Neil McIlhenney's mobile number. He pushed the call button.

'Andy,' the superintendent exclaimed briskly. 'Have you just been listening to the radio?'

'Yes indeed. What happened to him?'

'I can't speak right now.'

'I understand; too many people in earshot. But I do need to talk to you.'

There was a brief, loaded silence. 'You mean as a witness?'

'Yes. Look, I'm halfway home just now; I'll call Karen and tell her I'll be later than I thought, then I'll head back to Edinburgh.'

'You don't need to do that. Give Sammy a call when you get home and let him have whatever information you've got.'

'No, this has to be face to face; you and me. Maybe Mario, too, but that's it.'

'Mario's in Australia, on holiday with Paula. How about Bob, although he won't be available for a while; he's picking his kids up from the airport.'

'Then it's just the two of us for now; no Sammy, not yet at any rate.'

'Is it that important?' asked McIlhenney, a trace of doubt in his tone.

'It could ruin your whole fucking day,' said the deputy chief constable grimly. 'That's how important it could be.'

Twenty

'Do you have any idea what time it is?' asked Mario McGuire.

'By my reckoning it'll be about half past ten at night where you are,' Neil McIlhenney replied calmly.

'Exactly. We've not long finished dinner, we're sitting under a space heater in an open-air bar, with drinks in our hands, looking across Sydney Harbour at the bridge, and at the moonlight on the water, and it's bloody magnificent even if we are both half asleep, practically falling off our stools. We haven't got to grips with the jet lag yet. Paula says hello, though.'

'And hello back to her. What's the weather like in Aussie-land?'

'It's OK, considering that in our climate terms it's the middle of February. It's dry, it's sunny and it's quite warm during the day; cold at night, though, hence the space heater.'

'How much longer are the pair of you spending in Sydney?'

'Three more days after this, then we're going up the Gold Coast on Thursday. It'll be warmer there, I'm told, even though it's still their winter. How's it back home?'

'Sunny and warm. I had planned to take the kids to the beach this afternoon. I might still do that.'

'What's holding you back?' asked the head of CID. 'You're allowed Sundays off, aren't you?'

'That's a nice concept, but at the moment I'm sitting in an effing Mongolian tent at the Book Festival, waiting for Andy Martin to arrive and tell me something that's supposed to be for my ears only.'

'Oh yes? Suddenly, I get the impression that this isn't a social call. What's up? Why are you at the Book Festival, and what the hell has our pal the Tayside DCC got to do with it?'

'I can't answer your last question yet, but as for your first, somebody's won the Festival some extra publicity by bumping off a crime writer. And to give the media a bonus, this one happens to be an MSP as well. You asked me to let you know if any heavy stuff happened; I reckon you might hear about this on the BBC World Service telly, so best you get it from me first.'

'You said an MSP as well as an author. It's not Ainsley Glover, is it?'

'That's the guy.'

'Aw shit,' McGuire moaned. 'I'm a big fan of his; I've read all his books. I met him once, at a signing. I asked him if his Strachan character was based on Willie Haggerty. He didn't admit it, but he didn't deny it either.'

'That's a laugh,' said McIlhenney. 'I know people who think he was based on you, and that Glover only put him in Glasgow to cover it up.'

'That's bollocks. You and I were both plods when he wrote the first book, so it couldn't have been me.'

'I know that, but other folk don't. I'm only telling you what's been said to me.'

'But Walter Strachan's a rough so-and-so; he bends the rules and he's ugly with it.'

'Like I said . . .'

'You're pulling my chain, you bastard,' McGuire growled.

'A wee bit,' McIlhenney laughed. 'But come on, Mario, you were flattered; admit it.'

'Not in the slightest.' The holidaying detective paused. 'What happened to the poor sod?' He listened as his colleague explained how and where Glover's body had been found and ran through the sequence of events that had culminated in Professor Hutchinson's eventual findings. 'It's just as well you got him to do the PM,' he said, when McIlhenney was finished. 'Another pathologist might not have been as thorough.'

'I agree, but as it is, old Joe's a bit embarrassed that it took two examinations before he got the whole picture.'

'He did get it, though, in the end, like he always does. Who's in the frame?'

'We're not looking hard at anyone at the moment; we've a bit to go before we get there. Mr Glover seems to have been a guy with no enemies . . . bar one.'

'Who's that?'

'Dr Bruce Anderson; apparently he had a grudge against the guy. He had a verbal go at him at the Festival party last night, just before Glover was killed.'

'Did he indeed? I can see the headlines being written right now. "Ex Secretary of State banged up for murder." The red-tops will go pure crazy. Mind you, I can think of one man who'd just love it if that happened.'

'Aye, me too. But I can't see it. This killing was very carefully planned; it was absolutely not spur of the moment. My thinking is that if Anderson had set it up, he'd hardly have drawn attention to his feud with Glover just before he bumped him off.'

'On the other hand, perhaps he would, knowing that your conclusion's the one simple polis like us are likely to draw.'

'In that case, Sammy can put that to him when he interviews him.' He glanced over his shoulder at Pye, who was studying the list of party guests that Randall Mosley had provided.

'Sammy?'

'Yes, he's lead investigator on this one. With Stevie Steele gone, he's pretty much our top DI,' he said quietly, not wanting his assessment to be overheard by its subject. 'I've brought him and Ray up from Leith. Alice Cowan too; she and Wilding have gone back out to see Glover's daughter, to take a formal statement from her.'

'Does she know her dad was murdered?'

'She will if she heard me on the radio. If not, she still thinks that he died from a heart attack. They've gone to fill in the blanks.'

'Fine,' said McGuire. He hesitated for a second, before continuing. 'Neil, bringing Sammy in, that's a good shout, but are you sure you want to put him in with Anderson?'

The detective superintendent sighed. 'Maybe not. I suppose I should take the lead on that one, or sit in at least. Bugger it; and there was me looking forward to getting the sand between my toes this afternoon.' He looked up as the door of the yurt opened and Andy Martin stepped inside. 'Got to go now,' he said. 'Sleep tight.'

'With luck. Keep me informed, chum.'

McIlhenney snapped his phone shut and rose to his feet.

'Hello, Andy,' he said, extending his hand to the newcomer. 'Good to see you, although I'm sorry your Sunday's screwed up too.' As they shook, he thought for an instant that something flashed in the other man's eyes, something he could not read, but it was so fleeting that he decided almost as quickly that he had been mistaken. 'You're sure we couldn't have done this over the phone?' he asked, moving on.

'Not unless it was secure.' The reply was abrupt, renewing McIlhenney's curiosity; his own eyes must have betrayed him, for Martin's face softened at once. 'Sorry, Neil. I didn't mean to snap. You're right, this day is not turning out as I'd have liked. I should have laid off the whoopee juice last night and gone straight home after the dinner.'

The big superintendent smiled sympathetically. 'So let's get this done,' he said, 'and then you can get home.'

Martin looked around the tent. He nodded briefly to Pye, who replied, 'Afternoon, sir.'

The DCC glanced at his watch. 'Don't remind me of the fact. Sammy, can you give us a minute?'

'No, he won't.' McIlhenney's intervention took the senior officer by surprise. 'I'm sorry, Andy,' he went on, 'but DI Pye is leading this inquiry. If what you've got to say is relevant to it then he's going to hear it. I'm not cutting him out of anything.'

'I told you, this is highly sensitive,' said Martin, his voice suddenly formal and commanding.

Pye looked at the two men. He had known them both for years, as his career had progressed. Martin had brought him into CID, and he had worked with McIlhenney in Special Branch. He had never known them to be at odds, yet there they were staring each other down.

'Look, boss,' he said to the superintendent, 'I'll step outside. I don't mind.'

'You'll stand your ground,' McIlhenney snapped. 'DCC Martin's warrant card was issued by the Tayside force, not this one. He's come here because he has information that he thinks may be relevant to your investigation and you are fucking well going to hear it.'

'I've got a long memory, my friend,' Martin murmured, 'and you know how good it is.'

'In that case you'll have DCC Skinner's phone number stored in there. You call him and tell him what we've got going on here and see whose side he comes down on. But you'd better tell him that now you've kicked this game off, you're not leaving here till it's played out.'

'Don't threaten me.'

'Sorry, sir; not a threat, but a promise.'

'Gentlemen!' Pye exclaimed, feeling totally out of his depth. He was ignored, by them both, and found himself wondering what he would do if Martin headed for the door.

And so a huge sigh of relief escaped from within him when instead he shrugged and said, 'Have it your way, but Bob will hear of this . . . and so will you, down the line.'

'You mean if you come back as deputy when he moves up? You think none of us have seen that one coming? Well, I don't give a shit about down the line, because I'm right and you bloody well know it.' He looked at the inspector. 'Sammy, do you have a notebook?'

'No notes, Neil,' Martin interjected, 'and no tape.'

McIlhenney frowned. 'OK, I'll give you that much. Tell us your story and maybe we can all be friends again.'

'Maybe.' Martin pointed to a table at the back of the yurt; Randall Mosley had left behind a kettle, half a dozen mugs, a carton of milk and a jar of Nescafé. 'Any chance of a coffee? The last one I had went cold, and the one before that . . .' he paused, 'it was way back.'

'Help yourself.'

'You?'

The superintendent nodded; the DI shook his head. They waited and watched the kettle as it boiled, and as their visitor filled two mugs, handing one to McIlhenney as if it was a peace offering.

The trio took seats at the small table near the entrance, Pye securing the door with a bolt.

'Right,' said Martin briskly and almost cheerfully, as if the confrontation had never happened. 'I believe it's possible that the security services were involved in Ainsley Glover's death.'

'What?' McIlhenney gasped. 'Have you been reading one of his books?'

'I can understand that reaction, but hear me out. I've never mentioned this before, probably because I was slightly embarrassed by the fact, being a serving police officer, but Ainsley Glover was a distant relation of mine. I know that he's always been regarded as very much an Edinburgh toff, and mostly he was. His father was Professor of

Medical Law at the university, but his mother was from Glasgow, and she was my mother's cousin. She was older than my mum, just as Ainsley was older than me, so they were never that close, but they'd meet up at family events. The first time I ever came across Ainsley was at his sister's wedding. I was about fourteen at the time, and so he'd have been late twenties. He was a nice bloke, distinctive-looking even then, chubby, and with that fly-away hair of his. His wife, Joyce, she was about the same size as him that night; she was pregnant with their first kid.'

'I know he was widowed,' said McIlhenney. 'What happened to her?'

'She died of viral meningitis, in her thirties. I believe that's when Ainsley started to write, as a form of therapy.'

'What was his profession before that?'

'He was an accountant at the beginning, but he did some part-time lecturing as well. After Joyce died, he concentrated on that, and became head of the accountancy school at Heriot-Watt. I didn't see him again for a few years after the wedding, not until I was at university myself, and playing first-team rugby. We had a game at Goldenacre one Saturday; I was getting a bit of a reputation by then, and he turned up with his kids. He hung around afterwards, and said hello when I came out. I won't say he was a regular attender, but he was in the stand on the odd occasion after that, at Edinburgh games, usually on his own. He knew fuck all about the game, but that's true of quite a few people who call themselves rugby followers. After I joined the police, moved through here and started playing for the Accies, I didn't have to jump straight on the bus home when the game was finished. If I saw him there, we'd have a couple of pints in the clubhouse afterwards. At least I would; Ainsley had to keep off the beer, not so much for his weight but because of his condition. Did you know that, by the way? That he was diabetic?'

'Yes,' McIlhenney confirmed casually, 'we knew that.'

'Fine. Anyway that was the extent of it. I stopped playing regularly because of the job, and so I stopped seeing Ainsley socially, until I got to the age when I found myself going to funerals as often as weddings. I saw him at his mother's send-off, but there wasn't much said between us that day. The only other time . . . that's right,' he exclaimed, his eyes glazing for a second as if he was examining a mental picture, 'was when I met him by accident in the Café Royal bar, about fifteen years ago. He was with Joyce and another couple; it must have been just before she died. I had just made CID, and I was with Bob; he was a DCI then on the drugs squad. Ainsley came over, I introduced them . . . and that's when Inspector Walter Strachan was born.'

'You are joking!' the superintendent gasped.

'No way am I joking; Strachan is based on Bob Skinner. He doesn't look like him, but that's deliberate. If you think about it, though, the basic connection's obvious: they're both hard bastards from the west of Scotland. I went to one of Ainsley's events in the Edinburgh Bookshop about ten years ago, once he had a few books out there. When he read from his latest, it was Bob's voice he was using for Strachan. I asked him about it when he was done and I had him in a quiet corner. He owned up to it. The popular belief is that it was Haggerty, and he didn't discourage that, but it wasn't.'

'Does Bob know?'

Martin shook his head. 'I promised Ainsley I'd never tell him . . . and I want the same undertaking from you guys, even though the poor bloke's dead.'

'You've got it. That night in the Bookshop, was that the last time you saw him?'

'All but two. I saw him at another funeral, then I had a call from him a few months ago, middle of April. He asked if he could come to see me. I was taken by surprise, not just by the call, but because he didn't sound himself. Now the truth is, I didn't fancy him turning up at the office in Dundee, for the same reason that I never spoke of our relationship before now. I was a bit embarrassed by it, and I reckoned it might get me a bit of ribbing from colleagues, if they knew I was related to Inspector Strachan. Ainsley said he'd rather not come to the house, so we wound up meeting for lunch in Rufflets Hotel, just outside St Andrews; that's about as discreet as you can get.'

'I know,' McIlhenney admitted. 'Lou took me there for a weekend break, when she found out she was pregnant.'

'Right, you get the picture. This was midweek, so we had the dining room to ourselves, apart from two elderly American couples who were sat well away from us. I should tell you that although I kept quiet about it, I'd been following Ainsley's career over the years, pleased for him as his reputation grew, so I knew what he was up to. I knew about the politics as well, that he'd set himself the objective of getting Trident out of Scotland. I read an interview with him in the *Saltire*, where he said that he reckoned he had a far more realistic chance of achieving that than any of the rabble-rousers or any . . . and here I'm paraphrasing as accurately as I can . . . of the born-again disarmers who thought that blocking the public highway was a sensible form of protestation.'

'Guess who he was talking about there?' said Pye.

'Bruce Anderson,' Martin countered. 'I'd guessed that even before he told me. I'd only ever heard Ainsley speak kindly of people before, so it was bit of a shock to the system, hearing him describe the guy as an arrogant self-promoting bullshitter. That's what he did, though. He said that normally he wouldn't be bothered with him, only he expected to be fighting him for a seat in the Scottish Parliament pretty soon.'

'It didn't work out that way, though,' McIlhenney pointed out.

'No, it didn't. The local Labour Party in Dunbartonshire insisted on one of theirs fighting the seat with the Trident base in it, so did the Nationalists, and that made it easy for Ainsley. He was afraid he'd have lost to Anderson.' Martin paused. 'But that wasn't all he was afraid of. We were on the dessert by the time he got round to it, and even then I could sense that he was hesitant. Finally he took a deep breath and asked, "Andy, does your remit cover Special Branch?" I had to think about that one, but then I realised that he wasn't the sort of guy to ask something like that out of the blue, unless he was pretty damn sure of the answer. So I told him that it did, and that quite a bit of my job involved overseeing covert surveillance on potential security risks. "Of which I may be one, it seems." That's what he said next. I could have cut him off at that point, but I didn't. Instead I asked him what made him think that, trying to take him seriously. Christ, Neil, you know that if a tenth of the people who reckon they're being watched actually were, there would be no unemployment, all the jobless would be in MI5, and on overtime at that. Plus, the guy was a crime writer, with all sorts of plots and sub-plots going on in his head. He was pretty rational, though. He took a letter from his pocket and handed it to me. I didn't recognise the stamp; it was from his publisher in Prague, he said. He'd slit it open with a blade, but he asked me to look at the flap. I did; it wasn't quite square on, as if it had been peeled back very gently, so as not to tear it, and then put back in place. He said that's how it had arrived and told me that he'd taken it to a lady friend of his at Heriot-Watt, in the chemical engineering department, and had asked her to look at it. She tested it, and reported back that she had found two different sorts of adhesive. And she'd done more, she'd lifted three different thumbprints from the letter inside. One would have been his, the second his publisher's, but the third? I asked him whether it could have been a secretary, but he said no, that the Czechs had a very small office, with part-time helpers, and they did their own mail.'

'Hold on,' McIlhenney exclaimed. 'This guy lived in Edinburgh. If he was under surveillance . . . Dottie Shannon and Tarvil Singh might keep an eye on him, but it wouldn't extend to opening his mail.'

Martin held up a hand. 'I'll get there, Neil. That letter was a month old when Ainsley gave it to me. Since then he'd been having all his mail examined in the same way, and half of it appeared to have been opened, everything but the junk and the official mail.'

'What did he want you to do about it?'

'He didn't ask me to do anything about it. He just gave me an envelope; he said it contained a list of names, and he wanted me to keep a copy, in case anything ever happened to him. I've got it in the safe in my office.'

'But did you look into the surveillance? Did you speak to our people, or to Bob?'

'That's what I should have done,' the DCC admitted, 'but I didn't. Instead I decided to keep it in the family; I looked into it myself. I spent a couple of nights watching Ainsley's place, but from a distance; it didn't take me long to spot them, and to know that they weren't from any Special Branch units I know. They were using at least three vehicles. I took the numbers, ran the plates, and guess what? All of them were phoney; they all went back to cars that had been written off in insurance claims. That's when I started to take my distant cousin's predicament more seriously.'

'I'm not surprised,' Pye muttered. He was visibly shaken. 'They were operating on our patch, behind our backs?'

'Yes. Now you're going to ask me again whether I alerted anybody at Fettes at that point, and the answer's still no. The next thing I did was lean on an old source in BT. After a bit of heavy persuasion, he did some digging and told me that there was a tap on Ainsley's phone, but that nobody was saying who had authorised it. There was only one place to go after that. I have my own contacts within the security services, from my time there and from my present position. I used them. I went to a section head I know, only two levels below Amanda Dennis, told him what I had and said that, one, the guy was a relation, two, he was on to them, and three, he was high-profile. He called me back within an hour and swore to me, as one officer to another, that it had nothing to do with them, or MI6 either.'

'And you believed him?'

'Yes, I did, and for sure once I had a call from Amanda Dennis herself a bit later on, confirming what I'd been told.'

'And you reckon now that they were lying?'

'Maybe, but not necessarily. At the time, I started looking in another direction. I was beginning to think that maybe there was something criminal going on. I was at the stage where I was going to talk to Bob, but before I got there, I decided to have another go at my BT source. So I went to see him and I told him that I wanted to know who had set up that phone tap and no fucking messing. I gave him two days to get back to me or he was getting burned.'

'And did he?'

'No, but somebody else did. Turned up in my bloody office, he did, and told my secretary that no, he didn't have an appointment but he had come from London on a matter of shared interest, and he hoped that I would have the time to meet him. He introduced himself as Mr Coben, but if that's his real name, then I'm Dorothy L. Sayers. He didn't mess about. He told me very politely that he was from the intelligence community, and that I was stepping on something outside my remit. He said that, yes, Ainsley Glover was on their watch list, and that he would remain so. With Scotland entering a phase of, as he put it, electoral instability, there was great concern internationally about the security of the deterrent. If he had simply been one of those protesters he detested, like Anderson, they wouldn't have been so worried about him, but it was his links to other countries, through his work, that had marked him out, and that the situation was being monitored internationally. So would I please back off and let them do their job. At that moment in time, Coben said – and do his words come back to haunt me now – he wasn't in any jeopardy. On the other hand, I had a career, a wife and child to think about, and I would do well to keep all three in mind.'

'Jesus, Andy,' McIlhenney gasped. 'How did you react to that?'

'In my mind, I picked him out of his chair and stuck the head on him. I was so steaming mad inside I almost did that very thing, but in the end I kept it to telling him to get the fuck out of my office. All he did was smile, tell me, "Take my message to heart, sir," and walk out.'

'And did you? Take his message to heart?'

Martin nodded. 'Oh yes, I did. What else was I to do? If it had just been the spooks, I'd probably have taken it to ACPOS, but the military, they're not subject to the normal rules. So I told Ainsley that there had been a pilferer on the Royal Mail and that they'd been dealt with, guessing that the watchers would be more careful with his letters in future.' He sighed. 'And that was that,' he said. 'I hadn't thought much about it since then; not till this morning.'

The superintendent leaned back in his chair. 'And what about us? You're suggesting that someone on our own side, national team, that is, might have had Glover killed. What are we supposed to do about that? How are we supposed to investigate it?'

'I wish I could tell you.'

'Never mind us, are you going to tell the boss now? Are we? Jesus, is there any question? Now that you've told us this story, we have to pass it on to him, even if you don't.'

The Tayside deputy chief constable ran his thick fingers through his hair. 'I've been thinking about that,' he said, 'and I have a problem with it, a big one at that. It's why I've said nothing about this to anyone, until now. If you or I do tell him, what's he going to do? Keep it to himself, or tell Aileen? He may feel that he has to. If he does that . . . I know her, and she won't sit still for it. Lads, these people operate on a need-to-know basis. I don't believe for a minute that Ainsley's surveillance was signed off by ministers. But Aileen's a minister, First Minister at that, and although defence isn't in her remit, Scotland as a whole is. Even if Coben's team had nothing to do with the murder, she will go straight to Downing Street, and the consequences ... they could be unthinkable.'

Twenty-one

'Come in, Sergeant,' said Carol Glover, 'but forgive me for hoping this will be your last visit.' She stepped aside to let Ray Wilding and DC Alice Cowan pass into the hall of her first-floor tenement flat. She had changed, from the T-shirt and jeans she had worn at their earlier meetings, into a black blouse and a dark grey skirt.

'I quite understand that,' the DS assured her. 'I wish I could guarantee that it will, but in the new circumstances—'

'New circumstances?' she exclaimed.

'You haven't been listening to the radio or had any calls from the media?'

'No, I haven't, and my number's ex-directory, so it'll take them a while to trace me. Are you telling me that my father's death wasn't caused by a heart attack? Did he overdose on insulin? Is that why you wanted those ampoules earlier?'

'Can we sit down and talk about this?'

'Of course, sorry; go on through into the living room.'

They preceded her, and as they entered they saw two young men standing in front of the hearth. One was short, dark and chubby, the other taller, slim, square-shouldered and fair-haired. Their only common feature was a day-old stubble. The smaller of the two was red-eyed; his companion was pale, and frowned as he approached the detectives.

'I'm Ed Collins,' he told them, 'Carol's fiancé. This is her brother, Wilkie.'

Wilding introduced himself, and Cowan. 'I'm sorry about your loss,' he said awkwardly. He had never been confident when dealing with the bereaved, always afraid to go beyond the most basic courtesies.

'It's unreal,' Wilkie Glover muttered, looking at Cowan, younger, closer to him in age, rather than the sergeant, as if he hoped to find more comfort in her. 'I saw my dad yesterday morning, and he was fine. Some bloody doctor I'm going to make if I couldn't see the signs.'

'Don't be hard on yourself,' the DC told him. 'There was nothing you could have noticed.'

'Things seem to have moved on,' his sister explained as she offered the visitors places on a low white sofa, then moved beside her brother to face them, both still standing.

'Listen,' Collins volunteered, 'I'll leave you to it. I'll go and get us a takeaway for lunch. A couple of pizzas maybe. What do you fancy?'

'No,' Carol insisted. 'I want you here.' He shrugged, and took a seat at a table by the window. She looked down at Wilding. 'So tell us. What happened to my dad?'

'When I came to collect your father's insulin supplies,' he began, 'I told you that there were some more tests we needed to run. They're now more or less complete. A short time ago we announced that his death is now the subject of a full-scale investigation. Mr Glover was killed by fatally high levels of glucose in his bloodstream—'

'Hold on,' Wilkie interrupted. 'I've just been studying that area. Like I said, I saw him yesterday and he was showing no signs of hyperglycaemia.'

'He wouldn't have been,' Wilding replied quietly. 'He was drugged, immobilised and then injected with massive quantities of the stuff.'

As both siblings stared down at him, he saw their faces go from pale to chalk-white. He rose from the couch. 'I think it's you two who need the seat,' he said.

Carol looked towards her fiancé. 'Ed,' she gasped, 'did you hear that?'

'I sure did.' He moved towards her, and put his arms around her, then eased her on to the space that the DS had vacated.

'We came to take a statement from you, Miss Glover, and we'll need one from your brother since he's here. They're not formal, but even so, the book says they should be done separately, I'm afraid. Do you have another room where we could interview you?'

'There's the kitchen.'

'You don't need to do that,' Collins declared, looking at the officers. 'Wilkie and I will go and get those pizzas, OK?'

'Fair enough,' the sergeant agreed.

'How long should we be gone?'

'Fifteen minutes will do fine.'

'It'll take us that long anyway.' He nodded to Wilkie and headed for the door.

'What do you want to ask me?' said Carol as it closed. 'I can't think of anything that I can tell you that would help.'

'Let's take it in stages,' Alice Cowan murmured. 'Let's begin with the last time you saw your dad.'

'Yesterday morning, like my brother; we were all here. The flat Wilkie's in just now is pretty crappy, so he's here quite a lot. I've told him he can have my spare room, but he says it would cramp my style . . . although I think he really means Ed's.'

'You're a close family, would you say?'

'Very. We always have been. Wilkie and I were both still at primary school when our mum died, but our father . . . he filled both roles, I suppose.'

'Did he have anyone else in his life?'

'You mean women? He had lady friends, but he didn't have a partner, if that's what you mean. There was Sandy Rankin, the *Herald* writer; they had dinner from time to time, but she couldn't be seen chumming him to book things because she's a reviewer and didn't want to be accused of bias. There was Karla Hiaasen, from the university; they were friendly. And of course there was June.'

'From the university?' the sergeant noted. 'Wasn't your father a full-time writer?'

'More or less, but he still lectured on some of the postgraduate courses in the accountancy school . . . so he could keep calling himself "Professor" mainly.' She smiled, faintly. 'He was very proud of that title, because my grandfather was one too . . . plus I reckon he was a bit of a closet academic snob. But back to the ladies; yes, he was closest to June Connelly, his agent. He used to stay with her when he went down to London, and she stayed at his place when she came up here. You don't ask your dad about his sleeping arrangements, but I suppose . . .' Her hand went to her mouth. 'Oh God, she's due here today. She'll be on the train. Dad said he was meeting her at Waverley at two thirty; she travels by train because she can work better on it than on aircraft,' she explained. 'She won't know about this.'

'Maybe Mr Collins could meet her.'

'He doesn't know June. Besides, he has to go to Tynecastle. No, it'll have to be me.'

'Don't worry,' Wilding assured her, 'we'll attend to that. But let's get through this first. How has your father's demeanour been recently?'

'He's been fine.'

'Has he mentioned any disagreements with anyone? Rows with his publisher, for example?'

'No, they love him; they make lots of money out of him, and he's happy with them.'

'How about the university? Any problems there?'

'No, he's a fixture there. He hasn't been Head of School for a few years, so he hasn't had any management role. There's been nothing to cause him problems.'

'Dissatisfied students?'

'No. I told you, his people were all postgrads. They finish the course, they get their Masters; that's it.'

'So there was nothing troubling him, and he had no enemies that you knew of?'

'No.'

'Did he ever mention Dr Bruce Anderson?' Wilding asked.

Carol Glover nodded. 'That he did. I know that Anderson didn't like him, and I know why, but Dad didn't take him seriously. He called him a shallow bully of a man. He didn't regard him as an enemy, though; he didn't regard him as anything, really. For fun, I asked him if he'd get me tickets for his event at the Book Festival so I could go along and heckle, but he took me seriously, and said he wouldn't do it. But why do you ask about Anderson? Is he a suspect?'

'He and your father had an . . . encounter . . . last night. But it was in a room full of people.'

'That doesn't answer my question.'

The sergeant met her gaze. 'It's as much of an answer as you're going to get, at this stage of the investigation at any rate. Let's change tack. Do you know who'll benefit from your father's estate?'

'We will. Wilkie and me. Dad told us about his will. He said there's money in trust for us already, there's a private pension fund that comes to us in the event of his death before its maturity, and then there's the house and everything else. It's split down the middle.' She paused, her hands trembling in her lap. 'Does that make us prime suspects?' she asked.

'Not unless you were hanging about the Book Festival at midnight last night.'

'We were hanging across the bar in Deacon Brodie's at midnight,' she retorted 'Wilkie, me, and a few hundred others, to judge from the noise in the place.'

'What about Mr Collins?'

'He was at a late-night Festival show, just along the road in the Bedlam Theatre; he joined us about quarter past.'

'Then you're all in the clear, no worries. So, to sum up, your father's been acting perfectly normally of late, and unconcerned about anything.'

Her brow creased. 'Not quite normally.'

'So what's been unusual about him?'

'He's been using my email, and using this place as a correspondence address.'

'What do you mean?' asked Cowan.

'What I've just said. For the last few months, mail's been arriving here for him, marked care of me.'

'Why?'

'It was to do with his website, he said. He gets . . . got . . . feedback from readers and sometimes they want to send him things. He didn't want them to have his own address, so he asked if once or twice he could use mine.'

'So instead they know where you live, and if he gets an obsessive . . .' the DC began, frowning.

'I'll be moving out of here in a few months, when Ed and I get married. We're buying a waterside flat in Leith.'

'Was there much of this mail?'

'Some, but not loads. A lot of it had foreign stamps.'

'What about the email?'

'He set up his own screen name on my AOL subscription, for the same reason . . . "Annie Wilkes watch" he called it. That's the name of the nutter in that Stephen King novel. He called himself *fatallyg*, as in Fat Ally G. Get it?' Cowan nodded. 'Ally was his nickname,' Carol went on, 'not generally used, though, only by his real friends, people like June, Fred Mount and Henry Noble, his author chums, and maybe Denzel Chandler . . . his partner's the new Book Festival director.'

'We know,' Wilding told her. 'She found your father's body.'

'Poor soul.' She looked up at him. 'Sergeant, you said earlier that Dad was found when they unlocked the author tent. If he had been found earlier . . .'

'Would he have survived? From what Professor Hutchinson, the pathologist, told us, he'd have been affected very quickly, beyond recovery.'

'Didn't he have that palm pilot thing of his? Wouldn't he have been able to phone?'

'He did use it. He sent Dr Mosley an email, but she didn't get it until this morning. That's what made her go to the yurt. I know,' the DS said, 'you're asking yourself, "Why didn't he phone her? Why email?" We're advised that he'd have been in a very confused state, not thinking normally. Plus there would have been a very small window before he lost consciousness.'

'I see.' Her eyes moistened. 'Poor old Dad,' she whispered. 'It's just horrible; I've got an image in my head that I don't think I'll ever lose.'

As she spoke they heard the front door open, and muffled male voices.

'Thanks,' said Alice Cowan softly. 'Unless there's anything else you can think of that might help, that'll do for now.' The dead man's daughter shook her head. 'In that case, maybe you could help Mr Collins cut up the pizzas, and ask your brother to join us for a couple of minutes.'

Twenty-two

Alex stepped past the smokers and through the doorway that led to Edinburgh Airport's arrivals gateway. During the day, even at weekends, the concourse area was always busy, a sign of the growing volume of traffic that was flowing into Scotland's capital. She looked for her father at the gate, but saw no sign of him. She frowned, wondering whether she had missed him, whether Aileen had given her the wrong time. Equally, and probably more likely, it was not unknown for flights to arrive early, and the capital city's baggage handlers were known for their efficiency. Her decision to come to the airport had been spur of the moment, and she had not called him; he had no reason to wait for her. She knew what had made her anxious to see him and her young half-siblings; her encounter with Andy had thrown her completely off balance, and she needed the equilibrium that they always gave her.

She was angry, too, angry with herself, at her weakness; for she had set herself up for the inevitable fall. She and he had split in shouts of anger, but that had been a sham on her part. In truth, it had torn her in two, and for all the active social life she had pursued since then, for all the sexual partners she had known, not legions, but more than she could tick off on the fingers of one hand, the torch that she carried for him still burned her, whenever she let it. Griff Montell had come closest to supplanting him, but he had fallen short too.

So she had set up their meeting, in spite of all the instincts that told

113

her not to. Her play for him in the kitchen had been unplanned, but once it had begun it had been unstoppable, neither of them thinking of what would come after. But as soon as he had gone, and the air around her had cooled to its normal even temperature, she had known within herself that nothing would come after. She could read him too well to believe that he would ever allow his betrayal of Karen to be more than a one-off. And so his call an hour earlier, his voice, metallic through his car's small speaker, telling her, apologetically, remorsefully, that it could never happen again, had come as no surprise. Yet still that torch burned, scorching her emotionally, and at that moment she could think of nothing, nobody who could ever put it out. To make it worse, the hurt would always be hers alone. She had never confided her deepest secrets to anyone but her father, and this one had to be kept, even from him.

She winced, and realised that she had been staring into space; for how long, she had no idea. She was on the point of turning on her heel and leaving when she heard a ringtone in her ear and remembered that she was still wearing her hands-free device. 'Yes,' she said, answering by voice command.

'Stand where you are, and look slowly to your right.' She did as she was instructed, and saw him, sitting at a table beside the coffee kiosk, phone held to his ear, the other hand waving. 'Come on over,' he said. 'The flight's delayed twenty minutes.'

'OK. I'll get myself a coffee.'

'Get me another one as well; filter, touch of milk, and since you're buying, I'll have a bun of some sort.'

She laughed as she walked towards him. 'I've always assumed I'd have to look after you in your old age,' she said, 'but I didn't realise it had started now.'

She went to the bar, waited while her order was made up, paid the inevitably Polish server, and carried a tray across to the table. When she arrived he was speaking on his mobile once again. 'Sorry,' he said. 'I was just letting Aileen know we'll be later than planned, and catching up with developments.'

'Yours or hers?'

'Both. We've had a sudden death this morning that's turned into a homicide. It'll also turn into a Holyrood by-election.'

'Ah! I heard something about that on the radio news as I was driving here, but I didn't really catch it.'

He updated her, explaining how Glover had been found and how the story had unfolded. 'Aileen's taken a double hit. She liked Glover, but on top of that, his death could have serious consequences for her politically.'

'She'll just have to win the seat.'

'How?'

'By putting up a candidate of her own who'll catch the anti-Trident vote as effectively as Ainsley Glover did.'

Bob smiled. 'Since when did you take an interest in politics?'

'Shortly after you started going out with the First Minister, or Justice Minister, as she was then. Plus it was on my university course as a fill-in subject, remember.'

'Then you should realise that Aileen's party's official line is pro-nuclear.'

'Doesn't matter,' Alex pointed out. 'Defence is a reserved power; it has nothing to do with the party in Scotland. She can put her own runner in there, throw up her hands in mock horror when he or she disowns Trident, then carry on, giving them full support against Anderson.'

'Anderson?'

'That's something I did pick up from the radio. I didn't understand the context but now I do. Bruce Anderson was on, saying that if the Labour Party doesn't select him this time, he'll fight the by-election as an independent candidate.'

'Bastard. It didn't take him long, but that doesn't surprise me.' He scowled. 'Maybe we'll have put a spoke in his wheel before then. Maybe we'll have charged him with murder.'

'Really?'

'I wish. Neil's interviewing him this afternoon, but more as a witness than a suspect.' He looked at her. 'Do you have anyone in mind for Aileen as a candidate?'

'That's her field, not mine. I'm sure she'll come up with someone.'

'How about you?'

Alex gasped. 'Me? That's the best laugh I've had all day; the first, for that matter.'

'Who's joking?'

'You'd better be.'

'Why should I be?' he challenged her. 'You're articulate, attractive, very clever, a fine analytical thinker, and you don't back off from anyone in debate. Plus you're anti-Trident yourself.'

'Dad, how do you know that I'm even a member of Aileen's party?'

He chuckled. 'I don't, but whether you are or not, that's a mere detail. You vote for her; you told me.'

'Because of her, mostly. Dad, stop it. What's put this crazy idea in your head?'

'I'm not sure. Just lately I've been a bit concerned about you.'

'In what way?' she asked cautiously.

'Like I say, I'm not sure. How can I put this? Looking at you, I'm not sure that your life is completely fulfilled. You say that you're totally focused on your career, and I believe you, but I find myself wondering whether these ambitions of yours, to be the world's youngest partner and so on, come from the heart, or from the drawing board. I want you to be all you can be, love, and I know you do too. I just wonder, your career . . . whether that's it.'

'So you want me to stand for Holyrood, to fulfil my subconscious desires, is that it?' There was a hard edge to her voice.

'No, no,' he protested, backing off hurriedly. 'That was just an idle suggestion, so don't take it seriously. But it must have dawned on you by now that I think you're the most talented person on the surface of the planet and that you could achieve anything you set your mind to achieving.'

As she looked at him, he thought for a moment or two that her eyes were a little blurred, but decided that the artificial light in the hall was patchy, and could be playing tricks.

'A real wee Wonderwoman, eh?' she murmured. 'Dad, let me just stick to my career, for I know where I'm going there, and, to be honest, blinded by love as you are, you just can't see that I'm fuck all good at anything else.'

He gazed back at her, trying to read her, realising that he may have stirred up something that might have been better left alone. 'Do you want to tell me about it?' he ventured.

'No,' she replied, but realised to her great surprise that she was lying. She really did want to pour everything out so that, as he always did, he could make it better.

'OK,' he said. 'When you do . . . You're my blind spot, Alex. I've built a career out of finding things that people try to hide from me, and I can be a holy terror at it. It doesn't work with you, though.'

For a moment, she came to the very edge of proving him wrong. And then a voice sounded on the other side of the arrivals hall.

'Dad! Sis!'

She and her father both turned, and saw running towards them the tanned, sturdy form of James Andrew Skinner, maybe an inch or so taller than when he had left for America six weeks before. They stood and went to meet him, and Alex was reminded of something that perhaps she had forgotten in his absence, that there was someone else who made her life worth living.

Twenty-three

'What's this guy's background?' asked Sammy Pye.

Neil McIlhenney looked up at the grey stone facade of the Georgian building in Darnaway Street, the short terrace that links Moray Place to Heriot Row. 'He's a doctor from Glasgow.'

'Even so, this is top end of the market. The man must be minted.'

'Not necessarily; there are always people buying property like this on huge mortgages and living on baked beans, because they think it's a good long-term bet. Then the interest rates go up and they have to start counting the beans.'

'Rather them than me,' the inspector confessed. 'I'll stick to my suburban semi, thanks, and the prospect of actually paying off my mortgage some day.' He followed his colleague up to the secure front door, and watched as he found the button labelled 'Anderson' and pressed it.

'Yes?' The answering voice was young, a child's, and female.

'Is Dr Anderson at home? This is Detective Superintendent McIlhenney, with Detective Inspector Pye. We'd like a word with him.'

'Can you wait for a minute, please?' the girl asked. 'Daddy,' the detectives heard her call out.

A few seconds later, a man's voice replaced hers. 'I've been expecting you people,' it said sharply. 'Come up. First floor.'

A soft buzz sounded close to them. Pye pushed the door open and led the way into a tiled hall, lit by narrow glass panels on either side of the entrance and by a cupola above. An unsupported stone stairway, one of those little-regarded engineering masterpieces that are commonplace in New Town buildings, led upwards.

The one-time Secretary of State for Scotland was waiting for them at the entrance to the flat. He was of medium height, but stocky, and his body language shouted impatience at them. The superintendent remembered him from his days in office, and noted that his hair had gone completely grey in the time since then.

'Come in, come in,' he said, leading them into a drawing room that would have been elegant with period furniture but in which a modern L-shaped sofa arrangement looked completely incongruous. A slim, auburn-haired, thirty-something woman stood beside the window, with a girl, an eleven-year-old female version of her father, at her side, both of them frowning at the officers as they entered. 'My partner, Anthea Walters,' he grunted, 'and my daughter Tanya. Leave us, please, girls; sit in the study if you'd like.'

For a moment it seemed that Walters would protest, but finally she nodded, murmured, 'If we must,' coldly, glancing at the officers as if they were of another species, and led the child from the room, burning Pye with her eyes as she passed close to him.

As the door closed, Anderson looked up at the older detective. 'McIlhenney, is it? Weren't you Bob Skinner's exec when he was my security adviser?'

'That's right, sir. I was a sergeant then.'

'Up in the world, eh? And how's Bob? From what I hear he's got over his antipathy to politicians in a big way.' There was no mistaking the sneer.

The big detective's eyes narrowed. 'DCC Skinner is very well, sir,' he replied. 'I'm not sure that he ever had a general antipathy to politicians, only those who tried to fuck him over for their own careers' sake.'

Anderson's eyes widened and for a moment Pye thought that he would fire back, but instead he chuckled. 'I see the grand master still inspires devotion in his acolytes,' he murmured.

'The respect and loyalty of his colleagues, I would sooner say, sir,' McIlhenney countered. 'And maybe he's due a bit more respect from you; after all, he did take care of your wife's killer and recover your daughter.'

'He did his job, that's all. He's still doing it. I always knew he was a careerist, but Christ,' he sighed, 'sleeping his way to the top.'

'Is that so?' The superintendent's brows knitted, and his normally amiable features darkened. 'Anthea Walters, you said. That would be Lady Anthea Walters, wouldn't it, eldest daughter of the Duke of Lanark and heiress to the family fortunes, the same Lady Walters who has two cautions and one conviction to her name for possession of cannabis and who was chucked out of the US a few years ago after an incident involving a white powder? So what would you be doing, Doctor? Sleeping your way to the bottom?'

Every trace of humour vanished from Anderson's face. 'That's out of order. Your police prejudice is showing. Anthea's put those days behind her. She's a remarkable woman, with much to offer society.'

'I'll look forward to watching her do that, sir,' said the detective. 'Now can we get down to business?'

'Yes, please, as quickly as possible. You're here to talk about Glover, yes?'

'That's right, the late Mr Ainsley Glover. You've heard of his death, yes?'

'I have indeed, courtesy, initially, of that little Glasgow journo Ryan McCool, who called me to ask if I would give him an expression of sympathy. I declined. Then he called me again, telling me that you are now regarding the death as suspicious.'

'Actually, sir,' Pye, no longer content to be a spectator, told him, 'we're regarding it as murder.'

'How, in God's name? Initially you were talking myocardial infarction. Can't you people tell the difference?'

'We don't have to, sir.' The DI smiled. 'We have doctors, like you, to diagnose for us, and pathologists, like Professor Hutchinson, to correct them when they fuck up.'

'I see you've been to the Skinner charm school as well, Mr Pye.'

'And proud of it, sir.'

'So how did Glover die?'

'We're keeping that to ourselves, for now,' McIlhenney declared firmly. 'However, I can tell you that he was killed, with premeditation, by someone with more than sketchy medical knowledge.'

'Are you working up to accusing me?' Anderson barked.

'If we were going to do that, Doctor, we'd be in an interview room in Gayfield Square, or Fettes, and you'd have a lawyer sat beside you. There are questions we need to ask you, that's all.'

'So let's hear them.' The man dropped on to the sofa. 'You might as well sit while you do it.'

The two detectives accepted the grudging invitation. 'Let's begin with your attitude to Ainsley Glover,' said Pye. 'You knew him, yes?'

'Yes, I did. I met him a few years back, when I visited Heriot-Watt University with some political colleagues, while we were in opposition.'

'How did you get on?'

'Get on? In truth he didn't make much of an impression on me. I must have made an impression on him, though, because a few years later, after my period in office, he published one of his penny dreadfuls, in which there was a fictional Secretary of State for Scotland. The physical description was me to a T and the character was very unpleasant: venal, vindictive and thoroughly evil. I thought about suing, but I was advised that it wouldn't be in my best interests.'

'Why not?'

'Counsel's opinion was that I'd have to prove my assertion, against

Glover's undoubted denial and assurance of no slur on my integrity. I'd have to prove bad faith on his part, and counsel felt that would be impossible. I didn't like it, but I had to live with it.'

'Did you ever challenge Mr Glover personally?'

'As in, "Come outside, you objectionable little man"? Hardly.'

'In any way?'

'I wouldn't call it a challenge. After I'd been told I had no legal recourse, I called him and accused him of blackening my reputation. He told me I was being preposterous, that actually he had someone else in mind when he came up with the character, but that he wasn't about to tell me who it was. I can't remember who hung up on who. Maybe we both slammed the phone down at the same time.'

'And after that exchange, when did you meet next?' asked McIlhenney.

'Now long afterwards, at an official functional. I ignored him, blanked him. Then last night, at the Book Festival party in Charlotte Square.'

'And you quarrelled?'

'Yes. I was going to ignore him again, but he came up to me and picked a fight. I think he'd had a couple of drinks.'

'He started the argument?'

'Yes he did. I'd have turned my back on him but he wouldn't let me. He asked me if I was out to live up to the characterisation in his book. I asked him what the fuck he meant by that, and he said, "Trident." I think he saw it as his personal campaign, and resented anyone else who opposes its awful presence in our country. It all got a bit heated after that, until finally I walked away from him.'

'OK. Now tell us this, and think carefully before you answer. When you went to the do last night, did you know that Mr Glover would be there?'

'I don't need to think about that one. I didn't know, I wasn't shown a guest list, and I never asked to see one.'

'Did you expect him to be there?'

'It never occurred to me to wonder whether he would be or not. I do not arrange my diary with Ainsley Glover's movements in mind, any more than I do those of Fred Noble.'

'Fred Noble?' Pye exclaimed. 'What's he got to do with it?'

'I've had a similar dispute with him. One of his books, the year before last, had a storyline about a politician whose wife was murdered. I thought that was far too close to home and I told Noble as much.'

'Did you ever think of suing him?'

'No, I'd had enough grief with Glover. I decided that the bastards were out to get me, but that I was going to let it all wash over me in future.'

'Did you see Mr Noble last night?'

'I saw him, across the room, but I ignored him, and happily he took the hint.'

'When did you leave the event, sir?' the inspector asked.

'About eleven thirty.'

'Alone?'

'Yes. Anthea would have accompanied me to the do, but we couldn't get a sitter for Tanya. They were in the audience at my event, but left afterwards.'

'Ah yes, you had a reading last night, didn't you?'

'I did, at six thirty in the main theatre; full house.' He allowed himself a small, smug smile.

'So you'd have been in the yurt?'

'Yes, we were all asked to go there to meet our chairperson, and be miked up.'

'And afterwards?'

'Yes, I was there again. I met up with Anthea and Tanya, before they left. I had a long queue in the book-signing tent; it was after eight before I got there.'

'So you'd have seen Mr Glover at that point? We know he was in the tent before the party started.'

'Well. Yes, I suppose I did. At least I was aware of his presence. I was talking to my daughter and to Denzel Chandler then, so I paid him no mind.'

'Was Lady Walters awake when you got home?' asked McIlhenney.

Anderson shot his inquisitor a furious exasperated look. 'Of course!' he snapped.

'Not "of course," Doctor. As you said, you left at eleven thirty. You're close to Charlotte Square, but it must still have taken you ten minutes to get home. I was asleep myself at that time.'

'Well, Anthea wasn't, OK? She was in bed, watching some crap on television. I let her know I was home but I was still boiling after the barney with Glover, so I read for a while, before turning in myself.'

'And was she asleep by that time?'

Anderson stared at the superintendent for several seconds, long enough for the detective to decide that he was going to ignore his question, until finally he replied, slowly and evenly, 'She was, but I woke her, and we had sex.' He rose to his feet, dismissively. 'Now, gentlemen, if you'll excuse me. We're due at Anthea's father's place in Biggar this afternoon, and it'll take us an hour or so to get there.'

McIlhenney stayed in his seat and looked at his colleague. 'Are you done, Sammy?'

Pye smiled. 'I think so, sir; for now, at any rate.' He pushed himself easily up from the sofa.

Anderson showed them to the door in silence; they felt his eyes upon them as they walked downstairs, and stepped out into the street.

McIlhenney drew a deep breath, then let it out all in one. 'Well,' he exclaimed, as they walked towards Moray Place, 'what did you think of that, Sammy my lad?'

'I wouldn't like to be in the same room as him and the boss, that's for sure.'

'I would, but tucked away in a corner. Apart from that, though?'

Pye frowned at him. 'Are you asking me if he's a viable suspect? He disliked the victim intensely, he has the medical knowledge to have planned the killing, and he was in the yurt with Glover earlier in the evening.'

The superintendent nodded. 'All of that, and by the way, that was pretty sharp, Sam. We only had the assumption that Glover was there before; we had no bloody witness. Now we have.'

'And Anderson could have seen him put his pouch in that drawer. On top of all that, he has no alibi worth the name. He could have got home, flagged up his presence to Anthea, then gone out again without her knowing and been back up at the square in time to rig the insulin pen before Glover picked it up. I can see how he'd have done it.'

'What about access to the Pavulon? You don't find that in Boots.'

'No, but Randall Mosley told me that he still consults at a private hospital in Midlothian; they do surgical procedures there.'

'Do you fancy him for it, then?'

'Let's wait for McCall and his young PC to find that ampoule and see what we can lift from that.'

'Every minute might count.'

'Agreed, but . . .'

'I know, Sammy. The next stage would be a warrant to search his flat for Pavulon and glucose. Based on what we've got at the moment, I can't see any sheriff, not even our tamest, giving us one. You're right; let's wait for the search to complete and see what that turns up.'

'Nothing,' said Pye gloomily, 'if the perpetrator is as smart as we reckon he is. It's not his flat, by the way. I checked the register before we went along; it belongs to Anthea Walters.'

'Hey,' the superintendent chuckled, 'given her history, do you think the drugs squad could get a warrant to search the place?' He paused. 'It's OK, I'm kidding. Still ... Bugger!' he swore as his mobile's ringtone interrupted him. He stopped in his tracks, took it out and flipped it open. 'Yes,' he said calmly, mastering his irritation.

'How's your day going?' a clear male voice asked. 'Caught the bad guy yet?'

'No, but we've got a couple of options already. You not asleep yet, pal?'

'Fat chance,' Mario McGuire replied. 'Paula's zonked, but I'm still staring at the ceiling. Fucking jet lag. And it doesn't just screw up your body clock: it slows your mind down as well. Since we spoke, there's been something trying to burrow its way out of my brain. Finally it's made it. I know who planned Glover's murder.'

'What?' McIlhenney exclaimed. 'Have you been smoking something that would get you arrested here?'

'I'm serious. I know who worked out how to kill him.'

'Man, if you're taking the piss, this is not the time.'

'Hear me out, Superintendent.'

'Tell me then.'

'He did; the man himself. Ainsley Glover did. I told you I've read all his books; well, in the third one, *Black Sugar* it's called, there's a murder where exactly that method is used. I'm surprised nobody's put you wise already.'

'We haven't told anybody how he was killed.'

'You might as well have.' McGuire paused. 'Oh dear, I'm in the shit. I've wakened Paula. Got to go.'

McIlhenney sighed as he put his phone back in his pocket.

'Complication?' the detective inspector asked him.

'You could say that, Sammy. Our head of CID has just widened the field of suspects from somebody with medical knowledge to take in anyone who's read one of Ainsley's fucking books!'

Twenty-four

'Where does that lot take us, Sarge?' asked Alice Cowan.

Wilding shrugged as he placed a chair behind the extra desk that the Festival administrator had supplied. It had been sited just beyond the entrance and to the left, facing the area where Glover had died; that had been blocked off with yellow crime scene tape. At the back of the tent, a whiteboard had been set up, but it was virgin. 'It rules out patricide, assuming Glover's kids really were getting tanked up along the Royal Mile when he died. It tells us that he liked to keep his fan base at arm's length. It tells us something about his circle of friends, lady friends at any rate. But in terms of a solution, it doesn't take us any further.'

'Wilkie's a medical student.'

'Sure, but not even they can be in two places at once.'

'Carol's a dentist; they do anaesthetics.'

'But not with the drug that was used on the victim.'

'Maybe it was a conspiracy; the two of them, and a third party. Their dad must have been worth a few bob.'

The sergeant sighed. 'You spent too long in Special Branch, Alice. Or maybe you've been reading too many crime novels.'

She looked at him disdainfully. 'I don't read crime novels; they're for saddos.'

'Like me, you mean? So what do you read?'

'Romance, mostly.'

'Jesus, and you're calling me a sad person.'

'Not you,' she said, backtracking. 'You're different. You've got a professional interest in the subject.'

Wilding laughed. 'When in a friggin' hole, Alice, stop digging. Are you saying that my approach to crime-solving is based on pearls of wisdom that I pick up from reading police procedurals? Do you think DI Walter Strachan's my mentor?' He winked at her. 'Because if you do, you're wrong; my professional style's based on somebody else fictional, but he's retired now, so I'm on my own.'

'Excuse us.'

They turned, startled by a voice that came from the entrance to the tent. Cowan looked out and saw two men standing there. The younger, forties, she reckoned, was tall, over six feet, with a small head on a long body, floppy dark hair and a narrow build; he was dressed mainly in black. His companion was an inch or two shorter but with a bigger frame, clothed in jeans and a red T-shirt, emblazoned with a devilish face she took for that of a bull, a first impression confirmed, once she could read it, by the name 'Cordoba' stencilled below. What little was left of the man's greying hair was cropped so close that at first glance he seemed totally bald, making it consequently difficult to guess his age.

'CID?' he asked.

'That's us,' Wilding confirmed, stepping into view past the DC. 'Mr Mount, is it?' The bald man nodded. 'And Mr Noble?'

'That's me,' his companion confirmed.

'I read your books,' the detective explained. 'You both look more or less like the photos on the cover.'

'That's good to know,' said Fred Noble with a tentative smile. 'It means we haven't aged much in the five years since they were taken. Randy Mosley said you wanted to talk to Henry and me about poor old Ainsley.'

Wilding nodded. 'That's right. We're talking to everybody who was with him last night.' As he spoke he noticed a thick and recently lit cigar burning between the first two fingers of Henry Mount's right hand. 'Sir,' he murmured, nodding towards it, 'I'm sorry, but even if it doesn't look it, this is a workplace, so . . .'

'Of course; excuse me,' the author responded. He lifted up his left foot, stubbed out the offending object on the sole of his shoe, and slipped it into his pocket. 'My vice,' he explained, his accent more than hinting at west of Scotland origins. 'Deeply non-PC these days, but I look on it as an aid to weight loss.' He smiled. 'It's a weak excuse, I'll grant you, but it's the best I can come up with. Wish I could give it up: they're bloody expensive, even abroad, where you're not giving most of the cost to that bastard in Eleven Downing Street.'

'You don't like politicians, Mr Mount?'

He looked at Cowan, appraising her, trying to read behind her question. 'I used to work in the world of politics, lady. I don't like politicians of a certain colour, especially not when they pursue policies that discriminate against the people they should be trying to help the most.'

'Mr Glover was a politician.'

'Hah!' Mount's guffaw filled the tent. 'Congratulations, officer, you've just won Henry's Golden Cigar for the unsubtle question of the week. My God, I could have written your dialogue. Come to think of it, I did; last book but one.'

'I must read it,' said the DC drily. 'I might pick up some more tips.'

'You do that; I can use the sales. Now, if you want a proper answer, I never regarded Ainsley as a politician, any more than he did. He was a sincere man, and when he got passionate about an issue, he could talk about nothing else.'

'Gentlemen,' Wilding intervened, 'come round here and have a seat, so we can do this like a proper interview.' He introduced himself, and his colleague, as the two writers each took a chair. 'You were saying, Mr Mount,' he continued.

'I was saying that while Ainsley might have been an MSP, he wasn't part of any machine.'

'Do you know if he had any enemies in Parliament?'

'None he ever mentioned; he was a man who made friends, not foes.'

'What about Dr Anderson?'

'Anderson?' Fred Noble spat the name out. 'It's an honour to have that man as an enemy. That's one thing that Ally and I had in common: we were both on his shit list.'

'Why?'

'Same reason in each case: he accused each of us of modelling characters on him.'

'And did you?'

'I didn't and Ally swore he didn't either. Truth is, the guy's ego is so big he couldn't park it in an aircraft hangar.'

'Were you aware that he and Mr Glover had an argument last night?'

'Everybody in the bloody tent was aware of it. There was nearly another one after it. Henry was going to go across and nut him after what he called Ally, but I persuaded him that there are better ways of getting your name in the papers.'

'Our poor old pal's found the best way of all,' said Mount gloomily. 'You guys are quite certain that this is murder, are you? There are precedents for pathologists getting it wrong.'

'The pathologist in question is Professor Hutchinson.'

'Joe? No doubt then, it's homicide, right enough. Are you going to tell us the cause of death?'

Wilding smiled, and shook his head. 'I like wearing a suit to work. The uniform does not flatter me at all. How about you, Mr Mount? Are you on Dr Anderson's shit list?'

The bulky author nodded. 'I am, actually.' Noble looked at him, surprised. 'Not for anything in a book, Fred,' he continued. 'I do a monthly blog on my website; it makes up for nobody ever having asked me to write a newspaper column, and paying me for it. I comment on anything and everything under the sun. A couple of years back, there was a media story about some rich waster, a duke's daughter, who got into bother in the US for possession of cocaine. Instead of banging her up for a few years, as they would have done if she'd been a hooker, they took her to the nearest airport and stuck her on a plane home. I wrote about it, said that although I don't believe in the criminalisation of drugs, I believe even less in the rich being exempt from the law. I went on to comment on useless prats like her being allowed to adopt one of daddy's old titles as a courtesy, and suggested that the best way to put a stop to the silly practice would be for the tabloids to stop referring to her as Lady Whatever . . . Lady Anthea Walters, it was . . . and just as plain Miss or, better still, by her surname alone, just like ordinary criminals and footballers and the like. That piece was very popular: I had a lot of positive feedback from readers, including several Americans, pissed off that she'd been turned loose. In among them, though, was a piece of vitriol from Bruce Anderson. It was threatening, only it wasn't; it said that he was a man of influence, and that he would put it to work against me unless a full apology appeared in the following month's blog, but it didn't explain how he thought he could hurt me.'

'How did you deal with it?' asked Cowan.

A look came into Mount's eye, as wicked as that of the bull on his T-shirt. 'First I sent him a private response by email. I told him that from what I knew of him, he and I were adherents of the same political party, and that as far as I knew it was committed to freedom of speech. I closed by inviting him to get back in touch if there was any part of "Go and abuse yourself with a lavatory brush" that needed explanation. The next month I published both his message and my response.'

'Was that the end of it?'

'Not quite. He phoned me, at home.'

'How did he get your number?'

Mount looked at the DC patiently. 'Research Document Number One, hen: the phone book. Everybody assumes I'm ex-directory, but I'm not, never have been. My wife took the call. She always picks up after the fourth ring; if I'm busy I let it get that far. She came through to my study and said that an extremely rude man wanted to speak to me. It was Anderson, of course. He said that he'd half a mind to come out to Gullane and thump me. I told him that I knew he'd only half a mind, and that if he ever put down the lavatory brush and plucked up the courage, he could find me in the local gym most lunchtimes. I'm still waiting, but it's been a while. I don't think he'll turn up now. He certainly didn't want to know me last night.'

'You live in Gullane?' said Wilding. 'So does our gaffer, DCC Skinner.'

'Yes, I know Bob. We frequent the same local.'

'Did you tell him about your run-in with Anderson?'

'I mentioned it, one Friday night. He said that if I wanted to make a formal complaint about his threat of violence, he'd have someone visit him and give him a warning. I told him I wasn't taking it that seriously.'

'Did you ever find out why the guy got so worked up about this Lady Anthea?'

'She's his girlfriend, Ray,' The quartet looked up as the newcomer spoke; they had no idea how long he had been standing there, in the entrance area. 'Mr McIlhenney and I have just left the two of them,' he added. 'But don't let me interrupt your interview.'

'We're almost finished, Sammy.' Wilding turned back to the two authors. 'Did Mr Glover say anything to you last night that struck you as odd? Did he give any hint that he felt threatened in any way?'

'No,' Mount replied, 'he was fine. A bit pissed towards the end, but that happened with him sometimes. He was looking forward to today, in fact. June, his other half, was coming up from London.'

'June Connelly?' Cowan asked. 'His agent?'

'She was a bit more than that. Didn't you know that?'

'His daughter thought that might be the case but she couldn't say for certain.'

Noble frowned; the expression seemed to add to the overall sense of blackness that emanated from him. 'Poor June,' he sighed. 'This'll be a bigger shock for her than for any of us. Henry,' he asked, 'can you remember when Ally said her train was due?'

Wilding replied for him. 'Two thirty. But it's running half an hour late. DC Cowan's going along to meet it.'

'Hell no!' Noble exclaimed. 'With respect, that won't do. She doesn't know you, Constable. If she's heard on the radio on the way up, she'll be in a hell of a state, and if she hasn't . . . it's better if that sort of news is broken by friends. Henry and I will go along there,' he glanced at his watch, 'straight away.'

Mount grimaced. 'Wish I could, chum,' he sighed, 'but I'm off to Melbourne this evening, remember.'

'Of course, I'd forgotten that. I'll do it myself, then.' He looked at the detectives. 'I imagine you'll want to interview her.'

The sergeant nodded. 'As soon as she's up to it.'

'Give me your number and I'll phone you. I'll take her up to my place; she can hardly go to Ally's now.'

'That's fine.' Wilding rose, and Cowan followed his lead. 'We won't detain you further, gents,' he said, handing Noble a card bearing his office and mobile numbers. They waited as the odd couple left the yurt. As soon as the door had closed, Pye came across to join them.

'Where's the super?' Wilding asked him.

'He's gone home, to try and rescue some of his Sunday and keep a rash promise he made to his kids. The older two are back at school in a few days, so he's under pressure.'

'Lucky him. Still, I suppose he didn't have to come in at all. You could have handled Anderson.'

'Maybe, but I was glad he was there in the end. Big Neil's a calm guy, mostly, but when somebody winds him up, he doesn't take any prisoners.' He described the interview of Anderson, and McIlhenney's exchange with the former Secretary of State.

'Ouch!' Alice Cowan grinned. 'What's she like, this aristocratic junkie girlfriend?'

'Pale and not very interesting, I'd have said. She doesn't like us, that's for sure; she looked at me like I was one of her dad's pheasants.'

'You mean peasants?'

'No, I mean what I said; she looked as if she'd like to shoot me.'

'Where did you leave it with them?'

'Unresolved. Anderson says he was home when Glover was killed.'

'Do you believe him?' Wilding asked pointedly.

'That doesn't matter; with nobody to say different, a jury would believe him when Lady Anthea confirmed that he was.' He paused, then went on briskly, deflecting attention from his own persistent vision of Dr Anderson creeping silently out of the Darnaway Street flat, retracing his steps back up the hill to Charlotte Square, and ambushing the unsuspecting Glover. 'How did you two get on with the daughter?'

'And the son,' the sergeant volunteered. 'He was there too; and the boyfriend, Ed Collins.'

'What do you know about him?'

'Nothing, other than the fact that he was in the pub with the Glover kids when the father was killed. We interviewed Carol and Wilkie – that's the lad – but Collins nipped off without telling us, before we could talk to him.'

'Did he know you'd want to see him?'

'To be fair, he probably didn't; we didn't ask him to wait. Carol said he had to get to Tynecastle for the game.'

Pye gasped. 'His fiancée's dad's just been bumped off and he goes to see the Jambos?'

'That's football for you,' said Cowan cheerfully. 'One of my aunts died a couple of years ago; the funeral was on a Monday morning, and in the evening my uncle flew out to the Ukraine for a Celtic Champions' League game.'

'Ah well, I don't suppose it matters. If you're happy he's not in the frame, we can catch up with him later. Did you learn anything worth knowing about Glover?'

Wilding shook his head. 'Not really. You picked up on the close relationship with his agent. Also he seems to have been pally with a lady journalist, Sandy Rankin, although there's no suggestion they were any more than friends. That's about it.'

'Apart from him using his daughter's place as a postal address,' Cowan pointed out. 'And setting up a guest screen name on her email, to keep potential stalkers at bay.'

The inspector stared at her. 'Run that past me again,' he said.

The detective constable repeated Carol Glover's story. 'It makes sense when you think about it,' she said. 'If I was in the public eye like that, I wouldn't want people to get too close to me.'

'I'm sure you wouldn't, Alice. But maybe this bloke was more worried about . . .' Pye stopped in mid-gaffe, but it was beyond retrieval. They were both ex-Special Branch and she picked up his meaning at once.

'Are you saying he thought he was under surveillance?' she exclaimed. 'Come on, sir. If he'd thought that, he'd have told his daughter surely.'

'I'm not saying anything,' Pye snapped. Cowan responded with an intake of breath, and a look that might have frozen the mercury in the thermometer mounted on a pillar behind her head. 'What did he do with this correspondence?'

'I can't say for sure. I assume he took the letters away with him, and I suppose the emails will be in Carol's computer, unless he deleted them.'

'Then find out, and retrieve what you can. How do you know there's nothing in that material that's relevant to our investigation? Answer: you don't till you've seen it. I know it's Sunday, Alice, but try to pretend it's just another working day and stay on the ball.'

'Yes, sir!' She strode out of the yurt, making no attempt to hide her anger.

'Hey,' Wilding murmured when she had gone. 'I thought that kicking the DCs was my job.'

'Do you think I'm being hard on her, Ray? Well, now it's your turn. The pair of you are equally at fault. Hell no, what am I saying? Ultimately you're the one to blame, for you're the senior officer. There. Now do you want to go and cry in the toilet as well?'

The reproved sergeant laughed. 'Sammy, if you think that's what she's doing, you don't know Cowan very well; more likely she's making a wax model of you and getting ready to stick pins in its eyes. Fact is, we've got a long list of people to interview. My judgement was that that came first, and I'm standing by it. But that outburst of yours just now, that had fuck all to do with the notion that Glover's killer might have been sending him threatening letters or emails, had it? You do think he was being bugged, don't you? Or do you know it for a fact? Is that it?'

'Leave it, Ray.'

'No, sir. We're supposed to be a team, and this is a murder investigation. No information that might relate to it can be on a need-to-know basis.'

As he looked at his colleague, Pye found himself recalling how McIlhenney had faced down Andy Martin on his behalf, over exactly the same point of principle. And he realised that he had learned another lesson. 'Go find Alice,' he said, 'if you can, and bring her back here – once she's cleaned the wax off her hands, that is.'

'Sure, boss.'

As he waited, the young inspector thought of calling his senior officer for clearance, then remembered something else he had said in that earlier confrontation. He was the lead investigator, and he would rely on his own judgement.

Wilding returned in no more than three minutes, with Cowan at his heels looking as angry as before. 'Found her in the bog, with a box of Kleenex.'

'That'll be the fucking day,' she hissed.

'Alice,' Pye began, 'let me make something clear to you. The next time you show me insubordination, either by word or attitude, you'll be back in uniform so fast it'll set a record.' He waited.

Gradually, the tension in her lessened and the flame in her eyes dimmed. 'Yes, sir,' she said quietly.

'OK, that's fine. Now, I apologise, to you and DS Wilding. The late Mr Glover was indeed being watched, not by our lot but by an outside agency. I'm telling you this on the same confidential basis that I was let into the loop. It doesn't go outside the inquiry team, and . . . I can't stress this enough . . . no hint of it can ever be dropped to the family. Now, I have no reason to believe this surveillance is connected to his murder, or that the people involved are, but you'll agree that the fact of it puts the arrangement he had with Carol in a different context.'

'Too right,' Wilding grunted. 'Sorry, boss. You were right earlier, we should have been covering this.'

Pye smiled. 'We're not going there again, Ray. You took a view, and in the knowledge you had at the time, you were right. But we do need to recover the back-door correspondence Glover received. That means we need to get into Carol's computer, and into Glover's house. I'm going to ask the duty inspector at Torphichen Place to put uniforms outside it, front and back, then as soon as we've got the family's permission, and the keys, we need to get in there. That's going to stretch our resources.' He glanced at Wilding. 'Do you think that DI Stallings would agree to lend me that bright young DC of hers, Haddock?'

The sergeant nodded. 'I reckon so . . . although there'll be a price to pay in the future, I'm sure.'

Once again, Pye thought of Andy Martin, and his threat to McIlhenney. 'I'll pay it,' he said. 'It'll be worth it. Give her a call, then if she okays it, raise the lad, wherever he is, and tell him he's come into an overtime windfall and to get his carcass along here. Then get back out to the daughter's place and get her co-operation for what we need to do.' He smiled. 'While you do that, I must pay a visit to Sergeant McCall and PC Knight, to see whether they're still up to their elbows in crap.'

Twenty-five

'It's funny,' Neil McIlhenney chuckled, 'but I've never taken you for a guy who'd sit on a beach filtering the sand through his toes.'

'Why not?' Bob Skinner replied 'I'm a dad just like you, and it's a nice Sunday. OK, maybe I'm a bit older than you, but my kids are younger than yours, apart from wee Louis here, of course.' He turned to the infant who sat beside him in a carry-chair, chewing earnestly on a teething ring, and tickled his tummy. 'Eh, wee man. Won't be long before you're on your feet and in the sea with the other four.' He pointed to the water's edge, where Spencer McIlhenney and his own adopted son Mark were superintending James Andrew and Seonaid as they played in the light surf. 'The bathing's always safe here,' he said. 'Just as well, for I don't know what Markie-boy could do if a big wave came in,' he murmured. 'The Jazzer's a better swimmer than he is.'

'Maybe better than Spence, too,' Neil conceded, 'and definitely better than Lauren, although you won't find her with this group any more. She sees her place as up at the house with Aileen and Lou.'

'That's all part of growing up, mate. I always think that puberty's a bigger thing for a girl than a boy. With lads the change is more gradual, but . . . She may be an early teen, but you better start thinking of your Lauren as a woman. You know, I'd never heard of PMT till Alex was that age, then I found out about it big time. Her mother was neither up nor down at that time of the month . . . although maybe she was in her teens, I don't know . . . but Alexis, Christ, from being a peaceable wee girl, she started throwing tantrums every four weeks, regular as clockwork. It was probably the worst part of being a single parent.' He broke off as a cry of 'Daddee!' split the air and Seonaid came running up the beach towards him, throwing herself into his arms as she arrived, soaking his shirt and shorts.

'Hey,' he called out, rolling backwards and throwing her in the air, then catching her again as she squealed with delight. 'I tell you, Neil, I'm making a point of cherishing every moment of this one's childhood, for it'll be over in the blink of an eye.'

The child soon tired of the game and returned to her brothers, and their friend, leaving the two men to their chat. 'Tell me,' said Skinner, 'for how long did you consider taking Andy's advice and keeping me in the dark about Glover's surveillance?'

'Two seconds, maybe.'

'Twice as long as was appropriate, I'd say.'

'Yes. Sorry I hesitated.' McIlhenney snorted. 'I don't know what he was thinking about, suggesting that I could keep a significant line of investigation secret from my reporting officer.'

'No, me neither. It's not like Andy to think that way. He's never been a pure book operator, any more than I have, but he's always come down on the right side of an issue.'

'Maybe this Coben guy got to him; maybe he really was scared for you and for Aileen.'

'Andy? Scared?'

'It would be unprecedented, I'll grant you.'

'Unnecessary too, all of it. Aileen and I agreed very early in our relationship that it was all right for each of us to keep operational secrets from the other. Plus, I knew about the surveillance.'

'You knew?' McIlhenney exclaimed. 'You mean they cleared it with you?'

'No, they didn't, for which omission somebody's probably had his arse kicked. I found out by accident. Andy's pal at BT was my source before he ever was his. When he got leaned on by Andy for a second time, he got pissed off, so he came to me and told me about it. So did Amanda Dennis, after he started poking around in MI5. It didn't take me long to figure out who was behind it, or why. Trident's an incredibly sensitive issue; anything, anything at all that might relate to its security is going to attract a degree of attention.'

'This defence intelligence heavy didn't come to see you, did he?'

'No, and I didn't know about his visit to Andy either, before you ask.'

'So what do we do? Regard the man Coben as a suspect?'

'Nah, I can't credit that. MoD intelligence don't go bumping off people like Glover.' He chuckled. 'Not as a general rule, anyway.'

'How do I proceed? This is not my usual line of work.'

'It's within your pay grade, though. Forget about Coben; I'll handle that. You get that list, the one that Andy has in his safe. Take a look at the names on it and follow them up; do what you can to check their well-being. If anything's happened to any of them, bring it back to me.'

'Will do. Incidentally,' the superintendent murmured casually, 'you might be getting a call from Andy, about me. He and I had a disagreement. He didn't want Sammy Pye in the room when he talked to me. It got a bit—'

'You had your way, I hope.'

'Yes, but there were things said, warnings given.'

'Then forget them; and forget about getting that list. I'll do that myself. Andy will be having a visit from me, tomorrow morning. He's crossed the line a couple of times today, by trying to keep secrets from me and by having a go at one of my officers. I want to know why.'

Twenty-six

'I'm as sure as I'll ever be, Inspector Pye,' Ian McCall declared. 'As you can see, I pulled in four extra bodies to help, and we've sifted through the morass not once but three times. We've found no ampoule in there, and no needle. It looks as if whoever planted it was thorough, and took it away with them once they were done with the victim. We'll do it again if you want, but . . .'

'No, Sergeant, that's enough. You're right. If you haven't found it by now, it's not there. You can dismiss your hired hands, then go and wash up. I know your shift ended officially a couple of hours ago, and I'll sign your overtime claims for the extra, but I'd like you back here tomorrow morning. We've still got a lot of witnesses to interview from Dr Mosley's list, and you can handle some of them. Don't worry, I've fixed it with Jock Varley.'

'They won't all be around here, these witnesses, will they?'

'Of course not, but telephone contact will be OK at this stage. If anyone comes up with anything significant, for example seeing someone follow Glover when he left the party with Ryan McCool, we can bring them in and sit them down.'

'McCool's not a suspect then?'

'No. When he left the yurt he met up with another couple of journalists and they all went along to the Oxford Bar. One of them was waiting outside the yurt; I've been in touch with him, and he says he heard McCool speak to Glover as he left, and Glover answer. He's in

142

the clear all right.' He paused, then looked at his watch. 'Go on, the pair of you. See you here tomorrow morning.'

'I'll need to tell Dr Mosley she can have this lot cleared away now.'

'That's OK, Ian, I'll do that.' Pye left the small pavilion where the detritus had been laid out and headed along the wooden gangway, making for the Book Festival office. The event was in full swing, and the gardens were full of people, some queuing for events, others perusing programmes, and more than a few heading purposefully towards the bars. He wondered how many of them were aware that they were in the middle of a crime scene, reckoning quickly that in the absence of an evening paper on a Sunday, the answer lay on the side of the minority. He was halfway to his destination when a voice called out, 'Sir!' The cry might have been aimed at any man there, but he stopped instinctively, looking towards the yurt. Framed in the gateway that led to it stood Detective Constable Harold Haddock, a tall, rangy young man, blessed with a nickname that he would carry throughout his career, all the way up to the Command Corridor at Fettes, some suggested.

'Sauce,' Pye exclaimed. 'You got the word? That's good.'

'Yes, sir. What's up? I mean I know about the murder inquiry. But why me?'

'Because you're available; and because I hear on the grapevine that you're a half-decent operator. Come with me just now; I have to pay a call on the director. Once that's done, I'll bring you up to speed on what's happening.'

The inspector led the way to the Book Festival office. As they drew close he glanced through its double glass door, and saw Randall Mosley, her back to him, in conversation with a tall, slim man, and a short, round-faced woman. Physically the two were diametric opposites, with only one common attribute: short, close-cut dark hair. The man wore chinos and a white, collarless shirt, while the woman

143

was dressed all in black, save for a pair of red moccasins. As he looked more closely, Pye saw the shock registered on her face, and guessed what was under discussion.

'Director,' he said as he stepped into the pavilion.

She turned to face him. 'Detective Inspector Pye,' she responded. 'How are things going?'

'Steadily. We're working our way through the list you gave us. We're done with the rubbish, though; you can have it cleared away, all of it.'

'Any luck . . . or shouldn't I ask that?'

'We didn't find anything of interest.'

'Is that a setback?'

'Not really. Our expectations weren't high, and our investigation wasn't dependent on it.'

'And what does it depend on?' asked the little woman fiercely.

Pye looked at her, and saw that the eyes behind her round spectacles were red-rimmed. 'I'm sorry,' he murmured evenly. 'You are?'

'This is Sandy Rankin,' the director told him. 'She's the lead reviewer for the *Herald*. Sandy was a very good friend of poor Ainsley.' She looked up at the man. 'And this is Denzel Chandler, my partner.'

'Pleased to meet you, Inspector.' Chandler offered his hand; they shook. 'This is a desperate business. I can't tell you how hard it's hit us.' The accent was North American but soft, possibly Canadian, Pye surmised, although in truth he had no real idea.

'I can imagine,' he said. 'Did you know the dead man?'

'Of course. I'm a writer too, but nowhere near as successful as Ally was.'

'What's your field?'

'I work across a pretty broad spectrum. I do a bit of journalism, I've had a couple of works published, but up until now I've earned most of my serious bread as a ghost writer.'

'Anyone I'd recognise?'

Chandler fired off half a dozen names: two musicians, two footballers, a golfer and a 'celebrity,' the source of whose fame was obscure.

The detective knew them all. 'That's a pretty solid list; meets my definition of success.'

'As I said, the money's good.'

'He's being too modest,' Mosley declared. 'He's a very gifted writer. A couple of the people he's ghosted for are virtually brain-dead. Coaxing worthwhile material out of thickos like that is a skill in itself, and as for turning it into readable prose . . . Happily it's a talent that's recognised. When the next collaboration is published—'

'Hey,' Chandler exclaimed. 'We can't talk about it yet.'

'We can to the police.' She patted his arm. 'When that one's done, it'll move Denzel to another level altogether.'

'Who's the . . .?' The inspector paused. 'What do you call them, the people you write for? Clients, subjects?'

'With,' the director corrected him. 'Write with. You call them what they want you to if the money's right, and it will be for this one. It's the autobiography of a Scottish High Court judge, Lord Elmore. That might sound dull, but it won't be. When he was a barrister he was very high-profile, defended a lot of notorious people and got most of them off. He was Claus Blackman QC then, and he was always in the press. Nothing much changed when he became a judge. He was a hard-liner and said some very pointed things about sentencing policy.'

Pye nodded. 'I know the story,' he said. 'He was a top silk, and a popular judge with the police after he went to the bench; he knew when to make an example of someone. Eventually his profile got so high he was nominated for the Yugoslav War Crimes Tribunal at the Hague, and wound up trying some of the worst criminals in living memory. I noticed he was at your reception last night; in fact, he's on my list for interview, eight thirty tomorrow morning at his house in Ann Street.'

'That's the man,' Randall Mosley confirmed. 'Well, he's on the point of retirement and he's been signed up for a book that's not only going to lift the lid on his entire career, but it's going to attack the entire culture of criminal prosecution in Europe. I've seen his agent's synopsis and it's going to be powerful stuff. Best of it is that Denzel will have front cover accreditation. That means he won't be anonymous; the author billing will be "Claus Blackman, QC, with Denzel Chandler." It'll make his name properly and lead on—'

'To an uncertain future, as with all authors,' Sandy Rankin interjected.

'You sound bitter.'

She glowered at the inspector. 'Call me a cynic, a professional cynic.' She shrugged. 'I'm a journalist, so that's what I'm supposed to be. Isn't it?' Her gaze switched to Chandler. 'Or shouldn't it be, Denz? Should I have assumed that Claus Blackman would write his own fucking memoirs, and be shocked when I find out that he won't? Nah, of course not. Because the whole fucking publishing business is sick, sick unto fucking death.'

'Oh, come on, Sandy,' Mosley protested. 'Look out there, look at all those people; we'll have up to a quarter of a million of them though this site over the next few weeks. That doesn't speak of a sick industry.'

'Randy, this is your first year, so you've still got to learn; that doesn't speak of anything. They're consumers; they're not driving anything any more. They're being fed what the retailers tell the publishers will sell best, and the publishers are nodding like fucking donkeys and going along with it. The whole fucking industry's about volume sales now; the big retailers and the online companies are screwing ridiculous discounts out of the producers, small booksellers are being driven out of business because they're not being offered the same deals so can't compete, and the people at the start of the supply chain, the authors, the essential creatives, are being screwed worst of all. They're being devalued. Randy, there's lots of seriously good work out there, more of it than ever before, with no fucking chance of ever being published. You know that as well as I do, but do the punters? No they don't. You go on about the size of your crowds, but you must have noticed that the people who sell out your big tent mostly aren't the proper authors, they're the celebs, like that girl with the ridiculous tits that calls herself a novelist, or the monosyllabic footballer of the month, or the tired old political has-beens like that wanker Bruce Anderson you had on last night. Yes, Director, you look out there, and you know what you'll see? People who shed tears about the plight of Nicaraguan coffee producers and always buy the Fair Trade range at fucking Starbucks, but who wouldn't dream of buying a hardback book unless it was remaindered or discounted down to less than the cover price of a paperback!'

Her voice had risen to a pitch just short of a yell; all work had stopped in the office, and its occupants were staring at her, but she was oblivious to their attentions. 'No wonder poor old Ally was so fucking worked up about it,' she ranted. 'Only two things ever got him close to mad, in all the time I've known him. One was Trident, and the other was what he called the conspiracy between the big-volume booksellers and the publishers' bean-counters to cut the balls off authors and their agents.'

Pye sensed that the time had come to channel her anger. 'Ms Rankin,' he said, 'I wonder if DC Haddock and I might carry on this discussion in private. We're interviewing all of Mr Glover's friends as part of our investigation.'

His intervention put an end to her tirade. 'How long will it take?' she asked. 'I'll need to do an obituary on Ally for tomorrow's paper. If I don't file it soon, the editor will give the job to one of the feature people or, worse, to one of the political staff.'

'We won't keep you long.' The two detectives led the journalist through to the makeshift investigation headquarters. As she looked around, they sensed her professional instincts coming back into play.

'This is where Ally died, isn't it?' she asked quietly.

'Yes. He was found lying in the area that's been taped off.'

'Isn't that a first, having the murder room in the crime scene itself?'

Pye raised an eyebrow. 'My idea was that we'd be doing the interviewing.'

Rankin returned his gaze. 'If I'm on the record with you, so are you with me.'

'In that case, I'll let you speculate about that, because I honestly don't know. However, we will ask all the questions for now. Beginning with, how close were you and Mr Glover?'

'We were friends of long standing.'

'How long exactly?'

'Twenty years; twenty years and one month, to be even more accurate. Earlier in my career, I worked on the *Saltire*, as a business reporter. I was on a story that needed an objective quote from an eminent accountant. Somebody suggested him; I got in touch, and he did the needful. After that, every time I needed that sort of involvement, I went to him.'

'How old were you then, Miss Rankin?' asked Haddock.

'What the fuck's that got to do with it?' she retorted.

'It's one of the things we're supposed to ask interviewees,' the young DC replied, unruffled. 'You know, occupation, date of birth, and so on.'

She softened. 'I see. And that was you being subtle, son, was it? Fair enough; it's a standard journo question too, although I've never really understood why. For the record, I'm forty-eight years old, but my birthday was last week, so if I'd answered your original question and you'd done your wee sum, you'd have got it wrong. People like you and me, we must always be precise. If we're not . . . journalists can get sued,

detectives can get their arses kicked by defence counsel and judges.'
She smiled. 'Like Claus Blackman, for example,' she mused. 'Imagine
Denzel landing his biography; can't get over that.'

'So,' Haddock continued, 'for the sake of clarity, what was the precise
nature of your relationship with the deceased?'

'That's better, son. Latterly, pure friendship, but there was a time,
after Ally's wife's death, it was more than that. Not for long, though. It
was never going anywhere on his part, and as for me, well,' she caught
the detective's eye, 'I bat for both teams, as they say. You can note that
down as "bisexual" in your wee book. Eventually we drifted back to
being pals again, closer than before. Ally's writing career started to
motor properly, I moved to the *Herald*, June Connelly came on the
scene, and everything settled into a nice wee rut.'

'You say his career was motoring,' Pye pointed out, 'yet when you
were talking to Dr Mosley you implied that he was unhappy with the
way it was going.'

'He wasn't alone. Ally did all right, no mistake about that; as well as
Mount, not as well as Noble, but all right. He was successful in Scottish
terms, but down south, he was a name but not at the top of the A list,
not by quite a way. It's those fucking supermarkets, y'see. A while back
they decided to sell books, but not in a considered way, as just another
commodity. So now they stock new titles and they'll sell them
discounted. They don't keep an author's back catalogue and they only
handle the top tier of authors, but that's enough to make a big hole in
the profits of the proper booksellers. So they shout for discounts too,
and they get them.'

'But don't authors get a percentage of cover price?'

'Yes, but that percentage declines with the discount, and unless
you're lucky enough to be a supermarket author, it's never made up by
increased sales.'

'And that frustrated Mr Glover?'

'That's putting it mildly.'

'Was he in financial difficulty?'

Rankin shook her head. 'No, he was well fixed, but not only from writing. His book sales were fine, and yet he could see his royalty income declining, the market being as it is. There's a bottom line, though; his advances were big enough for him to be able to forecast minimum income for a few years ahead. And, of course, for the last few months he had an MSP's salary coming in. Ach, Ally was rolling in it, truth be told, but he wasn't a man to get angry for himself. Last time we had dinner, he went on at some length about the silent majority, the authors who are being driven back to part-time writing or out of the business altogether. They were his . . . his second constituency, you might say.'

'And what about his first? His political career? How did he feel about that?'

The journalist laughed softly. 'Bewildered. When he stood for Holyrood, he never expected to get elected. He did it because he wanted to be a focal point for Scottish opposition to the nuclear deterrent, but that was all. He didn't anticipate that the Labour vote would collapse and swing behind him in the way it did.'

'I'm told that Dr Anderson accused him of doing it to sell books.'

For a moment, Pye thought the woman would spit on the floor. 'He's a fine one. He turned on his own party to sell his pathetic book, bastard that he is. Look at him now, trying to be the mouthpiece of the old socialist conscience and shagging a Tory duke's daughter at the same time.'

'Did you hear the exchange last night?'

'Only the end of it, when Anderson started shouting his mouth off.'

'And did you see Dr Anderson after that?'

'Yes. When Ryan McCool and Jock Fisher and I were turning into Young Street, I saw him.'

A frisson of excitement flickered in Pye's stomach, but he kept his tone casual. 'Heading home to Darnaway Street, I take it?' he asked.

Sandy Rankin shook her head. 'No,' she said, 'he was heading in the other direction, just before midnight. For an awful moment I thought he was going to the Oxford Bar as well, but when I took a look back over my shoulder, I saw him going past the entrance, carrying on up North Charlotte Street.'

Twenty-seven

The two fathers were stepping out of the lane that led from the bents on to Hill Road when Neil McIlhenney's mobile sounded.

'Probably Lou, wondering where you are,' said Bob. He was carrying the sleeping Seonaid, her fair curly locks resting against his chest, as his sons walked ahead of them. They had allowed the children to play until the first signs of tiredness from their transatlantic flight had appeared in the three Skinner youngsters, then headed for home.

'She'll have seen us by now,' his friend replied. 'Hello.'

• 'Boss,' Sammy Pye's voice sounded in his ear. 'Can you speak?'

'I can listen; let's try that first.' He stopped. Skinner watched him curiously as his expression changed. 'Mmm,' he muttered eventually. 'That might change things a little. My instinct is to pull him in but I wouldn't do anything yet if I were you. I'll consult with a higher power . . . yes, him, I'm with him just now . . . and get back to you.' McIlhenney pocketed the phone, swept the flagging James Andrew off his feet and lifted him up on to his shoulder, then began the short walk downhill to Skinner's home, steering Louis' pushchair with one hand. 'Pye,' he said. 'News from the battleground; a witness who saw Bruce Anderson heading in the wrong direction at the wrong time.'

'So your instinct was right.' They reached their destination and Bob unlocked the gate with a key. 'He did go out again. His so-called alibi is useless.'

'How do we play it?' Neil asked, as Spencer and Mark ran

ahead, their feet crunching on the gravel path.

'You play it, mate, you and Sammy. I'm keeping well away from this one, for all sorts of reasons.'

As they approached the house, the front door opened and Trish, the Barbadian nanny, emerged. As she took Seonaid from her father's arms, Neil set James Andrew back on his feet, to follow her indoors. Leaving Spencer in charge of the pushchair, the two men walked into the kitchen, where Bob took a beer from the fridge and handed his friend a can of Sprite.

'As I said to Sammy,' the superintendent continued, 'my gut says to lift him, but can we do it unobtrusively?'

'Why should you? Given all the circumstances, if this was Johnny-on-the-street-corner, he'd be in the cells by now.'

'Fine, but by now the word about his dust-up with the dead guy will have spread right through the media. They wouldn't be watching your man Johnny, but they'll be keeping an eye on Anderson, that's for sure.'

'Not right now, they aren't; he's at his girlfriend's father's place, or so you told me. Nobody will be camped there, not yet, at any rate.'

'Are you saying we should drive right into the Duke of Lanark's estate and arrest him?'

Skinner's grin was huge and wicked. 'I'm just helping your thought process, mate, that's all. Why should you hesitate to do that? This is a murder investigation, the man displayed hostility to the victim and he appears to have lied to you about his whereabouts at the time of the killing.'

'He appears to have, but he wasn't under caution.'

'So?'

McIlhenney nodded. 'So we visit him again and we take a formal signed statement. But we don't tell him about the Rankin woman seeing him in North Charlotte Street. If he tells us the same story and signs it . . .' He paused. 'But would we get away

153

with that? Would we need to disclose?'

'He hasn't been charged with anything; he doesn't have the rights of an accused person. So why should you?'

'True. But if we went charging up to the duke's baronial hall, he'd twig something was up, wouldn't he?'

'Unless he's a lot dumber than we think, he probably would.'

'In which case we play it quietly. We visit him again as soon as he gets back to Edinburgh . . . no, that might be late; we do it tomorrow morning.'

'This time you probably don't, not you personally; Sammy can see him, or even Wilding and Cowan, so it appears routine. But as soon as you have that signed statement . . . then he really is Johnny-on-the-street-corner.'

McIlhenney nodded. 'He gets lifted and we go in with a warrant to search the place. The search of the Festival rubbish turned up nothing. You never know, he might have taken the ampoule home, and the big syringe with the glucose in it.'

'That's if he did it.'

'You can't see him as a murderer?'

Skinner shook his head. 'I'm not going to say anything to influence you, or prejudice your investigation.'

'No, if you've got a view, I need to hear it. You know the man a lot better than I do.'

'OK, but bear in mind that this is just my impression of him. This killing was well thought out, well-planned, and the moment was well-chosen; it's one of the boldest crimes I've ever known. There's no doubt that Anderson is smart enough to have planned it, or that he has the medical knowledge to have carried it out. My doubt is whether he has the balls to have done it. My experience of the man, Neil, is that he's a coward.'

McIlhenney smiled. 'Backing off from you, Bob, doesn't necessarily make a man a coward. But . . .' he took a breath, 'what you say might square with something else that Sammy told me. I believe you know an author called Henry Mount?'

'Sure, he's one of our Friday crowd; known him for years.' He nodded. 'That's right, he told me he had a run-in with Anderson a while back. Bruce threatened to thump him, didn't he?'

'And Mount invited him to try it, only the offer was never taken up. The guy went all quiet. At the very least that marks him out as a blusterer.' McIlhenney looked at the unopened can in his hand, popped the ring pull, and took a long drink. 'But that doesn't change what we know about last night, and about his deception. We see him tomorrow, take his statement and if he's still saying that he didn't go out again, we knock on his door with a search team, and if the media spot us, then that'll be too bad.'

'Fine.'

'I'll let you know how it goes.'

'Don't be in any rush. Anyway, I might be out of town tomorrow morning. I might just take a run up to Tayside. You're busy, and we need that list from Andy's safe.'

'He could send it down with a courier.'

'I know he could, but like I said, I want to talk to him about a few things, including his trampling uninvited all over our patch, and the Coben visit. That in particular is something for me.'

'Do you take it that seriously?'

'As I said, not in the context of your investigation. Yet the intelligence community seems to have taken Glover seriously enough to threaten a senior police officer. That's worth looking into. And nobody's warned me off, or tried to, not yet at any rate.'

'I've been sent to ask whether you two are ever going to join us.'

Wrenched from their conversation, the men turned, so see Lauren McIlhenney standing in the kitchen doorway.

A child no more, Skinner thought, and more like her mother every day. 'There's only one answer to that one,' he said. 'Come on, Neil.' He led the way across the hall, and into the garden room.

'Was that fun?' Louise McIlhenney asked them. 'You've tired the kids out, that's for sure, even Spence.'

'That was our purpose,' said Bob. 'But I'll bet my three will waken in the middle of the night, nonetheless.' He smiled. 'But then so will Trish, so she can get on with it. And how about you two ladies . . . sorry, Lauren, you three. Got all your catching up done?'

'That'll never happen,' Aileen told him, 'not when you guys are the subject under discussion.' She held out a slip of paper, offering it to him. 'You had a phone call, about half an hour ago. A Mr Aislado; says you know him, didn't want to leave a message, but would appreciate a call. That's his direct line.'

Bob frowned as he took the note from her hand. 'I know him all right, and so do you. Big Xavi; he's the editor of the *Saltire*, remember. You should; his paper supported your party in the election – remarkably, given what it's called.'

'Now you mention it, I do. But that's a funny name for a Scottish journalist, isn't it?'

He laughed. 'Come on, you're from Glasgow, and your name's de Marco. You of all people should know that there's no such thing as a typically Scottish name any more. Aislado's . . .' he paused, 'Xavi's short for Xavier, by the way . . . his grandfather was a refugee from Spain in the thirties, at the start of the civil war, but he was born here, so that makes him just about as Scottish as you and me. Grandad made a small fortune in the pub trade. When he died, Xavi's dad Joe carried on the business and doubled it in size, then, when Franco died, he sold up, went back to Spain and invested in newspapers and radio stations. Xavi stayed in Scotland, though; he was a pro footballer for a while, with the Hearts mainly, and then he became a journalist. When he went to work for the *Saltire*, it was on its last legs, and being run into the ground by a crook. But just when it looked as if the paper was going down the toilet, Xavi went to see his old man . . . although as I understand it, he can't stand him . . . and got him to buy it. He was installed as managing editor, and the thing's never looked back since.'

'I wonder what he wants.'

'Let's find out.' He picked up a cordless phone from the coffee table and punched in the number.

The call was answered at once. 'Aislado,' said a deep slow voice.

'Xavi, it's Bob Skinner. What can I do for you?'

'First of all, thank you for calling me back.' The accent was Scottish and yet not quite, not one hundred per cent. There was a hint of his Spanish ancestry hidden there. 'I'm looking at a story here, Bob, filed by one of my people. It's about Ainsley Glover's murder, and it's got quite a bit of detail that I do not recall Detective Superintendent McIlhenney mentioning when he made his statement earlier on today. My reporters are good, as you know, yet I'm surprised by this piece, since the writer is a member of my sports staff.'

Skinner looked at his colleague, meaningfully, beckoning him closer. 'Xavi,' he said 'Neil's with me now. I'm going to put you on speaker mode, if that's OK?'

'Of course.'

He pressed the hands-free button. 'Could you repeat what you've just told me?'

'Sure.' The editor told his tale once more.

'So what does your story say?' On the couch, Aileen and Louise were listening, intently but silently.

'It claims that Glover was murdered by a massive injection of glucose after being paralysed by an anaesthetic drug. And it says that you are looking for a killer with specialist medical knowledge. Bob, I was at the party last night, and I heard Dr Anderson shout at the man.'

157

'Does your story attribute this information?'

'It refers to police sources, plural.'

'What is the reporter's name?' asked McIlhenney.

'Ed Collins. He's my top football writer.'

'Shit,' the superintendent exclaimed, 'that's Carol Glover's boyfriend. Wilding and Cowan went to tell her the cause of death, in confidence, and he was there. He left before they could interview him and discover for themselves that he was a reporter.'

'So the information's correct?'

'We can't deny it, Xavi,' Skinner admitted. 'Looks like you've got yourself an exclusive.'

'Will it inconvenience you if I run it?' The editor's question took the police officers by surprise.

'It would let certain people have information we'd rather keep to ourselves for now.'

'Would that include Anderson?'

'Yes, it would.'

'In that case I'm prepared to omit the sensitive elements from the story. Collins' relationship to the victim's daughter is enough of an exclusive for me. I'll tell him to do a piece from that angle.'

'Will he take that?'

'He'll take it from me,' the editor rumbled. 'He came by the information through a sin of omission. He should have told your officers immediately that he worked for the *Saltire*. I'll tell him that, forcefully, and I'll impress upon him that if he even thinks about passing the story on to a pal, he'll be yesterday's news as far as I'm concerned.'

'Thanks, Xavi,' said Skinner, sincerely. 'That's another one our force owes you.'

'Forget it,' said Aislado, with just a hint of a very rare chuckle in his voice. 'I don't like that man Anderson either.'

Twenty-eight

'Jesus, Sammy,' said Ray Wilding, 'that's a bit embarrassing. Are we in the shit? How are the bosses taking it?'

'Remarkably well, all things considered. They're taking the view that Collins should have made it clear to you that he was a journo.'

'Nonetheless, we should have found that out for ourselves. Schoolboy error, boss; I'm sorry.'

'Noted. The truth is, Mr Aislado's attitude probably let you off the hook. If he'd splashed it without warning the DCC, then there might have been an explosion.'

'I'll buy his paper from now on,' Wilding vowed. 'That seems the least I can do.'

'I'm sure he'll be grateful; his circulation's on the up from what I hear, but every sale counts. Now, where are you?'

'We're at Glover's house,' the sergeant told him, 'in his office, as I speak. And we've got a problem: somebody's beaten us to it.'

'What do you mean?'

'The place has been gone over, expertly. Wilkie, the son, brought us here. He's downstairs just now. When he let us in, the first thing I noticed was that the alarm wasn't set. I came here earlier, remember, with Carol, to collect his insulin ampoules. When we came in, there was a warning tone, and she cancelled the system. When we left, she reset it. I watched her punch the numbers into the keypad. When we unlocked it, no tone, no nothing.'

'Maybe she missed something out and it wasn't set properly. She was under stress, remember; she'd just had a hell of a shock.'

'Sure, that was my first thought too, until I got up here, into the office. Wilkie showed us his dad's filing cabinet. His personal records were there, payment slips, receipts, bank statements, all that stuff, but the file we really wanted, his correspondence, it's missing. There's a folder, sure, but it's empty.'

'Are you sure he kept paper records?'

'The son says that he did.'

'OK, but his outgoing stuff, letters he wrote, emails he sent, there will be copies of these on his computer, surely.'

'I'm sure there are. But the big problem is, it's not here. Glover's whole life, so Wilkie says, the originals of his books in various stages, his accounts, his photos, his music, was on a Dell desktop, with everything backed up on an external resource. Alice and I are looking at the computer now; the casing's been opened and the hard disk's been removed. There's no sign of the back-up disk either.'

'Who would want to do that? The daughter, the son?'

'I don't see that, Sammy. Why would they? Wilkie seemed totally shocked when we found this. He says that his father had three new works on the computer, and two of them hadn't been delivered to his publisher. The way he sees it, this is a disaster. We did ask him where he's been all afternoon, though. He said that he and Carol never went out of her flat from the moment we left them to the moment we returned. They spent most of that time fielding telephone calls from the media, so if we need to confirm their story it should be easy enough.'

'Have you looked at Carol's computer yet, at her dad's secret email address?'

'No. We came straight here.'

'Then you better had. Call me on my mobile as soon as you have.

Young Sauce and I are going out to Fred Noble's place to interview Glover's agent. She's ready to see us, but before that, I'll need to report this upstairs. If you're convinced it wasn't Wilkie and Carol protecting their inheritance, then it has to bring Mr Coben, Andy Martin's mystery visitor, right back into the game.'

Twenty-nine

'This is a pretty exclusive neighbourhood,' said DC Sauce Haddock, looking along the terrace of substantial grey stone houses. 'This writing game must pay pretty well.'

'For some,' Sammy Pye told him as he stepped out of the driving seat and closed his car door. 'I have a cousin who's trying to make a living at it. She's had three books published, but she's still teaching and not expecting to be giving up any time soon.'

'Would I have heard of her?'

'I doubt it.'

'What does she write?'

'Intense novels about women having a hard time.'

'Ah. No, I probably won't have heard of her.' He looked at the number on a low iron gate. 'Seven. This must be the house.'

'Yes.' The DI led the way up a pathway between two rose beds. As the detectives reached the front door, it opened to reveal Fred Noble. He was still dressed all in black, but the T-shirt he had worn earlier had been replaced by an open-necked shirt, and he had shaved.

'Inspector,' he began.

'And Detective Constable Haddock,' Pye continued; an introduction. 'You didn't meet earlier.'

'Haddock, eh. You'll have had all the "battered or breadcrumbs" jokes, I suppose.'

The young constable drew an imaginary line a few inches above his head. 'Right up to there,' he replied with a smile. 'But if you think you know a new one, I'm all ears.'

'That's not something you should say too often. Come away in; June's waiting for you.' He opened a heavy panelled door, and showed them into a drawing room. Pye had a quick glance around, taking in a high fireplace with a mirror above the mantelpiece, sash-cord windows, with secondary glazing, and a ceiling cornice that was a work of art. He wondered how many books his cousin would have to sell to attain such a lifestyle.

The woman they had come to interview swung round slowly to face them, in a red leather captain's chair, but she remained seated. She was middle-aged . . . she and Glover might have been contemporaries, the DI surmised . . . with expensively managed honey-blonde hair, not a telltale grey root in sight. She wore a trouser suit in a pale colour that might have been described as peach, over a tight white sweater that made no attempt to downplay a formidable bosom. And she was still clearly in shock. Her eyes seemed to be somewhere else as Fred Noble made the introductions, seated the detectives, then left to fetch a pot of coffee.

'I didn't know,' said June Connelly, with a crack in her voice. 'I thought it was funny that Ally hadn't called me while I was on the train, but I supposed he must have been busy. I expected him on the platform when we got to Waverley, and even when I saw Fred waiting, it never occurred to me that there was anything wrong. Not until I saw his face . . .'

'We are very sorry to have to intrude, Ms Connelly,' Pye told her. 'We understand that your relationship with Mr Glover was more than just professional.'

She nodded. 'Ally called us a New Age couple. We both had earlier marriages, him widowed, me divorced . . . it's Mrs Connelly, by the way . . . and our arrangement suited us. Occasionally he would talk about moving down to London, but Carol and Wilkie, still being youngish and single, tied him to Edinburgh. My son Mike flew the coop a while back. He's in America now.'

'Did you ever think of moving north?' Haddock asked.

'That was never an option, the publishing industry being what it is.' She paused. 'But that's only an excuse; I'm a Londoner, and I always will be.'

The DC was about to comment that his usual boss, DI Becky Stallings, had made the move for reasons that were more personal than professional, when Sammy Pye cut across him. 'Are you sure you're ready for this?' he asked.

'I'm ready for anything that will help you, Inspector.' As she spoke, the door creaked quietly as Fred Noble shouldered his way into the room, carrying a large tray. He poured mugs of coffee for each of them and then stood, eyebrows raised, as if waiting to be invited to remain in his own front room. The DI nodded, and he sat.

'When was the last time you spoke to Mr Glover?' Pye began.

'Yesterday,' she replied. 'Yesterday afternoon. He called me to check on the arrival time of my train.'

'How did he seem?'

'Same as always. Cheery.'

'As always, you say. So he hadn't been concerned about anything lately?'

'No, he'd been very up, excited even. He had a lot going on in his life; he had all sorts of new responsibilities as an MSP, he was getting to the end of the latest Strachan book . . . that always pumped him up . . . and then there was his new project. Actually, he was on such a high I was worried about him; he was overdoing things and . . .' She hesitated, and her eyes dropped to her lap. 'To be honest,' she continued, more quietly than before, 'when Fred met me at the station, and I saw the expression on his face, my instant thought was, "My God, Ally's had another heart attack; please let him be all right." But then he told me that he was dead, and that you believed he had been murdered.' Her eyes renewed contact with the inspector, locking on hard. 'You really do think that?'

'That's what the pathologist says, Mrs Connelly.'

'And I know him, June,' Fred Noble interjected. 'He's the top man in Scotland, probably in Britain.'

'So how did he die?' she asked.

'That's information we have to keep to ourselves for the moment.'

'You're not telling anyone?'

Pye winced, involuntarily; she picked it up.

'Nobody at all?' she persisted.

'The immediate family have been told,' he admitted. 'Mr Glover junior, and Miss Glover.'

'What about Ed?'

Sharp, the DI thought, noting a subtle change of expression. 'Yes, him too.'

'But he's a journalist.'

'Something we found out after the event. It's OK, though; there will be no leak from that source.'

'You don't know Ed Collins; I'm assured he's a shifty young chap. Ally wasn't at all keen on him, but he's Carol's choice, and he had to live with it.'

'Collins will behave himself from now on if he wants to go on collecting a salary at the end of the month. Turns out that his boss is more honourable than he is.'

'Are you going to tell me, in confidence?'

Fred Noble reached across and touched her on the shoulder. 'June,' he murmured, 'think about this. I'm happy to leave you to hear this on your own if you want, but do you want? You're going to be quizzed by half the journos in Scotland, and one of the things they're going to try to find out will be the cause of death. If you don't know, and if I don't know, we can't have it tricked out of us, can we?'

She took a deep breath and nodded. 'I suppose that's true,' she admitted.

Pye seized the moment, and moved on quickly. 'Was Mr Glover's diabetes a continuing problem?' he asked.

'It worried me from time to time, but he managed it pretty well. It presented in his early thirties, and he'd been on insulin since then. He knew the long-term risks, so he was careful with his diet. He still enjoyed fine wines, though, and knew how to adjust his daily dose to allow for different levels of consumption.'

'Was his condition generally known, or did he keep it to himself?'

'No, no, no; he didn't keep it a secret at all. Far from it, in fact; he referred to it often and he was a big supporter of diabetes charities. If you look at his website you'll find several links to them.'

'OK. Now, a few minutes ago, you said that Mr Glover was working on a new project. What did it involve?'

For the first time, June Connelly gave a hint of a smile. 'This might sound strange,' she replied, 'given our dual relationship, but I honestly do not know. Ally wouldn't tell me. He could be like that. He was open in every other respect, but when it came to his work he was often secretive. Some writers involve their agents in the creative process; they talk over ideas for stories and some let them see their work for comment every step of the way. Ally never did that; he'd work away on his own and when he was done he'd email me the finished novel, but it would go to CJ at the same time.'

'CJ?'

'CJ Carver, his editor at Smokescreen Publishing.'

'What contracts did he have with the publisher?'

'He was working on the third Walter Strachan story in a four-book deal. Once he'd delivered it, I'd have been sitting down with CJ to discuss terms for another four.'

'We've been told that he wasn't too happy with his publisher,' said Pye, 'over the way his books were being sold.'

'You've been talking to Sandy Rankin, haven't you?'

Pye nodded, with a small grin.

'She was Ally's other great sounding board. Well, it's true he wasn't ecstatic with the way the market's been moving, but he wasn't alone in that. Stop ten authors in the street . . . you could in Edinburgh at this time of year . . . and nine will tell you the same story. But the fact is that he was more successful than most, and his political exposure wasn't doing him any harm either; it got him on to a lot of chat shows. He was even on *Question Time* two months ago. Believe me, that would have counted in the discussions over the next Strachan deal.'

'But this new project, whatever it might have been, wasn't contracted?'

'Not yet. Ally was well in with Smokescreen but not even they would buy something without having the faintest idea what it was.'

'He hadn't given you any clues?'

'I had the impression that it was political.'

'To do with his role as an MSP?'

'Possibly.'

'To do with Trident?'

'Given his obsession with the subject, that would be a reasonable guess, but guess is still all it would be. Maybe I'll find the answer on his computer. More important, though, hopefully I'll find the whole of the Strachan novel. He told me a few days ago that he was pretty much finished with it. For sure, it'll be a best-seller; Smokescreen will want to milk every last penny out of it, so they'll put a big budget behind it.'

'That may be a problem,' said Pye heavily.

Thirty

'Are you sure you don't want me to come with you?' Aileen asked.

'Not this time,' Bob answered, smiling. 'But you never know, if it goes well I might invite them back for a bite of supper.' He felt her eyes on his back as he closed the front door behind him.

It was early evening, but there was still warmth in the day as he walked down Hill Road, flanked on either side by substantial stone dwellings, wondering what their owners would say if they knew where he was headed. Apart from Colonel Rendell, two other concerned neighbours had called him to discuss the travellers' arrival, and a check with the duty inspector in Haddington had told him that twenty-three other complaints had been made to the police. He had arranged, through Brian Mackie, the assistant chief constable responsible for uniformed operations, that patrol cars should drive by more frequently than was usual, but only as a public relations gesture. No police approach was to be made to the encampment.

He picked up his pace as he turned into Sandy Loan, then cut through Goose Green and across the Main Street. As he passed the parish church and turned the corner, the Mallard Hotel came into view. Fifty yards ahead, he saw two figures, the men he was meeting, Derek Baillie and Asmir Mustafic. The former still wore jeans and T-shirt, but his companion had changed into well-used dark trousers and a shirt that might once have been pristine white. He caught up with them just as they reached the conservatory that served as an entrance to the inn. 'Gentlemen,' he called.

Baillie turned, pausing in the act of opening the door. 'Mr Skinner,' he exclaimed. 'Am I pleased to see you; you've won me a bet.'

'How come?' the DCC asked as they stepped into the glass foyer.

'Hugo Playfair reckoned you wouldn't be here. He told us that all you wanted was to get us off the site, away from the rest. He said we'd find guys waiting to lift us when we got here.'

'How much did you have on it?'

'A tenner.'

Skinner laughed. 'In that case he's buying; that's enough for three pints. Mine's Seventy Shilling.'

They made their way inside but, finding the bar filled by day trippers, decided to return to the conservatory. They settled into armchairs, around a coffee table. A red-bearded barman, looking uncomfortably warm in a multicoloured waistcoat, served three pints of beer from a tray.

'Thanks, Andrew,' said the police officer as he left. 'So, guys,' he continued, 'how's the new pitch?'

'It's flat, and that's the main thing,' Baillie told him.

'Your first requirement, I guess. Those screens will go up tomorrow, and the sanitary arrangements will begin on Tuesday . . . unless you've decided to move on by then.'

'Or been moved? Mr Skinner, I'm neither so stupid nor so provocative that I'd choose to set up camp in front of the deputy chief constable's house . . . or the First Minister's, for that matter. I'd almost expect to be shifted.'

'Have you been doing your homework since this morning?'

'Didn't have to. Hugo Playfair told us all about you.'

'Don't believe too much he says. Mind you, he's got the basics right. When you speak to me, you also have, informally, let's say, the ear of our head of government. Now, as for moving you on, that won't happen, not at this stage at any rate. The policy of my force is to seek civil solutions to the problems your communities cause.'

'There you are,' Asmir Mustafic snorted. It was the first time the DCC had heard him speak; his accent was thick, not western European, he guessed. 'You hear, Derek, we are problem.'

Baillie held up a hand in admonition. 'Ssh. Hear the man out, Az.'

Skinner looked at the smaller of his companions. 'But you have to accept that you are just that. You have to realise that whenever you pitch a new camp, you cause real resentment in that neighbourhood. I'm not being judgemental when I say that; I'm stating a fact. I've read the statutes that cover camping. Pretty much wherever you go, the locals see you as lawbreakers, and on the face of it, they're right.'

'Not Roma law,' Mustafic muttered.

'No, Scots law, and like it or not, friend, you're living under the jurisdiction of the Scottish court. That said, we're not harsh. We'll only shift you on the order of that court, if you defy its interdict. As far as I can find out, your group has never done that.' He picked up his glass and took a mouthful before continuing. 'So, gentlemen, enlighten me; tell me what I should be saying on your behalf when Mr Angry of Gullane rings my doorbell on a Sunday morning.'

'Fair enough,' said Baillie, 'but let me ᵦgin by asking you something. We're always being directed to the nearest dedicated site for travelling people. It's not going to happen, but suppose we all wanted to go there, all at once, to be supervised by a local authority manager. Do you know how many you have in the area your force covers?'

'Three.'

'Offering how many places?'

'Just over sixty.'

The traveller nodded. 'Now it's you who's been doing his homework. Sixty serviced lots covering the city of Edinburgh and all the area around it. Across Scotland you've got less than five hundred traveller places, and of them, some are seasonal, closed in the winter. Now, do you know how many of our people there are in Scotland?'

'I can't say that I do with any certainty. The official figure puts the travelling population at a couple of thousand, but there are charities who reckon it's much higher. Some even put it at twenty thousand.'

'I'd doubt it's that many,' Baillie conceded, 'but you can take it that it's more than the two, Mr Skinner, for there are some of us who just don't want to be counted. I happen to be one of them. I don't think that makes me an anti-social person; rather I believe it makes me a free man.'

'Yes,' Mustafic declared. 'Is about freedom.'

'Freedom to do what?'

'To live as we choose.' Baillie looked the DCC in the eye. 'But leave that aside for now. My point is that suppose every traveller in the country said tomorrow, "OK, we'll conform, we'll all live in approved sites, be they run by councils or private people or what," there would be chaos, for there are nowhere near enough pitches for all of us. For decades, Mr Skinner, we've had people in government spouting platitudes about the need for provision, then passing the buck to local authorities without putting any firm obligations on them.'

'It's a circle, though, isn't it? Government doesn't know for sure how many of you there are so how can it know how many places to provide?'

'It might start by believing its own figures as a minimum level, and then taking charge of the provision. But if ever it does, one place per family will never be enough. We are travelling people; some of us may live in one spot for a year and more, but eventually we all move on.'

'So what we need is over-provision?' Skinner asked. 'Is that what you're saying? Estimate one place per caravan, then create a surplus, to allow for your mobile lifestyle.'

'You've got it, sir. But it's not going to happen, is it?'

'Given the political will to make it happen, anything's possible.'

'Well, that will hasn't been apparent up to now, and that's why you found us on your beach car park this morning. Without shifting our families to the other end of Scotland, which we do not want to do, we had nowhere else to go.'

'There is always somewhere else to go, surely.'

'Try to find it.'

The DCC smiled. 'I'm not in a position to do that.'

'Pah!' Asmir Mustafic spat. 'No, you can't and you won't. All you can do is come in the night, with your uniforms and your lights and your cars to waken us and our children. I came to Britain to be safe, but it is still the same. Police here no carry guns, but you hate us the same.' He drained his glass and stood. 'I sorry, Derek, I had enough of this talk that will go nowhere. I go somewhere else, then back to caravan.'

They watched him as he left. 'Sorry about that,' said Baillie as the self-closer pushed the door shut. 'Az is one of the old school, pure gypsy. He's been with the group for a couple of years now, but he's still suspicious of everybody and everything. I keep him close to me, otherwise he'd be isolated, even in our small group,'

'Where's he from?'

Baillie smiled. 'Where are any of us from? That's the essence of the traveller; he's a nomad. We may call ourselves different things. I'm a Scottish traveller, Az is Roma, then there are the New Age people, who left settled communities for a life on the road. We're all different, but we're all the same. Your question should have been, "Where's he from, last?" If it had been, I'd have said he came from Bulgaria. Hugo Playfair brought him in.'

'What's Hugo? New Age?'

'Mostly he's a wanker, but yes, that's the category I'd have to put him in.'

'If you don't like him, why do you let him stay with you?'

'I couldn't kick him out if I wanted. You seem to have me marked out as a leader, but I'm not. I'm a spokesman, at most. I don't command the group. Fact is, the traditionalists like Asmir Mustafic see me as a dangerous radical for speaking to a gorgio like you.'

'Gorgio?'

'That's the old gypsy word for . . . everybody else, I suppose.'

'Is Playfair a gorgio?'

'Most of our group would say he is. But the fact is, he can be useful from time to time . . . at least his charity can. If we need legal advice, Hugo can fix it. If we wanted to challenge your council's interdict, for example, he'd get us a brief.' He saw Skinner's expression darken. 'Not that we will,' he added. 'It would be a waste of his group's money.' He grinned. 'I suppose being a cop you've got a down on lawyers.'

'My father was a lawyer and so is my daughter. Mind you, I'm not sure I'd want her marrying another one.'

'How about another policeman?'

Skinner frowned. 'She nearly did once. Fucking disaster. People like me, we're too autocratic for Alex; we can't help it, it's in our nature. And Andy, her guy as was, is just like me.'

'So Az and Hugo were right; your natural reaction is just to move us on.'

'It probably is,' he admitted, 'or has been up until now. But my duty is not to give in to that instinct, rather to make an informed judgement. The hardest thing for people like me, for gorgios, as your man would say, is to understand you. We see your groups and instantly we have an image in our heads.'

'Cher.'

'What?'

'Cher. Remember that fucking song of hers, "Gypsies, tramps and thieves"? I bet that goes through your mind when you see our camps. Don't deny it; if you know it, you've thought it.'

Skinner nodded, sadly. 'No,' he said, 'I can't deny it.'

'Fucking disaster for our people, that song. Whatever her intentions, even if they were innocent, it gave voice to a stereotypical image, and it's been a millstone hanging on us since it was written.' For the first time, the DCC saw a flash of real anger in the man, but it vanished as quickly as it had flared. 'Why do we do it, you ask me?' he continued. 'Because for most of us it's our culture, our environment, our tradition, the way we were raised. For generations we've travelled, taking our labour and our skills wherever they were needed, wherever we could sell them, whether it be picking potatoes, vegetables, or berries, or if you go back far enough, mending pots and pans. My own specialty is machinery. I'm an engineer, and I service motorised lawnmowers, and even tractors and the like, on small farms. Sure, we've had our bad apples down the years, but so has your society and more of them, man for man, than in ours, I'll bet. My God, sir, they're what's kept you in a job, and what's put you in that fine house up the hill, to be outraged by the likes of us. Your own bad bastards, that is, not ours, for we can take care of our own troublemakers.' Baillie's voice was rising, but still he was smiling, challenging.

'Then there's the show people,' he continued, 'the funfairs, like you had here a couple of weeks ago on the Goose Green for your village games day. You welcome them, as much as you resent us, because your kids like them, yet they're travellers, just like us. That elderly couple whose dogs you had to walk this morning; chances are they took their grandchildren to the shows, paid them on to the merry-go-rounds and the waltzers, and bought them candyfloss till they had to hose it off them. Did they think anything of it? No. And the irony is that in a different year, for he's been here with his stall on occasion, my cousin Zak could have been taking their money. Mr Skinner, we are to be used when it suits your community and shunned when it suits you.'

He finished; the DCC sat quiet for almost a minute.

'Derek,' he said at last, 'you've given me food for thought. Maybe sometime you'd like to tell the First Minister and her colleagues what you've just told me.'

'I would in a minute. But for now, we'll still have to move on, again. Once the council has its interdict, you'll enforce it?'

'I'm afraid so. I might understand you better now, but that will still be my job.'

Thirty-one

'I hope I haven't inconvenienced you, Mr Pye. My diary is full today, and this was the only time I could fit you in.'

The DI nodded. 'I understand, Lord Elmore,' he replied, having detected nothing but sincerity in the judge's apology. 'And I appreciate you making the effort. But then you'll understand more than most the importance of a murder inquiry.'

'Mmm.' The judge pursed his lips. 'Indeed.' He paused, glancing through the first-floor window of his study, watching the neighbourhood postman as he made his way along the narrow, car-packed Ann Street. 'We've encountered each other before, haven't we?' he asked.

'Yes, we have, sir,' Pye replied. 'Six or seven years ago, in the High Court, an armed robbery trial; the accused was a guy called McTurk. I was a constable then.'

'That's right.' Lord Elmore, a small, trim, white-haired man, turned to face him, peering over the top of half-moon spectacles. 'Defence counsel gave you a bit of a going-over, as I recall, but you handled it pretty well.'

'Well enough for you to give him fifteen years.'

'Did you think that was too stiff?'

'You won't find many police officers complaining about sentencing being too severe, especially when the accused carries a sawn-off and threatens to blow a jeweller's head off with it.'

'The appeal court didn't share your view. They reduced it to ten, so Mr McTurk will be eligible for parole in a couple more years. Mind you, he was unlucky in one respect.'

'What was that, sir?'

'His counsel made a complete balls of the trial. If I'd been defending, I'd have got him an acquittal, or worst case a Not Proven verdict, which has the same effect. The conviction hinged on a DNA sample in a balaclava helmet found in a bin, along with the shotgun, a couple of hundred yards away from where the robbery took place. McTurk claimed that he had left the garment in a pub, and there were traces on it from another person.'

'Yes, but we found traces of lubricant from the shotgun inside his jacket.'

Lord Elmore smiled. 'You found traces of the same lubricant, that's all. I'd have established reasonable doubt with that, no question. That said, the thought doesn't keep me awake at night. The man was as guilty as sin, and I was quite happy to send him down. I only wish my brother judges had been as robust at appeal. The politicians didn't like the line they took, that's for sure. Bruce Anderson was particularly scathing.'

'Do you know Dr Anderson, sir?' asked Haddock, standing by the door.

'Ah, it speaks,' the judge exclaimed. 'Of course I do. I was appointed to the Supreme Court during his time as Secretary of State, and when Archie Nelson was Lord Advocate. I don't think Archie . . . Lord Archibald, as you will know him . . . was too keen on my appointment, but Bruce was persuaded that the bench needed toughening up.' He looked up at the young DC. 'I know what you're going to ask me next. Was I a witness to the spat between him and the late Mr Glover? The answer is yes, I was, well within earshot, in fact. Who started the argument? Ainsley Glover did, beyond a doubt; he had a penchant for mischief. Was Bruce in some way responsible for his death? Of course not; the idea's preposterous.' He turned to Pye. 'I know you're regarding this death as a homicide, on Hutchinson's say-so, but to be honest, you have more faith in him than I have. I've cross-examined him as defence counsel, I've presented him as a prosecutor and I've seen him as a witness from the bench. He's an opinionated little man and when he hits on a theory, nothing will shake it loose. Whatever tale he's fed you, if I were you I'd be looking for an alternative to murder as an explanation. Drunk diabetics run a risk.'

'Forgive me, sir,' said the DI, 'but you don't seem to have been too fond of Mr Glover from the way you speak of him.'

'I confess that I wasn't. For a start I disagree profoundly with his politics. This country needs Trident if it is to continue to punch above its weight internationally, as we always have done. We're a force for good in the world, gentlemen. We and the Americans shoulder the responsibility of keeping anarchy at bay. Without us . . .' He frowned. 'You're aware that I'm now a member of the Hague Tribunal?' Pye nodded. 'Well, if you saw some of the cases that are brought to us for trial. Ten years on and we're still rounding up these Balkan butchers. When we do manage to bring them to trial, their influence is still such that the witnesses. . . Ah!' he broke off, exasperated. 'Without us and our military strength they'd still be out there, killing people by the thousands, yet the bleeding hearts like Glover would have us throw that strength away. It's the nuclear deterrent that gets us to the top table; damn fool didn't realise that.'

'Dr Anderson professes to be anti-Trident as well.'

'That's the political coat he wears at the moment, that's all. Bruce is an opportunist, but sometimes there's no harm in that. He's an outspoken individual, politically, and that's the most important thing. I hear he's talking about fighting the parliamentary seat left vacant by

Glover's death. If he does, I expect him to win it. Once he's at Holyrood, sparks will fly, I tell you.'

'You're saying that he stands to benefit from Mr Glover's death, sir?' asked Haddock. 'Have I got that right?'

The little judge smiled at him, gently, without condescension. 'Young man,' he replied, 'in my opinion, all Scotland stands to benefit from Glover's death, so that line of questioning will get you precisely nowhere.'

Pye intervened hastily. 'If I can bring us back to the subject, sir. When was the last time you saw Mr Glover?'

'When Leona, that's Lady Elmore, and I left the party, at eleven twenty-five; I checked my watch and decided that enough was enough. I'd had a long day, starting with a meeting with Denzel Chandler. I'm retiring soon and will be doing a book. It'll be a retrospective of my career as a lawyer,' he explained, 'with emphasis on the judicial years, and he's my collaborator. When we abandoned ship, Glover was still there. As a matter of fact, now that I think of it, Bruce left at the same time. We walked home . . . no hope of a casual taxi pick-up in the city on a Saturday night . . . and saw him heading down North Charlotte Street, just ahead of us. We went our different ways and we were home by midnight, as my wife will confirm if you feel the need to ask her.'

'That won't be necessary,' said the DI. 'In fact, that just about covers it, sir, unless there's anything else you can tell us you think might be useful.'

The former Claus Blackman frowned. 'Useful? I don't know whether it is or not, but Ainsley was up to something.'

'What do you mean?'

'I'm not sure exactly, but he'd been asking around.'

'Asking around?'

'Yes, or so one of my brother judges told me. Glover called him and asked him a couple of questions about procedure at the Hague. He said that there was a line in a future book that he wanted to get right.'

'Did it involve you?'

'Not that he said, but after his altercation with Bruce, I can't imagine even him being so foolhardy as to portray me in one of his yarns.' He shrugged. 'But it's academic now, isn't it? Poor chap's dead.'

Haddock smiled at him. 'So's Elvis, sir, but his work lives on after him. And they keep coming out with new material, don't they?'

Thirty-two

'How are the kids doing with the jet lag?' asked McIlhenney.

'Not too bad,' Skinner replied; his voice had a slight echo, and there was road noise behind it. 'The boys were up before me . . . that's unusual, James Andrew could sleep for Scotland . . . but Seonaid went pretty much all through the night. The nanny's the one who's suffering most of all; seems to me that children handle travel better than adults. Maybe their body clocks aren't as firmly set as ours. But if Trish does go without sleep for a few days, she'll soon be back to normal. She's on holiday from Saturday, and then she's heading back across the Atlantic, bound for Barbados to see her sister.'

'Making you and Aileen full-time parents for a while?'

'Yes, and I have to say I'm looking forward to it. The boys will be back to school soon, plus tomorrow's Jimmy's last day, so I have good reasons to keep close to home and close to the office. This trip to see Andy's a bit of an inconvenience, truth be told, but I've got to do it.'

'Listen, boss, about what happened between him and me; it all worked out on the end, so maybe it's best left to stick to the wall, yes?'

'Don't worry, I'm not going up there to tear a strip off him. I need that list of Ainsley Glover's out of his safe. That's my main reason for going to see him, although . . . we might have a friendly chat while I'm there. That's if I ever get there; I'm stuck in a tailback on the Forth Bridge at the moment.' He paused. 'Any developments in the Glover situation? That's partly what I called to ask you.'

'One. I've just had a call from Sammy. Wilding and Cowan have taken a formal statement from Anderson, and he repeated the story that he got in soon after eleven thirty, and didn't go out again. And just in case he tries to retract and say he got the time mixed up, we've got a witness who followed him out of the Book Festival and down the street.'

'A reliable witness?'

'Lord Elmore reliable enough for you?'

'Claus Blackman? You couldn't get better. I take it that Wilding's having Anderson's statement typed up for signature.'

'He doesn't have to. The guy typed it up on his own computer and printed it out for them, there and then.'

'What do you do next?'

'We're going to re-interview Sandy Rankin, and get her story formalised. Then we can go to the Sheriff, present Anderson's account and hers, and get a warrant to search his premises.'

'Rankin's a journalist, remember; she may figure out what you're working up to.'

'Then let her. I don't care who Anderson is, he's lied to police investigating a homicide and thus put himself in the frame. If he gets his name in the papers, that'll be too damn bad. Many another force would tip off the media before turning up to execute the warrant; at least we're not going to do that.'

'It's a tempting thought, though,' said Skinner. 'I owe Xavi Aislado one, and Anderson as well, in a different way; it would be a good way to repay them both.'

'Are you serious? I could have someone make a call, if you want.'

'If I was serious, Neil, I'd make the fucking call myself. There was a time when I might have, but now I've got to be spotless.'

'Sure, you're going to be chief constable in two days.'

'Acting, Detective Superintendent, only acting. But still, examples have to be set, and I don't want our force to be known for pulling stunts for the TV cameras. Hey,' he called out suddenly, 'traffic's moving, at bloody last.'

'I'd better let you get your eyes back on the road in that case.'

'Not yet; I'm not finished. Something occurred to me, about that call from Aislado, and the story he spiked for us. Not about what was in it, but what wasn't. Thanks to DCS McGuire, that avid reader of crime fiction, we know that whoever killed Glover lifted the method of his murder out of one of his own books. The only people we've told about the cause of death are his son, his daughter, and his future son-in-law, the *Saltire*'s ace sports reporter. They all must have read the old boy's books, so doesn't it strike you as strange that Ed Collins didn't include the link to that plot line in the copy he filed?'

'He's a sports reporter, boss, not a news man.'

'Neil, I'm not a journo, but even I know a front-page headline when I see one. "Novelist foretold own murder!" Come on. Why would he leave that out?'

'Are you saying he didn't want to go too far in what he wrote?'

'No, I'm asking, that's all.'

'Then so will we. But first we'll do some checking up at Deacon Brodie's to see if anyone actually remembers Carol and Wilkie Glover being there on Saturday night. I'll make sure that Sammy does it too; he's never met the family, so he'll approach it with a harder edge than Ray and Alice. They spent half of yesterday with the kids.'

'Good thinking. Now I am off. See you when I get back.'

McIlhenney cradled his phone, but only for a second, before picking it up and calling Pye's mobile number. He had decided that the murder investigation should base itself in Charlotte Square Gardens for only one more day, before moving to the team's Leith office, and that there was no point in having landline telephones installed. 'Where are we with Rankin?' he asked, as the DI responded.

'Ray and Alice are with her now. They ran her to ground at a hotel up in Jeffrey Street, and went up there to see her.'

'And you?'

'Sauce and I have some more people to interview from the Saturday night reception, but mostly I'm waiting for Rankin to confirm her statement about Anderson.'

'I've got something else for you.' He briefed Pye on the question that Skinner had raised over the odd omission from Ed Collins's *Saltire* story.

'Yes,' the inspector conceded, 'it's a thought. I'd intended going to Deacon Brodie's anyway, to confirm their stories, but to be frank I regarded that as a formality so it wasn't at the top of my to-do list. Now I find myself thinking of something June Connelly said, that Glover hadn't really taken to Collins, and only tolerated him for his daughter's sake. Yes, I'll take a closer look at the guy.'

'Put a bit of pressure on him, Sammy. Have him come to you. Christ, have him brought to you if necessary.'

'Who has priority? Him or Anderson?'

'It isn't a question of priorities. Whatever manpower resources you need, I'll make sure you have them. Becky Stallings and Jack McGurk are round in Torphichen Place with a light caseload. You want them, I'll bring them in. Don't worry about Becky being a DI; you'll still be the lead investigator.'

'Thanks, sir. Let me think about that one.'

'Don't think for too long. This inquiry's complicated; we've caught Anderson in a lie, Collins may be a second suspect and, to cap it all, the victim's home's been burgled and all his data stolen.'

'Maybe not all of it. We've impounded Carol Glover's desktop for examination; could be we'll find something there. Then there's that mysterious list in DCC Martin's safe. That may relate.'

McIlhenney frowned, and took a decision. 'Sammy, we have to keep up the pace. Send the daughter's computer along to Torphichen. I'll brief Stallings and McGurk; they can handle that aspect of the investigation, and report to you on it.'

'Yes, boss.' Pye sounded relieved. 'I'll do that now.'

The superintendent hung up once more, but before he could pick up to call Stallings, the phone rang. He snatched at it. 'Yes,' he said impatiently.

'Sir,' a familiar voice began. 'It's George Regan, out in East Lothian.' On his return to duty following a family tragedy, Regan had been promoted to detective inspector and transferred to the rural area to the south and east of the city. McIlhenney knew that he was not a man to be calling him on a trivial matter.

'Yes, George,' he replied. 'What have you got?'

'A dead guy, sir, and what could be a nasty situation.'

Thirty-three

'What did he say?' asked Detective Sergeant Lisa McDermid, as Regan pocketed his phone. She stood close to him on a narrow path that led from a roadway down towards the beach.

'Word for word? He said, "Thank you, George, you've just made my fucking day." The investigation into that author murder is high-profile and using up more and more people. Our acting head of CID needed this like a rash on his face, as somebody said once.'

'What author murder?'

'Where have you been? It was all over the radio and telly yesterday, and this morning's papers. You ever heard of Ainsley Glover, the crime writer?'

'It was him? For a horrible moment I thought it might have been Fred Noble. I really like him, and so does my dad.'

'So you're not bothered that Glover's dead?'

'That's not what I meant, and you know it. Noble's my favourite, that's all; that character of his is absolutely brilliant.'

'Chief Inspector Ellroy? He reminds me too much of old Dan Pringle for me to take him seriously. I'm a Henry Mount fan myself; Petra Jecks, she's a proper detective.'

'We could do with them both here,' McDermid muttered.

Regan looked at her as she tucked a few strands of streaked blonde hair out of sight, and decided that she was one of those women who could look good in anything, even a disposable crime-scene suit. He turned to the uniformed officer by his side. 'How was he found, Sergeant Hope?'

'When? About forty-five minutes ago, just after nine. If you want it exact, the time will be logged in at the communications centre.'

'No,' said Regan patiently. 'How was he found, as in, has a member of the public trampled all over the crime scene before we got here?'

'Not as far as I know. It was a rider found him . . . as in, horse. There are quite a few in Gullane, and along at West Fenton. This lady had been on the beach and was heading home. This path's a bit narrow and windy, but it's used quite a bit by equestrians, more so than walkers, truth be told, because it tends to be covered in horse shit. She went to take it, but her animal refused. It just wouldn't go, whatever she did. So she got off, took a look and found this guy. She didn't have to get very close to see the blood on the back of his head and work out that he wasn't asleep. She got straight on her mobile and called us. She'd just done that when the guy from that house up there,' the sergeant pointed towards a wide, grey bungalow, 'came out to walk his dog. She told him what she had found and he had the presence of mind to block the path at the top, in Erskine Road, to stop any civilians getting down before we got there. My neighbour PC Reid's up there now, keeping guard.'

'Did you speak to the householder?'

'Soon as we got here. He saw nothing, heard nothing out of the ordinary; no shouts, screams, sounds of argument. It was him that told me about the tinker camp just along the way.'

'Traveller camp, Sergeant Hope. "Tinker" isn't an acceptable term any longer. Have you been to see them?'

'Oh no! That's a job for CID. Us uniforms have been told to stay away from there.'

'Have you indeed?' he murmured, wondering why. He turned round and looked across the field beside which the narrow path ran. Beyond it, he saw a golf course – Muirfield, he had been told – and at its furthest point a woman, holding a large grey horse as it grazed.

'That's the witness, yes?'

'That's right. I asked her to wait for you.'

'Thanks.' He turned to DS McDermid. 'Peel off your paper suit, Lisa, and go and have a word with her. I'll wait for the pathologist.'

'You don't have to. He's here.' The voice was soft, Irish. The DI turned to see a tall, youngish man, with a round face and distinctive brown hair; he, too, wore a crime-scene tunic and carried a small bag. 'Inspector Regan?' the newcomer asked. 'I'm Dr Brown, Aidan Brown.' The two shook hands. 'Have you had a look?'

'You mean have I touched anything?'

The pathologist smiled. 'I was trying to be discreet, since this is our first meeting.'

'That's OK. If you'd been here first I'd have asked you the same thing. I verified that the man was dead, that's all. I didn't need to look for a pulse; he's stone cold. You can tell us for sure, but I'm guessing he was killed during the hours of darkness.'

'You say "killed"?'

'Take a look at the back of his head. Either he was drunk enough to climb a tree and fall out, or someone bashed it in for him.'

'Are the SOCOs on the way?'

'Yes. Led by the self-proclaimed genius Arthur Dorward.'

'I'd better get finished before they arrive in that case.' Dr Brown headed up the path, approaching the body.

Regan followed, at a distance, and watched as he went to work on the little figure, pathetic in its dark trousers and dirty shirt; a sordid death, he thought. The pathologist was thorough; his examination took almost fifteen painstaking minutes as he peered at the body, using a torch on occasion even though the morning was bright and fair. Eventually he stood up and turned back to face the DI. 'Yes, you can indeed forget suicide or accident. There isn't a tree around here that's high enough for him to have fallen out and done that. Subject to detailed examination, I'd put the time of death between eleven last night and midnight, with the deceased having been on the way home from the pub. He's choked or vomited at some point and there is a strong smell of alcohol. It appears that he was attacked from behind. He has a couple of broken fingers in his right hand, and my supposition would be that after the first blow, he put it to his head in an instinctive but useless attempt to protect himself. He wasn't struck that many times, but enough to do the job. The skull is intact, but I've no doubt about the cause of death. He wasn't killed instantly, but the limited amount of bleeding indicates that he died quickly after he was attacked. I can feel indentations, and there's a clear, circular bruise on the damaged hand, all of which lead me to conclude that he was killed with a heavy hammer.' He paused. 'I'm probably straying into your area here, but unless the people of Gullane are routinely tooled up, in the most literal sense, when they go out for an evening, this was not an accidental encounter. Someone followed this man, with intent to kill.'

The detective smiled. 'That's pretty comprehensive, Dr Brown. Any other pointers?'

'None I'd take into the witness box, but. . . his face is undamaged, and going purely by his facial features, I'd take a guess that he might not be British.'

Thirty-four

'This is a bit cloak and dagger, isn't it?' Andy Martin murmured as he handed Skinner a mug of coffee, then settled into a seat, facing his visitor across a low table. His casual air hid his uncertainty. His friend's secretary had called his just after nine, and had made an appointment for ten thirty, no reason given, no agenda specified. He had spent the time since wondering what the motive might be, and whether there was any chance of it being personal rather than business.

'Deliberate on my part,' the older man replied, with a soft Sphinx-like grin. 'I wanted to keep you on edge, keep you guessing. Mind you, I'm surprised you haven't worked it out by now.'

Martin's anxiety deepened. 'Humour me,' he said, deliberately casual. 'It's Monday morning and I had a busy weekend.'

'So I gather.' In an instant Skinner's amiability vanished. 'Which brings me to the point. Did you really think you had any chance of keeping a secret from me, in my own city?'

He felt ice in his veins. Surely Alex could not have gone to her father? 'What do you mean?' he retorted.

'You know damn well what I mean.'

'I want to hear it from you.'

'Yesterday morning,' Skinner paused, his unblinking gaze locking on to the other man, 'you gave Neil McIlhenney and Sammy Pye information that related to a homicide inquiry that they have under way. For which I thank you. And then for some reason you suggested

190

that they might keep it from me. What the hell did you think you were doing?'

'Christ! Is that what's behind all this? McIlhenney ran straight to you and spilled it out. I might have bloody known.'

'Yes, you might have. We're not talking about friendship here, Andy, we're not even talking about loyalty, although if that was put to the test, I think you'd find that Neil's lies with me. We're talking about duty. It's his duty as an officer under my command . . . and I don't mean line management; in two days I'll be his acting chief . . . it's his duty to report to me. That's black and white, or are you going to argue there's a shade of grey?'

Martin shook his head. 'No, I'm not, but didn't he tell you why I made that suggestion?'

'He did, but I want to hear it first hand.'

'It ties in with Aileen. My thinking was, and still is, that if you knew about a secret surveillance, outside the knowledge of the local police force, and you told her, then given her position . . . there would be a huge political argument, she'd get hurt and your career would be crippled in the process.'

'Bullshit!'

'That's what I thought,' Martin insisted.

'No, it's what you persuaded yourself you thought. Do you think for one moment that I'd put Aileen in harm's way? If I'd a problem with military intelligence playing silly buggers on my patch, I'd have sorted it myself. As it is, I accept that sometimes national security has its own requirements. And in case you hadn't noticed, that isn't a function devolved to the Scottish Parliament, because like it or not, we ain't a fully self-governing nation, chum, not yet at any rate. My duty to Aileen is to keep her safe, and if that means shielding her from information that's outside her official remit, then so be it.'

'Wait a minute, are you telling me you knew about Coben?'

'I'd never heard of the guy before yesterday but I knew about what was happening. You came on to my patch and stirred it, instead of calling me and asking me to sort it out, as you should have . . . not just because of the territorial thing, but because you had a family connection with the man involved. Of course the ripples got back to me, man. When they did, I looked into it, and found out what was up. The people who ran the surveillance apologised but said it was necessary.'

'To the point at which they took my poor hapless cousin out of the game?' Martin snapped.

'Don't be fucking daft. The intelligence community had nothing to do with his murder, I'd bet the house on that. They may have been playing silly buggers after it, but that's as far as they're involved.'

'Did you tell them to have a word with me, though? Did you know about that?'

Skinner stared at him. 'Are you crazy?' he asked. 'No way would I do that, or countenance it. If I ever had a visit like that, the guy would leave the room in a fucking bin bag.' He frowned. 'Come to think of it, I did once, and he did. But that's what's at the heart of this, isn't it? That's what's behind your strange order to McIlhenney, isn't it? And that's why you tried to keep Pye out of the discussion. This man Coben got to you.'

Martin sat silent; then he nodded. 'He did, Bob. He sat there, military sharp, with is wee Union Jack lapel badge in his blazer, and he threatened me, professionally; that's no problem on its own, but he threatened my family too, and that's different. I lost it, and I told him to get the fuck out of my office before he left via the window. I meant it, yet he just smiled at me. What he was saying to me was, "I can reach right into your life and hurt you where it causes you the most pain." If you want me to come right out and admit it, yes, that scared me.'

Skinner sighed. 'You shouldn't have been keeping that from

me, son, you should have told me. National security or not, we can't have the state intimidating chief police officers. That's what I call a real excess of zeal. Look, I've been at this level for a lot longer than you, and I've got connections you haven't. Do you want me to put it right?'

'No, I want you to forget about it. You weren't there, Bob, and it isn't your family.'

'Andy, he takes orders like the rest of us, and he's exceeded them. A word in the right ear and he'll be reprimanded.'

'Leave it,' Martin insisted. 'It's all history now anyway. Ainsley's dead, so the surveillance is over and there's nothing for the spooks to get their knickers twisted over. I just want it to go away.'

'OK,' Skinner conceded. 'But I want something from you: that list your late cousin gave you.'

'No problem, but if you don't think the watching operation was linked to his death, what good's it going to do?'

'I won't know that until I've seen it, will I, but if the people he was in touch with were being watched themselves, his contact with them might have drawn attention from people we don't know about. It's a long shot, but it's a line of inquiry that has to be followed.'

Martin nodded. 'Sure.' He rose from his chair and stepped across to a small secure cabinet in the furthest corner of his office, unlocked it, and took out a white envelope. 'There,' he said as he handed it over. 'For what it's worth.'

'Thanks.' Skinner slipped it, unopened, into an inside pocket of his jacket. He picked up his coffee and drained what was left in the mug, making a face as he realised that it had gone cold. 'How's Karen?' he asked.

'Expanding, and it's pissing her off. She's a great mother, but she's not hugely fond of being pregnant.'

'I wouldn't expect her to be. As I remember, Myra and Sarah in the same condition were about as approachable as a wasp's byke. Myra, God bless her, was fond of declaring that if women and men took turns at being pregnant and giving birth, the maximum family size would be three, because no man would ever do it twice.' His forehead twisted into a frown. 'Not that she had the chance herself, poor lass. We'd planned to have four, she and I.' Bob Skinner looked at his friend. 'I've never stopped missing her, you know, even now when I'm happier than I've ever been since she died. I still have this daydream where she walks in out of the blue, and I have to explain to her all the changes in the modern world, the internet, satellite navigation, all that stuff her daughter takes for granted. That's something I miss too, not being able to share my worries about Alex with her.'

'You're worried about her?' Andy asked quietly, not yet sure of what might be coming.

'No, no, not really. No more than usual; it comes with the territory of being a dad, I suppose. She was a bit strange yesterday, and I found myself telling her that maybe she was getting too career focused, needed to broaden her interests.' He chuckled. 'Imagine me telling her that! I even suggested she should think about going into politics. The Aileen effect, I suppose.' He rose. 'Time I was back off to Edinburgh. The rest of today and tomorrow will be taken up by a handover with Jimmy.'

'Heard anything about rival candidates for the job?'

'I had a whisper from human resources that there might not be any. I'm not sure I want that. Coronations are for monarchs and, these days, prime ministers, not for cops.'

He headed for the door. Martin walked him downstairs, and out to his car.

'Remember what I told you, Andy,' Bob said as they parted. 'This Coben's a bully-boy, no more. If you change your mind about wanting him sorted, let me know.'

'I won't. But tell Neil I'm sorry for the way I behaved towards him. I regret that now.'

'Sure, I'll do that.' Bob waved goodbye, drove out of the car park and picked up the road that led west, then south, to Edinburgh. But as the miles passed by, he found that he could not stop thinking about his friend, and worrying about him, strangely concerned that one of the toughest people he had ever met should have confessed to fear.

'Is that all there is to it, Andy?' he asked himself aloud. 'A threat from a sinister stranger? Or is there more?'

Thirty-five

'What did the horse lady have to say?' Regan asked McDermid as she approached him along the foot-worn path that crossed the field.

'Nothing more than we'd heard from Sergeant Hope. She didn't see anyone near the scene; she'd been on the beach and had taken the track that skirts the second fairway, but nobody passed her by, no dog-walkers, nobody carrying a blunt instrument.'

'In this case a hammer, according to the pathologist. Not that she'd have seen the perpetrator anyway,' he sighed. 'This guy's been dead since midnight.' He glanced towards the course. 'Second fairway, eh? Have you played Muirfield, then?'

Lisa McDermid raised an eyebrow. 'That possibility doesn't exist. I'm a woman, George, in case you hadn't noticed.'

'I'd noticed; my wife's one, so I know what you lot look like.'

She looked at him, realising that it was the first time in their short professional association that he had mentioned anything about his private life. 'How does your wife feel about your new job?' she asked.

'She's pleased about it, especially the promotion and the extra money. She likes the new house too, and living in Longniddry; it's been good for us to get away from the old place. Too many reminders there . . . not that we'll ever forget him, of course.'

The DS did not know what to say; she was single, so she could not begin to imagine the pain of losing a child. But the moment passed. 'How do we take this forward?' she continued.

'We visit the travellers. I told Superintendent McIlhenney about them, but he knew already, of course, given their proximity to the DCC's house. We've got to keep a lid on this thing, for the natural inclination of the locals will be to blame them.'

'Maybe we won't have to visit them.' McDermid pointed over Regan's shoulder. 'They could be coming to us.'

The DI turned to see a tall man wearing denims and a T-shirt with a rock star logo that meant nothing to the Country and Western addict that was George Regan. He was walking not merely in their general direction but towards them, eyes fixed, and with a purposeful expression. The two detectives moved to meet him halfway, before he reached the turn into the path.

'Can we help you?' McDermid smiled at him but his face stayed set.

'Police?'

'Yes.'

'I thought so; one of our kids spotted you along here. Look, I thought we were clear to stay here for a while at least. Whatever happened to the civil solutions you're meant to be pursuing? Or is Mr Skinner's word not worth a stuff?'

'I don't know what you're talking about,' Regan told him.

'Sure you don't. When does the van arrive to lift us? I'd really like to know, because I've got some work lined up and I'd like to finish it before we get moved on. As a matter of fact, I'm due at the deputy chief constable's house at half eleven, to service his lawnmower.'

'We're not here to shift anybody. We're CID; DI Regan, DS McDermid. There's been an incident.'

'Where?'

'Just round the corner, up the path there. A man's been found dead.'

'What? As in had a heart attack?'

'I told you that we're CID, did I not? That might suggest different. Now, share with us please. Who are you?'

The man's manner seemed to change. 'My name's Derek Baillie.'

'You're a traveller?'

'I told you that.'

'Yes, sorry. Just making certain.'

Baillie nodded. 'Look,' he began, then paused. 'Bugger it,' he muttered, 'this is the last thing our lot needed. Tell your boss I'm sorry about his lawnmower but I reckon we'll be moving on.'

Regan shook his head. 'I don't think you will, Mr Baillie. Not until we're satisfied that none of your people had anything to do with this.'

'When you are, make sure you tell all the locals, because we'll get the blame regardless. Jesus, this is the first time we've ever been asked to stay somewhere. Who is the poor man anyway? Some local bigwig?'

'We haven't the faintest idea, but unless the toffs in Gullane make a habit of going out in shiny trousers and white shirts that are boiled grey, I doubt it.'

Baillie's eyes narrowed. 'Say that again. How's he dressed?'

'Dark trousers, formerly white shirt.'

'Can you describe him? Is he a big bloke?'

'No, he's a wee man,' replied Regan, interest awoken. 'Age, not sure; but our doctor thinks he might be foreign. Why, do you think you might know him?'

'I hope I don't,' exclaimed Baillie, suddenly agitated.

'The body's still there. Would you be prepared to take a look? I warn you, though, he's not pretty, lying like he is. If you like we could wait until the mortuary people come to collect him.'

The traveller looked at him, then at McDermid. 'I'm not a wimp,' he snapped. 'Let's get it over with.'

'You'll need to wear a protective overall like the DI's,' the sergeant told him. When she had taken hers off, to interview the horsewoman, she had tied it round her waist. She unwrapped it and handed it to him, together with a pair of overshoes. 'Use mine; it's uni-size.'

'Do I need to? If I'm just going in for a look . . .'

'We still can't run the risk of you leaving your DNA on the site.'

'Just in case it's there already,' Regan added.

Baillie glowered at him. 'It isn't. But that's what I mean about you people; we're where you look first.'

'We look everywhere, so don't take it personally. Suppose you were the parish priest, we'd still have to ask you to go in suited and booted.' He waited while the man fitted himself into the flimsy outfit and pulled on the slippers, then when he was ready he led the way up the path.

A tent, as wide as the path could accommodate, had been erected over the body; Regan raised its flap. 'OK to come in, Arthur?' he asked one of the two men who were working inside.

'I've got a witness who needs to see the body.'

'Is he properly dressed?' DI Arthur Dorward shot back.

'Of course.'

'Then OK, but tell him not to touch anything.'

Regan stood aside to let Baillie enter. Dorward and his assistant stopped what they were doing and watched as he bent over the body. They heard him gasp, then retch. 'Out,' the scene of crime chief shouted, 'if you're going to puke on him.'

'I'm all right,' the traveller assured him, straightening up. 'It was a shock, that's all.' He turned to Regan. 'I know him,' he said. 'His name's Asmir Mustafic, and he's a member of our group.'

'You sure?'

'Certain.'

'Come on then, let's get out of here.' He glanced at Dorward. 'Arthur, have your people recovered the murder weapon yet?'

'No, it's not in the immediate area. We'll need a squad of uniforms to search the surrounding land, and the gardens around here, in case it was chucked into one of them.'

'OK, I'll take care of that.' He followed Baillie out of the tent and down the path. 'Thanks for that,' he said as they rejoined McDermid. 'I know it can't have been easy, to see someone you know in such a state.' His face changed, for a fraction of a second; it betrayed nothing to the traveller, but the DS knew that he was speaking from personal, agonising, experience.

'He's a mess,' the man murmured as he stripped off the overall and handed it back. 'What was used on him? What sort of weapon?'

'I can't give you that detail, I'm afraid.'

'I suppose not. But this changes everything, you know. Instead of the locals blaming us, my people will be looking at them. Threats are nothing new to us; until now they've been hollow, though.'

'Listen, Mr Baillie, we're not jumping to any conclusions. This death will be investigated in the same way as any other, and that means we start by looking at the people closest to the victim, because statistically that's nearly always where we get a result. Did Mr Mustafic have any enemies within your group? Have there been any disagreements lately?'

'No, none at all. Asmir wasn't a disagreeable sort; he was a quiet wee man. He was old school, a gypsy from the east; that means he enjoyed a sort of respect within the community.'

'When did you see him last?'

'Yesterday evening. He and I went for a drink, then he left to go somewhere else.'

'On his own?'

'Yes.'

'You didn't follow him?' McDermid asked him.

Baillie smiled. 'And bash his head in, you mean? No, and I can prove that. There was a third person with us. He and I stayed on in the pub for a while, and then we left to walk home, both of us. We got to the foot of Hill Road, then he went his way and I went mine.'

'We'll need to talk to him.'

'I'm sure you will. He won't be hard to find; his name's Skinner and he's your deputy chief.'

Regan grunted. 'As soon as he hears about this he'll be finding us. Are you telling me that you and the DCC were the last people to see Mr Mustafic alive?'

'No, I'm not. I've just said he was going somewhere else when he left us. That tent back there was reeking of beer, and he only had the one with us. Az liked a drink, and he'd a few quid in his pocket; he'd have been somewhere till closing time. You ask around and you'll find out where. Bar staff and their punters give us the eye whenever we go in to a pub – and that's if they let us over the door. He'll be remembered.'

'No doubt,' McDermid's tone was sceptical 'but none of that gives you an alibi. As soon as you and Mr Skinner parted company, you could have gone and lain in wait for Mustafic, ready to smash his head in.'

'You could make the same suggestion to your boss, Sergeant, but I'm a gambling man and I'll bet whatever's in your wallet right now that you don't.'

'You will not even think about taking that bet, Lisa,' Regan warned her, before she could open her mouth to reply. 'Mr Baillie,' he continued, 'I take it that the dead man had a caravan.'

'Yes.'

'And a family in it?'

'No. Az was single.'

'Do you know anything about his background?'

'No more than I told Mr Skinner last night. He joined our group two years ago, and he's been travelling with us ever since. He never told us himself where he came from, but the man who introduced him to us said that he was from Bulgaria.'

'Who was the man?'

'His name's Hugo Playfair. He's one of us as well. He's a do-gooder, a big wheel in a charity that stands up for people like us.'

'Can we speak to him?'

'You can speak to whoever you like.'

'And we'd like to see inside Mr Mustafic's caravan,' McDermid added.

'Sergeant, as far as I'm concerned you can see inside every damn caravan we've got. I'm as keen to find the guy who killed Az as you are. Mr Skinner's lawnmower will have to wait for its service, but I'm sure he'll understand.'

Thirty-six

'The computer's arrived, Sammy,' said Detective Inspector Becky Stallings, her London accent unaffected by her lengthening stay in Edinburgh. 'Once Jack McGurk's managed to hijack a monitor and a keyboard, I'll be able to make a start. Do we need an administrator password?'

'Not as such; not to open the operating system. The daughter said you just switch it on and you're in. She's wireless capable, so you should be able to access the internet through our network. Once you've done that, the password for her email account is "rootcanal", all one word.'

'Yuk! I've had some of that. Is this girl a sadist?'

Pye smiled, imagining Stallings' expression at the other end of the line. 'No,' he replied, 'she's a dentist.'

'Same thing. Once we've got into her account, what next?'

'The second screen name you're looking for is *fatallyg*, all one word. That's . . .' He spelled it out. 'What I can't give you is the password he used.' In the silence that followed he could almost feel his colleague's frown.

'Mr McIlhenney didn't tell me that,' she sighed. 'Never mind, I might get lucky. It might be very simple, or he might have tried to be too clever in linking it to himself or someone he knows, that we trip over it quickly. A lot of people do that; I've had experience of this sort of stuff before. What I'd like you to do is send me an email with all the personal detail you can on Mr Glover: full name and date of birth, wife's details, children's details, his postcode, their postcode, and anything else you think might be relevant. Did he have a profession, apart from author?'

'He was an accountant.'

'That could mean it's number-based . . . but he was a wordsmith as well, so maybe not. I've never read any of his books. Might there be something in them he could have used?'

'I'm no expert either. All I can tell you is that his main character's name is Detective Inspector Walter Strachan.'

'Spelling as in the footballer?'

'The same.'

'That's something else to go on. As soon as we're up and running, I'll start playing around with combinations of that. Meantime, you put that email together and get it to me as quickly as you can.'

Thirty-seven

'Boss, where are you?' McIlhenney asked.

'I'm stuck on the Forth fucking Bridge again,' Skinner groaned. 'Roadworks this time. They can't build the new crossing soon enough for me.'

'Did you get the list?'

'Yes, and I have something else for you as well. An apology from Andy for the heavy-handed approach.'

'None needed. He had his viewpoint and I had mine.'

'Don't kid me, mate; your nose was well out of joint.'

'Maybe,' the superintendent conceded. 'I found myself wondering whether he would have acted the same way if Mario had been here.'

'He would, no doubt about it. He didn't take you for a soft touch, if that's what you're thinking. He'd have behaved in the same way and the outcome would have been the same. I didn't promote either of you guys to get rolled over by anyone on your own territory. McGuire might have been less diplomatic than you, that's all.'

'I shudder to think how McGuire might have been.' McIlhenney chuckled, then his mood changed. 'I've got some news for you now,' he said, 'and you're not going to like it. It's probably as well you're not moving at the moment.'

'What's up?' said Skinner, suddenly anxious. 'Has the Glover case gone bad on us?'

'Nothing to do with that. A name, Asmir Mustafic?'

205

'I know him,' the DCC confirmed, surprise undisguised in his tone. 'He and his travelling friends are camped almost right in front of my house; you must have noticed them yesterday. Don't tell me, there's been bother between him and the locals.'

'Between him and whom we know not, but he's come off a bad second. The guy's dead. He was found near the campsite this morning with his head badly dented. The pathologist reckons somebody took a hammer to him.'

'Jesus Christ!' Skinner gasped. 'When did this happen?'

'Midnight, give or take.'

'But I was with him last night. I had a beer with him in the Mallard.'

'I know that. He was identified by a man called Derek Baillie; he told the officers at the scene that they'd been with you.'

'That's right, although Mustafic didn't stay long. His ingrained suspicions of anyone with a warrant card were just too strong. Who's lead officer? DCI Leggat?'

'No, Graham's on holiday, like half the bloody force. George Regan and Lisa McDermid are running it.'

'George? I'm fine with that. McDermid's a bit new to CID, but he'll keep her right. Do they have any leads so far?'

'You and Baillie are their only suspects so far.' He paused. 'I'm joking, OK! But George says that Baillie's worried about how his people will take the news.'

'They'll take it quietly, or else. I'm having no confrontation between them and the village; tell George to make that clear to Derek Baillie. I assume that his investigation will begin in the encampment, with those who knew the guy. I'm not saying there's nobody in Gullane who'd do something like this, but I really would like to think there isn't. Step one, look at Mustafic's life and his relationships and establish a potential motive. It's unlikely to be robbery, I'll tell you that now. The man arrived from eastern Europe a couple of years ago, without a bean and without much English. He earned his keep doing casual jobs or helping other travellers with theirs. Plus I think he had a bit of charity support; there's a pushy wee guy among the group who fronts for a body called Rights for Ethnic Groups; name of Hugo Playfair.'

'But travellers aren't ethnics.'

'Not in Scotland, technically, but they're treated as if they are. I have the word of the First Minister for that.'

'Kid-glove treatment?'

'No. By the book, but nothing that smells of harassment. Regan will probably need a statement from me. Tell him I'll take care of it. What's he doing now?'

'Heading for the campsite to see what he can find out about Mustafic; to interview the travellers and, if he can, to check out their tool kits, to see who's got a big hammer, ideally one with blood, bone and brains sticking to it.'

'Hah,' Skinner barked, sourly. 'We should be so lucky.' He fell silent, but only for a few seconds. 'What about the Glover investigation? How's that going on? What about Anderson?'

'Even as we speak,' McIlhenney replied, 'the smooth young knuckles of Detective Inspector Pye should be chapping on his door.'

'Good. Let's hope he's in.'

Thirty-eight

'Not you people again,' Bruce Anderson exclaimed through the small loudspeaker in the doorway of the Darnaway Street building. 'I've given you my formal statement; now let that be an end of it and go away.'

'I can't do that, sir,' Pye insisted. 'Now let us in, if you please.'

'And if I don't please?'

'Then an officer will break it down.'

'Are you serious, man? You wait there while I phone your chief constable. We'll see what he has to say about this.'

'No, sir, I will not wait. Either you will open this door in the next ten seconds, or PC Childs here will; it'll be a lot quieter for the neighbours if it's you who does it.'

'This is outrageous,' Anderson snapped, but a second later a buzz came from the small speaker, and a click sounded in the lock. The DI pushed it open, leading Haddock and half a dozen uniformed officers inside and up the staircase to the first floor. The door to the flat remained closed. Seeing no bell, Pye knocked, softly, then took a pace back as it swung open, watching anger follow astonishment across the former Secretary of State's face as he took in the throng on the landing. 'Good God Almighty!' he shouted. 'What is the meaning of this?'

Sauce Haddock handed him a twice-folded sheet of A4 paper. 'This is a warrant to search these premises, sir,' he said, 'and also to search your clinic. It was issued by the Sheriff this morning.'

'On what grounds?'

'The search relates to our investigation into the murder of Ainsley Glover,' Pye told him. 'Is there anyone else in the house, sir?'

'No. Lady Walters and my daughter have gone to Harvey Nichols.'

'Good. That means we don't have to remove them from the premises while we search.'

Anderson scanned the warrant. 'This appears to be genuine,' he said, 'but you're searching nothing unless my solicitor is present.'

'Sorry, sir, but we are; the search will be filmed and you may remain present for the duration, but I'm not obliged to let anyone else in here, and I don't plan to do so. Now I suggest that you allow us to come inside and do our job. I assure you that we'll be as quiet, neat and discreet as we can.' For a moment the DI thought that Anderson was going to try to block his way, but finally he stood aside.

Pye led the squad into the flat. 'Begin with the bedrooms, Constable,' he told Haddock as the squad crowded into the narrow hallway, 'then the bathroom, kitchen, the study, and finally the living room. Dr Anderson and I will be in there while you're at work. Film everything you find, in situ, before you remove it. Doctor, if you'd like to come with me.'

'I'm going to have your nuts in the crusher for this,' the politician murmured, softly but with feeling, as he followed the detective into the room where he had received him and McIlhenney a little less that twenty-four hours earlier.

'Don't threaten me, sir,' Pye replied calmly. 'You're in a vulnerable situation; don't make it worse.'

'What do you mean vulnerable?'

'You've lied to us, yesterday, and again this morning when you gave my colleagues a formal signed statement.'

'Lied to you?' The man's eyes narrowed, and for the first time he looked unsure of himself. 'Regarding what, precisely?'

'I've got a problem with your account of your whereabouts at the time of Mr Glover's death. Your statement has you returning home from the Book Festival party at around eleven thirty, and staying put. That's right, isn't it?'

'Yes.'

The inspector looked him in the eye. 'So how does that tally,' he asked, 'with the version of a witness who saw you heading back up North Charlotte Street, towards the square, just before midnight?'

Anderson's facial muscles froze, but only for a second or so. 'It doesn't,' he snapped, 'which means that your witness mistook me for somebody else.'

'My witness wasn't alone, Dr Anderson.' He spoke the truth, without adding that he had still to ask Sandy Rankin's companions, Jock Fisher and Ryan McCool, whether they, too, had seen him. 'You really don't want to mess me about any longer,' he added. 'You are a suspect, make no mistake about it, a very strong suspect at that. You fit the profile of the person we're after; you showed strong antagonism towards the victim, you have medical expertise and you were seen heading towards the place where he was killed.'

'But I wasn't!'

'Doctor, I urge you to consider your position. You were seen in North Charlotte Street twice. Once by Lord Elmore and his wife, heading home around eleven thirty, and again by others, going in the opposite direction around twenty minutes later.'

'I wasn't going back to the Book Festival!' Anderson shouted.

'Then where were you going?'

'I cannot tell you that.'

'You have to, sir. I'll let you withdraw the statement you signed this morning, without comeback, but you have to be telling me the truth from now on.'

'I cannot do that.'

'In that case—'

'Sir,' Haddock called from the doorway. 'Sorry to interrupt, but I wonder if you could join us for a minute.'

'Right now?'

'Yes please.'

Pye rose from his seat. 'Excuse me, Dr Anderson.' He followed the DC from the room, into the hall, past the uniformed bulk of Constable Childs who stood leaning on his unused door ram, and through to a large bedroom. 'What have you got, Sauce?' he asked.

'Have a look, sir.' He pointed the DI into a small dressing room, where a woman police officer stood, holding a pair of high-heeled shoes.

'Not my style, Sauce.'

'I hope not, sir.' Haddock took one of the shoes and held it upside down. A packet fell out and he caught it neatly. It was clear plastic, filled with a brown powder. 'I don't think that's sugar, boss,' he said. 'There's the same again in the other shoe. Afghanistan's finest, going by that drugs course I did last month; if I'm wrong you can stick me back in a uniform tomorrow.'

'And me alongside you,' the inspector murmured. 'Have you got this locus on video? I want no suggestion that it was planted.'

'Too right we have.'

'OK. Bag the stuff, in the shoes, as you found it, then carry on with the search; I want to find any other drugs that are in here, and the paraphernalia that goes with the stuff. Tear this fucking place apart if you have to. I'll be busy with Anderson for a while.'

He turned and walked back through to the drawing room. It was empty. 'Dr Anderson?' he called out. He waited for a few moments, frowning, then returned to the hall and checked the bathroom, and then the kitchen. 'Oh no,' he whispered, as he retraced his steps. 'Don't let this have happened, God, please.'

There was a door at the far end of the living room. He strode across and threw it open, revealing a study, with a window that looked on to the back of the building, and two doors. The first concealed a cupboard, filled with books and papers. He tried the second, and found it locked, by a Yale, which he opened easily, and by a heavy mortice which he could not. He peered through the keyhole and saw enough to make out a stairway, narrower and less grand than the main entrance. 'Magic,' he moaned, 'a first-floor flat with a back door.'

He went to the window and peered out into a courtyard enclosed by the building in which he stood and by two adjoining streets. There were several parking places, some occupied, some vacant. Blue exhaust smoke hung in the air, and as his gaze found the exit road, he thought he caught a momentary flash of brake lights reflected in the dark polish of a stationary vehicle.

'Fuck it!' he swore, then dashed back through to the hall. 'Childs,' he called to the burly officer in the hallway 'I've got something needs opening; bring the ram that I threatened Anderson with earlier.'

Thirty-nine

'Wherever this guy came from,' said George Regan quietly, 'he didn't bring much with him.'

'Sorry, sir?'

The DI turned to his sergeant. 'I was just thinking that this guy wasn't big on personal possessions,' he told her. 'He has no photographs, no books, nothing at all, other than his passport and the letter from the immigration people giving him indefinite permission to stay in the UK.' He pointed to a tiny wardrobe, the door of which was open. 'As for clothes, apart from what he was wearing when he died, he's got one pair of work boots, a pair of shoes, four shirts, one jacket and two pairs of trousers.'

Lisa McDermid pulled open the drawer she had just searched. 'He didn't change his underwear or his socks too often either, if this is his entire stock in here.' She looked around the shabby caravan. 'Imagine living like this.'

'Most of us are pretty comfortable.' Derek Baillie was standing in the doorway. 'We're not all like Az. When he arrived here he was set up by Playfair's charity. They gave him the van, and his old truck to tow it.'

'And the clothes?' McDermid asked. 'The manky old pants here are from British Home Stores.'

'The jacket isn't,' Regan pointed out as he checked its pockets. He twisted it on its hanger to show the label. 'Whatever that is, it's not English.'

Baillie held out a hand. 'Let me see.' He took the black garment that the detective passed across, peering at the lettering. 'It's the Cyrillic alphabet,' he declared. 'Bulgarian, I guess, given that's where Az was from.'

'Did he ever talk about his origins?'

'Not much. I asked him about Sofia once; he said that for him it was a shit-hole with no jobs for casuals, and that he never went near it. He said he was a countryman, and having seen him at work, I can understand that. His skills were rural rather than urban. He was a pretty fair gardener; I took him out on jobs with me whenever I could. I'd service the machinery and he'd test it for me, cutting grass, trimming hedges and so on. He was good at that, but he hadn't a clue about what made the things work.' He smiled. 'Actually, he was a bit better than fair in the garden. He and I did a big house once, down near Lauder. It had a lot of topiary . . . hedge sculptures and such . . . that had been neglected. Az found a pair of shears and went to work; it took him half a day and everything was perfect. There was a vegetable garden too, and it was a shambles. The guy who owned the house was a stockbroker, and he hadn't a clue. Az told him that he'd no chance of growing maize in that soil, and the bloke said, "OK, sort it out." So he did. He tore the place apart, junked nearly all of it. I wound up labouring for him, and in a couple of days he had potatoes, carrots, cabbages and leeks, all in neat sections and rows. He was singing away as he worked, in his own language. That was the happiest I ever saw him, but when I said as much, he clammed up. It was odd.'

'In what way?' asked McDermid.

'The way he looked. It was as if he felt guilty about being so contented. Like I said, I've never seen him that way since, the poor wee guy. Resentment and suspicion were never far from the surface with him. I guess he was one of those old-fashioned gypsies, the sort who want as little as possible to do with the other world. Even last night, when we met your boss, I had to lean on him to get him to come, but it was a waste of time. The man was perfectly reasonable, perfectly polite; I understood his point of view, but Az wasn't having any of it. He drank up and left.' Baillie shook his head sadly, then handed the jacket back to Regan.

The inspector took it from him, and made to hang it on its rail; as he moved, the back of his free hand brushed the hem of the garment and felt something hard. He frowned, slipped it from its hanger, turned it inside out and felt inside the shiny lining until he found a tear inside the breast pocket, large enough for him to retrieve the hidden object.

It was a brown envelope, unsealed, its contents stiff. He drew them out, a small bundle of letters and two photographs, all held together by an elastic band which snapped as soon as he made to release it. He laid the letters on the caravan's kitchen work surface and looked at the first of the images. It was cracked and its colours had begun to fade, but the woman it portrayed, seated on a grassy hillside, was still strikingly beautiful, with dark hair, high cheekbones and eyes that seemed to grab Regan and capture him. He stared at her, until he realised that his companions were staring at him. The second snapshot showed the same woman, a few years older perhaps, but still as dramatic, standing, flanked by two small children, a boy, no more than a toddler, and a girl, taller and a year or two older; in the background were a caravan and a car.

The DI glanced at Baillie, then handed the photographs to him. 'Did he ever mention a family?'

'No,' the traveller replied. 'Never. Not once. Do you think this could be his wife and kids?' He passed the two prints to McDermid as he spoke.

'It needn't be. Could be his sister and hers.'

'His mother?' the sergeant suggested. 'Could the boy be him?'

'Look at the car in the picture with the kids,' Regan told her. 'It's a

Volvo. According to Mustafic's passport he was thirty-eight years old. So if that's him as a nipper ... Well, it couldn't be, end of story. I did enough time on traffic when I was a plod to know that model's ten years old, fifteen at most. If this is his family, and he left them behind when he came over here, no wonder he was a sad wee bugger.'

'If they are, they need to be told about this,' McDermid declared.

'In that case,' said Baillie, 'you'd better speak to Hugo Playfair. There's nobody else here who'll have the faintest idea how to trace them.'

Forty

'Are you telling me, Sammy,' Neil McIlhenney asked, in a quiet tone that Pye regarded as a masterpiece of restraint, 'that in the middle of an interview, in the middle of a search of his premises, you let our only suspect in the Ainsley Glover homicide inquiry walk out the door? That's the story, is it?'

The inspector sighed. 'That's what happened,' he confirmed.

The superintendent looked across his desk impassively. 'I might leave you to explain that to the big man when he gets back. I'm just heading off to Gullane to catch up on George Regan's investigation into a dead gypsy, before the media turn up in numbers.'

'Fair enough. I'm sorry, boss. I took my eye off the ball. It never occurred to me for a second that he'd do that. Even if it had, I wouldn't have worried, because I had PC Childs stationed at the front door. But I didn't know about the other way out, did I?'

'No, and I doubt if I'd have guessed that one either.' Pye breathed easier at the confession. 'And I suppose the guy had the right to leave without notice. He wasn't under caution, and you hadn't arrested him.'

'I was about a second away from doing just that when Sauce came in to tell me about the drugs find.'

'You were? I thought we were playing it cool.'

'The time for that was over. When I pinned him down he admitted that he had gone out again. He denied that he'd gone back to the Festival site, but he refused point-blank to tell me where he was going.'

'What's your feel for his denial? Genuine?'

'I don't have a feel as such. The man's a bully and a blusterer; he and I had a confrontation when we served him the warrant.'

'So why did he run for it?' McIlhenney mused. 'Did he kill Glover right enough, and realise that the game's up?'

'That's one possibility. The other is that he guessed we'd found his girlfriend's smack and decided he'd be better off out of there.'

'Maybe. Did you find anything else, apart from that?'

'Not what we went in there looking for. Nothing that could relate to the murder.'

'No syringes? I'd have thought she'd—'

'So did I, but as Sauce says, she could have been smoking the stuff. If you're rich enough you don't have to inject, and with the quantity she had, that may well be her habit.'

'We are sure it's hers, and not his?'

'It was in her shoes. Given her record, she has to be a user; mind you, that doesn't mean Anderson doesn't join in.'

'With his kid around? Surely to Christ . . .'

'We won't know till we ask him.'

'True, so what have you done about getting him back?'

'The first thing I did was to send a car to the clinic. Anderson knew we were going to search that too, so I reckoned there was a chance of him trying to beat us to it, get rid of the evidence before we could find it. He'll be apprehended if he shows up there, but he hasn't so far.'

'You've put a vehicle description out, though?'

Pye shook his head. 'That's my big problem, I don't know what the fucker's driving. I did a DVLA check. Anderson owns a blue Discovery; that's still sitting in one of his two parking spaces. The other one's empty, so my assumption is that he's taken his girlfriend's motor. A neighbour confirmed that she has one, but he didn't know the make or model. The only thing is, DVLA has no record of a car registered to Lady Walters, and only the one in Anderson's name.'

'Then it must be her father's.'

'I'd assumed that too, but which one? Seems that the Duke of Lanark doesn't have a personally registered vehicle either. All his cars are registered in the name of the limited company that manages his estates, and there are eleven of them.'

'Ask him which one she drives. Or do you want me to make that call?'

'I've done it already. The Duke's on his way to London. I spoke to his manager, but he pleaded ignorance. He said it could be one of half a dozen.'

'Was he lying?' asked McIlhenney.

'Probably, but I didn't have time to press him. All I could do was get him to give me the numbers of all the cars he knew to be on the estate. I've eliminated them and put out "Stop on sight" orders for all the others. But again, if he does know which car she has . . .'

'. . . he might well have included it on the list he gave you.'

'Exactly.'

'So where are you at?'

'Sauce has taken the search team to the clinic. The drugs squad are crawling all over Anderson's flat, with orders to be neither neat nor discreet, and I've got Ray Wilding and Alice Cowan going through Harvey Nichols, floor by floor. That's where Anderson said Anthea Walters was. At the very least, I'm having her!' He frowned. 'But there's someone else involved: Tanya, Anderson's daughter. She's with Walters. Her dad's on the run from the police and she's in the care of a junkie. The kid needs protection, and she's my top priority.'

Forty-one

'You know, Bob,' Sir James Proud confessed, 'this is a week that once I thought would never come; my last as a police officer before I go off to tend my garden.'

Skinner laughed. He looked around the room: rectangular patches showed on the walls, the places where personal photographs had been hung until a few minutes earlier. 'You reckoned you were immortal?' he asked.

The outgoing chief constable did not smile. 'No, no. Far from it. I had a secret belief that I would die in office. Damn near did too; that heart scare a few years back might have seen me off. But it didn't. Instead it showed me that too much time spent behind a desk is good for nobody. So now I'm three stone lighter than I was then and I can jog upstairs to this office.' He patted the arm of the rocker in which he sat. 'Watch this chair when you settle into it. It's bewitched; the longer you sit in it, the closer your belly gets to the desk, without either piece of furniture moving at all.'

'I'm bringing my own chair across the corridor, Jimmy. It's magic too. If I sit in it for longer than half an hour there's an ejector mechanism that fires me to my feet. If I'm confirmed in your job, my successor as deputy can have yours.'

'There's no "if" about it, son,' said Proud quietly. 'None of your brother Scots have applied for the position, in deference to you, or in acceptance of the inevitable, I reckon, and in the current political climate it's been deemed unacceptable by the Police Board that officers from outwith Scotland should be considered, unless they have a record of service north of the border.'

Skinner stared at him for several seconds as the import of what he had just been told began to sink in. 'I don't suppose you had any influence on that "deeming", did you?' he asked.

'Far be it for me to press my opinion on the Board.'

'If I had you under interrogation and you gave me a non-answer like that, you'd be waiting a long time for your next cup of tea. Were you asked for your opinion?'

'If I was, why do you assume that I'd have agreed with that view?' Proud Jimmy smiled. 'But to stop you pestering me about it, I played no part in the deliberation . . . my insistence, not the Board's. My last act as chief will be to attend the meeting tomorrow, at which your appointment will be confirmed, effective immediately.'

'I didn't want that, Jimmy,' the DCC said quietly. 'I wanted a contest.'

'I know, but since this is the way it's panned out, we'll just have to accept it . . . won't we? So . . . who's your deputy going to be?' he asked brusquely. 'Andy Martin, I assume.'

'That's one job there will be several valid applications for.'

'But none will stand up against him in interview. He is going to apply, isn't he?'

'That's the general expectation.'

Sir James's heavy grey right eyebrow rose. 'But not yours?'

'I have no reason to think he won't, but . . .'

'What?'

Skinner frowned. 'Maybe it would be just too chummy if Andy waltzed back in here. Like I said, I'm personally more than a little embarrassed to be taking over your job without a contest, if that's what's going to happen, but you are such a crafty old bastard that I'm not really surprised. If I'm seen to be trying to move my best mate into the number two job, that might be too much even for our malleable Board to swallow. Andy can apply, but I'll make damn sure he's opposed.'

'I suppose Brian Mackie will fall to be considered naturally as a serving assistant chief.'

'Yes, but there are others. For example, I've heard that Max Allan might be interested in a move away from Strathclyde. Then there's Eddie Burke up in Grampian. And one other who's entitled to a run at it, if she's interested.'

'She? You mean . . .'

'I mean Maggie Rose. I know she's only a chief super just now, but in my opinion she's the best all-round police officer on this force.'

'I won't argue with that view . . . if we're excluding you and me from consideration,' he chuckled. 'But would she be interested? Remember, she's a single mother and her recent medical history isn't too great.'

'I came through the ranks as a single parent. Fuck it, technically I'm a single parent right now. As for the health side, you've had a heart attack, I've got a pacemaker implanted and we're both fine. Mags had cancer, it's in remission and she's clear to come back to work as soon as her maternity leave's over, or before if she chooses.'

'Would she be interested?'

'That's her choice, but I'll be putting it to her.'

'And your choice, Bob, who would that be? Privately, of course.'

'To be honest, it would still be Andy, but I'd be happy with any of the people I've mentioned.'

'Then I hope you get one of them. I'll look on intrigued, from the sidelines.'

'I'm sure you will,' said Skinner, 'but you're not on the bloody sidelines yet, and there's stuff happening I need your view on.'

'The Anderson situation, you mean? Neil McIlhenney came in and briefed me on that just before you got back. There was no need for him to do that, incidentally, but I appreciated it, even if I am a virtual non-person.'

The DCC shook his head. 'You still have no real grasp of the respect your officers have for you, do you?' he murmured. 'Yes,' he continued, 'I mean the Anderson situation. The guy's a former leader of this country, and I have personal issues with him. Now he's a murder suspect, which I have trouble crediting, but not only that, he's behaving as though he actually did it. Up to now, Neil and Sammy Pye have kept the whole situation low key, but I have a decision to make. If Anderson isn't found soon, or doesn't give himself up, do I put out a public appeal for information?'

'And a "keep clear" warning to the public?'

'Maybe that too.'

'Has anybody tried phoning him? He's a politician, Bob; every bloody newspaper in Scotland will have his mobile number on record. I've met the fellow too, remember; can't stand him, but if you want a veteran's opinion, I don't see him as a murderer. So before you splash his picture all over the press, why don't you give him a call, or send him a text, and ask him what his problem is?'

A broad grin spread across Skinner's face. 'You know, Jimmy,' he drawled, 'I'm really going to miss you.'

'Why should you?' his soon-to-be predecessor replied. 'You've got both my phone numbers, and I've got no immediate plans to change either of them.'

Forty-two

Standing on the second of the steps that gave access to the caravan, Regan rapped on the door. 'Mr Playfair,' he called, loudly enough to be heard inside. 'Police. We'd like a word.' He jumped down and waited; the seconds ticked away, but there was no reply.

'Inspector.' He turned to see Derek Baillie approaching.

'Yes?' he snapped impatiently.

'He's gone. Don't you see? His car's not there. My wife heard him drive off, must have been over an hour ago, she reckons. Yes, because it was before you arrived.'

'Would that have been before or after the body was found?' McDermid asked.

'Afterwards. She said she saw Hugo coming back from that direction; he was talking to a policeman, then he turned and headed back to the camp, not to his own van, but to Az's. She thought nothing of it at the time, because, well, we didn't know then about him being dead. She wondered what the cop was doing there, right enough, but we see plenty of them, so she didn't dwell on it. About ten minutes after that she heard his car start up and drive off.'

'How did she know it was Playfair's car?'

'He drives a clunky old Peugeot diesel, noisier than a Meat Loaf album. It was him all right.'

'OK. Thanks again, Mr Baillie.' He reached up and tried the door handle; it was locked fast. 'I don't suppose you have a key for this thing, do you?'

'No, I don't, but he'll probably be back soon.'

'You reckon?'

'Sure.' Baillie stopped and stared at the detective. 'You don't think Hugo would have . . .'

'I haven't even ruled you out for sure as a suspect, mate, and you're still here.' He turned to McDermid. 'Lisa, I want you to find Sergeant Hope. An hour ago, there was only him and Reid here, and Reid was at the top of the lane, so it must have been him that Mrs Baillie saw talking to Playfair. Confirm that, ask him why the hell he didn't bother to tell us, and have him give you every detail of their conversation.' As she left, Regan's attention returned to Baillie. 'What's this guy like?' he asked. 'And what's his relationship to Mr Mustafic?'

'I told you. He's a pompous wee chap, but he's useful to us at times.'

'When did he join your crowd?'

'A couple of years ago; just before he brought Az along, in fact.'

'Did it strike you as strange that he should want to become a traveller?'

'We get people like him from time to time. "Fellow travellers", I call them, romantics who fancy the roving life. Unless they're real arseholes, we tolerate them for as long as they stick around, and that isn't long, as a rule. Our life is OK if you're born to it, but most of those people have left behind en-suite bathrooms in the south of England and do not have a fucking clue what they're letting themselves in for. Hugo stuck it out, though; he had his charity behind him, and like I said, he's useful for his legal knowledge.'

'Is he a lawyer?'

'I don't think so. I did ask him what his background was, a while back, one time when we'd all had a couple of beers and he was more relaxed than normal. Now that I think about it, I'm still waiting for a straight answer. "I suppose you could call it social work." That was what he said.'

The DI grinned. 'Do you think he'd object to my kicking his door in?'

'I'd wait for him to come back, if I were you. He has the capacity to make as much noise as his fucking car.'

'George!' The call came from the path, twenty yards away. Regan swung round to see Detective Superintendent Neil McIlhenney heading his way. He was dressed in summer mode: light slacks and a white short-sleeved shirt, open at the neck. His jacket was slung over his shoulder.

'Sir.'

'Any result yet?'

'No, boss. This isn't a simple domestic; the man was ambushed.'

'What have you got? Anything to go on?'

'At the moment, a problem. The man who owns this van, his name's Hugo Playfair, he brought Mr Mustafic to join the group, and I'd like to interview him . . . only he's not here. He shot the craw over an hour ago.'

'Magic, just magic,' McIlhenney groaned. 'Not another one.'

'Boss, we weren't here!' the DI protested.

'I'm not getting at you, George,' the superintendent assured him. 'It's been a trying day on more than one front, that's all. When Playfair left, did he have knowledge of Mustafic's death?'

'Lisa McDermid's confirming it, but we believe so.'

'What's your next move?'

'I'm considering whether to effect an entry in Mr Playfair's absence,' Regan replied stuffily.

'Without a key?'

'Nobody has one.'

'Then stand back.' The big superintendent smiled and handed his jacket to his colleague. 'It's been too long since I booted somebody's door in.'

Forty-three

'Why do you come to me for this information?' asked Xavi Aislado.

'Because I don't have time to ask my Special Branch team to get it for me,' Skinner told him frankly. 'They could, but they'd have to jump through a couple of hoops, maybe go through all the provider directories.'

'I'm a journalist, Bob, you're begging a hell of a lot of questions.'

'You'll get the answers before anyone else, Xavi; that's a promise.'

'I take it this has to do with Glover's murder.'

'And more. It involves possession of Class A drugs.'

'By Anderson?'

'We don't think so. Look, you give me the number and I'll give you a couple of hours' start on a front-page story for tomorrow's paper.'

'Yes, I can guess whose drugs they were. OK, take this down.' The editor recited a mobile phone number.

'That's up to date? You're sure?'

'One of my people used it yesterday, looking for a comment on Glover's death. He was told to fuck off. I don't like my staff being treated discourteously, Bob.'

'I'll bear that in mind for the future,' Skinner chuckled. 'I hope the thing's switched on.'

A soft, deep laugh sounded in the DCC's ear. 'It will be. People like Anderson only know how to keep their mobiles charged up, not how to switch them off.' Pause. 'Bob, before you go, can you give me anything about the incident my news desk tells me about, in your home village?'

'The dead man's an ethnic member of a traveller group, camped out there. That's all I know for now.'

'Suspicious?'

'Not any more. Confirmed as homicide.'

'Can you give me a name?'

'Asmir Mustafic.' He spelled it out. 'He was Bulgarian, a harmless wee man. We'll be going public on it pretty soon, I imagine. For any more, have your crime reporter call Neil McIlhenney; he's on the scene. I imagine you've got his mobile number too.'

The editor laughed again. 'Of course.'

Skinner sighed, making a mental note to have senior officers' numbers changed, and hung up. He took out his own mobile, which was set to 'caller details withheld' when his calls were picked up, and began to key in digits. When he pressed the 'call' button, it was with little hope. He heard three rings and then a click.

'Yes?' One short word, but filled with tension; no background noise.

'Dr Anderson?'

'Who is this?'

'Are you going to stay on line when I tell you?'

He heard a sigh. 'You don't have to tell me, Skinner. I'd know your voice anywhere. What is it?'

'I want to ask you something, one question, and I want you to tell me the truth without hesitation, because whatever that is, I'll be able to prove it. Did you murder Ainsley Glover?'

The reply was instantaneous. 'No.'

'I believe you. So why did you leg it?'

'The questioning was going into an area that I didn't want to discuss.'

'Something to do with drugs?'

'What drugs?' Anderson paused, and this time Skinner could hear an intake of breath. 'Oh no, let me guess. Bloody Anthea. Yes?'

'Yes.'

'That stupid twat!' he sighed. 'She promised me that she was clean. I should have known, I should have read the signs. What was it? Coke, as before?'

'No, she's moved on from the posh people's party stuff. This is heroin, enough for us to charge her not just with possession but with intent to supply, if we've a mind. She's been inhaling the stuff, "Chasing the dragon" as the Chinese say. As for the signs, you wouldn't have seen any needle marks or runny noses. I'm told she used a teapot. Pretty ingenious, from what my drugs squad leader tells me; you heat the stuff on the cooker and suck it in through the spout.'

'Bob, I promise you, I did not know. And I run an addiction clinic, too.'

'You do? That I did not know.'

'I don't advertise the fact. Actually I run two; one's operated through the NHS, but the other's at a private place. My patients there tend to be higher up the social scale. Truth is, that's how I met Anthea. What a mug I am; I really did think she was behaving herself.'

'Then she fooled you, big time. She was arrested in Harvey Nichols' restaurant half an hour ago. Your daughter was with her, I'm afraid.'

'Hold on, man,' Anderson exclaimed, 'you haven't taken Tanya to a police station, have you?'

'No, we haven't; give me credit, I'm a parent myself, man. I told Alice Cowan, who made the arrest with another officer, to take her back to Darnaway Street, and stay with her, pending further instructions.'

'What are you going to do with her? You're not going to stick her in some social work refuge, are you?'

'That's entirely down to you,' Skinner told him. 'Where are you right now? Don't be cute, tell me.'

'I'm in Gifford, parked next to the Goblin Ha' pub, trying to work out what to do next.'

'Then you can stop trying, right now, for this is the only answer: you're going home to your kid. I'm going to forget about your stupid runner from Sammy Pye . . . although he'll remember being embarrassed, so you'd better not cross him again.'

'Sure, I go home, and you charge me with possession along with Anthea. You'd love that, Bob.'

Skinner laughed. 'You know, Bruce,' he said, 'one of the many differences between you and me is that when you have a grudge against someone, you shout about it for everyone to hear, like you did on Saturday night apparently, with Ainsley Glover, in a hall full of people. I don't. To be honest, I like to think I don't bear grudges, but if someone does me a bad enough turn for me to be bothered about getting even, I don't tell a living soul, I just wait for my moment. You betrayed me back in our past, sure, but from that I took the knowledge of the sort of guy you are, and that was enough. You were a bad Secretary of State, because you were weak, and you were a liar. We both know that, and that's all the satisfaction I need. You're not on my hit list, mate; and you never were. I'm not going to charge you with possession, or anything else for that matter, out of personal spite. Go home and look after your kid, like you did once before; that's the only thing I've ever even half respected you for.'

'I'm not sure I want to go back to Darnaway Street,' Anderson murmured.

'I don't blame you. But that's not your only home, is it?'

'No; I still have my house in Glasgow, but it's rented out. But I also have a cottage near Oban.'

'Then if you want some advice, take Tanya up there until it's time for her to go back to school. But before you do that, you need to complete your interview with DI Pye. You say you didn't know about your girlfriend's drugs, and I'll accept that, partly because I'd have a bit of a job proving that you did, given where she'd hidden them. I could ask you to submit to a blood test to prove that you're not a user yourself, but I won't. You say you didn't kill Ainsley Glover; I believe that also, but we have a witness statement that contradicts yours, and that has to be dealt with. Understood?'

'If that's the way it has to be, yes.'

'OK. So this is what you do. Go back to Edinburgh, and take charge of your daughter; either stay at Darnaway Street tonight, or check into a hotel, if you can find one in the Festival month. Whatever you decide, I want you in my office, here at Fettes, at ten a.m. tomorrow morning, to be interviewed under caution by DI Pye and me, about your movements on Saturday night. You may have legal representation if you wish, but you will tell us the truth.'

'To do that, it may not be a lawyer I need.'

'Bring whoever you like, man. But be there or, trust me, you will be arrested. Your girlfriend will be a hot story in tomorrow's *Saltire*. Make sure you don't follow her on Wednesday morning.'

Skinner closed his phone, ending the call, then re-dialled Xavi Aislado. 'The one I owe you,' he began, as the Scottish Spaniard answered. 'It's not Anderson, and it doesn't have anything to do with him, but would I be right in thinking that a duke's daughter charged with possession of industrial quantities of smack might make the columns of even a quality newspaper like yours?'

Forty-four

'Don't be in a rush to climb the promotion ladder, Lisa,' Neil McIlhenney told the detective sergeant. 'When I opened the door back there, it took me three goes, where it used to be just the one. Rank softens you up; no mistake about it.'

'I doubt if your pal the chief super would agree with you,' Regan pointed out.

'McGuire? Ah, he's a special case; in the old days he could open them with his head. You know he wears a nineteen and a half shirt collar?'

'I didn't realise he had a neck.'

The superintendent chuckled. 'Only just.' In the next instant he was serious once more. 'This man Playfair hasn't left much behind him, has he?'

'No, sir,' the DI concurred. 'There's even less here than there was in Mustafic's van, and a hermit's cell's better kitted out than that was. Some dirty dishes and that's it; he's even cleared out the fucking fridge.'

'And he knew that Mustafic's body had been found?'

'We have to assume that,' said McDermid. 'He approached Sergeant Hope, casually, and asked him what was up. Kenny told him; he gave him a physical description and asked him if it meant anything to him. Playfair replied, "Nothing at all," and left.'

'And ten minutes later he was gone. What does that tell you?'

'That he's our prime suspect?'

McIlhenney frowned at her. 'Think that through, Sergeant. If it was Playfair that bashed our man's head in, then one, why did he ask Hope what the trouble was and, two, why didn't he clear off last night, straight after he had done it? It seems to me it makes him no suspect at all.'

'Then why would he run if he had nothing to do with it?'

'Exactly. We need to find out all there is to know about this guy. Lisa, get on to the charity he worked with . . . What was it called, Fred, or something?'

'REG, boss.'

'Near enough. Ask them exactly what he did for them; if they have a personnel file on him, find out what's in it. George, let's put a description of his car out there, and the number, and get it found.'

'Yes, but do you think he'll still be in it?'

'That depends what he's got for brains. If he's panicking, he probably is, but if he's thought it through, he's dumped it by now. Make sure that we check all the railway station car parks: North Berwick, Longniddry, Dunbar, Prestonpans.'

'And Drem, that's the nearest.'

'Fine, get it done, soon as possible.' He paused. 'George, we've got a dead guy on his way to the mortuary. Have we got any physical evidence at all at the scene, or any witness sightings that take us anywhere?'

The DI shook his head solemnly. 'Dorward's people have found nothing up around the body. The uniforms have searched the encampment for a murder weapon, with Derek Baillie's cooperation, and found nothing. The crime scene is fairly isolated, but we've spoken to the nearest neighbours and none of them can help us.' He reached into his pocket, produced the envelope that he had discovered in Mustafic's jacket, and held it up. 'All we have are these, the only personal items he had: two photos that might be his family, but equally might not, and a couple of old letters written in Bulgarian. To make it even less decipherable, the lettering's Cyrillic.'

'Then let's find someone from our list of approved translators and turn them into English, pronto.' The superintendent hesitated, as if considering an afterthought. 'Where were they, George?'

Regan described how he had found the packet, accidentally.

'Interesting,' he said. 'The only things that tell us anything about the man were hidden away. Could that have been deliberate on his part?'

'It's possible. He could have cut the lining.'

'Then let's find out. Send the jacket to the lab for examination, but cut the label off and send that to the translator. Maybe that will tell us where he bought the bloody thing. Less than twenty-four hours ago, that poor wee dead guy was having a pint with our chief. He's got a personal interest in this one, so he'll expect us to pull out all the stops as we normally would, then look under the pedals as well.'

'Will that include speaking to him, sir?' asked McDermid. 'He met the man, so maybe he has knowledge that's important to the investigation. In which case . . .'

McIlhenney nodded. 'The answer is yes,' he told the young sergeant. He smiled. 'Is that an interview you'd want to carry out yourself, Lisa? Or would you rather delegate it to me?'

Forty-five

'You know what really pisses me off, Anthea?' Sammy Pye asked angrily. 'No, and you don't give a shit either, but let me tell you. We're in the middle of a murder investigation, and we've got some important questions that need answering, but we can't, because DC Haddock and I have been sidetracked to deal with you and your miserable little habit, because we had the misfortune to be the officers who found your stash.'

'My client denies having a habit.' The woman leaned across the interview table as she spoke, blonde, sharp-faced and just as sharply dressed, in a silver suit. Her name was Susannah Himes, nickname, the 'Barracuda'; she was Lady Walters' solicitor, instructed by her father, and the interview had been delayed by half an hour to await her arrival, to the detectives' intense annoyance. The DI had never met her, but he knew of her reputation as a 'fixer' at the top end of the criminal market. ('The poor people get Frankie Bristles,' he had told Haddock, 'the well-off call Himes.') 'And it's Lady Anthea, by the way,' she added.

'Your client can deny all she likes, but the blood test results that I have before me say different. So do the packets of brown that we found in the toes of her shoes, in her house. So does the copper teapot, liberally dusted with heroin and with her fingerprints . . . and nobody else's . . . all over it. As for her title, Ms Himes, welcome to the twenty-first century. I'm doing her the courtesy of addressing her by her forename; be happy with that.'

'I'm not happy at all,' the lawyer replied with a show of belligerence.

'Aw, cut the bluster, please,' the DI told her. 'We both know the game: you'll earn your fee by persuading the fiscal to reduce the charges against your client in return for a guilty plea, and you'll keep her out of jail on the back of a promise to enter rehab. Plus, you're expected to persuade me to bail her this afternoon, pending a court appearance. The first of those aren't within my control, but the last is, and I'm not playing. Your client will be held in custody overnight, and she'll appear in court tomorrow; you can make your bail plea to the Sheriff, not to me. But when the fiscal tells her that Lady . . .' he paused '. . . Anthea, was in charge of a child while zonked out of her head, you might find that your task is that bit tougher.'

'And what of Dr Anderson?' Himes shot back. 'My understanding is that he fled the scene when the drugs were found. When will he be charged?'

'There isn't a scrap of evidence linking Dr Anderson to the heroin. It was in her wardrobe, in her shoes, on her premises, not his, and he denies all knowledge. As for his leaving, it's been established that he had other reasons for that. He's on his way home as I speak, to collect his daughter. If I were you, I'd be trying to persuade the Duke of Lanark to turn up in court tomorrow in person, to put in a word for his daughter. The Sheriff might just be persuaded to release her into his custody, and we might not oppose that.'

'How very gracious of you,' the accused woman exclaimed. 'Bloody little policeman. As if my father could be summoned to—'

'Ah, shut the fuck up!' Pye snapped, silencing her, and startling DC Haddock by his side. He stared hard at the lawyer. 'We're finished here, Ms Himes,' he said, rising from his chair. 'See you tomorrow morning. Sauce, take the prisoner back to the cells and hand her over to the custody sergeant.'

'Susannah!' Anthea Walters protested, but her solicitor looked at the desk top and shrugged her shoulders.

'I'm sorry,' she murmured, 'but if the inspector chooses to take this line, there's nothing I can do at this stage.'

'My father knows a couple of High Court judges. He'll call them if you ask him.'

'That would not help, I promise you.'

The woman's eyes flashed, as if an inspired thought had broken the surface of the cloudy pond that was her mind. 'He knows Sir James Proud too; the chief constable. Get him to phone him and tell him to put a stop to this nonsense.'

The DI and the lawyer exchanged glances. 'Lady Walters,' Pye explained, 'the chief retires tomorrow. I think your father would find that his call would be referred to his deputy. But it wouldn't matter, because either one of them would back me up.' He glanced at Haddock. 'Sauce, take her back. I'll escort Ms Himes out of the building.'

As the DC stepped towards her, he thought for a moment that the woman would resist. He smiled at her, saying, wordlessly, 'Help me, please.' Finally her shoulders slumped, and when he took her lightly by the elbow and guided her towards the door, she went with him, meekly.

'This isn't a class thing, is it, Detective Inspector?' asked Himes as they walked back to the Torphichen Place front office.

'No,' he replied, sincerely, 'not in the slightest. I don't care who she is, and even less who her father is. With the amount of heroin she had in her possession, it's automatic that the Sheriff decides whether or not she's bailed. And don't tell me you don't know that.'

Himes smiled, and suddenly her face did not seem quite as sharp. 'I won't,' she said, 'and don't tell me you don't know when you see a lawyer performing for the cameras either . . . even if there wasn't one in your interview room. Will you oppose bail?'

'Truthfully, I've got no interest. You won't see me tomorrow morning. I'm involved today because I found the stuff, that's all. The drugs people will make the running from now on, ours and probably the Scottish Drug Enforcement Agency, given the media profile this will attract. They'll interview her as well before she goes to court; if she gives up her supplier, they might ask the fiscal to take his foot off the gas. If not, it'll be full speed ahead, and you will have some job keeping her out of prison.'

'But I will, don't you fret.'

'We'll see. I'll tell you one thing, although you probably realise it anyway. I wouldn't let her anywhere near a jury; she'd be her own worst enemy.'

'What about Anderson?'

Pye made a face. 'I don't think she'll find him rushing to be a character witness; his daughter told my DC that she saw her using the kettle once. When she asked, Anthea said it was an inhaler for a chest cold, so she didn't mention it to her dad. Apparently Tanya's worldly-wise for her age, but dragon-chasing's a bit beyond her, thanks be.'

'Thanks for sharing that, but what I actually meant was what about Anderson and your murder inquiry? Am I likely to be having a call from him?'

'He says you're not. I'll hear the rest of his story tomorrow morning.'

'What made him stop running?'

'Not what, who. My DCC did.'

The blonde solicitor whistled. 'That's a surprise. The word is that if Dr Bruce is ever crucified, Skinner will hammer in the nails.'

'Our big boss is full of surprises,' said Pye as they reached the main entrance. 'Good luck for tomorrow.' He paused. 'And one more thing: I might know when somebody's playing to the gallery, but my young DC doesn't, not yet, so when it happens, I have to do the same thing. Next time our paths cross, let's agree a truce before the interview, not after it.'

'That would be nice,' Himes agreed, 'but you know how it is with clients. They like to see a bit of drama for their money. So I'm sorry, Mr Pye, it looks as if we'll always be going to each other's throats.'

Her smile stayed with him for a while after she had gone, until he turned and jogged up a nearby flight of stairs, to the CID suite. Becky Stallings was in her office as he reached it, sat behind her desk, frowning at a flat-screen monitor.

'Sammy,' she exclaimed as he entered. 'Just the man I want to see. Your victim's daughter's computer.' She reached down and slapped the top of a PC tower by her side. 'It's been a bit of a bugger, but I finally got into Mr Glover's files. I went through all the obvious passwords, daughter's name, son's name, combinations of names and birthdays; nothing worked. And then I went back to basics, tried the screen name *fatallyg* as password. No joy there either, but when I reversed it and keyed in *gyllataf*, then "Bingo", as we said in the Met, or "Ya fuckin' beauty", the local equivalent, or so I understand from my Ray.' And then her pleasure seemed to evaporate before his eyes. 'But you know what? It's been largely a waste of time.'

'How come?' Pye asked.

'Your victim was a very thorough man. He wasn't content with hiding an email entity on his daughter's internet service, he left barely a trace on that of what he's been up to. The programme Miss Glover uses automatically files incoming and outgoing emails, not within the computer itself, unless you tell it to do that, but on line, in the provider's main server. You'll find them there for a couple of months, until they go off line,' she grimaced, 'or until the user deletes them manually, as your murder victim appears to have done. I've checked and there's damn all there; incoming, outgoing, it's all been wiped.'

'But you can recover deleted files, can't you?'

'Not these ones, because they were never stored inside this computer.'

'How about the service provider's terminal? Won't they still be there?'

'Not with the one that Miss Glover uses. I've checked, and customer deleted files are gone for all time.'

'Is that usual?'

'I don't know and I don't care. I'm only interested in what's happened here.'

'No, I meant is it usual for email users to do that?'

'I'm guessing, but I wouldn't have thought so. Your man's been super-careful. He has not wanted anyone, not even his daughter, apparently, if she couldn't give you his password, to find out what he's been up to.'

'So we've got nothing?'

'Not quite,' said Stallings. 'There's one thing he didn't delete, presumably because he needed to keep it somewhere and this was his most secure location. His mailing list, his address book; that's still intact.' She handed him a sheet of paper. 'I've printed a copy. That's it, the sum total of my labours.' She glanced down at the computer. 'The box itself can go back to its owner.'

Pye frowned. 'Not yet, Becky,' he murmured. 'I'm sorry to be so persistent, but I'd like you to go back in there, into Carol's files.'

'Why?'

'To see if it's possible that anyone else has been rummaging around in there. If they had done, would they have left a trace.'

'It's possible,' she conceded. 'OK, I'll have a look. Don't hold your breath waiting for results, though. Chances are you'd go blue in the face.'

Forty-six

'Have you ever felt like a traveller?' Lisa McDermid asked George Regan as she stood in the doorway of the mobile crime-scene office that had just been delivered to Gullane bents, and parked halfway between the encampment and the path where Mustafic's body had been found.

'I might right now,' the DI conceded, 'if not for the fact that this thing has "Police" painted on it in big letters and black and white check all around it. I reckon the public will be able to figure out who's who. But the same thought's occurred to Baillie's group, in reverse. He's just asked me if it's OK for them to move on.'

'Has he? What did you say?'

'I checked with the super; he says that he's willing to let them, as long as they agree to go to the official site just outside Musselburgh, so that we don't have to search the county for them if we need to talk to anyone again. Baillie's accepted that; whether they do it or not remains to be seen, but I'll be happy when they're gone.'

'I'd have thought they'd want to stay close to us, for protection. After all, one of their people's just been attacked.'

'These people aren't used to asking for police protection; I doubt if the thought occurred to friend Baillie.'

'Maybe not.' McDermid looked at the steel desks, bolted to the floor, and to the stack of chairs tethered for transit against the side of the unit. 'Will they put phone lines in here?' she asked.

'I doubt it. We won't be here long enough; rest of the week, at most. Our next task will be to find out where Mustafic went last night after he left Baillie and Mr Skinner. We know he had more drink, and there's only three other pubs in the village, so that won't take us long. Then we interview bar staff, locals, anyone who remembers him from last night. This is a small place, so that won't take long. Hopefully we'll get a lead from that; if not it's door-to-door.'

'What do you think happened?'

Regan stared at her. 'What's that got to do with it, Lisa? The obvious is that somebody who doesn't like gypsies followed him out of the boozer and stove his head in. But we don't make assumptions in CID; we take statements, we gather any physical evidence there might be . . . in this case, that would be fuck all . . . and we see where they lead us. So when we go down the village shortly and start making inquiries, please keep an open mind. Don't just go looking for a thug with a hammer tucked in his belt. Discount nothing; if somebody tells you they thought they saw a Martian eyeing him up . . .'

McDermid grinned. 'I'll keep a straight face and try to find out where he might have parked his spaceship. I get the message, George.'

'Good.' He checked his watch. 'Ready to go?'

'Give me a minute. I still have to call Playfair's charity. Do we have phone books?'

'They're usually in a desk drawer.' He tossed her the keys that the delivery driver had given him and watched as she matched each one to a lock.

At the third attempt she found what she was looking for, two thick volumes, Edinburgh Yellow Pages and the residential directory. She picked up the former and turned to 'C'. 'Got it,' she declared, and keyed in a number.

'Rights for Ethnic Groups,' a bright high-pitched male voice sang in her ear, in an accent that contrived to be both Asian and Scottish.

'Hello, this is DS McDermid, East Lothian CID. I need to speak to somebody about one of your workers, a Mr Hugo Playfair.'

'I'm sorry,' the man replied. 'We don't have anybody of that name here.'

'I didn't say that he worked there, only that he's associated with your group.'

'You better speak to my director.'

'And he would be . . .?'

'She. Ms James. Hold on, please.'

McDermid did as she was told, happy that at least she did not have to listen to recorded ethnic music while she waited.

If she had, she would only have heard a few bars. 'This is Peedy James,' a new voice said briskly. 'How can I help you, Ms McDermid?'

From Asia to Australia, the sergeant reckoned. 'You can tell me about a man named Hugo Playfair. I understand that he's one of your field workers.'

'You do? Who told you that?'

'That's what I've been led to believe.'

'Well . . . sounds as if Hugo's been getting a bit flowery. We're a small charity, Sergeant, dealing with pretty diverse client groups. We can't afford to have field workers out with each of them. Hugo Playfair doesn't work for us; he's a supporter, sure, and he acts as a helpline for travellers, but it's entirely voluntary on his part.'

'Can you put me in touch with him?'

'You could try and trace the group he travels with.'

'We've done that; he's not there. Do you have a mobile number for him?'

'As far as I know he doesn't have one. Too new-tech for him, he told me once.'

'How long have you known him?' McDermid asked.

'A couple of years, I suppose. He pitched up here in the office, and made a donation to our funds. I gave him a coffee in return, and a Tunnock's Caramel Log as a bonus. He told me that he was adopting a travelling lifestyle, and that he hoped that he could help us by being a disciple . . . yes, that was the word he used . . . among the travellers. I told him that was fine by me, but that he'd better not look for anything other than no-cost or low-cost support from me, as I don't have the budget. He told me, "No worries," and headed off. Since then I've heard from him a few times, about nothing specific, just calls to say hello, and let me know how his group was doing.'

'Would it be fair to describe himself as a representative of REG?'

'It wouldn't be entirely accurate,' James replied, 'since I never gave him that mandate, but as long as he's not pledging money in my name, I wouldn't object to it.'

'I understand,' said the sergeant. 'The first time you met Mr Playfair, when he said he'd "Decided to adopt a travelling lifestyle", as you quoted him, did he say what he'd been doing before then?'

'Not that I recall, and I didn't ask. I've seen a few guys like him back in Australia; wankers, basically. They either made a few quid or inherited it, and decided to try the outback life, but they never lasted long before they scurried back to the town. I put Hugo in that category, but I have to admit, he's stayed the course.' As she spoke, McDermid recalled Derek Baillie saying something very similar.

'Does the name Asmir Mustafic mean anything to you?'

'Not a thing.'

'Mr Playfair never mentioned him?'

'No.'

'So you don't provide him with a caravan and a vehicle?'

'Are you crazy? Of course not. Who is this guy anyway?'

'He's a Bulgarian gypsy immigrant, or he was until last night. Mr

Playfair introduced him to the traveller group, not long after he joined himself.'

'Hold on,' the director told her. 'I'll check my database just in case; it has thousands of names of immigrants. Asmir Mustafic, you said, yes?'

'Yes. You want me to spell it?'

'I don't think so; I've come across a few Asmirs, and a few Mustafics, but never in tandem. But the way, what do you mean he was an immigrant? Has he been deported, is that what this is about?'

'No, he's dead. He was murdered last night.'

'Jesus! A racist killing?'

'We're still looking into that.'

The detective heard her blow out a breath. 'Bastards!' she swore, quietly, as if she had reached her own conclusion about the murder. 'No,' she continued. 'He's definitely not on my files. Listen, if Hugo should contact me, do you want me to ask him to get in touch with you?'

'No,' McDermid replied quickly. 'I want you to say nothing at all about me. If you can, find out where he is, then let me know.' She recited her mobile number, slowly, so that Peedy James could note it. 'Thanks for your help,' she concluded.

She felt Regan's eyes upon her. 'Well?' he asked quietly.

'It's a front,' she told him. 'He's used REG as a . . . a . . .' She searched for a phrase that would not come.

'Flag of convenience?' the DI suggested.

'Yes, one of those, whatever it is. His relationship with Mustafic didn't derive from the charity, as he told Baillie. It's weird, the whole business.'

'Too right, which makes it all the more important that we find out exactly who this mystery man is.'

'Which one?'

'What do you mean?'

'I mean that if Hugo Playfair isn't what he said he was, then why should we take it for granted that Mustafic was either? Like you said, George, we make no assumptions in CID.'

Forty-seven

'I'm going to miss this view,' Bob Skinner whispered to the room that had been his since his promotion to chief officer rank. He had taken over the office as an assistant chief, and had insisted on retaining it on rising to deputy. For how many years had it been his? Not being one for calendars or metaphorical milestones, he found that he was unable to recall off the top of his head.

In an ideal world he would have stayed there for good, but the chief's office had added privacy, in that his secretary's office was en-suite. More than that, there were the security considerations that suggested he should be at the back of the building rather than the front. He knew them well, since he had put the argument forward himself.

He was still turning over Proud Jimmy's revelation, that he would inherit the accommodation across the corridor without opposition. He had expected that there would be a contest, and had hoped genuinely that it would be so. Why? Perhaps, secretly, because it offered his last escape route. For years, his gut feeling had been to stay where he was, for a few more years at least, perhaps pitching for the Strathclyde job once he was past fifty. Conventionally, he would not have been promoted to head his own force, but circumstances, and Sir James's machinations, had made him eligible, and since then all of the counsel of those closest to him had pointed him in the same direction, until he had no counter-arguments left. So he had declared his candidacy, but with the thought in the back of his mind that he might not be the

247

certainty everyone assumed, and that a stronger runner than he might emerge and win through in the interview process. If Andy Martin had decided to contest the position, he would not have held that against him, although he knew that if the younger man had been successful, he could not have worked for long under his command.

But all of that had become academic. Barring an upheaval within a generally supportive Police Board, he would be chief constable in twenty-four hours.

He looked down the driveway that led to the main entrance to the police headquarters. He saw Sammy Pye park his car in one of the visitor spaces and climb out, heading, Skinner guessed, to brief Neil McIlhenney on the Ainsley Glover investigation. The detective superintendent would be waiting for him, having just returned to his office after giving the DCC an update on the murder of Asmir Mustafic, and on the disappearance of Hugo Playfair.

'I knew there was something about that wee bastard that didn't ring true,' he had told his colleague. 'I thought he was watching over the travellers as a group like a mother hen, but now, it seems, he was only looking out for one of them.'

'But why?'

'That's why we're detectives, mate . . . and make no mistake, when I'm across the way I will still be a detective, because we answer questions like that. Find Playfair; at least, do the best you can. From what you've told me, it might not be that easy.'

He watched as Pye turned left at the top of the crest and headed for McIlhenney's office. The next time he saw the DI, they would be facing Bruce Anderson across a desk. There you go again, Bob, he thought, letting instinct override common sense. He knew that most officers would have arrested the fugitive and held him for questioning, until he had been eliminated as a suspect. But he knew the man and he knew his weaknesses, and in his judgement, his lack of moral courage made it inconceivable that he could plan and execute a crime as meticulous and cold-blooded as the killing of Ainsley Glover. He hoped that he would not be proved wrong, but decided he would rather deal with that than with the consequences of a highly public arrest, followed by a vindication. He nodded, as if in confirmation; at the same moment there was a soft knock on the door. He had no need to call 'Enter,' since his green light was on, but he did anyway, out of habit.

Gerry Crossley, the secretary he would inherit, stepped into the room. 'Sir, I've got the Duke of Lanark on the phone. He's come through on the chief's line, but he's left for his farewell tour of the divisional offices, so he's asked to speak to you. I've tried to press him, but he won't say what it's about. Can I transfer him to your line, or would you rather be unavailable?'

Skinner smiled. 'What would Sir James have done had he been here?'

'He'd have growled a bit but taken the call. He always does.'

'Then that's how it'll continue, Gerry, probably with the growling as well. Put him through. And don't worry, I reckon I know what it's about.'

'Do you want me to listen in?'

'No, not to this one.'

'Understood.'

He left. The DCC stared at his phone, waiting for it to ring. He had no problem dealing with the aristocracy as a rule; he had met the Duke of Lanark once, at a reception hosted by his friend the Marquis of Kinture, but the encounter had been brief.

'Mr Skinner.' The voice was softer than he had recalled, or expected. 'I assume that you can guess what leads me to call you.'

'I tend to keep my guesses to myself,' he replied. 'So why don't you tell me, formally.'

'Of course. It's about my daughter; she was arrested today in connection with the possession of Class A drugs.'

'Yes. She's been charged and she's being held in custody overnight. She'll appear before Sheriff Morgan tomorrow.'

'You endorse the decision to detain her?'

'Absolutely. I have no problem with it, none at all.'

'Mmm,' the Duke murmured. 'In that case, I simply want to assure you that I don't either. I will of course support her, in that I'll pay for her defence, but I have no expectations and I will not attempt to exercise any influence on the court. I'm in London just now, and I have no intention of returning for her appearance. I want Anthea to get what's coming to her. My daughter is a self-indulgent brat who is an embarrassment to me, to her mother and to her siblings, and I've had enough of her behaviour. I've tolerated her past indiscretions, but she's gone too far.'

For a few moments, Skinner sat silent, wondering how he would have dealt, as a parent, with a similar situation. 'I see,' he said finally. 'For our part, I have to tell you that we're not out to make an example of her just because of who she is. From what I'm told, a guilty plea would be very appropriate, but that won't be expected tomorrow. I won't oppose bail; if you like I can ask the fiscal what his attitude will be.'

'No, no, you misunderstand me. You go ahead and oppose bail. I mean it; I don't want to see Anthea go away for years or anything like that, but a short spell in custody might concentrate her mind . . . if she has one left, that is.'

'I hear what you're saying, sir,' the DCC replied, 'but you can hardly propose that in court. Let's leave it to the fiscal and the judge to decide the issue, shall we?'

'I would like you to ask the fiscal to oppose; I really would.'

'OK, if you feel that strongly, I'll make that call.'

'Good man. Thanks. You must come to dinner some time. I'd appreciate a chat with you, and with the First Minister, in calmer circumstances.'

'That would be interesting,' Skinner replied, with a smile.

'Excellent. I'll have my secretary contact yours when I get back to Scotland.' Just as he thought the conversation at an end, the Duke continued. 'What of Bruce Anderson?' he asked. 'I've already had him on the phone, assuring me he knew nothing of this awful heroin. He doesn't feel that he can spend another night at the flat, so I've invited him and Tanya to stay at my place, until he sorts himself out. They can sleep in the big house tonight, and there's an empty cottage on the estate that they can move into tomorrow.'

'I'm glad about that; I've cut him some slack, but I confess that I'm more comfortable knowing where he is . . . just in case I've made a major mistake about him. I'm seeing him tomorrow in connection with the Glover investigation. He won't be implicated in the drugs business, though.'

'That's good. He should have been more careful, but I can't be too hard on him. People like Anthea are incredibly devious; I know, because I've made it my business to study them. I encouraged her relationship with Bruce, because he has skills in that area. In fact I put them together initially. I employed him, truth be told; their thing developed from there.'

'So he was her counsellor first?' said Skinner.

'Initially he was, before they became partners. If you're worried about the ethics of the relationship, I'm not. He did her good for a while, even though he's a bit volatile himself. If you ask me, he never had a good counsellor himself when he needed one. Don't be too hard on him, Mr Skinner. Thank you and good day. I look forward to entertaining you.'

The DCC was thoughtful as he replaced the phone, still surprised by the Duke's unexpected attitude, and wondering if there was another way of looking at Bruce Anderson. He was so preoccupied that he almost forgot the business that had been on his mind earlier. Almost.

He took out his most private diary, and ran through the list of numbers that he would not trust to a computer; it included several with no names attached, and it was one of those he dialled, on his secure telephone.

'Yes? How can I help you?' The call was answered by a woman, her voice pleasant but completely bland.

'I'd like to speak to Piers Frame. This is Bob Skinner, up in Edinburgh. If you have a problem, call me back; Piers has my number.'

'No problem, Bob.' He was picked up instantly, and the Scot could tell that he had been on speaker-phone. He wondered how many other people were in the room, but was put at his ease instantly. 'It's OK, I'm clear to speak. What's up? Have my unruly Ministry of Defence colleagues been annoying you again?'

Piers Frame was one of the most senior intelligence operatives in the country; when the matter of the Glover surveillance had broken surface, he had helped Skinner root out the truth.

'Christ, I hope not,' the DCC replied earnestly. 'The guy they were watching was murdered at the weekend. Very cleverly, a pro job, I'd say, one that we might well have put down as an accidental death. Way too subtle for the soldiers.'

'Stone me!' Frame exclaimed. 'I . . . No, no, no; no way would they be involved in something as drastic as that.'

'I wouldn't have thought so either, but the housekeepers have been at work since then. Someone broke into his house and stole the guts of his computer, and his back-up hard disk. I don't imagine for a moment that they took him out, but if they heard about it and decided on a precautionary clean-up, then I don't appreciate that. Apart from the commercial value of what's been stolen, Glover's files might be essential to my investigation and I fucking well want them back.'

'Understood. If they did that, it sounds like excessive zeal, even if they were working in association with the Americans. Leave it with me and I'll make some discreet noises.'

'Fine, thanks. By the way, while I've got your attention, have you ever heard of a man called Coben, or of anyone who might on occasion use that name?'

'Coben? Not one of this department's, I can tell you that. Why do you ask?'

'He's more likely to be military than one of yours. Don't worry about it; he's just someone who came up on my radar. That said, if your MoD friends do know of him, it might be worth warning him that he doesn't want to show up there again. If he does, I won't appreciate that either.'

'In that case, if he is connected to HMG in any way, he will definitely be told. I've seen what you can do when you're annoyed. I'll be in touch.'

Forty-eight

George Regan was still getting to know his new patch, and Gullane was a sensitive area for him. Normally one of his first acts on moving into an area would have been to put himself about, to make his face known. He had done as much in Musselburgh, Tranent and Haddington, but the coastal townships had a low priority, not least the one where the deputy chief lived.

He parked opposite the Old Clubhouse Inn and looked across at it. The design of the building indicated that once it had been what its name implied, a starting point for golfers, before the construction of larger and more opulent premises at the west end of the village. Even on an early Monday evening it was busy; the tables set outside, with chairs and ashtrays for smokers driven into the open air by the law, were all occupied, with space heaters ... little used in August, Regan guessed ... scattered between them like elongated mushrooms.

He pulled his key from the ignition and stepped out of the car, locking the door electronically a bare second after it had closed behind him. He headed for the pub, but had not taken more than two steps before his phone vibrated in his trouser pocket. He took it out, checked the caller and put it to his ear. 'Yes, Lisa,' he said, turning and stepping off the roadway.

'I've just had a call back from the Department for Work and Pensions,' the sergeant told him, without preamble. 'They're emailing me a list of all the people in Britain called Hugo Playfair, with national

254

insurance numbers and current known addresses. There aren't a hell of a lot, and only three aged between thirty-five and forty-five, which we reckoned were age band outer limits for our guy. One of them is drawing full disability benefit and lives in Dorset, so we can rule him out. I've cross-referenced the other two with the passport agency, and I'm waiting for photographs. I've also run an NCIS check like you said. It's blank.'

'How can you pick up an email down there in the van?'

'Cleverly. One of the people in a house across the way has a wireless set-up and he's let me piggy-back on it with my laptop.'

'He won't have access to your files, will he?'

'No, they're secure.'

'In that case, good thinking. Any sightings of Playfair's Peugeot?'

'No, and all the station parks have been checked. If he has dumped it, could be at the airport.'

'Aye, but which one? He's had time to get to Newcastle by now. Gimme a call if you get anything positive. I'm just about to start my trawl of the pubs.'

He pocketed the phone and crossed the street, picking his way between the tightly packed tables and into the Old Clubhouse. Inside, he had to blink hard before his eyes became accustomed to the light and he could see that the saloon was empty, apart from himself and a lone barman.

The man was massive, not exceptionally tall, but with the frame of a weightlifter, dark-skinned with a spectacular cascade of dreadlocks that suggested West Indian origins, an impression that was confirmed by his accent.

'What can I get you?' he asked, with a welcoming smile that Regan read as sincere.

'Do you know how to make a rock shandy?'

'Which kind you like? Mine has ginger beer, bitter lemon, angostura.'

'That'll do it.' Regan frowned as he looked at the man. 'Have we met?' he asked.

'Could be,' he conceded, 'if you ever went clubbing in Edinburgh. I used to do door security there.'

Regan scanned his past. 'Buster Brown's when it was called that?'

'Among others. You wouldn't be a policeman, would you?'

He nodded. 'I was uniform in those days. Do you remember me?'

'No, but you remember me; that tells me enough. If you'd been a punter, chances are you'd have been too pissed to recall it.' He reached out a hand. 'My name's Tony Bravo, by the way.'

As they shook, the police officer expected his hand to be crushed, but the big man's touch was soft. 'George Regan, detective inspector. Have you heard about the discovery near the beach this morning?'

'Word got around. Who was he?'

'A gypsy, from the camp down on the bents. We reckon he was attacked on his way home after a night out drinking.'

'And you reckon he might have been here?'

'Yes. Were you on duty last night?'

'Sure, all the evening, through to midnight, and then after, cleaning up. Do you have a photo of the guy?'

'Not one that you'd like to see. He was a little guy, skinny, badly dressed.'

'British?'

'No, Bulgarian.'

'Then I reckon he was in here. I saw him come up the road from the Mallard. I thought he'd head for Bissett's or the Golf, but he came in here.'

'Are you saying you hoped he'd pass you by?'

'No, everybody's welcome here. He came in, asked for a pint.' Bravo smiled. 'He blinked when he saw what it cost, mind you.'

'Did he speak to anyone?'

'No, not at first. The regulars ignored him; they guessed where he was from, and so did I, to tell the truth. This is Gullane; travelling people stand out.'

'No trouble, though?'

'Inspector George,' said the barman mildly, 'I don't have trouble.'

Regan understood why not. He laid a five pound note on the bar and picked up his rock shandy. 'Not at first, you said.'

'That's right.' Bravo picked up the banknote, folded it and slid it into the detective's breast pocket. 'Another guy came in just after; stuck his head round the door as if he was looking for him, then when he saw him, came in. Bought two pints, one for him, one for the little guy. Then they went over and sat in the window.'

'Can you describe the second man?'

'Ginger,' the barman replied at once. 'Red beard, red hair, stocky guy, thick wrists, looked quite strong. Wore a work shirt; looked hot in it. Wore boots too. Reckon he might have been a soldier.'

'What makes you think that?' Regan asked. The description matched Hugo Playfair, beyond a shadow of a doubt, but no one had ever suggested that the man might have had a military background.

'The boots. They were polished. I see a lot of guys come through here, and a lot of them wear boots, especially in the winter. But I never see anybody polish them, save for soldiers.'

The DI took a drink, and filed the thought away.

'Could you hear the conversation?'

'No, but I could see them. I thought they were both on edge. They didn't stay long. Finished their drinks and headed off together.'

'What time?'

'By then? About nine.'

'And Mustafic had the two pints while he was here, that's all?'

'Yes.'

On top of one in the Mallard, Regan thought. There was more than that in him when he died, for sure. Must have gone somewhere else. Oh, Mr Playfair, I really do want to talk to you.

He finished his rock shandy and nodded farewell to Tony Bravo. 'Thanks a lot, big man,' he said. 'I'll see you around.'

He left the pub and, leaving his car parked, walked back to the main street, where the other two village pubs stood, on opposite sides but only around a hundred yards apart. He decided to stay on the south side of the road, although Bissett's bar was the further away. As he reached it, he saw a powered wheelchair parked outside, flanked by two men, smoking. He nodded to them as he passed and stepped inside, into a big square bar, complete with dartboard and pool table, although neither was in use.

'What can I get you?' the bartender asked him. The contrast with Tony Bravo could not have been greater; the man was shorter, overweight, and looked as if he spent too long indoors.

The inspector decided against another soft drink. 'Information,' he said. 'Police, DI Regan.'

'The murder, eh.'

'That's right. We're trying to establish the dead man's movements last night. I know he was in the Mallard and the Old Clubhouse, but I'm pretty sure his drinking didn't end there.'

'Well, he didn't do any of it in here.'

'And how would you know that?'

'It was Sunday night and the Fire Training School was empty. I knew everyone who came in here last night.'

'Everyone?' Regan asked sceptically. 'On a nice summer evening you only had locals in?'

'Pretty much.'

'But not entirely?'

'Maybe not,' the man conceded.

'The victim was a small man, skinny, not very well dressed, and he probably wouldn't have been alone. My last sighting has him with another man, stocky, red hair, red beard.'

'Oh aye. I remember them.'

'So they were here.'

'Not for long. I wouldn't serve them.'

'They were the worse for drink?'

'The wee man probably had had a couple, but no, that's no' why. I didn't fancy them, that's all. I reckoned they were travellers. There's bad feeling about these people around here, and I didn't want any of it in this bar. If I let trouble develop, my boss would be down on me like a ton of breezeblock. So I showed them the door.'

'How did they take that?'

'The wee man didn't take it too well, but him wi' the red hair, he hustled him outside.'

'He did?'

'Aye, no argument.'

Regan was surprised, given Playfair's position as a self-appointed champion of the people of the road, but he realised that there was no point in pressing the barman further. He headed for the door himself, wondering who, among the half-dozen drinkers he had seen perched on stools, was the owner of the wheelchair, and trying to recall any applicable law about driving under the influence.

He crossed the road and walked into the public bar of the Golf Inn. Its layout was different, split into two areas, the first equipped with comfortable seating, some of it around an unused fireplace.

'Evening, Inspector,' said the thin, fair-haired steward.

'That obvious?'

The man smiled. 'No. There's a guy in the back bar who just came in from Bissett's. You wanting to know about the dead guy and his pal?'

'They were here?'

'Yes. They came in around half nine. Two pints of Eighty Shilling. My name's John, by the way.'

'Who paid?'

'The red-haired bloke. It's the other fella that's dead, right?'

Regan nodded. 'Yes. How long did they stay?'

'The wee man was there until after eleven; the pair of them sat over there.' He pointed to a corner of the bar, next to the window.

'The red-haired guy left first?'

'Yes, about half ten. They finished those pints, red-haired guy got another couple in. They were halfway through them when they had some sort of a barney. We were fairly busy on Sunday night . . . the good weather brings out some of the older people as well as the regulars . . . so I couldn't hear what they were saying, but the wee man started shouting at the other bloke. Not in English, but I could tell he wasn't complimenting him on his dress . . . or anything else for that matter. I was about to tell them to pipe down or piss off, but Red-head beat me to in. Got up and walked out with a face like . . .'

'Angry?'

'Oh aye, he was all that.'

'And the other guy?'

'He finished both pints, his and his mate's, then got another in for himself; and another after that. He might have been only a wee guy, but he could put it away.'

'What sort of state was he in when he left?'

'About one more pint short of dazed and confused, I'd say.' John looked at the detective. 'Was Red-head waiting for him, then? Is that what happened?'

Regan smiled, grimly. 'Let's just say that's a possibility I'm starting to consider very seriously.'

Forty-nine

Bob pulled into the driveway, coming to a halt a few feet short of the garage door, which was closed, as usual. He glanced in the rear-view mirror to ensure that the gate had closed properly behind him, in response to his remote signal, then eased himself from behind the driver's seat and retrieved his jacket from its hook in the back.

He frowned, wondering why for a few seconds, until he realised that his usual welcoming committee was conspicuous by its absence. Normally, when the children were at home, at least one of them would be in the doorway to greet him before the car had stopped moving. And if not them, Aileen, whose high office carried with it chauffeur-driven travel to and from the Parliament, and who usually made it home before he did.

He opened the door and stepped into the hall, but still there was no rush of feet, nor the sound of any presence. He turned to his right and looked into the kitchen, but that too was empty. 'On the beach, I guess,' he murmured, feeling a tinge of disappointment. He transferred his mobile to a trouser pocket, slung his jacket as usual over the post at the foot of the banister, and headed for the garden room.

It was full, of his family: Aileen, the children, Trish the nanny and Alex.

'What the hell's this?' he asked, with a huge smile.

'Let me give you a clue,' Aileen replied, as she took a bottle from the ice bucket and began to pour. 'This is not Asti Spumante, this is the

261

Widow Cliquot.' She handed him a glass, rose up on her toes to kiss him, and whispered, 'Congratulations, my darling,' in his ear.

'Congratulations,' five voices echoed, although Seonaid's version, screamed above the rest, was missing at least one syllable.

He took his glass and acknowledged the toast, noting that while the two younger children were waving glasses of cola, Mark had been allowed a small amount of champagne, then slipped an arm around his partner's waist. 'That's me kept my side of the bargain,' he told her. 'Now it's your turn.'

'A deal's a deal.' She nodded. 'October suit you, in the next parliamentary recess?'

'You set the date, and I'll be there.'

'Who'll be your best man?' asked Alex.

He was surprised by the question, and paused, for he had not considered it. But he looked her in the eye and said, 'I'm not having one. I'm having a best person, and you're it.'

'Pass!' she exclaimed.

'Refusal is not an option. No embarrassing speeches, though.' He caught Mark looking at him, a little quizzically. 'Don't worry, kid,' he laughed, 'that doesn't mean that you and the Jazzer have to be bridesmaids.'

'Or pageboys,' the boy begged. 'Please not, Dad.'

'You can be ushers,' Aileen announced, 'not that there'll be many people to ush,' she added. 'And the wee one can be a flower girl.'

Alex picked up her sister. 'If she's trainable,' she chuckled as the child wriggled, and a small amount of cola spilled on to the floor.

Two thoughts occurred to Bob. 'How did you know?' he asked.

'Jimmy called me this afternoon,' his fiancée replied.

'And where have you hidden your car, daughter? I had no notion that you were here when I came in.'

'It's in the garage; the last place you'd be likely to look.' She set Seonaid back on her feet and herded the children in the direction of the kitchen, where their evening meal had been set out for them by the nanny.

As they left, Bob dropped into his armchair. 'You realise this is premature?' he murmured. 'The Board doesn't meet until tomorrow. The recommendation could be overturned.'

'There is no chance of that,' Aileen declared firmly. 'No chance at all. It will be endorsed unanimously. If I had enemies within the Labour group, then there might be some sort of stunt, but I don't. My reach is long, when I choose, and I made damn sure there were no rebels appointed. I wouldn't give anyone the chance to attack you to get at me.' She smiled. 'But I agree, we should keep the celebrations in-house till it's all official. That's why we're having dinner in La Potinière tomorrow, rather than tonight.'

'We are? Just the two of us? Or have you asked Jimmy and Chrissie too?'

'I did, but they send their apologies; they're going somewhere else. Brian and Sheila Mackie are coming, Neil and Louise, and Alex, of course. Andy and Karen too, if you'd like and they can get a sitter.'

'Veto the last,' said Bob quickly. 'If word got out, that might be seen as a public endorsement. Brian's a close colleague; he's different, I can live with that. Jimmy would tell you the same thing.'

Aileen gazed at him, intrigued. 'Since when did you bother about things like that?' she asked. 'Not that I'm arguing with you, but I'm surprised.'

He met her eyes with his. 'I'm glad I can still do that . . . surprise you, that is. Since this afternoon, I reckon. Until now, everything's been hypothetical, but now it's about to become real . . . maybe I'm kidding myself, but I feel my thinking starting to change. It occurred to me as I was speaking to Jimmy about my possible successor; I found myself taking new factors into account, that wouldn't have occurred to me before.'

'Welcome to the club. You've just described how I felt when I became First Minister. All of a sudden, I had all the responsibility, no filters, nobody to hide behind when it came to the difficult decisions. It was scary until I accepted that, in truth, it was what I'd wanted from the day I entered public life.'

'Ah well,' said Bob, 'I don't know that I have accepted that yet. Maybe it isn't true of me.'

'Are you feeling self-doubt? If you are, love, then the last thing I'd want is for you to do something that would make you unhappy. It's not too late to withdraw your application. I can scrap the dinner.'

He savoured his Veuve Cliquot and stared out of the window. 'And if I did that, how would I feel about myself for the rest of my life? I know we made our deal, honey, I go for chief and you marry me, but both those things were going to happen anyway. I don't think anyone has ever made me do something I didn't want to do, or didn't feel that I should.' He looked back towards her. 'No, they can appoint me, and once they have done, we'll all have to take the consequences of that, until I'm done with it or they're done with me. So let's gather in La Potinière, enjoy it, and prepare for the mayhem to come! Are you bringing a partner?' he asked his daughter as she returned.

'No,' she told him.

'You can if you like,' Aileen pointed out.

'Ah.' Alex eyed her father. 'But what if I brought Griff Montell?'

He laughed out loud. 'Now you are being mischievous, kid. Do you think he'd come, even if he wasn't in South Africa with his gay sister? A detective constable at that table? The guy would run a mile rather than accept that invitation, and you know it. But bring somebody else if you like, someone from the firm, maybe.'

'No, I'll come alone.' She flashed him a sharp glare. 'You were right, of course: I wouldn't have dreamt of inviting Griff, and not just because of the company. It would be implying something that isn't true; we're not that close.' She paused. 'And what's with the crack about Spring being gay? That's rubbish.'

Her father shook his head. 'No, it isn't. I've seen Griff's vetting report; it was done when he applied for a transfer from South Africa. You can imagine why we looked into her. Single guy living with his single sister; I didn't demand it, but I understand why it was done. That's what showed up; in fact, it was the main reason for her wanting to leave. She drove the move more than he did. Fine, it means nothing to me, which team she bats for; it doesn't make her brother a security risk. As it happens, I have gay people on my force right through the ranks, and I'm comfortable with it.'

'Griff's not one of them,' Alex muttered. 'I can tell you that.'

'I know; he left an ex-wife and two kids in South Africa.' Her mouth fell open. Bob nodded. 'It's true.'

'You knew that and you didn't tell me.'

'I didn't feel that I could tell you at the time, given how I got the information. Plus, the man got you out of a very nasty scrape, you'll remember, so maybe I made some allowances for him. When I realised you were sleeping with him, I was in a bit of a quandary, but again, I decided that all I could do was let it play itself out.'

'But he didn't tell me either.'

'Yet you still cooled off the relationship. See? Your instincts were right, you sensed something, and you made the right decision. There's a lesson I learned from the failure of my second marriage, a lesson that Aileen and I have both taken to heart, and it's this. We know everything about each other, she and I. Why? Because you can't build on hidden truths; they'd bring the whole fucking house down.'

'Jesus!' Alex gasped. 'And as Chief Constable Bob Skinner

you'll have access to even more secrets, and even more power.'

'That's what gets to me, my dear. It's a hell of a responsibility; now you can see why I was ambivalent about it for a while. This morning, Andy Martin told me about something that had scared him. I could have made the same admission to him; but I've got over it.'

'And has Andy?' she asked, curious, frowning.

'Don't know about that.'

Silence hung between them, until it was broken by the sound of Bob's ringtone. He put his glass on a side table, fished out his mobile and took the call, from an undeclared number.

'Piers here,' he learned. 'Can you speak?'

'Yes. I'm just sat here cuddling a Widow, and getting ready for some more of her.'

'The lives you Jocks lead,' Frame drawled. 'I've made some inquiries, Bob, and the fact is, your chap was pretty low down the watch list. Indeed, once he was elected to your parliament, surveillance stopped altogether. The thinking was that if we wanted to find out what he was doing about Trident, it would all be on the public record, so the resources involved were reallocated. So I'm assured by MoD that they haven't done any housekeeping at your chap's place since his death; neither they nor anyone else we know about, if you get my meaning.'

So not the CIA either. 'Yes, I do. Thanks, although that leaves me with a puzzle.'

'Which I'm sure you'll solve. Oh, and also, that name you mentioned; not a member of our community, either real or assumed. Bit of a mystery caller, it seems.'

'Indeed. For his sake he'd better stay that way. Thanks, chum.' He pondered Frame's message as he closed the Motorola. Yes, the dead man had been watched for a while, but that had stopped, and no, Coben wasn't one of theirs. So who was he? Why did he visit Andy to warn him off? How did he even know about the surveillance? Or . . . had other eyes been fixed on Ainsley Glover?

He laid the phone on the table, picked up his flute and waved it at Aileen. 'Since I seem to be the star of the show,' he began, '. . . is there any chance of some more of that stuff?'

Fifty

'I don't want to put pressure on you, Inspector,' Denzel Chandler began, 'but Randy's having a really hard time. The pod she's using as a makeshift author reception centre really isn't big enough. She'd kill me if she knew I was asking, but can you give me an idea of when she might be getting her yurt back?'

'I reckon we'll clear out this afternoon,' Pye told the tall, dark-haired author, noting that he had shaved since their last encounter. 'We've done all we can here. I'd like to have the carpeting removed from the area where Mr Glover died, and the bench he was lying on, and taken to our lab, just as a precaution, in case the forensic people need to take another look at any of it. Once we've done that, we're out of here.'

'Thanks,' said the director's partner, his face brightening, 'you've made my morning.' Then his smiled disappeared. 'God, that sounds terrible; poor Ainsley died here and I'm going on about our inconvenience. How's your investigation going? Can you talk about it?'

'I don't have a lot to tell you. We've done a lot of elimination, so much that there's nothing positive left standing.'

'There was a rumour doing the rounds yesterday that you were searching Bruce Anderson's place.'

'No rumour, only it isn't his place, as such, it's his girlfriend's. We recovered a quantity of drugs; she's been charged with possession.'

'So Bruce is in the clear?'

'I didn't say that, but I won't say different. Mind you, he didn't make it easy for himself with that carry-on at the opening night party.'

'Bruce doesn't seem to have a gift for making things easy for himself. But I'm glad he's not in trouble . . . not least because Randy's asked him to appear on an extra panel next Monday, discussing the fictional approach to the drugs question.'

'Ouch!' Pye chuckled. 'She may find that he's less keen to do that, given that Lady Anthea's up in court this morning. The connection between them's bound to be reported.'

'Oh hell,' Chandler sighed. 'Maybe I should tell her to draw up a plan B.'

'The way things have gone in the last couple of days, if I were her I'd have C as well.'

'I don't envy Dr Mosley,' said Ray Wilding as Chandler left. 'This event must be a real bugger to run in an ordinary year, so what it's been like with this going on all around her . . .'

'And not just that,' Alice Cowan added. 'It's her first year in charge.'

'Where was she before?' asked Pye.

'She was with the European Commission in Brussels, in the culture directorate.'

'Bet she wishes she was back there.' Pye clapped his hands. 'OK, team,' he called out. 'I'm due up at Fettes before ten, to hear what Dr Anderson has to say for himself. Let's have a summary of where we've got to.' His three colleagues gave a collective sigh, and shifted in their seats. 'I know, this isn't one of the easy ones; it's going to be a hard slog, but we have to go on. As far as the family are concerned, I've checked their story myself. Yes, Carol and Wilkie were in Deacon Brodie's on Saturday night as they said. Wilkie was pissed as the proverbial, according to the manager. He remembered him when I showed him a photo; he stopped serving him drink before midnight. Carol was OK though; she took charge of him.'

'What about Collins?' Wilding asked.

'The staff don't remember seeing him before twelve thirty, but I've checked with the *Saltire* and he did file a review of the show in the Bedlam Theatre that Carol said he went to.'

'Have you checked with the theatre company that he was actually there? I know that might seem like overkill, but . . .'

'Of course I have,' Pye declared. 'I'm seeing the boss soon, and I don't want to be sitting there looking like Homer bloody Simpson when he starts asking me questions. I haven't confirmed it, though. I spoke to the director, they didn't have a performance last night, so he couldn't speak to his front of house staff, but there's a matinee on today. Have one of the DCs check with them.'

'Will do,' said the sergeant. 'I might as well have been at the theatre last night. Becky brought that computer home with her. She was at it until after ten, and from the effing and blinding that was going on, I could tell she wasn't having any joy.'

'There may be nothing for her to find,' Pye conceded, 'but it has to be covered.' He reached into his pocket and drew out the envelope she had given him the day before. 'Thanks to her, we've got this . . . which I confess I forgot to read until now.' He opened it and scanned its contents, a single sheet, frowned, then handed it to Wilding.

'Looks like five email addresses,' he said as he peered at it. 'Two of them are dot com, two are dot yu and one's dot ba. What the hell's dot yu and dot ba?'

'Dot yu used to be Yugoslavia,' Haddock volunteered. 'Serbia still uses it. I don't know about the other one.'

'Then check it, Sauce,' Pye ordered, 'and trace these addressees, without approaching them or alerting them if you can avoid it.'

'Yes, boss.'

'Fast as you can. I'd like some answers by the time I get back from seeing Dr Anderson.'

'Providing he's not heading for the hills again,' Alice Cowan chuckled.

The DI whistled. 'I don't think even he would be that reckless.'

Fifty-one

'Is this the biggest day of your life, Bob?' asked Assistant Chief Constable Brian Mackie.

Skinner looked at him, eyebrows raised. 'Shit, no, not even close. The day I married Myra; the days my children were born, the day I met Aileen; they all rank way above today.'

'Professionally, man; I meant professionally.'

'I know. I'm only pulling your chain. Maybe you should ask me after the Board meeting, when they call me in and tell me to my face, either that I'm chief or that they've realised in the nick of time what a terrible mistake they almost made. Until that happens, I won't know. As of this moment, I rank the day that Mario and I arrested Dražen Boras and charged him with Stevie Steele's murder as the best of my career. That was some buzz, seeing the look in his eyes when he knew he was done.'

'Yes, I can believe that all right. When does he come up for trial?'

'Before the year's out; that's all I know for sure. It'll be in Newcastle, since Stevie died in Northumberland and that's the nearest Crown Court.'

'Will you be a witness?'

'As of this moment, that's not certain; if the CPS feels the need, they may call Mario and me to give evidence about his arrest. Becky Stallings and Ray Wilding will be for sure. They were directly involved in the investigation on the day of the murder. Jimmy and I were at the scene, but only after the event. Arthur Dorward's going to be the star turn. It was his forensic work that nailed Dražen.'

'Will he be all right under cross-examination?'

'Arthur? Absolutely rock solid. I'm in no doubt about that. He's built a model of the trap that was set, and it'll be introduced as an exhibit. The Crown case will be absolutely watertight.' He paused. 'Anyway, going back to the present, however this day ends, there'll be sadness in it, for it'll be the last time that Sir James Proud will walk out of this building as a serving police officer. When he does, and I expect him to leave around four, after the Board lunch breaks up and after he says his final farewells along the command corridor, I want every available colleague, from you and me down, and the senior civilian staff as well, to form a guard of honour. Will you take care of that, get everyone along?'

'Sure, Bob, my pleasure. But come on, tell me, how do you feel?'

Skinner shrugged his shoulders, an uncertain gesture that sat strangely on him. 'Nervous,' he replied, 'if you want the truth. I suppose I should be happy about that; it's how I reckon I should feel.' He grinned. 'I'll have something to take my mind off it, though, in about half an hour. I have Dr Bruce Anderson calling on me, by appointment, for interview under caution by me and Sammy Pye. I'd better go and prepare for him.'

He left the room, and Mackie found himself looking at the door long after it had closed. He had known Bob Skinner for a long time, had even been his executive assistant for a spell, but he had never seen him so edgy. It was a momentous day, undoubtedly; end of an era, and the new one would bring change. How much? Maybe less than people expected, the ACC mused. The new chief was inheriting a highly motivated force, in good shape. He was too smart to stand that on its head.

The ringing telephone broke into his thoughts. 'Mackie,' he replied automatically as he snatched it up, feeling instantly foolish as he realised that the call had come from his outer office and that he had no need to identify himself.

Chief Inspector David Mackenzie, the senior officers' adjutant, ignored the slip. 'I've got someone on the line from Melbourne, sir. She says her name is Assistant Commissioner Gabrielle Robotham, and she's asking to speak to her opposite number. The control centre reckons that's you.'

The ACC frowned. 'Are we sure it's genuine?'

'Yes, it's been screened; she's calling from Victoria State police headquarters.'

'Then put her through, David.' He sat back in his chair and waited.

'Mr Mackie?' she began briskly. 'You're an assistant chief constable, right?'

'Right. In charge of uniformed operations throughout the force area.'

'Fine, sounds like you're the guy. I'm Gaby Robotham, and I need your help with something. We've had an incident here, and a man is dead. He's Scottish, from your territory, I understand, and next of kin need to be informed fast, because this could leak . . . in fact the story's bound to break sooner or later . . . and his name's going to be all over the media.'

'Why? What is his name?'

'He's been identified as Henry Matthew Mount, he was aged sixty-one, and according to his driving licence his address is number ten, Broadgreen Gate, Gullane, Scotland. His next of kin is shown on his passport as Mrs Trudy Mount, same address. He was travelling alone, so I'm hoping she's at home or close to it.'

The name registered with Mackie, somewhere, but he was unable to place it, as he thought through the logistics of the request. 'No problem,' he told the Australian. 'We have an operation in that village as we speak. I can take care of that. What happened to the man? How did he die?'

'That's the damnable thing. It appears that he's been shot, but none of my officers at the scene are prepared to tell me how, or even confirm that he was, until our forensic people report. It's a pretty public place, too. The guy's a visiting author, and he was killed at the Melbourne Writers' Festival.'

Fifty-two

Neil McIlhenney sat at his desk and brooded on his misfortune. The normal pattern of crime in the force area had made it unlikely that his time of deputising for the holidaying head of CID would be blighted by a homicide investigation. Murder tends to be a winter pastime in Edinburgh. 'I should be so lucky,' he hummed, 'lucky, lucky, lucky.' One death was bad enough, but two, that was calamitous. And for both to remain complete mysteries after more that twenty-four hours . . . he shook his head as he imagined Mario McGuire's dark satanic smile fixed upon him.

'Stuck in the fucking mud, mate.' He could hear his friend's gently mocking tone. Not that Mario would blame him, for he and his teams had done their best, but he had definitely fallen behind in the game of one-upmanship that had been played between them throughout their police careers. George Regan had just called him to advise him that not only had the chief suspect in the Mustafic killing, Hugo Playfair, vanished without trace, it seemed that he had never existed in the first place. Sammy Pye was on his way to Fettes, but would he accuse Bruce Anderson, or would he eliminate him? True, there were other leads, but none of them pointed to a quick conclusion.

'Stuck in the fucking mud,' he said aloud, just as his door opened and ACC Mackie, tall, bald-headed and shirt-sleeved, stepped into his office.

'Are you indeed?' he murmured. 'In that case I don't know whether I'm about to give you a hand out or push you deeper in.'

'Go ahead, then,' the superintendent challenged. 'Things can only get better.' My morning for dodgy pop songs, he thought.

'Want a bet? The odds against a best-selling crime author being murdered at a major festival are pretty astronomical, you'll agree?' McIlhenney nodded, with a sudden certainty that the nineties group D:Ream had been entirely wrong, and that things were, in fact, about to get significantly worse. 'In that case,' Mackie continued, 'what price against it happening twice?'

'What?' The big detective gasped, pushing himself to his feet. 'Another killing in Charlotte Square?'

'No. This one happened in Melbourne, Australia, at a similar festival there. The victim's a man called Henry Mount, from Gullane. Apparently he was standing in a place called Federation Square, where they're having their own festival, signing books for admiring readers, then next minute he was on the ground, stone cold bloody dead. I've just sent George Regan . . . hope you don't mind me pinching one of your people, but tact and a gentle touch is required . . . to break the news to the widow, and I've just told the DCC. He and Mount were near neighbours and regular pub chums. Naturally, he's distressed; he said you'd know what to do.'

'Sure, but is there any evidence that this wasn't a natural death?'

'The Australian assistant commissioner who called me said that the hole in the back of his head points in a certain direction. Plus, if you're going to shoot yourself you tend not to do it in a square full of people, with a bottle of beer in one hand and a cigar in the other.' The ACC laid a note on McIlhenney's desk. 'These are the numbers for the Victoria State Police, main switchboard, and for the mobile of the lead investigating officer, Inspector Michael Giarratano. It's pretty long distance . . . they're nine hours ahead of us . . . but I imagine you'll want to touch base.'

'I can do better than that,' McIlhenney murmured. 'Thanks, Brian. The boss was right, I do know what to do.'

'I'll leave you to get on with it, then.' He smiled, running a hand over his shiny dome. 'Of course, if you need a senior officer to go out there and liaise . . .'

'I may have that covered. Cheers.' He was reaching for the phone as Mackie left, and punching in a mobile number on the console. It took longer than normal for him to hear a ringtone, but only a couple of seconds for it to stop.

'What now?' Mario McGuire sighed.

'Where are you?' McIlhenney asked.

'In the QVB, having a beer.'

'QVB?'

'Queen Victoria Building. Everything has an acronym here, mate.'

'Is Paula there?'

'Of course.'

'Then put her on.'

'If you insist, but when the bean-counters spot the cost of this call . . . Here she is.'

'Neil, my love,' Paula Viareggio exclaimed breezily. 'How are you?'

'I'm fine, for now, but you're going to kill me shortly, and I wanted to tell you why. There's a dead man lying on the ground in Melbourne as we speak, he's Scottish, and it's almost certain that it relates to a murder investigation that we have under way here. I need your man to get on a plane as fast as he can, team up with the locals, take a look at the situation and report back to us. I'd send somebody else, I'd even go myself, but it would take a couple of days to get there, and this has to be handled now, right now. Sorry, Paulie.'

'So far,' she replied, 'I'm taking this quietly, although from the expression on Mario's face as he's watching me, I might not be looking too pleased. Tell me more.'

'The dead man's name is Henry Mount.'

'Henry Mount!' she squealed. 'Oh no. He's one of my favourite authors, just like Ainsley Glover was one of Mario's. I've read all his books; most of them twice. Of course he can go. What happened to him?'

'That's the damndest thing. Nobody's sure. He was standing in a public place, happy as Larry, and next second he was on the ground. It seems as if he was shot, but nobody saw anything and nobody heard anything.'

He waited for Paula to reply, or to pass the phone to Mario, but there was only silence on the line. When she did speak, her tone was quieter, tentative. 'Neil,' she said, 'this might be a strange thing to ask, but was he smoking a cigar?'

Fifty-three

Sammy Pye was mildly surprised when he was met by Gerry Crossley at the entrance to the command corridor and shown into the DCC's room, since Ruth, his wife, was secretary to both the deputy and assistant chiefs, and he knew that she should be in her office. But he assumed she was involved in a task for Mackie, and put the thought out of his mind.

For once, Skinner was not seated behind his desk. Instead his frame was half-sprawled on a long sofa, set against the wall facing the window, and he seemed barely aware that he had company. He was frowning, gazing at the floor, with a mug in his hand, held so carelessly that Pye hoped it was nowhere near full.

'Morning, sir,' the DI ventured.

The big man blinked, and looked up, with a momentary flash of annoyance at being caught off guard. 'Morning, Sam,' he responded. 'Sorry, I was miles away there. Grab yourself a coffee from the machine and have a seat.'

'I won't, thank you, sir. Ruth has me on a ration.'

Skinner grinned, and was himself again. 'She's tried that with me too,' he said, 'but since I control the means of production around here, she was doomed to failure. So go on; I won't shop you.'

The inspector shrugged, poured himself a mug from the half-full filter jug, added a very little milk and lowered himself on to the sofa.

'Have you spoken to Neil in the last few minutes?'

The DCC's question took him by surprise. 'Not that recently, sir. I called him about half an hour ago, but that's all.'

'Then you won't know. The Glover investigation's just gone global.' Quickly, Skinner told him of the Melbourne incident, that a second of Edinburgh's triumvirate of mystery authors had gone to the great publishing house in the sky.

'We're sure it's not a sudden death?' Pye asked tentatively.

'From what I'm told, no chance of that. I know Henry Mount . . . knew him. He looked after himself; OK, none of us have any certainty of continuing good health, but he didn't abuse himself, worked out pretty well for a man of his age . . . we belong to the same gym . . . and he didn't have any major vices. Yes, there were those cigars of his, but he never smoked cigarettes, and they're the real killers.'

'I'm very sorry, sir. I can tell you're upset.'

Skinner nodded. 'Yeah, I admit it, I am. I've just told you that it wasn't natural causes, but when someone you know dies, someone who may not be a contemporary but who's not that far off it, it's always a reminder of your own mortality. And you know what, Sammy? The older you get, the sharper that reminder is.'

'Stevie Steele.'

'What?'

'You made me think about Stevie. Young guy, walks though the wrong door and *bang!* that's it. There are wrong doors waiting for any one of us, I suppose.'

'Yeah.' Skinner straightened himself on the sofa. 'But you and I are still on the right side of ours, so let's get on with it.'

'Do you want me to contact the Australian police, sir?'

'They've already been in touch with us. Neil's handling the follow-up and he'll let you know all that's relevant to your investigation. I want you to take a look at this.' He reached out, picked up an envelope from the coffee table and handed it to the DI. 'It's the list that Ainsley Glover gave Andy Martin, his distant cousin, for safe keeping. I retrieved it yesterday from Dundee.'

'What is it? What's the list?'

'Four names, none appear to be British, and none means a damn thing to me. See what you can find out about them. They must be important, given the lengths that Glover went to to keep them hidden.'

'That's interesting,' Pye mused. 'Becky Stallings recovered a number of email addresses that Glover kept on his daughter's computer. Some of them appear to be foreign.'

'Then see if they relate to any of the names on the list.' The DCC laid his mug on the table and rose easily to his feet. 'But that's for later.' He checked his watch, retrieved his jacket from the back of his chair and slipped it on. 'We have another priority.' He stood for a second or to, then stepped across to the window and looked out, checking the section of the driveway car park that was reserved for visitors. As he did so, there was a knock, the door opened, and Gerry Crossley entered.

'Your visitors have arrived, sir,' he announced. 'I've put them in the meeting room, as you said. And there's a dual recorder on the table, plugged in, with a clean mini-disk in each drive.'

'Visitors plural?' Skinner mused. 'So Dr Anderson had the good sense to bring a lawyer with him. Wonder who it is? Can't be the Barracuda, though; she must be in court with the bad Lady Walters around now, getting ready for some really unwelcome news from the Sheriff.'

'I'm not sure it's a lawyer.'

'Then I'm not sure that whoever it is will be hanging around too long, not even if it's the Duke of bloody Lanark himself. If Dr Anderson thinks he can piss me about, he's making a big mistake. Come on, Sammy. Let's go see him.' He led the way into the command corridor and along to the small conference room at the far end. He opened the door, stepped inside, then stopped, so suddenly that Pye bumped into him. 'Jim!' the DI heard him exclaim. 'You're the last person I expected to be chumming our interviewee. Are you his confessor? Because if you are, I have to tell you, this will be on the record, and I'll be deciding the penance.' He stepped to one side. 'Detective Inspector Pye, you know Dr Anderson, but I don't believe you've met His Excellency James Gainer, Roman Catholic Archbishop of St Andrews and Edinburgh.'

The man with whom the DI shook hands was mid-forties, as tall as he was, and more heavily built, with big shoulders and a thick neck. He wore blue chinos, and a light cotton jacket hanging open over a white T-shirt with the simple message, 'Souls saved; apply within', printed in two lines on the front. Pye had heard tales of the charismatic priest, stories of a wild youth, redemption, and of late-night cruising round the city on a high-powered motorcycle. He had written them off as media fantasy, but as he looked the man in the eye, he realised that they were almost certainly true.

'My pleasure,' said the archbishop with a smile, then turned back to Skinner. 'Bruce doesn't take confession,' he went on, 'any more than you do. He isn't one of mine either, any more than you are, but I like to think that we all play in the same team, just in different positions, that's all. I'm here because he's asked me to be, to help him out with a little ethical difficulty he has.'

'Ethical? Jim, we're investing a breakage of the sixth commandment. As far as I'm concerned, that sets all other considerations aside.'

'I wouldn't quote commandments if I were you, chum,' Gainer chuckled. 'You break the third one all the time. I don't agree with your statement either; there are areas of unshakable confidentiality reserved for doctors, as Bruce is, and for priests, like me. You've got a murder on your hands. We're here to help you, but you have to understand his position.'

'His position would have been easier if he hadn't lied to my officers.'

'I know that, Bob,' said Anderson. 'But I had a reason. Can we explain it to you?'

Skinner nodded. 'Let's hear it.' He moved towards the square table in the centre of the room. 'Take a seat, you two back to the door, us facing.' He touched the black recorder box as he sat. 'I was going to do this formally, under caution, but your presence changes that, Jim. We'll leave this thing switched off for now. If I feel the need to go on the record, we can do that later.' He looked at Anderson. 'Tell us about Saturday night.'

'From the beginning?'

'No, your argument with the dead man has been well covered. Let's start from when Lord Elmore and his wife saw you walking away from Charlotte Square.'

'OK. I did go home, be in no doubt about that. I didn't want to bring her into this but if you need reliable confirmation, my daughter can provide it. The light was still on in her room; when I looked in, she was reading. *Harry Potter and the Goblet of Fire*, as I recall. I told her to turn it in and go to sleep. Then I went to my own room; Anthea was asleep already . . . although given what I've learned since, I suspect she may have had help.'

'We don't need to go into Lady Walters' problems,' said Pye.

'We might later,' Anderson countered.

'But go on for now,' Skinner told him. 'Lady W's in the land of nod.'

'Yes. I wasn't remotely tired, so I was a little annoyed that she hadn't waited up for me. However, I had set the television to record *Match of the Day*, so I went off to catch up on that. And then the phone rang.'

'The phone rang,' Pye repeated. 'Going on for midnight?'

'Yes. It happens. I have calls at all hours of the day, and sometimes at night.'

'Professional?'

'To do with my profession, yes.'

'That's a carefully worded reply, sir.'

'True.' Anderson shifted in his seat.

'So who was the caller?'

'It was me, Inspector,' said Archbishop Gainer.

'You, sir?'

'Yes. Someone I know needed help, so I rang Bruce, knowing that if he was available, he'd provide it.'

'How long have you been an addiction counsellor, Dr Anderson?' Skinner asked.

'I've been doing it for years, since my days as a GP in Glasgow, even when I was a Member of Parliament. A few of my colleagues at Westminster, and some party staffers, had problems, and I helped them, very discreetly though. When I dropped out of politics and went back into medical practice in a limited way, I went back to counselling in my old stamping ground in Glasgow, and worked with charities too.'

'How did you come to take your services upmarket? It was news to me, I have to admit.'

'I have always been discreet, Bob. I have never mentioned that side of my work to anyone, always taken pains to keep it confidential. I take the view that these people are ill, and as such they have the same right to medical confidentiality as any other patients. Of course, when I helped colleagues in politics, that was never going to be an issue. Front-bench spokesmen are never going to own up to a drug problem, are they?'

'Not while they're still there, that's for sure,' Skinner conceded.

'That said, it was one of those people who made me broaden my patient base, if I can use the term. An MP I had helped to get himself clean found himself on the board of a quoted company; its managing director had a bad cocaine habit. They thought about sacking him, but if they had, the share price would have dived. As a last resort, my friend approached me. I arranged to treat him in a clinic in the borders that's best known for providing a haven for rich alcoholics. I got him straightened out, and afterwards the clinic asked me if I'd continue to work with them. I do, and they're the only patients from whom I take fees. All the others are *pro bono*, as lawyers call their freebies.' He paused. 'I met Anthea through the clinic. Archie ... that's her father ... went there looking for help for her, about three years ago, and was referred to me. We had a chat, he brought Anthea along, and I put her on a withdrawal programme. She was badly hooked, so I had to stay very close to her. When she was in recovery, I carried on seeing her, and eventually moved into her place in Darnaway Street.'

'And yet you've still kept this part of your life a secret?' the DCC exclaimed. 'I'm astonished.'

Anderson shook his head. 'It hasn't been that difficult. I'm known in the clinic as Andrew Bruce, and it's Mr, not Dr. Many of my patients never get to know my real name; those who recognise me realise very quickly that we have a mutual interest in confidentiality.'

'There's no threat implied, is there?' asked Pye.

Anderson scowled at him. 'You mean do I threaten to "out" them if they "out" me? Certainly not, and I resent the suggestion.'

'Nothing's being suggested, Bruce,' the DCC intervened. 'It was a legitimate question, and you've answered it.' He glanced at the archbishop. 'How did you two meet?' he asked.

'I have a parishioner,' Gainer began, 'and a friend, a very well-known and respected public figure, who has an addictive personality. You name it, he's ingested it. I can't tell you how I found out about it; I'll just leave you to speculate. When I did, I spoke to another parishioner, who is on the board of the clinic. He mentioned Mr Andrew Bruce to me, and I facilitated a meeting. My friend was rescued; in the aftermath Bruce and I had a number of meetings and I became involved in his charity and public sector work, as an additional counsellor. Sometimes we even work together. On Saturday night, I had a call from my friend. He had relapsed, and he was in a bad way. His cry for help was more of a scream; I called Bruce, and asked him to come with me to see him. He agreed, but he'd had a couple of drinks, so couldn't drive. Rather than be seen picking him up in the house, I agreed to meet him in George Street, at midnight.'

'That was where I was heading when your witness saw me,' Anderson interposed. 'Jim picked me up on his bike, outside Brown's . . .' He looked at Pye. 'Yes, he had a spare helmet, Inspector. We visited our patient, I sedated him, called an ambulance and had him taken down to the borders and admitted. That's why I bolted yesterday. I did not want to get into that area. I didn't want to involve Jim today either, but I knew you'd insist.'

Skinner waited until he had caught his eye. 'You're not going to tell me who this patient is, are you?' he said.

'No. Under no circumstances.'

He looked at the archbishop. 'You're not bound by the doctor-patient relationship, though, Jim.'

'Maybe not, but I can claim another privilege.'

'Fair enough. The matter is closed, Dr Anderson,' he said abruptly, then paused. 'Jim, do you mind if Bruce and I have a minute alone?'

'How can I?' Gainer chuckled. 'Private conversations are at the heart of my priesthood.'

Skinner sat quietly as the cleric and the DI left the room. 'Tell me this, Bruce, please,' he began after the door had closed. 'How can a man who does the sort of work that you clearly excel in be such an abrasive, lying, manipulative arsehole of a politician, with both entities crammed into the same body?'

Anderson smiled, sadly. 'Do you think I don't ask myself that question every so often? I have the occasional glimpse of my own faults. My only answer is this: I believe that I'm so good at my private work because I have an addictive personality myself. My drug is politics, and in its pursuit I'm a different man to the one my patients meet. My judgement goes out the window sometimes, as it did when we had our differences, long ago, and again when I lost my temper with Glover the other night. What the man said was true. I saw my flirtation with the rebellious side of my party as a way back in; that's why I reversed my position on the Trident issue. That's why, even now, I'm tempted to contest the by-election for the newly vacant Holyrood seat . . . which, I repeat, I had no hand in causing.'

'Well, physician,' said Skinner slowly, 'my advice to you is this. Heal yourself of your addiction; get rid of your Mr Hyde. Don't yield to that temptation. Focus on doing good, and nothing but good. For if you don't, then pretty soon you're going to come into conflict with the lady I'm going to marry, and I won't like that. I told you yesterday that I don't bear grudges for myself, but anyone who goes out of his way to hurt her . . . and, Bruce, that's how you play the game . . . that person's letting himself in for more grief than he could ever handle.'

Fifty-four

'What I don't understand,' said Colin Mount, shaking with what George Regan recognised as a combination of shock and anger, 'is why, after Ainsley Glover was murdered, you could allow this to happen to my father.'

'Col, please, not now.' Trudy Mount's voice was cracked as she spoke from the depths of an armchair.

'It's a fair question,' the DI told her. 'All I can offer as an answer is that we had no reason to think that the attack on Mr Glover was anything other than a one-off.'

'But wouldn't it have been wise to consider the possibility?'

'What possibility, sir? That some madman is acting out a fantasy about crime writers and using literary festivals as a background? Let me ask you, do you think your father would have come up with a plot like that?'

A soft chuckle came from the chair, where the new widow held a tall glass, gin and tonic, ice, no lemon, mixed by her son. The likeness between them was striking: both fair-haired, tall, slim built, she in her mid-fifties, he around thirty. 'No, he wouldn't, Mr Regan; his work was more concerned with financial crimes. His lead character, Petra Jecks, was an accountant, turned policewoman. But he'd have been well pleased if he had, I can tell you. The more complex the mystery, the better Henry liked them.'

'Who were his favourites?' Regan asked.

'What's that got to do with the investigation?' Colin Mount snapped.

'Almost certainly nothing at all, it's a straight question. I don't expect to be involved in the inquiry; my assumption is that my colleague DI Pye will be linking with the Australian investigators, since he's senior officer in the Glover case. I was asked to break the news of your father's death because I'm working a homicide locally.'

'I appreciate the way you did it, Mr Regan,' Mrs Mount told him, 'with great sympathy and compassion. Please excuse my son's abruptness.'

'I have no need to. I understand it.'

'You ask about Henry's favourites; you'll find them all on the shelves in his office. Most are American, but the two old stagers were at the top of the list. You'll know who I mean, Ainsley and Fred Noble. They were friends, but he admired their work. They were called The Triumvirate; Henry was very pleased to be counted among their number, although he'd never have admitted that publicly.'

'Have you been aware of any threats to your husband?'

Mrs Mount shook her head. 'No, none at all. And I'd have known if something had been troubling him. I could read him like one of his books.'

Regan looked at her son. 'How about you? Had your father mentioned anything to you?'

'I thought you weren't involved in the investigation?' he shot back.

'I said that I don't expect to be, but I'm here now. I'd be letting myself and you down if I didn't ask the obvious questions.'

'Fair enough,' said Colin Mount, mollified. 'No, Dad was business as usual before he went to Australia. He was sorry that Mum couldn't go, but still excited about the trip.'

'Normally, I would have gone with him,' Mrs Mount explained. 'But I've just had a small operation, and the medical advice was to stay at home.' She frowned, deeply. 'If only . . .' she murmured.

'It would still have happened, Mum. It's probably as well you weren't there.'

Sudden ferocity shone in the woman's eyes. 'That he should have died alone? Is that what you're saying? If I'd been there . . .'

'What, Mum? You think whoever killed him would have thought twice because you were there?'

She subsided as quickly as she had flared up. 'No, but . . .' Her voice tailed off.

'My mother has a very protective nature,' her son explained. 'She gave me hell when I had a motorbike, until I sold the bloody thing just to get some peace and quiet. She was the same with Dad. She's probably the only person in Gullane, maybe even in the whole damn world, who thinks he stopped smoking.'

'What do you mean?' she protested. 'He did.'

Colin laughed. 'See what I mean? He told you he did, sure. But not even you could separate my old man from his Havanas.'

'Oh, I knew that, really,' Trudy Mount exclaimed, with a smile that did not fool Regan for a second.

'So your husband was in good humour,' the DI continued.

'Exceptionally. He had just finished a Jecks book, for publication next year, and he was working on a new project. I'm not sure what it was . . . he could be secretive about his work, even with me . . . but it was something different. Still financial, though; he'd been talking to Ainsley.' She caught Regan's puzzled expression. 'Henry used him as an informal, unpaid consultant on accountancy matters; he knew quite a bit himself, having trained to be a CA before going into the diplomatic service, but if he needed advice on anything, Ainsley would happily provide it.'

'Mr Mount was a diplomat before he was a writer?'

'Yes. He retired when he did his first big book deal, about ten years ago. We retired to Gullane then; Henry had always wanted to live here.

It made a pleasant change after some of the places we'd been. Venezuela, for example, you would not have liked, or Berlin, back in the early eighties. It's transformed now, of course.'

'But he didn't write about that part of his life?'

'No. He said that he wanted to keep both sides of his career completely separate.'

'Can I see his office?' Regan asked.

'Of course.' She looked at her son. 'Colin, drive the inspector along there, would you?'

The detective was taken by surprise. 'He didn't work at home?'

'No. Henry was very disciplined when he wrote, and he didn't like the inevitable domestic disturbances: doorbell ringing, me hoovering, that sort of thing. He had an office on the outskirts of the village, and did all his writing there. I never went near the place; it was an understanding we had. I used to tease him about keeping a mistress down there; he said that he did, and her name was Petra Jecks.'

Colin Mount smiled sadly. 'And one other,' he sighed. 'La Gloria Habana, his favourite cigar; when he was working, he used to kiss her all day.'

Fifty-five

'How are you doing with those lists?' asked Ray Wilding. 'Sammy will be back soon and he'll want to know.'

'Not helluva well,' Sauce Haddock admitted. 'I've been trying to identify the holders of the email addresses, but it's not easy. The first one, *pr876@whe.com*, could be a journalist. *www.whe.com* is the web page of the *Washington Herald* newspaper. *Margotthreecool@ hotmail.com* is a listed member but doesn't have any information on her profile. *Ratko7@belp.yu*, again, may be a journo, since that's the address of a radio station in Belgrade. The other two, *VsnaP@inet.yu* and *adilkovac6@saranet.ba* could be anything. I'll need an interpreter to correspond with those service providers. The "*ba*" suffix is Bosnia, by the way.'

'What about the names on the other list?'

'That's weird. All four appear to be Yugoslav: Mirko Anđelić, Danica Anđelić, Aca Nicolić, and Lazar Erceg. I've run them through every search engine I can find and come up with sweet eff all. The only thing I can say is that they don't seem to cross-reference with any of the email addresses.'

'Still, we've got a Yugoslav connection, and that's something. Let's make an assumption, Harold, that Glover didn't speak the language, and that when he communicated with these people . . . if he did . . . he did it in English. Fair bet, agreed?'

'Yes.'

293

'OK, I want you to send a message to all five addressees, on the force's email, telling them who you are and that you're investigating the murder of Ainsley Glover. Try that and wait to see what comes back.'

Haddock looked back at him, more than a little diffidently. 'Actually, Sarge,' he replied, 'I've done that already.'

Fifty-six

'Take a right turn into the main street,' Colin Mount instructed, 'then carry on into the village.'

Regan waited for a break in the traffic, then did as he was told. He had decided to drive, with the dead author's son directing. 'So your dad and Ainsley were close,' he said. 'How about your two families? Did you know Carol and Wilkie?'

'Yes, I've met them,' the younger man replied. 'Carol's my dentist.'

'NHS?'

'Are you kidding? When my old dentist retired, I found out very quickly that there are damn few of those left. I complained to Dad; he said that's how it is now, and he suggested that I speak to Carol. I'm on Denplan. My teeth are in pretty good shape, so it's not that expensive. Mind you, they need to be, so whatever the cost, I'd bear it.'

'Why are your gnashers important?' the DI asked.

'Because of my evening job. I'm a television presenter, with STV.'

'Oops, sorry. I'm afraid I'm mostly a BBC viewer, that and Sky. What do you present?'

'News features, documentaries, arts programmes.'

'Not *Scotsport*, then?'

'Definitely not *Scotsport*. I barely know a football from a rugby ball.

One's got points at the end, I think. Take a left here,' he exclaimed, 'at the bank, then go straight on.'

'So you're the opposite of Ed Collins?'

'Who?'

'Carol Glover's boyfriend; he's a sports writer, I'm told by one of my colleagues.'

'Oh, him. Yes I suppose, although I barely know the guy. I did meet him at the Book Festival launch. I was there with Dad, and he was with Ainsley. He quizzed me about how to get a start with STV, but I told him that these days most of our sports guys were ex-players. The guy is football fixated, so I was surprised to see his by-line on a couple of Festival reviews. It was probably the Ainsley connection that got him in there. I read one yesterday, in fact, of a show at the Bedlam Theatre. I saw that show myself; I'm afraid his review was fucking rubbish. He might as well not have been there; he could have done it from a publicity flyer.'

'Where do I go now?' Regan asked. The road seemed to be coming to an end.

'Go through the gate ahead, then park anywhere. Dad's office is just around the corner. It was his pride and joy,' he said sadly. 'He designed it more or less himself; the architect drew up plans to his instructions.'

The area looked to be the approach to a farm, but its use was no longer confined to agriculture. Regan pulled up alongside a van, with the name and telephone number of a local construction firm painted on the side. They stepped out, into the midday warmth, the inspector following his guide past a building that looked like a workshop, or tiny factory, and past a Portakabin, stopping finally at a big hexagonal wooden structure, with a pointed roof. There were windows in each of the six walls, apart from the one that held the door, which was itself part-glazed. Colin Mount produced two keys from his pocket, and unlocked it. 'Carry on,' he murmured, standing to one side to allow Regan to enter.

The DI looked around, impressed instantly by his surroundings. The floor was high-quality hardwood, with rugs scattered around. Beside the door was a small kitchen area, with sink, kettle, microwave and fridge below. Beyond, an area was closed off. 'Toilet?' he asked.

'And shower. Dad went for a jog from here occasionally, if he needed to think through a piece of a story. He called it running, but I knew the truth.'

The rest of the area was open. Henry Mount's desk was set against a window which looked out across open fields, or would have if it had not been obscured by a large LCD screen. 'Is that a monitor or a television?'

'Both.'

There was a second desk, not far away. The DI pointed to it. 'Whose is that?'

'Mine,' the young man replied. 'As well as my television job, I look after all my dad's affairs.'

Regan's gaze moved on, taking in an ashtray, complete with a cigar butt, a keyboard, a mouse, a telephone, a clay pot containing pens with a variety of logos, gathered, he guessed, from hotels around the world, a thick notepad, a side table on which sat a printer and a modem router, and photographs of his wife and son. But something was missing. 'Where's the computer?'

'Dad used a laptop, but more or less as a hard disk. The monitor plugged into it; the keyboard, mouse and printer are all wireless.'

'Did he take it to Australia with him?'

'No. He decided not to; too much hassle. It'll be in his safe.'

The inspector frowned. 'I don't see a safe.'

Colin Mount smiled faintly. 'No, you don't.' He stepped to the door, and flipped over the rubber-backed doormat, set to catch the first footfall. 'Now you do. Another piece of my dad's design.' It was there, set flush to the floor. He found the keys once more, slipped one of them into a lock, turned it twice, and lifted the heavy lid. He frowned. 'Or I thought he'd decided not to,' he muttered to himself. He looked up at Regan. 'It's not here. The bloody thing's empty.'

Fifty-seven

'I have to say this, sir, this is impressive,' Michael Giarratano drawled. 'After my boss spoke to Scotland, I was expecting a phone call from somebody in Edinburgh. Three hours later, you're here. Did you beam down here, Scotty?'

As the massive detective chief superintendent stared down at him, the Australian realised that he was several chuckles short of being amused. 'Let me explain something to you, Inspector,' Mario McGuire said, in a voice that made the winter night seem even colder. 'Just because you and I happen to make up one complete Italian name between us, that doesn't imply any kinship, and it sure as hell doesn't entitle you to patronise me like some hick from the bloody outback. I'll tell you how I got down here. I was on effing holiday in Sydney when I had a call from my oppo back home, telling me about this situation. I left my partner back there, and caught an effing plane at about an hour's notice, with one minute to spare. Now I'm standing here, at going on eleven at night, in an effing crime tent with an effing comedian, freezing my effing nuts off, and there's no effing body. So why the fuck,' he barked, 'did your people bring me here?'

Giarratano straightened as if he had come to attention. 'I'm sorry, sir,' he replied formally, 'I was ordered to offer full cooperation, and my assumption was that you'd want to visit the crime scene.'

McGuire shivered. 'Inspector, it's dark, any potential witnesses are long gone and I'm looking at a chalk outline on the ground. I've seen chalk outlines before, although mostly in dodgy movies. I'd like to make the acquaintance of the late Mr Mount, preferably before your pathologists start carving him into sections. Can we do that?'

'Yessir. I'm sorry.'

The Scot relented. 'Ah, me too. I shouldn't have yelled at you. I'm a lousy traveller at the best of times, and I had to pass up the Proclaimers live at the Sydney Opera House to come down here. Where have you taken him?'

'The deceased has been taken to the city mortuary.' There was still a certain stiffness about Giarratano's tone as they stepped out of the tent that covered the spot where Henry Mount had fallen. 'It's not far away, just across the Yarra River, down in Southbank.'

'And where's the Yarra River?'

'Federation Square, where we are now, backs on to it.' He pointed to a large, baroque building on the other side of the street. 'And that over there, that's Flinders Street station. It looks pretty good in the daylight.'

'I'll check it out, if I'm still here when the sun rises.'

The Australian led the way across the square, to a waiting police vehicle. 'They're not doing the post-mortem till tomorrow morning,' he told McGuire as it moved off. 'Our pathologist takes the view that they won't be any less dead after a few hours, or any more.'

'I'm not so sure about the "any more" part,' the DCS grunted. 'Check him out after a couple of weeks and see how bloody dead he'll look then.'

As the inspector had promised, the mortuary was no more than a couple of minutes away. Their driver used the ambulance entrance and parked in a yard. Giarratano was familiar with the layout; he went straight to an unmarked door and rapped on it, then spoke briefly to the attendant who opened it. He looked over his shoulder. 'OK, sir,' he called. 'Come this way and they'll bring him out of the fridge for us.'

Just as well we know when he died, McGuire thought. Refrigeration wouldn't help determine a time if they needed to.

The two men were shown into a room. If he had been blindfolded, the Scot would still have known that they were in the autopsy theatre, from the overpowering disinfectant odour. Behind them a double door crashed open, as Henry Mount's body, on a trolley, was wheeled in.

The attendant pulled off the covering sheet and they could see that the corpse was still clothed, in jeans, a casual shirt emblazoned with a crest that McGuire recognised as that of Archerfield Golf Club, and a light jacket of smooth black leather. He frowned. 'Wouldn't he have been cold in that gear?'

'He'd only just stepped outside,' Giarratano told him. 'But it was quite warm for August, this afternoon. He'd just done a panel discussion. The Festival director told me that once they're finished on stage, the writers go outside to sign books. The desk was set up in the sun, so he'd have been OK.'

The big Scot leaned forward, examining the dead author's big head, shaved close by clippers. Bereft of life, the skin of Mount's face was like parchment, emphasising a faint stubble along the jawline, and it was unmarked, save for an old scar on the chin, a relic of a childhood fall, perhaps. 'Where's the wound?' he asked.

Giarratano nodded to the attendant, who stepped forward and turned the body on to its side, so that McGuire could see the back of the head. At the base of the skull, the remaining hair had been darkest and there, just at the point where it met the spinal column, was a dark mass of blood, flecked with white chips of bone.

'Indeed,' he said.

'Quite a shot,' the Australian murmured, professionally dispassionate, as if he was admiring a display of sporting skill. 'We don't have a witness who saw it fired, or who saw the moment of impact, but we think we've worked out the spot from where the shot was fired. Our

301

ballistics people reckon the victim must have been bending forward at the time. They reckon it's a small-calibre bullet, maybe soft-nosed, since it's still in there. A heavier calibre would have taken half his face off.'

'I can't fault that thinking,' the DCS murmured. He raised Mount's right hand, examined it, nodded, and laid it down again. 'Tell me, what was he doing when he was killed?'

'According to his publicist, and his Book Festival minder . . . I didn't get much sense out of either of them, they were both so shocked . . . he'd just signed a book for the last lady in his queue.'

'Yes, but what was he doing?'

'His publicist . . . she's from Sydney . . . had just handed him a bottle of beer, James Squire's Pilsner. You should try it while you're here; bloody good. And he was smoking a cigar.'

'What happened immediately after he went down?'

'The guy from the Book Festival leaned over him, and saw pretty quickly that there was plenty wrong. He ran off inside and found a doctor in no time at all. She felt for a pulse, didn't find one and started to give him CPR. When she went to tilt his head back to try mouth-to-mouth, she felt the blood at the back, took a look and figured out that he hadn't done that when he fell. She was pretty good; she took charge until we arrived, and had all the people moved back.'

'There were people gathered around him after he went down?'

'Yes, naturally.'

'Sure, but after you arrived and your crime scene team, what happened?'

'Standard procedures. We roped off the area, covered the body, took photographs from all angles, and began to interview witnesses.'

'Did you do a ground search?'

'Of course. We were looking for a shell casing, until the ballistics guys worked out that any casing must be on the roof of Flinders Street station. By that time it was too dark to search up there; we do that tomorrow morning, first light, before the commuters start to arrive.'

'You'll be wasting your time,' McGuire told him. 'You won't find any shell casing up there.'

'What makes you say that?' asked Giarratano, clearly resenting the dismissal of his pet theory.

'My partner, the lovely Paula ... she has an Italian name too, Viareggio. She's my guiding light. Your people bagged up everything they found at the scene, yes?'

'Sure they did, sir. It's all gone to the lab.'

'Do you remember if they found a cigar stub, the one that Mr Mount was smoking when he was shot?'

The inspector shook his head. 'I remember that they didn't. I asked them about it specifically. It must have been blown away by the wind, or carried off on some bystander's shoe.'

'Neither of those. It wasn't there.'

'Eh?'

McGuire sighed. 'I'll explain ... it's Michael, isn't it?' The Australian nodded. 'But first and foremost, Michael, I'm fucking starving, and if you've been working all night you must be too. I've got a room in the Grand Hyatt. Let's go there to check me in, find a place to eat, and then I'll tell you what happened to Henry Mount.'

Fifty-eight

Chief Constable Bob Skinner leaned back in his familiar chair and stared at a less familiar ceiling. 'Well,' he whispered, 'there's no going back now, young man.'

He thought back to his recent conversation with Brian Mackie; he was no longer in doubt as to the most momentous day of his career. It had arrived. The call had come at ten past twelve, an invitation to join the Police Board meeting, at Edinburgh's city council headquarters. When he had entered the room, the first thing that he had noticed was the smile on the face of the chair, Councillor Terence Secombe; that was the only sign he needed. There had been no last-minute upheaval.

'Mr Skinner,' the councillor had begun, as soon as he had taken his seat, 'given that you are the only suitable applicant, and that you have qualifying service outside this force within the meaning of the regulations, the Board has decided, unanimously, to offer you the position of chief constable for a period of seven years. As you know, we are required to seek approval of the Scottish Government; that has been given, by the Justice Minister, the matter having been delegated, on personal grounds, by the First Minister. Do you accept the post?'

He had taken a deep breath, and looked slowly round the table, before replying, 'Yes, sir, I do.'

And that had been all there was to it. He had lunched with the Board members, and with his predecessor (he could not recall having seen Jimmy look so relieved, or so relaxed), seated next to the chairman.

The discussion had been light, mostly about the relative fortunes of Heart of Midlothian and Motherwell football clubs, but at one point Councillor Secombe had leaned close. 'One thing, Bob,' he had said softly. 'During our discussion of your appointment, the only reservation that was raised, by one of the SNP members, concerned your relationship with the First Minister. I don't need to tell you about the regulation prohibiting serving officers from getting actively involved in politics; all I will say is, watch your back in that respect. Say and do nothing that might compromise you, and make sure that Aileen doesn't either. When's the wedding, by the way? It hasn't gone unnoticed that she's been wearing a ring.'

'Soon, Terry, soon,' he had replied. 'But nobody outside our circle will know about it until after it's happened.'

'Wise man.'

Oh, but am I? he thought, making a mental note to change the ugly light fittings in his new office. If I was a target before, through Aileen, what am I now?

Sir James had stayed with the Board members, but he had declined coffee and had returned to Fettes. The first thing he had done was to tell Brian Mackie, Gerry Crossley and Ruth Pye what had happened. The second was to wheel his chair across the corridor and put the outgoing chief's big black rocker in its place. The third was to transfer the contents of his safe, his personal records and files, and his computer to their new home.

He was still contemplating the future when there was a knock on the door and Alan Royston, the force's media relations manager, was shown in, offering congratulations. Skinner sensed that he was a shade nervous, as relations between them had not always been cordial. He decided to clear the decks. 'Thanks, Alan,' he said. 'I'm looking forward to working with you in the future. What's first?'

'You should see this release, sir. It's being issued any time now by the

Board, through the city council press office, announcing your appointment, with immediate effect. We'll have the media on our backs, and I'd recommend getting that over within one hit, by holding a general press conference at four o'clock.'

'Set it up. I'll wear the deputy's uniform. The new one won't be ready for a few days.'

'Do you want Sir James to be there?'

'That will be his decision. But I don't want the Board chairman, even if he asks to be there. He's warned me to steer clear of politics; he's going to find that I'm taking his advice from the off.'

Fifty-nine

The restaurant was called Cento Venti. 'I thought Italian was appropriate,' said Inspector Giarratano as he led the way into the square dining room, not huge, but crammed with tables, of which half were occupied, 'and this is the best. Is your hotel room OK?'

'It's fine, thanks, Michael. I'm sorry I kept you waiting, but I had to check in with Paula. She's taking this interruption pretty well, and I want to keep it that way. I told her I still plan to be on a plane back to Sydney tomorrow.'

'What about your other investigation in Edinburgh? How's that going?'

'No arrest, and not even the sniff of one, that's all I know.'

The head waiter appeared before them and showed them to a window table. 'Would you like a drink?' Giarratano asked, as the man handed them menus.

'I'll try some of that Squire's Pilsner, if they have it.' He glanced at the list. 'As for food, I'll have spaghetti the way a whore would make it.' The Australian's eyes widened; the waiter smiled. 'Ah,' said McGuire, 'so the name's just for show. You don't speak the language.'

'*Prego* and *grazie*; that's my limit,' the other man admitted. 'I've never been to the northern hemisphere, never mind Italy.'

'Spaghetti alla puttanesca,' the Scot explained, 'or any other sort of pasta for that matter. What I just said is what the name of the sauce means, literally. It originated in Naples, and there are a few theories

307

about why it's called that. One is that it's a cheap meal that prostitutes could make quickly, between punters, so to speak. Did you know, by the way, that in Italy, brothels were once state owned, which made the hookers civil servants? This place isn't too precious to have it on the menu. Some are, or if they do they choose to call it "Pasta alla buona donna", that's "Good woman's pasta" in English, but there's a lot of irony in that name.'

'I better have it too,' Giarratano decided. 'It'll give me bragging rights in the office tomorrow.'

The head waiter left, reappearing almost instantly with McGuire's beer, and with a Victoria Bitter for Giarratano, and explaining that since the sauce was freshly prepared, it would take a few minutes.

'That's fine,' the big DCS told him. 'That's the way it should be.' He took a mouthful of his lager. 'You weren't kidding me,' he declared. 'This is damn good.'

'We're proud of it,' the inspector replied. 'Bet you don't get that in Edinburgh.'

'No, mostly it's Fosters.' He smiled at the reaction. 'I'm serious. We do; that and four X.'

'Edinburgh's pretty cosmopolitan, is it?'

'Very. I'm a walking example; the half of me that isn't Italian is Irish.'

'But which are you, mostly?'

'Actually, I'm entirely Scottish. I was born there and brought up there. My parents were both second generation. My Italian grandmother's still alive; Nana Viareggio, a fearsome old lady.'

'Didn't you say your partner's name was Viareggio?'

'It is. We're cousins; her dad . . . he's dead now . . . was my mum's brother. Paula says she carried a torch for me all her life, and that a couple of years ago it finally set fire to my shirt tail.'

'And you?'

'I was married for a few years, to another police officer. It didn't work out. Finally, I figured out why, and Paulie and I got together.'

'Funny,' the inspector murmured. 'I'm married to a cop, and we're fine. The job didn't have anything to do with your problems, did it?'

'Not at all. Mags outranked me for most of the time we were together, but that was no big deal. We're both chief superintendents now, but I suspect she may get ahead of me again, when she goes back to work . . . she's just had a daughter, by another detective.'

'So that marriage worked; that's a relief.'

McGuire's face darkened. 'That marriage was perfect, but he was killed on duty.'

'Oh no. I'm sorry.'

'Me too.' He realised that his beer was finished and signalled the waiter for another. It arrived with the food.

The two men ate in virtual silence, broken occasionally by questions from the Australian about the visitor's first impressions of his country.

'I'm told you have a saying,' McGuire responded, 'that Sydney's like your tarty sister and Melbourne's like your mum. I can see what they mean about Sydney. There's something else we have to do before I go, so maybe if I'm here long enough tomorrow, I'll get to see how this place feels.'

Giarratano waited until they were both finished before going on. 'So what is it?' he asked, as the Scot wiped the last traces of the puttanesca sauce from his mouth. 'This thing we have to do.'

'We need to have a look at the late Mr Mount's hotel room. Do you know where he was staying?'

'The Festival puts its guests up in the Sofitel, just along the road. Mount's room's been sealed, so hopefully no housekeepers will have been in there, touching anything. Are we looking for anything specific?'

'Yes, and this is where I come back to my clever partner. Paula and I are both great readers of crime fiction. The guy who was murdered back home, Ainsley Glover, he was a big favourite of mine. Paulie, she's read the entire Henry Mount catalogue, and she's got it filed away in her big brain.'

'And?'

'I'll get there, but let me stay with Glover for now. When he was found dead, the first thought was "heart attack"; and that's what it seemed like until the pathologist took another look and found exactly what had happened to him. But the odd coincidence was that in one of his books, there was a storyline which might have described his death exactly, and it was a murder. He'd been drugged and injected with a fatal dose of glucose, not insulin. He was diabetic,' McGuire explained. 'Moreover, after his death, someone broke into his house and stole his computer, with all his work on it.'

Giarratano's eyes narrowed; he leaned across the table. 'Go on,' he whispered.

'Right. So early this evening I have a call from my mate, my deputy, telling me that Mount is dead in Melbourne and asking me to get down here and report. A scenario of two top Scottish crime writers being bumped off within three days of each other, with no connection between them, strikes us both as highly unlikely. Paula was with me at the time, and when she heard what had happened, she dug into her Mastermind-sized Henry Mount database and remembered something from a book called *Havana Death*. Before I tell you what it was, I should also tell you that the guy didn't make it up. He borrowed the idea from things that actually happened, in Vietnam, and other places. In it, there's this guy, chairman of the US Federal Reserve, who upsets the Mafia. But he's powerful, and he's well-protected so they can't get to him. Then, one night, he's at home, in his study, behind bullet-proof glass; his wife goes in and he's dead, shot. Turns out the guy was a cigar smoker, and that he always bought his supply, the same brand, all the time, from the same store. When they examine him, and the forensic people go to work, they discover that one of his cigars was rigged. There was a cartridge inside it, bullet pointing inwards, and when the cigar burned down to a certain point . . . bang!' He slapped the table and Giarratano jumped.

'Michael, when the pathologist does the post-mortem tomorrow, he's not going to find a bullet inside the cranium, because what we saw tonight was an exit wound, not entry. On the other hand, he will find traces of burnt tobacco inside the man's mouth, and in the wound itself. Trust me, these devices exist and they work. The Vietcong used them in cigarettes, thirty years ago, to take out American soldiers. So did the Khmer Rouge, in Cambodia. Simple, nasty, deadly. Your people didn't find Mount's cigar butt, because it disintegrated. But if they'd looked, as I did in the morgue, they'd have seen that the first two fingers of his right hand were scorched on the inside from the flash when the detonator was triggered.'

The inspector frowned. 'I'm trying to recall whether there were any other cigars on the body.'

'Maybe yes, maybe no. That's why we need to look at his room. In the hotel, I made a call back home from my room, for an update. There are two new developments. Just like with Glover, Mount's computer and his records have been stolen from his office. Also, I'm told he always smoked the same brand of expensive Cuban cigar. Now I don't believe he'd come out here on a trip like this assuming that he could find them here. I reckon he brought his supply with him. If there's any left, and we find it in his room, we can possibly trace the source, and we'll be that much closer to his killer.'

'So whose investigation is this?'

McGuire smiled. 'That, my friend, is a hell of a good question. Mount died here, yes. But the crime was committed by the person who put the device in the cigar, and I'm as certain as I can be that happened in Scotland. So what do you want to do? Toss for it?'

Sixty

'How are you doing, Becky?' asked Sammy Pye.

'I'm at the end of the road,' his colleague confessed. 'There is nothing I can say for sure, nothing I'll be able to declare under oath. It's possible that somebody tried to access the victim's files on this computer, but nobody will ever prove it, far less who it was.'

'The daughter could have done it, but she's eliminated as a suspect.'

'She is, but there's one other. There was a second guest screen-name on her internet account: *sllinco*, with two "l"s. What's the boyfriend's name? Ray mentioned it, but it's slipped my mind.'

'Collins.'

'There you are, then; it's an anagram.'

'You haven't been in touch with Carol about this, have you?'

'Of course not. This is your investigation, Sam; I'm only on the periphery. I wouldn't go interviewing your witnesses without asking you.'

'Sorry, Becky, course you wouldn't. Do you think you can get into *sllinco*'s files?'

'I can have a go, but ideally I'd need the same sort of information you gave me on Glover.'

'That would be difficult.'

'Then I'll try with the basics. You never know . . .'

'Thanks.'

Pye was about to hang up when Stallings spoke again. 'Before you go, when am I getting my DC back? I gather he's been kidnapped and taken down to Leith.'

'Hey, he came of his own free will. We no longer needed to be based in Charlotte Square, so I decided we might as well go back home. Look, I'm grateful for the loan of Haddock. He's in the middle of a specific task right now; I'll look at releasing him once that's done, unless . . .' he said, heavily, 'we get sucked into the Henry Mount investigation. That's going to break in the media eventually, although the Aussies have helped us by keeping a lid on the name. From what I hear, they're going to release it at a press conference in Melbourne at ten a.m. local time.'

'What's that with us?'

'One a.m. Alan Royston's going to have a busy night, with journalists looking for the connection between the two murders.'

'Have we established one?'

'The head of CID reckons we have.'

'Neil McIlhenney?'

'No, the real head of CID, DCS McGuire. He's on holiday in Australia; he's gone to Melbourne and he's seen the body. He's convinced; so much so that he's told me to get up to Fred Noble's place sharpish, and offer him protection.'

'Who's he?'

'Ah, I forgot, you're a newcomer. Three days ago, this part of Scotland could boast of three internationally famous crime writers. Now we're down to one, and that's Noble.'

'He must be nervous.'

'I hope he is. If he is next on some nutter's list, being nervous will be no bad thing. Give me a call if you get any more out of the Glover daughter's computer.' He hung up and walked out of his office, into the CID suite, where Haddock had taken over the desk vacated by the holidaying Griff Montell. 'Sauce,' he said, 'any feedback from those emails you sent?'

'Three results, sir,' the DC replied. 'Two of them are negative; the Bosnian message and the one to *Ratko7* were both returned as undeliverable, addresses closed down. But while you were on the phone, I had a call from a woman in Cambridge, Massachusetts, Dr Mary Warmly.'

'Odd name, even for America.'

'Yes, but it explains her email, *Marythreecool*. She's a historian, on the staff at Harvard University, and she says that she's an expert on the wars that followed the break-up of Yugoslavia. She told me that she didn't know Glover but that she had an email from him, in April, asking if she knew anything about the four names on the list in DCC Martin's safe. She replied, saying she couldn't help him. A couple of days later, he phoned her. He asked if she was sure about this, and gave her the names again. She repeated that she didn't recognise any of them, and she asked him what it was about. He got quite excited, she said, and told her that he was afraid that two of them, Danica Anelić and Aca Nicolić, were dead, and that he was trying to find the other two, if they were still alive. He knew that she had contacts in Serbia and Bosnia and visited there, and wondered if she had heard anything at all that might help him. She said no, yet again, then she asked what was behind it all, but he said he couldn't tell her that and hung up.'

'Did she ever hear from him again?'

'No.'

Pye frowned, and scratched his head, pondering. He looked across the room, to find that Wilding was watching him. 'April,' the sergeant murmured. 'Wasn't it April when Glover had lunch with Andy Martin up in St Andrews, and gave him that list to put in his safe?'

'Yes, it was. But why did he do that? Because he had twigged that his anti-Trident views had brought him to the attention of the intelligence services, and that he was being watched.'

'And he was right. We know that from the new chief constable himself, don't we? Didn't he tell Neil McIlhenney that he had checked, and that it was true?'

'Yes, he did,' the DI agreed. 'But when he had his sit-down with DCC Martin and told him his story, did Glover ever mention the word Trident? I was there on Sunday when Andy let us in on it, and I don't remember him saying that he did.'

'You're suggesting what exactly?'

'That Andy assumed, correctly as it turned out, that it was the Trident connection that had attracted the spooks to Glover but that the man himself might have believed he was being watched because of something else, something unrelated. This list he left with him clearly has fuck all to do with Trident, not unless Serbia has a fleet of nuclear submarines that we know sod all about.'

'So what are we going to do?'

'First we're going to see Fred Noble, make sure he's still intact, and work out a plan to keep him that way. That's top priority. After that, I'm taking this up the line, all the way to the top if I have to.'

Sixty-one

The pictures on the wall have been changed already, Neil McIlhenney noted as he took his seat alongside ACC Brian Mackie around another innovation, the new chief constable's meeting table. Opposite was Chief Inspector David Mackenzie, with Skinner, in uniform, between them.

'I'm about to face the media,' he explained, 'hence the silver braid, but I wanted to speak to you guys first. I won't be taking too many questions down there, but one or two things might be said that you should hear first.' He glanced around. 'What I don't need to tell you is how sad part of me is feeling; there's going to be a ghost in this room for a long time to come. Jimmy has decided that he wants to leave quietly, and so as soon as Alan Royston has all the press gathered in the gym,' he checked his watch, 'in about ten minutes, he'll make his exit. Brian's told everyone else, and we'll all be there too, lined up to say farewell. Gerry will give us the word when he's ready.'

'The press might be miffed when they realise they've missed it,' Mackie suggested.

'They'll get over it. Until he leaves it, this is Jimmy's building, and things will happen as he wants them to happen.' He smiled. 'After that . . . what's going to be different?' He looked at each of his companions in turn. 'It may be that a new deputy will come in and affect my thinking on this, but my intention is that change will be minimised. You all know that in his later years as chief, Sir James

316

effectively delegated control of criminal investigation to me.' He paused, as if inviting comment, but there was none. 'Well, guys, I'm keeping it. My intention is that the head of CID,' he nodded towards McIlhenney, 'and in his absence, you, Neil, will continue to report directly to me. I will also take personal command of special operations as they arise, state visits, EU ministers' meetings, and the like. Special Branch, though, will continue to report to the deputy, whoever he or she may be.' He took a deep breath. 'I know there's been a lot of speculation, assumptions, even, that Andy will come back to fill that post, but that is a decision for the Police Board to make. I know the regs say they consult me, but I won't try to influence them in any way, unless I really do not fancy a particular candidate. However, whether the job goes to him, or to you, Brian . . . I can't order you to apply for it, but I hope you will . . . or to someone else, the new person will find himself . . . or herself . . . handling some of the things that were previously in Sir James's court. There are politics attached to my post, and I want to keep as far away from them as I can, at least for long as my other half remains First Minister. The new deputy will be responsible for day-to-day relations with the Police Board, with Scottish Government, and with cross-border matters involving the Home Office.' He turned to Mackenzie, immaculate in his chief inspector's uniform.

'That person's going to take time to settle into the job, David, even if it's Brian, or someone else from within. While he, or she, does, and beyond that, they will need support, and you will be the guy who provides it. Your job at the moment is command corridor adjutant; and you might still be called that, but you will have more clout. If the new deputy is on leave, or for any other reason can't handle, let's say, a meeting with government civil servants, he won't pass it up the line to me, he'll delegate it to you. And just in case the mini-mandarins feel slighted at being palmed off on to a chief inspector, you will be promoted to superintendent, with immediate effect, so get your epaulettes changed.'

Mackenzie's face flushed with pleasure, but before he could speak, there was a knock at the door. Gerry Crossley's head appeared. 'That's the press checked in, sir.'

'OK,' Skinner replied. 'Spread the word, and get everyone in position at the front door. Sir James is in my old room. I'll collect him and escort him downstairs. We'll be a couple of minutes, that's all.' He turned back to his colleagues. 'Anything else, before we wind up?'

'Two things . . . Chief,' said Neil McIlhenney. 'One's for information, on the other I need a decision. First, Mario's established, for sure as far as he and I are concerned, that Henry Mount's death is linked to Glover's.'

'Fred Noble?' The question was instantaneous.

'He's being taken care of. The second thing is this. The only potential suspect we have for the Mustafic murder is Playfair, the guy you met. He's disappeared, but in trying to trace him, the only thing we've established for sure is that he's been using a false name. DS McDermid has been to see Derek Baillie at the official site where his group's stopping, and she's come back with a photo that has Playfair in it. It's good enough for us to extract an image for issue to the media. George Regan has asked if he can do that. What do you reckon?'

'Do it. Issue the image, but have an artist play with it to come up with an impression of what he would look like without a beard and with his head shaved. He'd stand out like a pillar box the way he looked when I met him, so if he's on the run, there's every chance he's tried to change his appearance. But first,' he cautioned, 'you have to get Crown Office permission. Get hold of the Lord Advocate or the Solicitor General; tell them I've authorised the request as I believe it's in the public interest. Get on to it as soon as we've seen Proud Jimmy off into retirement.' He stood, and the others followed his lead automatically. As if I was a head of state, he thought.

As they headed for the stairs, he crossed the corridor, to the room that had been his, and stepped inside, with yet another pang of regret. He heard the phone ring, somewhere behind him, but ignored it.

Sir James Proud stood at the window; he had changed out of the uniform that he had worn for the Board meeting . . . worn for the last time, in fact . . . into a pale green linen suit. It struck Skinner that he had shed five years in age, along with the blue serge. 'Christ, Bob,' he exclaimed, 'you look like the prison governor come to take me to my doom. Where's the chaplain?'

Skinner laughed. 'Thanks for the warning. I feel like an old friend, come to send you on a long holiday; I must make sure that's clear to everyone.'

'You are sending me on holiday, of course, since I don't start drawing pension until the middle of next month. Better to go out this way, though.'

'What's your first act as a free man?'

'Chrissie and I are being picked up this evening by a chauffeur-driven car, and taken to Manchester. That's why we can't join you for dinner later. We spend the night in the airport hotel and tomorrow we fly to Singapore, first class. We spend a few days there, then we go to Penang for a week, and finally back to Singapore for what's left of a fortnight. It's my lovely wife's retirement present to us both: she's been saving in secret for years for it. Once that's over, we get on with the rest of our lives. Do you know, I've had three offers of company directorships already?'

'It doesn't surprise me. Are you going to accept them?'

'If I think them appropriate, I'll consider them. Chrissie says she's not having me lolling around the house all day. She wants to move, too; somewhere down your way, she says.'

'If Lady Chrissie wants it, then it'll happen. I'll look forward to having you as a neighbour, boss.'

'Boss?' Proud Jimmy chuckled. 'Not any more, son.'

Skinner grasped the older man's right hand in both of his; for a moment his eyes moistened. 'Sir James,' he said, 'you will always be the boss to me.'

'That's nice to know. I'll always be available to you, of course, whenever you need to bounce things off someone outside the office, and away from home. I've never told you this, but I admire the way that you and Aileen have handled your growing relationship. As Terry Secombe told you, I think, it worried some of the Board members, but he and I damped that down pretty firmly. Now,' he declared, 'I mustn't keep that car waiting. Lead on, Chief Constable.'

His successor nodded, opened the door and stepped aside. Gerry Crossley was waiting outside, ready to accompany them downstairs, although he and Proud had already said a private goodbye. 'Two calls for you, sir,' he told Skinner. 'One from Mr Laidlaw, at Curle Anthony and Jarvis, and the other from DCC Martin. Neither left a message, but Mr Martin did say his call was urgent.'

'Not more urgent than this, though, Gerry. I'll return them both when I get back upstairs, after I've sparred with the media and had my picture taken.'

The three men walked slowly downstairs into the foyer of the headquarters building. Police officers of all ranks, CID and uniform, and civilian staff formed two lines. They broke into spontaneous applause as Sir James appeared. He paused, smiled, then made his way through the honour guard, shaking hands with each person and thanking them, by name. Finally, he stepped through the door, with Skinner behind him. A police car waited outside, its uniformed driver, Sergeant Ian McCall, who had won a ballot for the honour of taking the old chief into retirement, standing at attention. Proud Jimmy returned his salute, shook hands with his protégé for the last time, then slid into the back seat. A few seconds later, he was gone.

Skinner stood, looking after the car as it cleared the gateway. Eventually he became aware of Royston standing beside him. 'On with the new, Alan?' he murmured.

'We better get to it, Chief,' said the civilian. 'The natives have figured out what's been going on, and they're restless.'

'Let's chuck them a few buns, then.'

The two men walked back inside, turning right and heading for the gym, where major press briefings were held. 'Before you go in there,' Royston murmured, 'I get the impression that there's something up. Nobody's said anything, but I have a feeling that you might have more to deal with than your own agenda.'

The chief constable frowned. 'Maybe they've got wind of Henry Mount's death earlier than we thought.'

'That could be.' The media manager pulled open one of the double doors. 'Whatever,' he said 'we'll find out soon.'

Skinner stepped into the hall. As usual, his place was at the far end, beneath the force crest on the wall. He made his way past the crowd, television cameras positioned at the back, press and radio reporters towards the front, and photographers to the side. His table was littered with the usual array of microphones. He took his place facing the crowd, surprised once more by the number of journalists that Edinburgh could turn out, and a little flattered that they had come because of him. But was that the only reason? Bearing in mind Royston's warning, as the cameras flashed, he studied the faces, trying to read them. Most were smiling, but one or two were sombre. Expectant? Maybe. His bellwethers sat in the front row: John Hunter, the ancient freelance, unchallenged doyen of the press corps, and Jock Fisher, chief reporter of the *Saltire*. Many years before, there had been an *Evening News* reporter called John Gunn, and it was a source of regret to the two veterans that he had not survived to their time, otherwise, as they put it, often, 'You'd have had hunting, fishing and shooting sitting side by side.' He smiled at them; Hunter nodded back, amiably, and Fisher gave him a brief smile, but yes, there was something behind it, an awkwardness, perhaps.

'Good afternoon, ladies and gentlemen,' he began. 'I'll take your questions, but first I'd like to say a few words. As you've been told, today the Joint Police Board offered me the position of chief constable of this force, and I'm pleased to say that I have accepted. I feel sad and proud . . . yes,' he grinned, 'I should use that word . . . all at once: sad to see the departure of a great police officer, and a great friend, in Sir James, but proud to be given the honour of succeeding him.' He stopped, leaning back and looking Hunter in the eye. His seniority was rarely challenged; if it was, by an outsider who did not know the ropes, the intruder was always ignored. 'John,' Skinner invited.

'Is this the culmination of your career, Bob?'

'I hope not. I have a seven-year contract and plenty to do.'

'Will there be changes in the way the force is run?'

'None that you or the public will notice, I hope.'

'When will the new deputy be appointed?'

'That's a matter for the Board.'

'On your advice.'

'No. The rules don't go that far; they say I may be consulted.'

'Is the First Minister pleased?' a woman asked. He looked in her direction, and recognised her: Rebecca Unthank, the *Daily Mail* political reporter, not a regular presence at police briefings.

'OK,' said Skinner. 'Here's the ground rule for this and all future occasions. I will be as open to the media as possible, but my private life is off limits. I won't answer questions about my partner under any circumstances, and the best that's going to happen to anyone who persists in asking them is that they'll be ignored.'

'Does that apply to every member of your family?' Unthank shot back.

The chief constable's eyes turned to ice as he stared at her, unblinking. He said nothing, but she seemed to shrink and her eyes went to the floor. A ripple seemed to go through the crowd, a faint collective sigh. 'What?' he snapped.

When no one replied, he looked at Hunter. 'John, what's up?'

The old man shook his head. 'This is not for me, Bob,' he replied. 'I wouldn't touch it with the proverbial.'

He moved on to Fisher. 'Jock,' he asked, 'are you going to let me in on the joke?'

'No joke, Bob,' the *Saltire* reporter sighed. 'I wish it was; I hate these things.' He reached into a side pocket of his jacket, took out a brown envelope that only just fitted, and passed it across the table. 'About half an hour before this meeting was due to begin, every news desk in Scotland received these by email, from an unknown address, with no covering message. I had our IT people trace the source. They were sent from an internet terminal in a café in Leith. Apparently you don't have to register with it; you just sit down, put money in the slot, and go ahead.'

Skinner ripped the envelope apart; two photographs fell on to his table, face up. He picked them up and stared at them. The first was a location shot, showing a building, centred on an uncurtained window. Alex's apartment building: Alex's apartment: Alex's bedroom. In the shot, there were two figures, close together, indistinct, but one, a dark-haired woman, was wearing a blue robe, and the other, a fair-haired man, was naked from the waist up. The second image, taken with a telephoto lens, was much closer. The blue robe was gone, and the woman was unfastening the man's belt. The figures were recognisable, all too recognisable: Alex, with Andy Martin.

'There were others,' he heard Jock Fisher say, somewhere. 'I chose not to bring them with me.'

He stared at the images, then turned them over. He was about to rip them into shreds, he was about to slam them on to the table, he was about to explode with rage, when he remembered that he was under the scrutiny of a room full of people, that the video cameras were still running, and that the stills photographers were still snapping. And so, albeit with a great effort, he laid the pictures down, and looked up at Fisher. 'Yes?' he asked. He spoke quietly, but in that instant, the air in the room seemed to have been chilled.

'My paper wouldn't dream of using those, Bob,' the *Saltire* reporter replied, 'but their very existence is a story and we can't ignore that.'

'Is that your daughter?' Rebecca Unthank shouted, her courage seemingly restored.

'I didn't answer your earlier question,' he told her. 'For the avoidance of doubt, I will not discuss any family matters in this forum with you or anyone else.'

'Were you aware that she's still seeing DCC Martin, even though he's married?' the woman persisted.

'Are we speaking the same language?' he fired back. 'Are you short of comprehension as well as manners?'

His gaze returned to Hunter and Fisher. 'Listen,' he began, in a voice loud enough to be heard at the back of the room, 'I understand and respect the job that the responsible media have to do, but I won't tolerate irresponsibility, wherever I find it. The only other personal comment I'm prepared to make is this: I regret that people who take and disseminate photographs like those I've just been shown are not subject, in this country, to criminal prosecution.' He paused, frowning, as Alan Royston approached, and handed him a folded note. He opened it, read it, nodded, then looked back across the crowd of reporters. 'Some news for you,' he told them. 'I've just received this message from Mitchell Laidlaw, chairman of Curle Anthony and Jarvis, solicitors. Any newspaper or broadcast organisation that publishes those images, or names the people in them, will be in breach of an interim interdict that has just been granted to my daughter by the court.' He stood. 'Any other questions you can put to me through Mr Royston,' he said. 'I have a job to be getting on with.'

He swept from the room, impassive, as a young journalist tried to block his way, only to be swept aside by the media manager. He was aware of eyes upon him as he walked from the gym and along the corridor, until he turned the corner and was out of sight.

He took the stairs two at a time, and strode along to his new office, pausing to open the door of its anteroom, where his secretary sat. 'I'll return Andy Martin's call now, Gerry,' he said. 'I want you to listen in to this one,' he added.

He had just eased himself in behind his desk when the phone rang. He was about to snatch it up when he stopped himself, and took a deep breath. 'Calm,' he whispered.

'Bob,' said Andy Martin.

'Do you know what you've done?' he asked, conversationally, as if his toe had just been stood on, nothing more. 'My introduction to the media as chief constable, and I find myself looking at my daughter, in the buff, easing her way into your jockeys.'

'Christ, Bob, listen—'

'I don't want to listen to you, Andy,' he said. 'I know it takes two to tango, but you have to understand that I'm biased here. I will do anything to protect my daughter, and her interests, private and professional. I'm going to assume that Karen knows about this, or will find out. Well, you make fucking certain that you give her my sincere, personal apologies for Alex's involvement with you. And this is personal too; you can be sure that I will do everything in my power to thwart any thought you might have of ever working in the same city as my kid again. You will not see her again, you will not approach her, you will not accept any misguided calls she may make to you. Now, I don't imagine that you rang her doorbell and asked her if she fancied a shag. You were in her house, so I must assume that she invited you there. Well, she's got my genes, so in her personal life she's going to make a few mistakes. To be honest, I always regarded you as one of them, although I kept that to myself when you were together. I'll help her through this. What you have to do now is get your sorry arse home, get down on your knees, and rescue what's left of your marriage, if you can. As for your career, you've crossed me, so that's fucked.'

He replaced the phone in its cradle, gently. A few seconds later, Gerry Crossley came into the room, his face paler than before. 'Boss, did you really want me to hear that?' he asked.

'Oh yes,' the chief constable replied. 'If I hadn't known you were on the line, I reckon I would really have lost it with my former best friend. Now, get me my daughter, please . . . but don't listen in this time.'

It took the secretary a few minutes to make the connection, but finally he buzzed through. 'I have Ms Skinner for you, sir,' he said.

'Hi, kid,' Bob murmured, as she came on line. 'You've had a tough afternoon, I hear.'

'Oh, Pops,' she sighed; he wondered if she was in tears. 'I'm so sorry; for this to have happened today of all days, and for it to have embarrassed you. I heard about your press briefing from Alan Royston; it's just awful. There's nothing I can say to excuse myself. It was a one-off, a meeting between the two of us, for a chat, as it was for a while, until it got out of control. I should never have put us in that position. It was my fault, so don't be too hard on Andy.'

'Alexis,' he told her, 'I couldn't be too hard on Andy, short of killing him. You're vulnerable where he's concerned, and he took advantage of you. The guy's got a pregnant wife, for Christ's sake.'

'Dad, don't make me feel worse. You and he have been friends for ever. He even gave you a clear run at your new job.'

'I never asked him to do that. Anyway, the truth is, he wouldn't have had a prayer against me, and he knew it.'

'I'll give tonight's dinner a miss,' said Alex suddenly.

'Then it's cancelled,' her father replied firmly. 'If you're not there, it doesn't go ahead, and Aileen will back me in that. You'll be among friends, so you're coming.'

'I need them,' she confessed heavily. 'I've just had Karen on the phone. That's why I was delayed taking your call. Mitchell Laidlaw wasn't going to let the switchboard put her through, but I insisted.'

'How was she?'

'Icy and tearful, all at once; not surprising, in the circumstances. She told me that I was a treacherous slapper, and that she'd like to tear my hair out by the roots. I told her more or less what I've just told you, and said that Andy was mortified afterwards, that he called me later to say it could never happen again.'

'He did that?' Bob barked. 'Better to have said nothing at all than to rub your nose in your own mistake. The bastard! I tell you, they're going to be selling tickets at the next ACPOS meeting.'

'Dad, stay away from him!' she said apprehensively.

'It'll be the other way round, baby; I'm pretty sure of that. I saw him yesterday; if he was my true friend, and yours, he would have told me about what had happened between you, and apologised. But he didn't have the balls to do either. He won't come near me for a long time, if ever.'

'Oh, Pops!'

'That's how it is, wee one. Subject closed. Now, this interdict of yours; that was fast work.'

'The photographs arrived in my email,' she told him, 'followed shortly afterwards by a call from a *Sun* reporter. I told Mitchell at once, of course; what affects me affects the firm. He went straight up to the court and got the interdict preventing publication.'

'Is he happy that it will hold?' he asked.

'He said that if it doesn't, the editor who publishes the pictures, or even our names, will wind up in jail for contempt. We'll go for a full interdict in due course.'

'In a couple of days, kid,' her father assured her, 'this will have blown over as far as the media are concerned. They'll have some sort of a story today and tomorrow, but with no names and no pictures, it won't feature very high up the news schedules. Still, you're staying at our place tonight, no question.'

'If you say so.' She fell silent for a few moments. 'Pops, what I don't understand is who would do this, and why? Those pictures weren't taken by accident. Somebody was watching my flat. And the timing too . . . just before your unveiling as chief constable. Is somebody out to get me? Have I upset a client that I don't know about?'

Bob chuckled, taking her by surprise. 'Alex, from what I know of your firm's client list, it's unlikely to include someone who'd take it out on a junior member of staff by photographing her in an intimate situation. You're a bystander in this business, even if you're not entirely innocent. Don't worry, I've been wondering the same as you. Whoever's behind this is either after me . . . but when I ask myself who would be that crazy, I can't come up with a name . . . or it's Andy who was the target. I promise you this, I'll find this character. When I do I'm going nowhere near him myself, but I'll have him charged with breach of the peace, that wonderful Scottish catch-all which lets you do just about anyone for just about anything. And the first person I'm going looking for is a man who calls himself Coben. See you tonight, babe,' he said softly. 'Keep your chin up, but most of all,' he laughed, 'please keep your bedroom curtains closed in future.'

Sixty-two

Fred Noble stood, his right hand grasping the high mantelshelf of the Victorian fireplace in his drawing room, so hard that his knuckles shone white, contrasting sharply with its black marble, and with his customary dark clothing. 'Henry?' he murmured. 'You have to be kidding me.'

'I wish I was,' Sammy Pye told the author, watching as his wife, Amanda, handed him a large malt whisky. She waved the bottle at the DI and at Ray Wilding, but they both declined the unspoken offer. 'One of our colleagues happens to be in Australia; he's in Melbourne right now, he's seen the body and he's established the cause of death, subject to autopsy confirmation.'

'What was it?' asked June Connelly, from an armchair.

'Before I go into that,' Pye replied, 'I must stress that what's said here has to stay here, within this room.' He looked up at Noble. 'But the time has come for you to be fully in the picture . . . especially you, sir. I know that you were friends with Mr Mount, but did that extend to reading his work?'

'Of course. I've read the lot, I think.'

'In that case, do you remember a book called *Havana Death*, and how one of the characters is murdered?'

The tall man frowned for a second, then his eyes widened. 'The old CIA trick, with the bullet in the cigar? That's how Henry died?'

'So it seems.' Pye turned to Connelly. 'You were Mr Glover's

329

agent,' he said, 'so you'll be familiar with a story called *Black Sugar*.'

She nodded. 'I'm familiar with it, but I confess I read a hell of a lot of crime novels; not all the details stick in my memory.'

'The victim's a diabetic,' Wilding explained. 'He's drugged, and then killed by a massive injection of glucose. That's what happened to Ainsley Glover. That information's been withheld from the public, and we'll be asking the Australians not to go into too much detail about Mr Mount's death. We don't have too many cards in our hands in this investigation. That degree of confidentiality might help us along the way.'

'Plus' Pye added, 'the last thing we need is a press contest to see who can write the most garish headline.'

Noble lowered himself into the empty chair that faced Connelly across the hearth, taking his wife's hand as she came to sit on the arm. 'First Ainsley, now Henry,' she said. 'This is like Agatha bloody Christie, Ten Little What-nots. Are you telling us that Fred's next on the list?'

'I hope we're not,' the DI replied, sincerely. 'But we don't need to spell out the need for caution. I've been authorised to offer you both protection at any level you'd like. You could move to a safe house, we could move a personal protection officer in here, or we could have uniforms outside, round the clock. Everywhere you go, they'll go, although, Mr Noble, you should probably think about cancelling your public engagements.'

'I won't do that,' the author declared instantly. 'I've got two gigs at the Book Festival and I'm doing them both.'

'Wait a minute,' Amanda Noble retorted. 'This is no time to be going all macho on me.'

'I'm not turning chicken on you either, though. We'll have protection on the doorstep, fine, but I won't be made a prisoner. My first event isn't till Sunday; maybe the police will have caught this nutter by then.'

'We might, we might not,' said Pye. 'Think about it, please. In the meantime, I'll have a protection team organised.'

'But won't that give the media the hint that there's a link?'

'Mr Noble, as soon as the Victoria State Police announce Henry Mount's identity, and the fact that he was murdered . . . at the moment their media seem to be assuming that some bloke had a heart attack, so no big story . . . the most downmarket tabloid will assume that there's a link, and your phone will start ringing to melting point. It's the connection between the methods used in each case that we hope to keep under wraps.'

'Point taken.' He paused and looked up at his wife. 'Switch on the answer machine, love, as soon as we're done here, and turn off our mobiles.' His eyes swung back to the DI. 'I'll think about pulling out of those events . . . the first one's a panel discussion anyway: it can go on without me . . . but even as we speak, I'm thinking about this too. Ainsley and Henry both liked to go in for dead clever murders . . . so to speak.' He grinned. 'In one Jecks book there's a female Egyptian bank manager called Cleo who's poisoned by the bite of an asp. My homicides aren't that prosaic or elaborate; they usually involve sharp objects, blunt instruments, or the occasional firearm, and they're nearly all committed at close range. The most sophisticated thing I've ever done was have a bloke,' he glanced at the detectives '. . . a police officer actually . . . walk in front of a bus, under hypnotic instruction.'

'In that case, don't go crossing the street on your own,' Amanda told him. 'At the best of times, you're the most accident-prone man I've ever known.'

'Maybe Fred isn't next in line,' June Connelly murmured. 'Maybe this person was only after Ainsley and Henry.'

'But why?' Wilding asked. 'As I understand it, of the three of them, Mr Noble's the biggest seller. If you're going to start knocking off Edinburgh crime writers, surely he'd be at the top of the list.'

'Or maybe it's one of my readers,' the dark figure brooded as he nursed his whisky in the depths of his armchair, 'thinking that he's doing me a favour by taking out the opposition.'

'Or maybe it's you yourself, Fred,' said the woman opposite, mischievously. 'That's the question these gentlemen are being too delicate to ask.' She glanced at them. 'Isn't it?'

The sergeant shook his head. 'When Mr Glover was murdered, Mr Noble was appearing live on the BBC2 Edinburgh Festival review programme. Even at that time of night, I reckon he has a few witnesses to his alibi.'

'Then perhaps it has to do with the project,' Connelly persisted, her voice thick. Wilding found himself wondering how big a share of the bottle of malt she had consumed.

'Hey, that's a point,' Noble agreed.

The DI looked at them surprised. 'What project?'

'Ainsley and Henry had a joint thing going,' the agent told him. 'I have no idea what it was, only that it was contemporary, non-fiction. I asked Ainsley what it was about, more than once, but he'd only smile and mutter, "Due course, due course," in his most infuriating tone.'

'But just the two of them?'

'They approached me,' Noble confessed. 'In January, I think it was. They said that there was something they wanted to do together and that it would involve a lot of investigation. They felt that it wouldn't be right not to offer me the chance to join them ... Henry did say they reckoned they'd need a third person anyway ... but I said to them that I was going to be way too busy this year to think about taking on anything else.'

'Did they tell you what it was about?'

'I wouldn't let them. I told them that if I didn't know, there was no chance of me getting too comfy at a writers' festival somewhere and blabbing about it.' He looked at Pye. 'So what do you reckon? Am I off the hook?'

'It's a line of inquiry,' the young inspector conceded, 'and we'll follow it up; but off the hook? No. Those officers will still be at your door, front and back, until this investigation is over.'

Sixty-three

'Bob,' said Piers Frame, 'I've told you. Military intelligence deny all knowledge of this man Coben.'

'I'm sure they do, and I'm inclined to believe them, for once in my life. But he exists, Piers. Andy Martin's not an excitable type, and he never makes a mistake over a name. If he says that's what the guy called himself, you can bank on it.'

'But he's irrelevant now, isn't he? The man Glover is sadly no longer with us, and therefore this Coben will have no interest in Martin.'

'Unless he really didn't take to being offered the window exit from his office, and decided that he'd exact some form of retribution. Or unless he decided simply to discredit him, as a precaution.'

'Are you saying he has done?'

'I'm saying that somebody has. It involves Martin, it involves my older daughter and I've been stuck right in the middle of it.' He described the sending of the graphic and compromising photographs to the media, and their disruption of his press briefing.

'I see,' Frame murmured. 'Yes, I can understand now why you're following this line. However,' he drawled, 'hasn't your interest in the fellow, and your pursuit of him, turned into a personal vendetta, old chap?'

'Certainly,' Skinner agreed. 'I'm looking forward to spending a few minutes with the man in an interview room. But there is an overiding professional need to find him. The MoD spooks were watching Glover, in a routine way. This man goes to see Martin to warn him off, goes to the length of threatening his family, and yet you tell me he's not a spook himself. If that's so, it suggests to me that he was involved with Glover in another context, and puts him right at the top of the list in terms of murder suspects. Now, with the second death, if I can connect Henry Mount to Coben—'

'Mount? Yes, I saw a note about that in a Foreign Office bulletin this morning. Are you telling me you can link a murder in Edinburgh with a suspected shooting in Melbourne?'

'We have done. We know how he was killed, and if I'm right about this Coben, we probably know who did it.'

'So what do you want from me?'

'I want you to trawl through the entire intelligence community until you find something that connects with this man, or with the name. I want you to look under every one of the stones where these people hide, and get me a lead to him.'

Frame sighed. 'All right, Bob, I'll do that for you. If I refused you'd probably go over my head anyway, and get what you want. However, it does seem to me that if this person is behind your two killings, then he's exposed himself rather recklessly with this stunt involving your daughter.'

'You can say that again, Piers, because by doing that he's got my keen personal attention. He may think that I'll be flying a desk for the rest of my career, and that I'm no longer a threat. If he does, he's got it wrong . . . and if he looks at my record, he'll find that when it comes to getting my man, even the fucking Mounties have nothing on me.'

Sixty-four

'I didn't go too far, did I, boss,' Pye asked, 'offering Fred Noble round-the-clock protection? When I told him I was authorised to offer it, I knew I might be stretching it a bit.'

'As far as I'm concerned, Sammy,' Neil McIlhenney replied, smiling across his desk, 'that warrant card in your pocket gives you all the authority you need. It was a matter for your judgement and it was the right call. His wife was bound to have asked for it anyway, and we couldn't have refused. How's Noble taking it?'

'I don't think that his own situation's really dawned on him yet. He's lost two good friends; that's all he's thinking about. When we left, he and Glover's agent-cum-ladyfriend were looking at the bottom of two whisky glasses and thinking about changing the view. Mrs Noble's a diamond, though; she'll keep them on line.'

'What if he decides to go to the off-licence to restock; or, worse, what if he decides to go to the Oxford, where these writers seem to hang out?'

'Then his protection officers will insist on going with him, in full uniform. It won't come to that, though. His wife won't let him over the door.'

'What about this project you mentioned? Neither he nor Connelly had a clue about it, you say?'

'No. I pressed them, but Noble was adamant that neither of the dead men had dropped a clue. Connelly said that she'd only really have been interested when they had something ready to sell. She also said that the buggers were so carried away with the thing that they'd never considered who was going to sell it for them, as in which of their agents.'

'Or if it would sell at all, I suppose.'

'Oh no,' said Pye firmly. 'They'd considered that all right. Glover told Mrs Connelly that if it worked out, it would be the biggest thing that he and Mount had ever done in sales terms, and that it would make them both international names.'

'Indeed,' McIlhenney exclaimed. 'It's done that already, if it's the reason why they're fucking dead. What's our next objective?' he asked.

'We have two, sir, haven't we? We need to ask Mrs Mount what she knows about the project.'

'Her son may be a better source, from what George Regan said; Mount seems to have kept secrets from his wife . . . his continuing cigar habit, for one. Mario should be sound asleep right now, but tomorrow morning, his time, he'll be looking to see what useful traces the late Henry might have left behind him. I'll let you know as soon as I hear from him. What's your second step?'

'It's got to be this man Coben, hasn't it? Andy Martin's visitor. We now have two computer thefts, following on each murder. They point straight to this mysterious project as the reason for the killings. Fuck all to do with a vendetta against crime writers . . .'

'Don't you prioritise Coben; the boss is dealing with that himself. But are you telling me now that you needn't have offered Noble protection?'

'No, not at all. One, maybe I'm wrong and the thefts have nothing to do with the project, and maybe there is a lunatic at work. Two, if they have, if that's the motive, it's possible that the killer will assume that if Glover and Mount were involved, then Noble is too.' He paused. 'Unless, of course,' he murmured, 'he knows who the third partner is . . . Noble told us that they reckoned they night need another person, even if it wasn't him.'

McIlhenney grinned. 'Or unless,' he said slowly, 'the killer is that third man.'

Sixty-five

'I like your hair,' said Alex quietly to her table companion, in the exclusive restaurant on Gullane's main street.

'Thanks,' said Maggie Rose Steele, an addition to the party, at Skinner's request. She touched her short red locks. 'It's curlier than it used to be, before I had the chemotherapy.' She smiled. 'There aren't too many bonuses from having cancer, but . . .'

'You're looking great.'

'I'm feeling great too,' she admitted. 'Perverse as I am, sometimes I'm scared by how well I've recovered. I'm over the surgery, I'm off all medication, my weight's back to what it was before I became pregnant . . . maybe not quite, but that's no bad thing . . . I'm in the gym three times a week, and I'm ready for action as soon as my maternity leave's over.'

'How's the baby doing?'

'Stephanie Margaret is doing even better than me, thanks. She's a handful already; I just hope my sister can cope with her tonight.' She looked sideways at Alex. 'This is the first time I've been out on my own since she was born.' And then she frowned. 'Come to think of it, this is the first time I've been out on my own since . . . do you know, I can't remember when. As a divorcee I found that I wasn't invited to many hen nights . . . not that I'd have gone. As a senior cop, I wasn't asked out on too many dates. As a widow: I'll have to find out.'

'Next time I'm on a girlie night,' Alex promised, 'I'll make sure you're invited.' A dark look crossed her face. 'There won't be any of the other kind for a while, that's for sure. You know what happened, don't you?'

'Yes,' Maggie murmured. 'Your dad told me . . . better I heard it from him than through the rumour mill; that was how he put it.'

'I still can't believe how stupid I was, in every way. He's been great about it.'

'Death to the man who harms his little girl.' She looked around. 'I wasn't going to comment, but I see one notable absentee tonight.'

'That's broken beyond repair, I'm afraid. Hell no, I'm not afraid at all. I plan to steer well clear of Andy from now on; for good. And not just him either. It turns out that Mr Montell next door, my Mr Reliable, has a past that he didn't choose to share with me, so he's definitely off the escort list. Then there was that disaster I had not so long ago; the one who's in jail now. No,' her jaw set firm as she spoke, 'I'm firmly back on the list of Edinburgh's eligible singles.'

'Want a tip from an older woman?'

'If that older woman is you, sure.'

'Don't go looking. Be the person you are and trust to your luck. Don't put yourself in the market for a man. I suppose I did, long ago; I felt that single was not how you're supposed to be. Then I got together with Mario. It was OK for a while, I admit; I was never anything like a housewife, and we socialised quite a lot. But if I'd really considered both pros and cons before marrying him, I wouldn't have. When Stevie happened, it was out of the blue.'

'He came looking for you?'

'That's just it, he didn't. It just clicked between us. Listen, Stevie was a babe magnet, we both know that. I bet you fancied him yourself, just a bit.' Alex smiled, and looked into her wine glass. 'Go on, admit it,' Maggie teased.

'Well,' she giggled, 'maybe just a wee bit.'

'Of course; no shame, everybody did, all the girls. And he got into scrapes too, just like you. There was Paula Viareggio, for example; she used him to send out signals to Mario.'

'Paula's not that devious.'

'Not consciously, granted, but that's what her and Stevie were about. Mind you, that was minor league. There was somebody else made a pitch for him, and that would have been big trouble, huge trouble.'

'I think I can guess who that was,' Alex whispered. 'My former stepmother? Not that she ever said, but I saw her look at him once, and that told me plenty.'

'See you lawyers?' Maggie rolled her eyes. 'I'm saying nothing. No names, no pack drill, even though the lady in question has gone from among us. Anyway, then Stevie and I clicked . . . and that's what happened. We were friends, away from the job. That was first, and then one night I just realised, God, I am so horny with this man. And he was gazing at me, thinking the same thing. So we screwed each other's brains out; I'd never had sex like that in my life before. Afterwards . . . I'll never forget it . . . I had this great surge, and I felt, "I'm safe. At last I'm safe." As I was thinking it, Stevie said just that, out loud. That was it, the beginning of what should have been Happy Ever After . . .' she paused '. . . only there's no such thing. There can't be; it's a nonsense saying.' She looked along the table at six people, heads bowed in conversation. 'There you see three couples who are together for life. But that's all it is, for life; there is no "for ever". Some day three of those people will be in the front row at a funeral, the principal mourner. Come to think of it, three of us at this table have been there already: me, your dad and Neil.' She reached across the table and squeezed Alex's hand. 'This might sound like a weird thing to say, but I really hope that one day in the dim and distant, you're sat there too, in the worst seat in the house, and that like the three of us, what you've had in between makes the hurt of the moment bearable. The Queen, God bless her, once wrote that grief is the price we pay for love.' She smiled, and simultaneously her eyes filled with tears. 'And you know what?' she said. 'It's a price worth paying.'

Glancing along the table at that moment, Bob Skinner felt a pang of anxiety, but then Maggie laughed, and washed it away. He picked up his coffee spoon and tapped his wine glass, to attract attention. 'I promised,' he began, 'that there would be no speeches tonight, and this isn't one. It's only a few words of thanks, to Maggie, Neil and Brian, for your part in shoving me into my new office . . . we are a team, and you three, along with our big Irish-Italian chum, and others who can't be here tonight for different reasons, have been among its most valuable players . . . to my lovely Aileen, who bribed me into it with the promise of eventual matrimony, and not least to Our Kid, who, although she doesn't realise it, has been my constant, my foundation stone throughout my police career, apart from the first year or so when she wasn't born . . . although maybe even then . . . and without whom the sun would cease to shine on my world.' He raised his glass and took a sip. 'A toast to you all.'

'You forgot all the bad guys,' Alex called out.

'Eh?'

'It's true,' she said. 'You should be toasting all the people you put away, all the Jackie Charleses, all the Big Lennies. If it wasn't for the likes of them, you wouldn't have had a career.'

'And maybe you should switch from corporate law to criminal defence. Then the Skinner family would cover both ends of the business.'

As the laughter subsided, he switched places with Aileen, to be next to Neil McIlhenney. 'Speaking of bad guys,' he murmured, 'did we get Crown Office clearance for the use of those images of Hugo Playfair?'

'Yes,' the superintendent replied. 'And the artist did a good job of removing his beard and most of his hair. He even did a third version, sans beard but with sunglasses. They're all in place, with every newspaper and TV station in the country.' He checked his watch. 'The early editions will be on the streets pretty soon. They'll be well used; the papers love this sort of thing.'

'Good luck, then. You never know, we may get a result.'

'You don't sound too optimistic, Chief.'

Skinner winced. 'The King is dead, eh. I wonder how long it'll take me to get used to being called that.'

'Could be worse, could be Guv.'

'Not on our force. My first decree: the terms "Guv'nor" and "Neighbour" . . . worse still, "Neebur", the *Taggart* version . . . banned. Optimistic? I'm hopeful, but the way this guy disappeared, and the fact that he's left not a trace of himself behind, tells me that he's going to be bloody difficult to find, if not impossible. On top of that . . .' He stopped abruptly.

McIlhenney persisted. 'On top of what?'

'I don't want to put a damper on George Regan's first major investigation as a DI, but I don't honestly believe that finding Playfair would wrap it up.'

'Come on. He's the last guy the victim spoke to; their conversation ended in a public argument. Playfair's the clear suspect. He had time to go back to his van, get a weapon, his hammer, then lie in wait for Mustafic.'

'Granted. But if he'd bashed his head in, why did he hang around till morning, waiting until the body was found, before he buggered off?'

'There's a counter to that. Why didn't he hang around to help Regan with his inquiries?'

'Not necessarily because he was guilty.'

'But he may have assumed he'd be our main suspect, and realised that he'd have trouble proving his innocence.'

'Did Dorward's team find any trace of Mustafic's blood in his caravan? You told me it was all over the bushes round the body.'

'No, I'll grant you that . . . but he could have gone for a swim in the sea straight after the killing.'

Skinner laughed softly. 'You are good, Neil,' he admitted. 'When I think of the big DC that I first took on the team, and I listen to you now, I'm proud of us both, me for picking you out, but mostly of you, the way you've grown as a detective. I'll give you that one. He could have. But . . . Playfair is a barrack-room lawyer; he's the sort of guy who will know very well that it's about us proving his guilt, not the other way round. Let's go back to that argument in the bar. What language were they speaking?'

'I don't know. But not English, according to Regan's report.'

'That's what I thought. And that brings me back to the great unknown. What was the nature of the relationship between these two men? From the little we've found out about how they came to join the group, it seems to me that they were partners of some sort. Partners in crime? Maybe, but partners in hiding. If you ask me, these guys were on the run, and when Playfair found that Mustafic was dead, he did the obvious . . . he kept on running, for his life. No, my friend, he's not going to be easy to find.'

'Who's not?' Aileen demanded. 'Are you two talking shop?'

'Comparing notes, that's all,' Bob replied defensively.

'Well, stop it,' she ordered. 'Back to our place for coffee and a nightcap. The shop is closed for today.'

McIlhenney laughed. 'It reopens pretty soon, though, Aileen . . . in Australia.'

Sixty-six

As Mario McGuire and Michael Giarratano walked along Collins Street from the Grand Hyatt towards the complex that housed the Sofitel, Melbourne seemed to be coming to life. The morning was bright, but an Antarctic breeze was blowing in off the sea, and the Scot was discovering how cold winter can be in Australia. He checked his watch: eight thirty-five, twenty-five minutes to midnight in Edinburgh, same local time in Sydney, where he had wakened Paula from her first sound night's sleep of the trip when he had called her an hour before.

The inspector climbed a few steps off the pavement, then led the way between two tall blocks into a courtyard filled with cafeteria tables, and round to an escalator that rose into the foyer of the late Henry Mount's hotel. He walked up to the reception desk and showed his badge, then waited, while a key card was cut for him. 'Forty-seventh floor,' he said, as they stood in front of the lifts. 'This hotel starts on thirty-five. The floors below are all offices.'

The elevator was lightning fast; McGuire felt his stomach flip as it came to a stop and was glad that he had skipped breakfast. As they turned into a corridor, open on one side and looking down on to a central area below, with a canopied bar, he spotted the author's room long before he could read the number, from the orange tape that was stretched across it. Giarratano stepped up to the door and ripped it off, then slid the key into the slot.

The bed had been made up. 'Housekeeping must have been in

345

before it was sealed off,' the Australian murmured. 'I hope they haven't screwed anything up.' Nevertheless, before they stepped inside, the two men donned white, sterile gloves, as if they were as anxious to leave no mess as not to contaminate any evidence.

'I'm only looking for one thing,' the DCS told him as he stepped into the room, and saw the view through a wall of windows. 'Jesus Christ,' he exclaimed. 'What's that?' One side of the hotel looked out on to a great circular stadium surrounded by six floodlighting towers.

'MCG, mate.' Another acronym. 'Melbourne Cricket Ground, the greatest stadium in the world, we reckon.' Giarratano pointed to its right. 'And that is the Rod Laver tennis centre, where they play our Open. The MCG's used all year round; they play Aussie rules footie there in the winter.'

'I didn't know you had any.'

'Winter? Come on, it's freezing today.'

'No, rules. I saw a sports paper in Sydney on Monday: before they got round to telling you the scores, they listed the weekend's injuries.'

Giarratano grinned. 'Maybe so, but the MCG holds a hundred thousand, and we can fill it for a game.'

'So did the Colosseum, and the Romans filled that too. That's blood sports for you. OK,' he said, 'let's see what Mr Mount's left behind him.' Quickly and methodically the two detectives searched the room. McGuire checked the dead man's suitcase, half-filled with fresh clothes, then picked his way through a plastic bag, crammed with used garments, but found nothing. The Australian checked drawers and wardrobes, but saw only a jacket and two pairs of trousers, draped over hangers, a pair of black shoes, and another bag, containing trainers and gym clothing. The room had a desk, by the window. On it sat a pile of books, a programme for the Writers' Festival, a copy of the previous day's *Age* newspaper, a notepad and two pens. But nothing else.

'Did he have his passport on him when he died?' the Scot asked.

'No, but he could have left that with the concierge. Wedding ring, Breitling watch, wallet, change purse, mobile phone, cigarette lighter and a Fuji pocket digital camera; those were all the personal items he had on him. I checked the list this morning, before I came to collect you.'

'No more cigars?'

'No. That's why I checked.'

'Then they're here,' McGuire declared. 'He'd another five days to go on this trip. This man would not run out of his favourite brand.'

'We should try the safe deposit box.'

'There is one?'

'This is a five-star hotel, Mario; of course there is. The receptionist gave me the emergency unlock code. All we need to do now is find the damn thing.'

'Let's check the wardrobe.' He stepped across, opened the unit that Giarratano had just searched, and looked in, seeing nothing at first . . . until he moved the gym bag. 'Got it. Damn thing's on the floor.'

He stood back as his smaller, nimbler colleague squatted beside the rectangular safe and keyed in four numbers, then swung the steel door open. He reached inside, fumbling, then smiled as he withdrew a wooden box and held it up for McGuire to take.

The DCS read the name on the lid aloud. 'La Gloria Cubana, Medaille d'Or number two.' He opened the box, and a rich odour seemed to explode from it. 'Jesus, these are good,' he murmured. He looked inside and counted. Originally it had held twenty-five cigars; there were twelve left.

'Are you a smoker?'

'Not any more, but when I was I never had the palate for these things. Papa Viareggio did, though. He loved his cigars; I suspect that if he hadn't died when I was sixteen, he'd have done his best to get me

347

hooked. He'd have loved these, I know.' His eyes narrowed. 'But the thing is, Papa didn't just smoke them, he imported them.'

'Through the internet?'

'Don't be daft, Michael. I'm talking about way before that was created. No, he imported them and he sold them. The family business that he started began with fish and chip shops, but he diversified over the years, into cafés and delicatessens. In the delis, he always stocked good cigars, the kind he smoked himself; he reckoned it made good business sense. You got the cigar aficionados through the door, you got their wives afterwards.'

'What happened to the business?'

'When Papa died, Paula's dad took it over, my Uncle Beppe. He didn't ruin it, but he didn't move it forward either. But then he died, Paula succeeded him, and she did. It's bigger now, with property holdings as well as the shops. Yet it's still family owned, and it still follows the model that the old man established, including the importing of cigars. If Henry Mount bought his Havanas in Edinburgh, there's a fair chance he bought them from my family.' He frowned. 'But he didn't get them with a special bonus, though. Somebody rigged this box, some bastard with a dark sense of humour.' He looked inside. 'These come without cellophane wrappers,' he said, 'and they're handmade, so it would have been relatively easy to rig a bullet trap in one and put it back without Mount being any the wiser.'

'So where does the sense of humour come in?' Giarratano asked.

McGuire passed him the box. 'Take a look,' he told him. 'The cigars are packed in three layers, eight, nine and eight. The top layer's gone and there are four cigars left in the second. That means the one that did the damage was number thirteen . . . unlucky for Henry.'

'Shit.' The Australian paused. 'Are we going to fight over who gets this box, Mario?'

'I hope we don't have to. Obviously you have to look for prints and

DNA other than Mount's, but if you get a result I promise you that the match will not be in Australia but in Scotland.'

'Unless your assumption is wrong, and he bought it here, or even in the duty free in Dubai.'

The big DCS grinned. 'If they were duty free, it would say so on the box, but the rest is easily sorted. Bring it over to the window and hold it up.' As Giarratano obeyed, he took a camera from his pocket. 'Let me see the side with the bar code.' He stepped in close, zoomed in on the black and white strip, focused and took a photograph, then a second, then a third, 'For twice the luck,' he said. 'Find me internet access in this place. I'll send these back to Edinburgh right now, and I'll warn my people to expect them. I'll copy them to you at the same time. You can both get checking, and by this evening we'll know for sure.'

'If it's Edinburgh, do you want the box?'

'At this stage, all we really need are any prints and DNA you lift from it. Did you bring an evidence bag, as well as these gloves?'

'Yes.' The inspector pulled a large clear envelope from his pocket, unfolded it and slid the cigar box inside. 'Let's take this back to my office. You can send your email from there.'

'No chance, mate. I send it from here, then I go back to the Grand Hyatt and check out. I'm on the first plane back to Sydney. I'm on holiday, remember.' He smiled. 'But to be honest, I have one more job to do. Paula never travels anywhere without her tiny wee Sony laptop. I need her to use it to access her files back home and find out for sure if Viareggio and company sell La Gloria Cubana cigars.'

Sixty-seven

Gerry Crossley prided himself on being an early starter. His job description read 'nine to five', but he always made a point of being at his desk at least fifteen minutes before the appointed time, so that everything would be ready for the chief constable's arrival. There had been heavy overnight rain, and a brief shower had caught him between the bus stop in Comely Bank and the headquarters building; standing in the corridor, he shook surface water off his raincoat before stepping into his compact office and hanging it on one of the two wall hooks. The other was occupied; a short car coat hung from it.

The connecting door to the chief's room was slightly ajar. He popped his head round, to see Bob Skinner seated at his meeting table, with the daily newspapers spread out before him, and a mug in his hand. He looked up and smiled. 'Morning, Gerry,' he called out.

'Morning, sir,' the secretary replied. 'I'm sorry I'm late.'

'You're not; I'm early.' He paused. 'And listen, we've got to get something sorted out. You're a civilian colleague, not a serving officer, and you're certainly not a servant, so don't go "sirring" me all the time.'

'How should I address you?'

'In any way that makes us both feel comfortable. You want to call me "Bob" in private and "Mr Skinner" in front of the troops, I'm fine with that.'

'I'm not sure the head of HR would approve of me being on first-name terms.'

'The head of HR reports to me; her approval or disapproval isn't of any consequence.'

Crossley stood for a few seconds, thinking. 'Well,' he said at last, 'if it's all the same to you, Mr Skinner, I'll call you that, or "Chief", as appropriate. That's what you are now, to police and civilians alike, and that's how I addressed Sir James.'

'Fine. That's agreed. Now, as for my daily routine, I plan to be here by eight thirty, partly because the traffic's slightly easier, and partly because it'll let me do what I'm doing now, catch up on what the press are saying, before this place comes alive. Once that's done, I'll look at any urgent mail, then at nine fifteen, with effect from tomorrow, I want a quick morning meeting with the deputy . . . when appointed; until then Brian Mackie's acting . . . the ACC, head of CID, or in his absence Neil McIlhenney, and David Mackenzie. No agenda, just a review of current business.'

'Understood. I'll do a note for your signature, for circulation.'

'Nah, do it yourself; I want you to be seen as an executive more than as a secretary. We'll maybe give you a new title. *"Chef d'équipe"* sounds a bit flash, but something along those lines. Frame the circular "The chief constable requests," and so on. It'll have the same effect as if I sign it. Tell them I don't anticipate it lasting any longer than fifteen minutes and that if anyone wants coffee or tea they can bring it themselves.'

Crossley grinned. 'They'll love that.'

'They'll have to. I'm not making it for them, and neither are you. However, I'll cater for the head of HR this morning. Ask her to come and see me at nine thirty, to brief me on procedures for appointing the new deputy. It has to be advertised, but tell her I want to know whether we can frame it in such a way that if Brian Mackie's promoted deputy, we can select an assistant to replace him from the same list of applicants.'

'Will do, Chief. Will you want to talk to her about designating an acting ACC?'

'No, Gerry, I'm not going to do that, not yet, at any rate; Maggie Steele comes back from maternity leave next month, and it's going to be her. HR doesn't need to be consulted on that, just told.' The secretary said nothing, but his eyes expressed approval. 'One other thing,' said Skinner, 'while I remember. I'd like you to check Brian Mackie's leave sheet. Aileen and I will be taking time off in October, while Holyrood's in recess.'

'Very good. I'll leave you to get on with the papers. How was the coverage of your briefing?'

'Restrained,' Skinner told him. 'There are news reports of my appointment, and a couple of photos, but nothing about the interruption. Mitchell Laidlaw's interdict is pretty comprehensive in what it prohibits. One of the tabloids has done a background piece on me that includes a picture of Alex, but that's as close to the wind as anyone seems to have sailed. I'm nearly finished. Just the *Herald* and the *Saltire* to read.'

He picked up his mug as Crossley left. It was half-full, but the contents were cold, and so he tipped them into the basin in his private bathroom, then poured himself a refill. Coffee was one of his vices, and he knew it. Only Aileen's firm instruction had made him switch to decaf.

He was studying the *Herald* when his phone rang. His appointment was reported on page three, but his attention was focused on the front. He reached across to his desk and took the call.

'I have a call for you, Mr Skinner,' said his assistant, 'but I'm not sure you'll want to take it.'

'Why wouldn't I?'

'It's from Brankholme Prison, near Darlington; the deputy governor who put it through here told me that it takes high-risk remand prisoners from the regional courts. The caller's Dražen Boras, the man who's awaiting trial for—'

'I know who Dražen Boras is, Gerry. Why would that bastard want to speak to me? To congratulate me on my appointment?'

'He says he has information, and that he'll only give it to you, nobody else. He says it's vital, and that you'll be very interested in it. The deputy governor said she reckons he's genuine.'

Skinner took a deep breath and gazed out of the window, at the uninspiring view of an empty playing field. The last time he had seen Dražen Boras, one of only two meetings, he and Mario McGuire had arrested him in a hotel in Monaco, and had charged him with the murder of Stevie Steele, Maggie's husband. The Bosnian-born millionaire had thought himself beyond their reach, thanks to the help of American friends who had repaid favours owed, but he had been wrong. Skinner knew that there was a good chance he would have to see the man again, to give evidence of his arrest, but in truth, if he could have tossed him from the balcony of his room in the Columbus to save the expense of a trial, he would have done so without a second's thought.

'Vital, is it?' he murmured, feeling the anger welling up within him. 'OK, Gerry, I'll take Mr Boras's call, but you be listening in. Tell him he'll be recorded.'

'But we don't have that facility, Chief.'

'Doesn't matter. Dražen's the sort of bloke who'll assume we do. I wouldn't want to ruin our image in his eyes.' As he waited, he realised that he was gripping the phone as tightly as he might if he had his hand round Boras's throat. He forced himself to relax, to be calm.

'Mr Skinner.' The voice was smooth, the accent that of an English public schoolboy, as he had been. 'I'm slightly surprised you're speaking to me, since I know you and your people would like me dead.'

'You're being dealt with as we would wish, Mr Boras. You'll have your day in court, then if you're convicted, as our evidence says you will be, you'll have your thirty years, or whatever, in jail.'

'Thirty years, you reckon?'

'Less than the time my colleague might have had left. Did you know his widow has a baby daughter that he never saw?'

'That's a great pity. Without making any admission for your tape, I assure you that I am genuinely sorry about that, as I am about the unfortunate death of DI Steele. If I send you a gift for the child, will you pass it on?'

'No, I'll have you charged with attempted bribery. Now what is it that you want? What's this information that you have for me?'

'I won't give it to you over the phone, or in any environment where I can be recorded. I'm a sitting target here.'

'Be sure you stay close to the window,' said Skinner, drily.

'They don't let me do that. I need to see you, Mr Skinner, to tell you what I know. If you have me brought up to Edinburgh, I'll tell you there.'

'There's no chance of that.'

'I thought not. Then you come to me, you and that gorilla of a colleague who thumped me in Monaco.'

'You're kidding. You really don't want to meet DCS McGuire again. Anyway, he's away just now.'

'Then someone else.'

'Are you trying to work a plea bargain? If you are, talk to the Crown Prosecution Service, not me.'

'No, I'm not. Maybe I'm just looking for some credit, when it counts.'

'Like when it comes to sentencing?'

'No comment.'

'You'll get nothing from me.'

Boras sighed. 'OK, if you come to me, I'll take you on trust.'

'I repeat, why should I? What have you got for me?'

'This morning,' Boras replied, 'when they woke me at the usual ungodly hour, they gave me my usual newspapers. In the *Daily Mail*, I saw a photograph, three actually, of a man you are looking for, someone calling himself Hugo Playfair.'

'Yes?' said Skinner, feeling the hair on the back of his neck start to prickle.

'I know who he is.'

Sixty-eight

'What do you think, Sarge?' Sauce Haddock asked. 'Will things be much different now that Mr Skinner's chief constable?'

'In theory, no,' Ray Wilding replied, 'not for us, at any rate. The word that's filtered down from Neil McIlhenney is that he's going to keep hands-on with CID, just like he did before. But there are bound to be changes. There'll be somebody new in the command corridor, for openers.'

'Someone from outside?'

'You'd assume so, especially with the big man's being promoted internally, but I wouldn't put money on that. He's loyal to his own, and it'll take a good candidate to beat Brian Mackie for the deputy job. If that happens—'

'Mr McGuire for ACC?'

'Wait and see, lad; I don't expect anyone will give us a vote.'

'What about Andy Martin?' Alice Cowan called out across the CID room.

Wilding stared at her. 'Are you pulling my chain?'

'No,' she replied innocently. 'Why not him?'

'If you don't know, I'm not going to be the one to tell you. Let's just say that Judas bloody Iscariot's got more chance.'

Cowan turned to Haddock. 'Sauce, what have I missed?' she demanded, but the young DC was saved by the ringing of his phone.

He snatched it up. 'Yes?'

356

'DC Haddock, Leith? Communications Centre. I have a call for you, foreign, from Belgrade.'

His heart jumped in his chest. 'Put it through.' He heard a click. 'This is DC Harold Haddock,' he said.

'I received email,' a woman replied, 'from you, yes?'

'Yes. Are you Vsna?'

'That's my name, Vsna Vukic. You tell me the man who email me before is dead?'

'Yes, I'm afraid so.'

'How?'

'Murdered.'

'Shit! Then I shouldn't be speaking to you.'

'I won't take long.'

'He ask me about some people, give me names, Anđelić, Nikolić, asked me if I knew them.'

'Why did he ask you?'

'I am journalist in Sarajevo. Someone we both know sent him to me, a lady in America.'

'Did he say anything else to you?'

'When I reply to his mail I ask why he want to know anyway. He send me another. It said, "It's about the cleaner." That's all I need to know. I delete his mails, just like I'm going to delete yours now. Don't send me no more. I going to close that address.'

'But . . .' There was a sound, louder than a click, the sound of a phone hitting its cradle, hard. And then the dialling tone.

'That's a load of help,' he sighed. 'Thank you very much.'

Sixty-nine

'Where's Neil?' asked Mario McGuire 'When I called Fettes they said that he and the chief went off somewhere in a hurry, and that I was to call you instead. Where the hell's he gone, and what's he doing with Proud Jimmy?'

'You are indeed out of touch, boss,' Sammy Pye told him. 'Sir James is gone. The new chief constable took up the post yesterday.'

'Big Bob?'

'Of course.'

'Acting chief?'

'No, permanent. For once in this place, nothing leaked in advance of it happening.'

'In that case, I won't be too hard on McIlhenney for not tipping me off, especially since it's the result we all wanted. Now, where are they off to?'

'I don't know. All he told me is that it has nothing to do with our investigation.'

'Investigations, plural. There's no longer any serious doubt that Glover and Mount were killed by the same person.'

'You're sure?'

'Sammy, I'm the fucking head of CID. If I tell you something as gospel, you're not supposed to ask me if I'm sure, even if I am giving you information from the other side of the planet.'

'Sorry, sir,' said the DI, chastened.

'That's OK,' McGuire chuckled. 'I'm taking the piss because I'm pleased with myself. You have no idea the buzz you get from swanning into somebody else's territory and clearing up his crime for him. His boss was so pleased she even picked up my hotel tab in Melbourne.'

'Paula's premise held up, about how he was killed?'

'One hundred per cent. They've done the post-mortem and confirmed it. There were powder burns on his fingers and lips, and tobacco in his mouth. His uvula was missing, shot off, and there was an exit wound behind where it used to be. They've actually found the bullet. They dug it out of a window frame behind where he was standing. After it went through the top of his spine and into the wood, it was flat as a pancake.'

'So it's our investigation, officially,' said Pye.

'We pretty much knew that as soon as George discovered his computer had been stolen, but yes, it's ours, Inspector.'

'And like with Glover, we've got bugger-all forensic evidence.'

'Ah but,' exclaimed McGuire, in a voice so exultant that Pye could almost see him beam, 'we do, my son, we do.' Without pausing he launched into a step-by-step description of the discovery of the cigar box, 'You should see the MCG from that room, mate; some view,' and of his photographing the bar code. 'Those images will be in McIlhenney's mailbox right now. He must have gone off in such a rush he didn't have time to open it.'

'I'll see if I can access it,' the DI volunteered.

'No need. We've cracked that too, thanks to my old grandad, dead these twenty years and more. Paula's IT traced the bar code. That very box was stocked by the Viareggio deli just off St Andrews Square. It's six thirty in the evening here in Sydney, so they'll be open by now. These babies are very rare items; that lot cost going on for two hundred quid the set, and even in Edinburgh they don't turn over many of them. If we discount the bizarre notion that Henry Mount decided to kill himself by doctoring one of his own Havanas, that means that someone either tampered with the thing after he'd bought it, or they bought it for him. You need to get somebody up to that shop to pinpoint the sale, and get the credit card details, and you need to reinterview Mount's family.'

'What about the box, and the cigars?'

'We're getting them. My new friend the chief commissioner of Victoria State Police herself has decreed that. They're in a secure container on their way to the airport even now. You'll have them tomorrow.' He laughed. 'Mind you, I don't envy the lab, trying to lift DNA off the cigars that are left. They're handmade, in Cuba; we might have bother summoning witnesses from there.' He chuckled. 'Almost as much trouble as you'll have trying to find me for the rest of my holiday. As of tomorrow, we're up in Queensland, in a Nissan Movano, and our mobiles will be switched off.'

Seventy

'This is not how I imagined I'd be spending my first day as chief constable,' said Bob Skinner to Neil McIlhenney as he swung off the A1(M), heading for Darlington. They had made good time from Edinburgh: it was still well short of midday.

'I don't imagine it was,' his friend replied. 'Your time's even more valuable now. Then there are the perks of the job; you could have had a driver take us down here, and take you to and from the office, for that matter.'

'I don't plan to use that privilege unless it's official and there might be alcohol involved; an ACPOS dinner, for example. Aileen gets picked up from home by her government car. If I had one as well, how long would it be before the tabloids caught on? I'm probably not flavour of the month with them, after our pal Laidlaw crapped all over their big picture special yesterday.'

'Yeah,' McIlhenney chuckled, as they joined a line of traffic on a single-carriageway road. 'Too bad Mitch retired from our Thursday night football in North Berwick. I miss his silky skills.'

'He'd probably sue you for describing him that way.' Skinner sighed. 'Maybe I should quit too; that would be a good picture for the sports page. I can see the headline: "Superintendent kicks fuck out of Chief Constable". Yes, maybe enough's enough.'

'Away you go. You need it; we both do. It lets us mix with guys outside the job on a regular basis. Taking me along there was the second biggest favour you've ever done me.'

'I needn't ask what the biggest was.'

'No. Introducing me to Louise tops the lot.' McIlhenney hesitated. 'She has told me about you two, you know, that you went out with each other at university. You never mentioned it.'

'Of course not. It was for her to do that.'

'Do you ever wonder what would have happened if you'd stayed together?'

'It wouldn't have worked. We were too career-minded, both of us. If we had, though, I suppose you and I might have wound up with pistols at dawn.'

'Like you and Andy?'

Skinner winced. 'No. That's different. That won't be a duel; if it comes to a fight, it'll be my rules.'

'You mean if he applies for the deputy's job?'

'I mean if he applies for any fucking job in Scotland; as from October, that'll be the First Minister's stepdaughter in those photographs. Aileen hasn't seen them, nor will she, but she's nearly as angry as me. But let's not dwell on that.'

'October?'

'Yes. A quiet do; registry office wedding, just us and witnesses, then a blessing by Jim Gainer, with guests, then a reception in the Parliament building . . . for which we will be paying the standard fee, incidentally. Keep it to yourself, but look out for the invite.' As he spoke, a sweet female voice from his satellite navigation system told him to turn right in three hundred yards. He obeyed and found himself heading north once more, for a mile or so, until a structure that could only have been a prison came into view. 'HMP Brankholme,' he said. 'Looks pretty secure; it would take a battalion to break in here, so getting out would be something of a challenge.'

'If you have the money . . .'

'Nah. The staff here are meant to be incorruptible, and bribery's the only way you could do it.'

'I bet Ainsley Glover or Henry Mount could have dreamed up a plan.'

'Maybe, but I doubt if Dražen Boras is a reader of either of them. They're too parochial; he moves internationally, just like his old man Davor does.' He frowned. 'Now there is a guy I really do not like.'

'Are you saying you like Dražen?'

'I like some people I've put away,' said Skinner. 'Lenny Plenderleith for one. Dražen? No, I never could, because he killed my friend and he has to pay the full price for that. But in terms of evil, of ruthlessness, I reckon the father's a league above the son. From our conversation this morning I'm coming to believe that Dražen genuinely regrets that Stevie died. But from my meetings with his dad, I don't believe that he gives a fuck.' The navigation system interrupted again, advising him that he had reached his destination. 'You can form your own view of junior in a few minutes.'

Entry to the prison was complicated. Their warrant cards were checked . . . Skinner's still showed him as deputy chief constable . . . and Skinner's car was checked, engine compartment, boot and beneath, before they passed the second gate, where a second layer of security awaited. Eventually they were greeted by a tall woman in a dark suit, with close-cropped brown hair, and a manner, as she introduced herself, which indicated that she had no problem functioning in a predominantly male work environment. 'Ngaio Arnott, Deputy Governor. I processed Boras's call to you.'

'Did he have trouble persuading you that he was serious?' asked Skinner.

'Yes, especially since you're possibly going to be a witness in his trial. If it had been anyone other than you, I'd have refused on those grounds, but he assured me that he has essential information unrelated to his own case, so I decided on public interest grounds to let you decide whether to speak to him or not. You're here, so I guess I made the right decision.'

'He could still be taking the piss, but if he is I'll look like a mug, not you.' The chief looked at her. 'What sort of a prisoner is he?'

'Exemplary. He's courteous, he does what he's asked rather than what he's told . . . and that makes a huge difference in a place like this, as I'm sure you'll know.'

'Does he mix with other prisoners?'

'He's not isolated, as such, but he keeps himself to himself. As a remand prisoner, he's not required to work, so he exercises a lot, in his cell and in the gym, when it's available to him. He reads the business press every day, and his library withdrawals show an interest in foreign affairs.'

'Is he resented by other prisoners?' McIlhenney asked her.

'Do you mean has anyone ever had a go at him? No. He's not a man to invite that sort of attention. As you're about to find out for yourself; he should be in the interview room by now.'

Arnott led the way through a series of corridors, until she stopped outside a plain grey door, and peered through a spyhole. 'Yes,' she murmured, 'he's here.' She opened the door, and ushered the police officers inside, announcing them both by name and rank.

Dražen Boras sat at a table, facing them; it was fixed to the floor and he was shackled to it, handcuffs through a bolt in the surface. He smiled as they entered. Skinner gazed at him, appraising him. He wore a skin-tight black Nike vest, and the evidence of his gym work was clear to see in well-defined musculature. He was clean-shaven, and somehow, even in prison, he had managed to maintain a tan. 'Welcome, gentlemen,' he greeted them. 'I'd rise, but they won't let me.'

The chief constable looked at the deputy governor. 'I think we can lose those,' he suggested. 'We'll be fine. Dražen knows I'd just love him to have a go at me.'

Boras nodded. 'True, and I have no thought of it.'

Arnott nodded to a guard, who stepped forward and unfastened his cuffs.

'Is this room bugged?' he asked. 'I don't see anything, but you may be more subtle than I give you credit for.'

'There's nothing here,' the woman promised. 'This room is kept for lawyers and clients; we couldn't use anything we taped so there would be no point doing it.'

'I can see that. You can leave us.' He pointed to the guard. 'He can go too.'

'No,' said Skinner firmly. 'He stays; he can stand as far away as this room allows, but he stays. I want him as insurance against you banging your head off the wall then accusing us of helping you do it.'

The prisoner chuckled. 'I can see that too. OK, I agree.' As Arnott left the room, the warder went to its furthest corner and the two police officers took seats at the table.

'Right,' Skinner began briskly. 'We didn't come here for the drive, Dražen.' He took three photo prints from his pocket and laid them on the desk. 'So tell us, who is he?'

'First, what's in it for me?'

'I told you, we're not here to do a deal with you.'

'That's what you said, but you've got here in under three hours. It seems that you need the information I have. I'm right, am I not, Mr Skinner? Maybe I'm right too in that you have a personal interest in this case. The *Daily Mail* report said that you live in the village where a man was killed, for which this guy is on the run.'

'Yes and no. I live there, but the man isn't necessarily on the run because he did the killing. In fact I don't believe that he did. Dražen, you have no cards in your hand. You know this man? OK, from where?

Was he a business acquaintance? I doubt that, not going by the way he lived. Were you at school together, or university? Possible, but if you were we could have checked that without driving down here, you know that. So that leaves your other activity. Let's summarise that. Your father was a Bosnian immigrant to Britain who made it big here. When his country was torn apart and NATO got involved, he volunteered his services to the intelligence community, placing agents in the Balkans as employees of his business. Eventually, so did you, when you set up in business for yourself. Don't ask me why, but I'm certain I reckon you know this man from those days. If you choose not to give me his name, I can ask your father, or your former associates in America.'

Boras's eyes darkened. 'You can ask my father if you can find him. A few days after my arrest, he disappeared. He hasn't been seen or heard from since, not even by my mother.'

'Because he was afraid you'd incriminate him in Stevie's murder?' asked McIlhenney.

'Not for a second. Because there are forces still at work in our region who would kill him if they could, for the things that he and I did against them, just as they'd kill me if they could get to me. As for the other people your boss mentions, you'd get nothing out of them. They have too many others still at risk to give one up. Plus, I think you'll find that they've disowned me. I'm probably as much at risk from them as from my enemies in Serbia.'

Skinner frowned. 'You know,' he murmured, 'I believe everything you've just said. But you're going to give us that name, with no promises or inducements; I believe that too. I'm Scottish, Dražen. My writ doesn't run down here, and you're well aware of that. No, you're going to talk to us, because your conscience is going to make you, because you owe, not us, necessarily, but a widow and a baby up in Edinburgh. This morning you said something about sending a gift to wee

Stephanie. You can't. This is all you can do; all that it's in your power to offer in atonement . . . without, of course, admitting your sin. So, let's have it.'

Boras leaned back in his chair and clasped his hands behind his head. He looked towards the guard in the corner. 'He has to go now,' he said.

Skinner nodded. 'If that's what you want.' He turned to the man. 'Leave us, please.'

As the door closed, Boras laid both hands on the table. 'I believe you're a fair man,' he told the chief constable. 'If this helps the Crown not to press for a heavy minimum sentence if I'm convicted, so be it, but I don't expect you to try to fix that.'

'I won't. I can't. Go on.'

'About four years ago, the people you referred to, in America, asked my father and I for help. They had an agent they wanted to place in Bosnia-Herzegovina, and were looking for a way in. The man had a specific task: he was to go into Serbia to look for witnesses to an act of genocide ordered and presided over personally by a notorious general, a beast, a piece of shit named Bogdan Tadic. He was confident that he'd killed them all, but there was intelligence that a very few had slipped the net and that they were in hiding, near Uzice, in fear for their lives. The operative was briefed to find them, and keep them safe. With them in safe hands, Tadic could be arrested and sent for trial at the International Tribunal at the Hague. My father and I were happy to help with that, but he had placed three people through his office in Sarajevo within the previous year. His business, Continental IT, was big, but yet another appointment might have attracted attention. So we decided that I would handle it through my company, Fishheads. We were supposed to be deadly business rivals, he and I, so my building up a presence there seemed quite natural.' He stopped and looked Skinner in the eye. 'You don't give my father enough credit, you know. He's a genuine Bosnian patriot, and through him so am I.'

'I've never doubted that,' the chief constable told him. 'However, I also give you both credit for being murderers, and not for patriotic motives.'

'Be that as it may,' Boras retorted. 'Ah, let's not get into a debate. I met the agent in Washington,' he continued. 'His name was Lazar Erceg, born in Tuzla to a British mother and to a Yugoslav, a professor of modern Balkan history. He was perfect for the job, and I could pass him off as an employee, no trouble, given his upbringing. When he was eleven the father managed to arrange a move to Cambridge, and young Lazar completed his education there. Then Yugoslavia exploded, Milosevic came to power and things were bad for anyone who wasn't a Serb and for some who were. Professor Erceg went home, to help found Bosnia as an independent nation, became a member of the first government, and was promptly killed, shot by a sniper. They never caught the assassin, but nobody needed a picture to be drawn. Young Lazar was in the British Territorial Army. He wanted to go home to fight, but his mother said, "No way!" and he obeyed her. He stayed in Cambridge and became an academic like his father, within the same area, supplementing his income by writing scripts for the BBC World Service. By this time he sounded as English as I do, so he was never asked to broadcast, but he came to the attention of the Foreign Office, and eventually of other people as well.'

'He was recruited then?'

'He was never recruited. He volunteered, for any job, as he put it, that needed doing and for which he might be suitable. Then he waited; while the war ended, while the Kosovo insurgency happened, he waited. Not in Cambridge, though, not all the time; he went back home whenever he could. He visited the family he still had there, and he came to know the country his father had died to found. While he was there, he heard of Tadic, and what he did. It isn't one of the most notorious atrocities, because the dead were numbered in dozens, not in thousands, but that didn't matter to them, how many were piled into the mass grave. It was an ethnic Bosnian enclave, in Serbia; people in a couple of small villages, minding their own business when Tadic warned them to get out of the country. They ignored him. He didn't give them a second chance. It was brutal, horribly brutal.'

'Wasn't he arrested as soon as the war was over?' asked McIlhenney.

'In Serbia, with Milosevic in power? No chance. Besides, no witnesses. That's what Lazar Erceg was sent in to put right. And I was happy to help.'

'You sent him in?'

'I appointed him Balkans regional sales development manager of Fishheads Ltd. I gave him an office, and a supply of business cards. The name on them was Hugo Playfair,' he pushed the photographs back towards Skinner and McIlhenney, 'and that gentlemen is him.'

'You're sure?' McIlhenney murmured. 'You're not just feeding us a line here?'

'There is no doubt about it,' said Boras, smiling. 'Come on, Detective Superintendent, you think I don't know my own employees?'

'What happened to him between then and now?' Skinner asked.

'Search me. I never saw him again, and they didn't give me operational feedback. All I know is that Tadic was eventually arrested, and put on trial before the International Criminal Tribunal for the Former Yugoslavia, to give it its full title. He was convicted . . . must be at least two years ago . . . and sentenced to life imprisonment, as in, not to be released until dead.' Suddenly he winced. 'If he wasn't a genocidal bastard I might feel some sympathy for him, in my situation.'

'So why should Playfair show up in Scotland, going round the country with a band of travelling people?'

'I take it that question was rhetorical, Chief Constable,' the prisoner exclaimed. 'For I haven't a fucking clue.' He paused. 'However, there is one person I can think of who might give you some more background.'

'Who's that?'

'One of Tadic's trial judges. From your own city, I believe: Lord Elmore.'

Seventy-one

'This is a nice set-up,' said Ray Wilding. 'I confess that I've never been in a Viareggio deli before. Are they all like this?'

'As far as I know they are,' Sammy Pye told him. 'They always were pretty classy, but since Paula took over from her old man, she's moved them further upmarket.'

The sergeant whistled. 'Why's our head of CID in the police force if he's part of the family that owns this? Why isn't he in the business?'

'I think he could have been, but he chose the police. So Neil McIlhenney told me.' He pushed the door open. 'Fancy lunch in the coffee shop?'

'Sure. It's going on one, and we might have to hang about anyway if this manager isn't back soon from her family funeral.'

'Let's find out.' Pye stepped up to the counter. 'Is Miss Hammett in?' he asked an assistant, showing his identification. 'We'd like a word.'

'Hold on a minute,' the man replied. 'Is Mickey back?' he called to a colleague at the cash desk.

'She's back,' a woman's voice announced. The detectives looked around to see a black trouser suit approach, a hand within it outstretched in greeting. 'Michaela Hammett. You the police?'

'DI Pye, DS Wilding. We're here to ask you about a particular box of cigars we believe was sold here.'

'La Gloria Cubanas, cabinet of twenty-five. I had an email from my

371

boss asking me to trace details of the purchase. Monday last week, that's when the transaction took place.'

'That's impressive.'

The manager frowned. 'That's as impressive as it gets, I'm afraid. It was a cash sale, so I've got no credit card details for you, I'm afraid.' She waved a hand to attract the attention of the counter assistant, then beckoned him across. 'This is Eddie McBain,' she said as he joined them. 'He's our cigar specialist, believe it or not.' He smiled bashfully, interpreting her remark as a compliment. 'Box of La Glorias,' she said, 'ten days ago. Your name's on the sale slip.'

'That's right.'

'Can you remember anything about the buyer?' Pye asked him.

'I remember he'd about five hundred quid in his bankroll. I saw it when he paid me; he peeled them off in twenties.'

'Anything else?'

McBain frowned. 'Thirty-something, maybe just, maybe a year or two younger, white; wore a blazer, as I remember, with a wee lapel badge, and a pale blue shirt with a white collar. Sharp guy, looked like a soldier rather than an office worker.'

'Clean-shaven?'

'No, he'd a moustache. His hair was neat too, dark and wavy, but he'd used foam on it. Aye, and he wore glasses, the kind that react to the light.'

Pye frowned, remembering . . . 'Thanks,' he said. 'That's helpful.'

'Do you no' want his name?' the assistant asked, surprised.

The inspector stared at him. 'I thought it was a cash sale,' he retorted.

'It was, but when I gave him his change, I said tae him, "These are cracking cigars. I hope you enjoy them, Mr . . ." and then I realised I didnae know his name, and felt daft, until he said to me, "Cockburn, the name's Cockburn," and left.'

The detectives exchanged glances. 'I want you to think about this,' said Wilding. 'Instead of "Cockburn", could the man have said "Coben"? Is that possible?'

Eddie McBain's face lit up. 'Aye,' he replied, 'it's more than possible, it's likely. I just thought he was mumblin' when he said it.'

Seventy-two

'What did you think of him, then?'

McIlhenney glanced momentarily to his left from behind the wheel; he had volunteered to drive back to Edinburgh, and Skinner had accepted. 'I think he's a remarkable man; if he hadn't been influenced by his corrupt and wicked father . . .'

'He's a murderer, Neil. He didn't plan to kill Stevie . . . that's not in doubt . . . but he had killed already and the trap he laid was set for somebody else.'

'Granted,' the superintendent acknowledged, 'but he's locked up now, the evidence against him is strong, and that's that. What I was going to say is that he gave me the impression of an inner strength that I haven't encountered too often before. There's a calmness about him that's almost monastic.'

'He's no monk.'

'He might as well be, in that place. I can understand why nobody's had a go at him; he looks bloody dangerous. There's an aura about him that will let him come to terms with his sentence. How long will he get, do you reckon?'

'That'll depend. His defence counsel will probably argue that Stevie was collateral damage, an innocent victim of a trap laid for villains. If the judge buys that, I could see a tariff of as little as fifteen years. But if he takes the hard line, then recent precedent says it could be as much as thirty-five years. Do you see him meditating his way through that?'

'Maybe. Look at the Birdman of Alcatraz.'

Skinner laughed. 'You've been watching your wife's favourite movies again. There's no comparison. Stroud, the real Birdman, was a murderous bastard who caused chaos in American prisons. My guess is that Dražen's so calm because he's been told by his very expensive legal team that they'll be able to cast reasonable doubt on the forensic evidence that we expect to convict him. But they're all Londoners, and they've never seen Arthur Dorward in the witness box. You wait till he's convicted; see then if he still has that aura about him.' He shifted in his seat. 'However,' he continued, 'you misunderstood my original question. What I meant was, what did you think of what he had to say? Did you believe him, or was he spinning us a yarn, knowing that we'll probably never be able to check it out?'

'Yes, I believe him. I accept the idea that his willingness to help us is penance in some way for Stevie's death. He knows Playfair, and he gave us his real name. It shouldn't be hard to check, starting in Cambridge, so he knows we'd see through a lie very quickly.'

'True. So what does it tell us about the man? What was he doing travelling around Scotland with a Bulgarian under his wing?'

'You and I can only speculate about that,' McIlhenney pointed out. 'Our best hope is that Lord Elmore can tell us more . . . or tell me more, at any rate.'

'You reckon I'll leave that to you, do you, that I'll be too busy in my new office? I don't think so. It's great being Supreme Leader; you get to cherry-pick. I'm going to sit in on that meeting, for two reasons. One, I've a personal interest in catching the killer of a man who was my companion only three nights ago.'

'Granted. What's the other?'

'I have a funny feeling that I can see the way this thing is headed.'

'Achh!' the superintendent snorted. 'You and your intuition. It's a bloody sight more than I have.'

His boss beamed. 'I guess that's why I'm chief constable,' he said mildly.

They drove on, circling Newcastle to the west, Skinner bemoaning the fact that the city's notorious Brown Ale had passed into foreign ownership. 'Not that I drink the stuff,' he admitted, just as the ringtone of his mobile sounded through the car's Bluetooth system. 'Yes,' he replied, his voice activating the call.

'Bob? Piers Frame here; your secretary told me you were travelling. Can you speak? Are you alone?'

'Not alone, but we can talk. My companion's a senior officer and in on the investigation.'

'OK, I'm happy with that. I don't need you to identify him. Let's leave the snoopers at GCHQ, who listen to my every word, I'm sure, something to puzzle over. I have some information for you, about the name Coben.'

'Have you by God? I wasn't hopeful, I admit.'

'What I have to say won't change that. He's dead.'

'Then he's not the man I want, unless he's been culled very recently.'

'No, this happened a few years back. There is very little known about him, but Frankie Coben was a Serbian national, from a wealthy family with a part-Hungarian, part-American background. He seems to have been very much a background figure, though. The current Serbian government can't tell us anything about him; all the records of him have been expunged. By whom? Nobody's sure. He was a nasty piece of work; the anecdotal evidence . . . and that's all there is . . . says that he was a state security fixer, torturer, and killer. He was also very bright; he was said to have been educated at the University of Belgrade, a student of literature.'

'What happened to him?'

'He was reported killed about seven years ago, during an assassination attempt that was blamed on the Americans. There was nothing intact in the building after the explosion, only body parts, but later, Coben's papers and ID card were found among the wreckage.'

'But nothing else, no physical confirmation . . . like his head, for example?'

'No, that was all.'

'I see.' Skinner glanced across at McIlhenney; his eyes were on the road ahead, but he had eased his speed and was listening intently. 'Can you get me a mugshot of this guy?' he asked.

'There aren't any. They went with his records.'

'Was he the target of the hit?'

'No, no. Coben was always a low-profile figure, never more than a background whisper; he didn't attract that level of notoriety. They were after a bigger fish, and the best evidence that it was indeed an American effort is that they ballsed it up. The man they were after was Coben's boss, who was then in hiding under protection, but he was elsewhere at the time . . . in a brothel, they reckoned after the event.'

'What was his name?'

'Tadic, General Bogdan Tadic.'

Seventy-three

'Has our cigar salesman finished with the artist?' Pye called through the open door of his cubicle as Wilding walked back into the CID office.

'Just.' The sergeant waved a printout at him. He stepped into the room and laid it on the inspector's desk. 'There you are,' he said. 'McBain reckons that's spot on.' The image could almost have been a photograph, it was so detailed. 'What do we do with it now?'

'We do two things. I've just had my instructions from the chief constable himself. He called me from his car to ask whether we'd heard from Mario in Australia, then hit the roof when I gave him my news. He and Neil McIlhenney have been away on a trip. He didn't tell me where, but he did say it's given them a clue to who the man might be. You've got the likeness on computer, yes?'

'Of course.'

'Good. I want you to send it to Andy Martin's email, up in Dundee. Call him, warn him it's there, wait till he opens it and ask him to confirm that it's the man who called on him. The other task, I'll handle; he wants the photofit faxed to a guy in London, who might be able to fill in some blanks on the guy.'

'MI5?'

'One number up from that.'

Wilding's eyes widened. 'Jesus, this is serious. Big boy's games.'

'We can play them too.'

As the sergeant left, Pye turned to his computer and keyed in a note, as dictated earlier by Skinner. '*For the attention of Mr Frame. There follows verified likeness of the man calling himself Coben, seen in Edinburgh Monday last week. Chief Constable Skinner requests your assistance in determining any links between him and the person of the same name, believed killed seven years ago in Serbia.*' He sent it to the unit's printer; by the time he had crossed the office, it had emerged. He signed it, keyed a number that Skinner had given him in a second call from his car into the fax machine, then fed it in, followed by the photofit.

'You're right, Ray,' he whispered to himself as he walked back to his tiny glass-walled room, 'this is heavy-duty.'

He had barely resumed his seat before his phone rang. He snatched it up, thinking that it might be Skinner, checking that his orders had been followed. But the voice in his ear was female, and English. 'Sammy? Becky. I bet you thought I'd given up on you and gone back to checking stolen cars.'

'You want to know the truth?' Pye asked, then confessed, unprompted. 'I've been so busy chasing other leads and angles that I'd forgotten about you.'

'Then let me remind you. I'm the colleague who's been letting crime run rampant through west Edinburgh while she tries to crack the mysteries of a computer you and her boyfriend dumped on her.'

'Yes, I know, I'm sorry. But this investigation has had me chasing fugitive former secretaries of state, banging up dukes' daughters with huge heroin habits, and now, when I thought I had only one mystifying homicide to clear up, I find that I've got two. That might seem like just another week at the office to a veteran of the Sweeney, but to us provincial hicks . . .'

'Stop it!' Stallings chuckled. 'I get enough grief from 'im indoors without hearing it from you too. He called me this morning to tell me that Mount is now officially on your caseload as well.'

'Are you going to help us with it?'

'To be honest wiff yer, as that annoying bastard always says on the football commentaries, I don't know. However, I am going to make your fucking hair stand on end, as my beloved would put it. I have finally got into the boy *sllinco*'s box on his girlfriend's computer. I'm sorry it's taken so long, but sometimes you crack a password easily, sometimes the obvious takes forever; in this case, the latter. I won't bore you with all the names and combinations I tried, but finally I recalled which paper Mr Collins works for and used that. No joy first up, so I reversed it, tried *eritlas* . . . sounds like a place in Middle Earth, doesn't it . . . and bingo.'

'Well done, Becky. What did you find?'

'He didn't use it much; only for one purpose as far as I can see, to communicate with someone using the screen name *neboc@redmail.com*.'

Pye gulped. 'Spell that, please,' he asked, quietly.

'All of it?'

'No, just the front end.' He noted the letters as she read them out, then reversed them. 'Fuck,' he whispered.

'Pardon?'

'Sorry, go on. What was in his files? I need the text of all the messages he sent.'

'Apart from one message, he didn't send text, just images.'

'That word-message. What did it say? When was it sent?'

'Sunday afternoon, just; ten past twelve. It said, "Got it. Left as arranged." Whatever that may mean.'

The inspector considered the words. 'I think I might be able to guess: the disk drive from Glover's computer, and his back-up. He must have done a dead drop. What about the images?'

'They're stored within his mailbox facility,' she told him, 'so they don't show up on Carol's hard disk, but I accessed them no problem. They're dated, and they go back for a few months.'

'What are they?'

'That's the strange thing. I'd say they're surveillance photos. They're all of one bloke, and they're all really boring, just day-to-day stuff: him at work, him with wife and kid, and so on. And then you get to last Sunday morning. Boy, was he busy on Sunday, being photographed through an open window giving a very athletically built young lady a real seeing-to.' She paused. 'Is your hair standing on end yet?' she asked.

'You're getting there,' Pye replied, holding down his impatience. 'Go on.'

'Well, here's the clincher. I've seen the bloke, when he did an inquiry at Fettes a couple of months back. He's the Tayside DCC, Andy Martin. I don't know who the girl is, but it is definitely not his wife. The images were sent to *neboc* on Sunday, at half past ten, a few hours before the text message. How's the hair?'

'Erect.'

'Mmm. And how does that relate to your inquiry?'

'It takes us well along the road. Becky, I'll tell Ray he owes you a large one.'

'A large what?' she murmured archly.

'A large whatever you fucking like. Got to go.'

He hung up, and looked out into the CID room, where Haddock and Cowan were both at their desks. 'Who was checking on Ed Collins being at that play on Saturday?' he shouted.

The female officer jumped to her feet and crossed the office. 'I was, sir. The people who were on the box office don't remember him, but that doesn't mean he wasn't there. The lighting isn't great, they said; they don't see faces, just people. But I do know one thing: he definitely didn't get to Deacon Brodie's until after half twelve. I found a staff member who was having a fag at the door and saw him come in; he recognised him from his picture in the paper. It appears with his reports apparently.'

'OK. Ray,' he called to Wilding, but saw that he had his phone to his ear. He waited until he had finished. 'Andy Martin?' he asked, as he hung up.

'Yes. Our Coben and his are one and the same.'

'Then he should definitely not have upset him. The guy got even big time, with the help of Ed Collins. Come on, we're off to the *Saltire* offices to lift their ace sports reporter.'

Seventy-four

As they approached the ugly grey monolith that was Torness power station, and the even uglier cement factory beyond, Bob Skinner sat in the passenger seat of his car and fretted. 'This is one single inquiry, Neil,' he muttered. 'I don't know how, but I feel it in my water. The deaths of these two authors and of Asmir Mustafic are tied together, I'm sure of it. The link is General Tadic, indirectly, through the man Coben, and through Hugo Playfair, or Lazar Erceg, as Boras says he's really called. But I don't know how they tie together, and I don't know why they were killed.'

'Or by whom?'

'No, that's easy. Coben's our man; thanks to the cigar salesman, we know he was in Edinburgh last week and that he bought Henry Mount's cigar box. We know his background, and that tells me that he's well capable of rigging that Havana. He's moving among us, Neil, this fucking man, openly, and yet we don't know who he is. Come on, chum, help me here. What else don't we know?'

'This joint project,' McIlhenney replied, 'that Glover and Mount are supposed to have been involved in: we don't know what that's about. The only hint is that Glover was asking questions about people in the Balkans.'

'There you are, that ties in too. Go on.'

'According to one of young Haddock's sources, Ainsley said that it was about "The cleaner", whoever the hell he is, she is, whatever.'

'More information, good. What else?'

'There might have been a third person in the project. Sammy says that Mount and Glover asked Fred Noble if he wanted to play, but he said he was too busy.'

'Did they tell him what it was about?' Skinner asked eagerly.

'He says no, that he didn't want to know, so that he couldn't let anything slip accidentally.'

'Noble said that? Can anyone confirm it?'

'Glover's agent can't. All he told her was that they were working on it and it was big.'

'What do we know about her?'

'We know she didn't kill Glover. She was in London when he died. Forget her.'

'What do we know about Fred Noble?'

'He's a best-selling author, the most successful of the so-called Triumvirate, although he hasn't been around for as long as Glover or Mount. He moved to Edinburgh six years ago, and—'

'Six years ago? After Frankie Coben was supposedly killed?'

'Yes, but he didn't kill Glover either. He was on telly when he died.'

'Who says our man is acting alone? Didn't you tell me you were looking into someone's movements on the night?'

'Ed Collins, Carol Glover's fiancée.'

'The boy who works for the *Saltire?*'

'Right.'

Skinner snatched up his mobile from the central console, retrieved the direct number of the Leith CID office and called it. DC Alice Cowan's strong voice filled the car as she answered.

'Alice,' he said, 'DCC here . . . sorry, chief constable here. Is DI Pye there?'

'No, sir. He and Ray, sorry, DS Wilding, are out.'

'Do you know if they've got anything solid on Ed Collins yet?'

'Hell yes, sir. They've just gone to arrest him. He's been working with Coben. I'm on to Collins's bank just now. He's been receiving regular payments for months and not from his employer. We're trying to trace the source.'

'What's he been doing for Coben? Do we know?'

Cowan hesitated. 'Surveillance, sir.'

'What do you mean, surveillance? Be specific, Alice.'

'He's been taking photographs, sir,' she replied, her voice for once expressionless, 'of DCC Martin.'

'Has he now,' Skinner growled. 'When Sammy and Ray pick him up, you tell them I want him brought up to Fettes.'

As he ended the call, McIlhenney glanced across at him. 'Is that a good idea, boss?' he asked. 'You interviewing the guy?'

'Don't worry,' the chief constable replied. 'I'm not going near him. He's for you.'

'Even so, the thought of you being in the same building as the guy who photographed Alex . . .'

'Hmmm.' A low growl seemed to fill the car 'This boy's fucking lucky I'm not sending him up to Dundee.' Then he brightened up. 'Come on, Neil, we're on a roll here. I love it when that happens. What else do we need?' Almost instantly he answered his own question. 'We need to know about Henry Mount's role in this mysterious project. And we need to know something else, maybe the key to wrapping up this whole business. Who's his agent?'

'His son, Colin.'

'Colin? I knew he was his father's manager, but not that he acted for him.'

'The previous agent retired last year; Colin took over from him. George Regan discovered that when he spoke to him.'

'Regan.' He picked up his phone again, opened his seemingly unending contacts folder and found a mobile number for the East

Lothian DI. He grinned, 'No one's beyond my reach, chum,' then called it. 'George,' he said into the microphone above the rear-view mirror. 'Skinner here. What are you up to?'

'Hoping for a miracle sighting of Hugo Playfair, sir. Otherwise we're completing door-to-door inquiries. I've followed up everybody who was in the Golf Inn on Sunday evening, and I've found half a dozen people who remember seeing Mustafic leaving there, then turning into Middleshot Road.'

'That's an odd way back to the bents,' Skinner mused. 'But with all that beer in him, he was probably a bit wandered. When I think about it, Middleshot would have led him to the top of the path where he died. Any sightings of Playfair, or anyone else following him?'

Regan sighed. 'None, sir.'

'No, that's the way it goes sometimes. George, this investigation has moved into the stage where we do everything the book says, then hope we get lucky. Your DS can keep an eye on it for a while. I've got another task for you. You've met Henry Mount's family, I believe.'

'Yes, sir.'

'Good. We know for sure how Henry died; the cigar that was used to kill him was in a box bought in Edinburgh last week from one of Paula Viareggio's luxury delis, for cash, by a man going by the name of Coben. I want you to go back and see them, Trudy and Colin . . . I know them both, by the way . . . and to ask them about a few things. The first is a project we believe Henry was working on with Ainsley Glover, something new, nothing to do with the Petra Jecks books.'

'His wife mentioned something yesterday,' the DI remarked. 'She said he'd been speaking to Glover about it, so she thought it was financial.'

'Maybe it was, but I doubt that. We need anything we can get on it, however trivial you or they might think it is. We need to know also whether Henry's career before he became a writer took him anywhere near Yugoslavia. Finally, and this is definitely one for Colin, for Trudy won't have a clue: we need to know how that cigar box got into Henry's possession, and whether the name Coben rings any bells.'

'Understood, sir,' Regan replied. 'I'm not far from their house; I'm on my way.'

Seventy-five

'He must be in.' Ray Wilding pointed to a motorcycle, sitting by the kerb, secured by a heavy chain which tethered its front wheel. 'I'm pretty sure that's his: a Triumph Tiger. I noticed one parked at Carol Glover's and they're pretty scarce machines.'

'Great job being a football reporter, isn't it?' Sammy Pye remarked as he pushed open the door and stepped into the apartment block. It was a modest building, in the west of the city, close to a railway line. 'Hibs have a midweek game so he doesn't have to go into the office at all today. And you have enough spare time to earn some extra money by spying on cops.'

'And maybe more,' said the sergeant. 'The images in his folder were all timed. He snapped Andy leaving the ACPOS dinner, getting into a taxi at ten thirty and going into Alex's at ten forty-five. Nothing after that till the stuff through the curtains, next morning. He had plenty of time to get back up to Charlotte Square and kill Glover. There was nobody better placed to know how he dosed himself, or to swap the insulin capsule for one with the drug.'

'That's true, but be honest, Ray; you've met Collins. Is he a methodical, cold-blooded killer?'

'I wouldn't rule it out. He was good enough to trail an experienced police officer for months until he caught him dipping his wick were he shouldn't have.' He whistled. 'Lucky man that he is.'

His colleague grinned as they climbed the stairs. 'I'll tell the new

388

chief you said that,' he joked. 'Worse still, I'll tell DI Stallings.'

'Ah,' Wilding countered, 'I didn't say he was as lucky as me, though.'

'Slippery bastard.' Pye stopped on the second-floor landing, facing a blue-painted door. A nameplate read 'E. Collins'. Wilding reached out and rang the bell. The detectives waited, listening for footfalls inside the flat but hearing nothing. 'I hope this place doesn't have a back door, like fucking Darnaway Street,' Pye muttered. 'Or maybe the sports editor broke his word and called him to warn him we were coming.'

'Want the door kicked in?'

'Let's not go that far just yet.' The DI reached out, turned the handle and pushed. The door opened. 'Your way looks great, my way's easier.'

They stepped into a small hallway; its only pieces of furniture were a coat stand, on which hung two jackets and a grey metallic crash helmet, and a telephone table, but the walls were festooned with football posters, all of them featuring the same club. 'There's no such team as Glasgow Rangers, you know,' said Wilding. 'It's just Rangers FC; that's the proper name.'

'Bluenose,' Pye grunted.

'Aye, and so's this boy. Hardly your impartial sports journalist, is he?'

Ally McCoist, aged twenty-something, smiled at them, larger than life, from a facing door; from the layout of the block they guessed it was the living room.

'Mr Collins,' the sergeant shouted. 'Police.'

But there was no sound within the flat. 'Excuse me, Coisty,' said Pye, as he opened the door and stepped into the room. 'Oh shit,' he exclaimed.

'Yes, I can smell it,' Wilding murmured as he stood beside him and looked down at the body of Ed Collins, clad in a Rangers replica top, lying in the centre of what a less experienced witness might have taken for a red rug. His eyes were only half open as they gazed lifelessly at the ceiling. There was a cut on his forehead, and a lump. But those wounds were superficial. Collins had been nailed to the floor, through the centre of his chest, by a short samurai sword, a souvenir, the sergeant imagined as he surveyed the scene, from a foreign holiday. He glanced to his right and nodded, indicating its scabbard, which sat on top of a television set in a corner of the room.

'Somebody's been taking precautions.'

'No, Ray, not just somebody; Coben has.'

'And there's nothing subtle about this one, it's not an imaginative death like Glover's or Mount's.'

'No,' the DI agreed. 'This one's from the Fred Noble school. What was it he said? "Sharp objects, at close range", or words to that effect.' He paused, pointing to the floor. 'But maybe there is some subtlety here. Look what's lying beside him; it's a ballpoint.'

'So?'

Pye shrugged. 'Maybe nothing, except there's a line somewhere, at the back of my mind.' He nodded. 'I remember now: "They may say" he quoted, '"that the pen is mightier than the sword, but when it comes down to it, that's never the way to bet." It's from a book called *The Sharp End*, and yes, it's by Fred Noble.'

Seventy-six

'I'm sorry,' said Colin Mount. 'Mum's asleep; she had a bad night, so the doctor called again and gave her a pretty strong sedative. I could wake her if it's really necessary, but I don't know how much you'd get out of her. I can talk to you, though; I'm on compassionate leave from the station. They've been very good about it.'

'Then let's you and I have a chat first,' Regan told him, 'and hope we don't have to bring your mother into it. Yesterday, she mentioned a project that your father was working on, something away from his usual thing. Can you tell me anything about it?'

The younger man exhaled loudly. 'This is going to make me sound like a bloody awful agent, but I can't. He was involved in it with Ainsley, though, that much I do know. It was a joint venture, and there may even have been a third person, but I do not know what they were doing. He never dropped any hints.'

'None at all? Do you know what sort of research he was doing?'

Mount shook his head. 'Not really. Occasionally I'd hear him on the phone to Ainsley, but I couldn't decipher what they were saying . . . not that I was trying to. My father often chose to keep me in the dark about his fiction as a plot developed, so why should this have been any different?'

'Think hard, did you overhear anything at all?'

'I heard names mentioned, foreign names, but you could quiz me all day and all night and I know that none of them will come back to me.'

'OK, but if you do have a flashback recollection, I want you to let me know soonest, OK?'

'Sure.'

'Now,' Regan continued, 'your father was a retired diplomat.'

'Yes. He spent quite a bit of his career abroad.'

'Your mother mentioned Venezuela, and Berlin during the Cold War.'

'Those were two of his more glamorous postings, yes, but others were more mundane. Neither Ireland nor Iceland were a barrel of fun and laughter.'

'What about Yugoslavia? Was he ever there?'

'Not on a posting, no. But when he came off the road, so to speak, he was an undersecretary in the section of the Foreign Office that kept an eye on the place. I was only a kid then, but I know it affected him very badly. There was some terrible stuff going on there, ethnic cleansing, real atrocities. He'd come home from the office some nights and wouldn't say a word to my mother or me. If you'd known my father, you'd have understood how untypical that was, how worrying it was. Even if he hadn't sold his first two books, I think he'd have taken the early retirement package when he did.'

'I see. Colin, this project, could it have been related to Yugoslavia, or to what it became?'

Mount considered the question for a few moments. 'If I said yes,' he ventured 'I'd only be . . .' he stopped in mid-sentence, 'except, there was that visit to England. A couple of weeks ago he went away for the day, in the car. I asked him where he was going; all he said was that there was a man he needed to see. "About a dog?" I asked him. He smiled and said that was right. He didn't say anything when I saw him next morning, but I did notice something on his desk. It was a photo pass, it said, "Visitor. HMP Brankholme", wherever that is, and it had the date on it.'

'Would it still be in his office?'

'No. When he caught me looking at it, he picked it up, winked at me, and put it in the shredder.'

'OK, that's worth knowing. We'll be able to check out who's there. By the way, Brankholme's in Darlington.' He paused. 'My last question,' he said. 'We've confirmed that your father was killed, as we thought, by a method lifted from one of his own books, a bullet or similar projectile planted in one of his cigars.'

'He made it easy for whoever did it,' the younger Mount sighed. 'Everybody in the bloody world . . . the literary world at any rate . . . knew that he smoked nothing but those La Glorias.'

'So it seems. But we know where the cigar that killed him was bought: a specialist shop in Edinburgh. It was one of a box of twenty-five, and we know that your father didn't make the purchase himself.'

'No, it was a present. He told me so when I saw it, down in the office.'

'Did he mention the name Coben?'

The dead author's son looked at him, blankly. 'No, he said it was a gift from the Edinburgh Book Festival; a token of their thanks.'

Seventy-seven

'How long does the pathologist reckon he's been dead?' McIlhenney asked, speaking to the air, in the driving seat of Skinner's car as he parked it in Ann Street.

'She's estimating time of death at between eight and nine this morning,' Sammy Pye told him though the hands-free speaker. 'There's a box of cornflakes, an unused bowl and a carton of milk on the kitchen table. It looks as if the guy was about to have his breakfast when he was interrupted. There are no signs of forced entry; the door was unlocked, and we were able to walk right in.'

'Any signs of a struggle?'

'None. It looks as if Collins knew the caller, let him in. From the head wound . . . caused by a blow hard enough to stun but not kill . . . the guy hit him with something, knocked him out and then skewered him with the sword.'

'Did he bring it with him?'

'We don't know, not yet. He could have; it's a wakizashi . . .'

'A what?'

'Short sword,' said the chief constable.

'That's right,' the DI confirmed. 'I've got Ray to thank for that; he's studied Japanese martial arts. Wakizashi's the name for a short sword, no more than two feet long, the samurai equivalent of a sidearm. It could easily have been hidden under a jacket if it was brought here. We'll need to ask Carol Glover, or somebody else who knew Collins and who's been here, before we'll know for sure. All I can say is that it's the sort of weapon you'd expect to find displayed on a wall or on a cabinet, and we haven't found any empty hooks or stands.'

'What are you doing about Carol?'

'I've sent Alice Cowan to break the news; the poor lass knows her, so it's probably best.'

'Yes, fine,' McIlhenney agreed. 'What do we know about Collins' family?'

'Next to bugger-all. There are a couple of photographs on his sideboard. One's of him and Carol, taken at a formal dance, and the other's a graduation photo, taken at what looks like Glasgow University, with him in a gown, and with a middle-aged couple who could be parents. Again, Carol should be able to help us with that. I hope so. I don't fancy having to ask her to make another trip to the city mortuary to look at a loved one on a slab.'

'I wouldn't fancy asking anyone to do that job,' said Skinner, 'but you're right. Even if the parents aren't available, you should get somebody else to do it rather than her. Xavi Aislado, the victim's editor; he'd be acceptable. When he learns that one of his people was doing homers for a murderer, he'll probably be happy to see him dead . . . or as happy as Xavi ever gets, at any rate. That reminds me, indirectly; what progress have you made on tracing those payments into Collins' account?'

'I think we've got as far as we're going to get, sir. The payments . . . twelve grand in total . . . have come from a numbered account in a bank in Luxembourg.'

'Damn it. You're right, Sammy, we're stuffed. It's against their law to disclose account information, even to us, unless we can show clear evidence of money laundering, which in this case we can't. It's a pity; anything that would have reinforced the link between Coben and Collins would have been useful.' He paused, looking at the microphone. 'Hey,' he exclaimed, 'the pen that was dropped beside the body: have you touched it?'

'No, sir, I couldn't stand the grief that Dorward would give me if I did. It's still on the floor; I'm looking at it now.'

'Then look a bit closer, and see if it tells us anything. Touch it if necessary; I'll clear you with Arthur.'

He waited, with McIlhenney, in silence for a few seconds.

'Yes, sir, it does,' said Pye at last. 'I had to roll it over to see it, but there's something on it. It's a hotel pen, the kind you find in your room, with the stationery. It's from the Novotel World Forum, The Hague.'

'Good,' the chief constable declared. 'Your next step is to find out from Aislado and from Carol Glover whether Collins has ever been to The Hague, for a football game or on holiday. If not, then there's a better than even chance that our Mr Coben has. Let Superintendent McIlhenney know as soon as you can. Meantime, he and I have an appointment with a judge.'

'Before you go, sir,' Pye said hurriedly. 'We haven't got to the bad news yet.'

Skinner frowned. 'Then get to it,' he said tersely.

'Ray and I have done a quick search of Collins' flat. Not touching, not moving, just looking. There's only one bedroom, and in his wardrobe we found a blazer, with a Union Jack lapel badge. In a pocket we found a pair of gold-rimmed glasses, bought from Boots, light-reactive, minimum strength. And in the bathroom, in his cabinet, we found an aerosol: hair styling foam for men. When we met Collins, his hair was loose, just like it is now. Then there's a photo, of him and Carol at a dance, framed on the sideboard. There's a date on it, in the corner; it was taken the Saturday before last, two days before the cigars were bought. The guy's got a beard in it. Sir—'

'Stop, Sammy,' McIlhenney sighed. 'We get the picture. It wasn't

Coben who bought the La Gloria cigars, or went to see Andy. It was his message boy, Ed Collins.'

'OK,' said Skinner briskly. 'We know this man is smart. We shouldn't be surprised by this. Now we really have to go.'

He ended the call and stepped out of the car with his colleague. As McIlhenney tossed him the keys, a perspiring traffic warden rushed towards them, ticket machine in hand. The superintendent whispered in his ear; he turned and shuffled off, with undisguised disappointment.

Lord Elmore was waiting in his open doorway as they walked up his drive. 'I wish I could do that,' he said smiling, extending his hand to Skinner.

'Hello, Claus,' said the chief constable. 'We don't normally pull that stunt; only when it's necessary. It's good to see you. How's The Hague?'

The little judge reflected on the question as he ushered his visitors inside, and up the stairs to his study. 'Not as varied as the Court of Session or the High Court of Justiciary,' he confessed as he closed the door behind him, 'and completely lacking the black humour that you find there, particularly on the criminal bench. But that wouldn't be appropriate, would it? The cases that we have to try are usually brutal; very harrowing crimes, and atrocities. I don't know what I did to upset the Lord President who recommended me for appointment to the Tribunal, but whatever it was, he got his own back.'

'I know,' Skinner told him. 'You ruffled plenty of feathers in your time, Claus, both as counsel and on the bench; you were bound to cross the wrong bloke eventually. Don't blame the Lord President; it had very little to do with him. Your views on the relationship between the judges and politics didn't go down well with a certain ex-First Minister.'

'Little Mr Murtagh, now fallen in disgrace? Yes, I was aware his dirty little hand was in it somewhere.'

'All over it; he pulled all the strings.'

Lord Elmore smiled. 'In that case, he'd be frustrated to know that although it's grim, and I'll be happy to retire when my stint is over, I feel privileged to be doing the job. Can I offer you a drink?' he asked abruptly.

'Something soft if you have it.'

'Superintendent?'

'The same for me, please.'

The officers took seats and watched as their host poured lime juice into two glasses, then topped them up with soda water from an old-fashioned siphon. 'Now, chaps,' he said as he handed them over, 'what can I do for you? Have you got something on our friend Anderson after all?'

Skinner shook his head. 'He's off the pitch. Bruce is a fool, and the worst sort of politician, but in the rest of his life he's well-intentioned, it seems. No, Claus, we've just come from a meeting with a man, someone you don't know and never will, who says that you're the man to ask about a certain General Bogdan Tadic; Serbian.'

Lord Elmore stared at him in astonishment. 'Why in God's name would you want to know about him?' he exclaimed.

'His name's come up in connection with a suspect in the deaths of Ainsley Glover and Henry Mount.'

'Then if I didn't know that the swine is behind some very thick solid bars indeed, I'd tell you to look no further. Of all the sordid villains my colleagues and I have tried, he's the one who made my blood run the coldest. Absolutely ruthless; a pure psychopath, surrounded by other pure psychopaths who did his bidding.'

'We know Tadic isn't in circulation. It's one of those associates we're concerned about, someone called Coben.'

'Coben?' The judge's forehead wrinkled in concentration. 'Coben? Yes, there was a person of that name in his circle, mentioned in the passing by a couple of witnesses. But the stories they told were second-hand, no more than legends. Frankie Coben was said to have carried out some of Tadic's more sadistic orders, those that he delegated, for the general was very hands on ... hands, feet, teeth, prick, knives, you name it, he used it on his victims. The evidence put before us was that Coben was much less crude that Tadic ... indeed was his cultural antithesis ... but capable of equal, if more sophisticated, violence.' He paused. 'In fact, I recall a story that was told during the trial. It was second-hand, so ultimately useless as evidence, but interesting nonetheless. Tadic ordered Coben to get rid of one of his own people he suspected of disloyalty. So the unfortunate was sent out with a mine, with orders to plant it under some enemy fortifications. But just as the man was setting about his task, Coben detonated the thing, using a remote trigger. The witness at the trial said the tale was that when the explosion was heard, Coben laughed and said, "Hoist by his own petard." So, not just a murderer, Coben was a Shakespearean scholar, with a black sense of humour.' Lord Elmore gazed at Skinner. 'But it's all academic, so to speak, isn't it? Coben's dead, killed by the Americans when they missed Tadic.'

'So they say,' the chief constable replied, 'but the name keeps cropping up in this inquiry.'

'It can't be the same person. And if it was, what possible interest would someone like Coben have in two crime writers?'

'We can't answer that yet; that's why we're here. Claus, what can you tell us about Tadic's trial?'

'We're going to have to do it again,' the judge glowered. 'That's the first thing I can tell you. His legal team have won a retrial, courtesy of an obscure blunder by the prosecution in preparing its case. We're going to have to uproot the witnesses from wherever they've been resettled.'

'All of them?' McIlhenney exclaimed. 'Isn't their evidence on the record?'

'Yes, but we reckon that we'll have to recall at least one of them, the key witness, who saw Tadic kill seven people, personally.'

'Can you remember his name?' the superintendent asked.

'Of course; I remember the whole trial, vividly, all the awful stories. His name was Mirko Andelić. He and two others were in hiding when Tadic and his men went on the rampage; all three saw him go into a building. Mirko got to a window and saw him . . .' he drew a breath, '. . . do it. He gutted them all with a sharpened sickle, one by one, four men and three women . . . another piece from the Bard, by the way, maybe suggested by Coben. The wounds matched those on bodies found well after the event, by NATO forces. At least the other witnesses didn't get to see that. One of them was Mirko's wife, Danica; the other was her brother, Aca something.'

'Nicolić?'

Lord Elmore stared at Skinner. 'Yes, that's it. How did you know that?'

'The names you've just mentioned were all on a list compiled by Ainsley Glover.'

'Jesus, how did he get those?'

'No idea, but why does it surprise you that he did?'

'Because the trial was held in camera, at the request of the American government. They didn't want attention to focus on their attempt to assassinate Tadic. Besides Frankie Coben, there were many civilian casualties; their action could be construed as a war crime itself.' He hesitated, thinking. 'So what the hell was Glover up to?'

'Glover and Mount. We know they were working on a joint project, perhaps with a third party. It looks now as if they were planning a book on Tadic.'

'And his secret trial?'

'I suppose so. It's pretty clear they were looking for the witnesses.'

'But where would they get the lead, their names?'

'Henry Mount was a retired diplomat. Could he have had access?'

'Oh my. If he had the right contacts in the Foreign Office, indeed he could.'

'That's it. They were looking for witnesses, they tripped over Coben and were taken out.'

'So what's Coben's purpose?'

'I'd been wondering the same thing, Claus, but now it's obvious, from what you've just told us: Coben is looking for the witnesses too, before the retrial can begin.'

'In that case, Bob, Superintendent, please run the sod to ground!'

'We will, I promise you.'

'Is there any other way I can help?'

'There is one thing,' McIlhenney responded, 'something that's been puzzling my people. Does the term "the cleaner" mean anything to you in this context?'

Lord Elmore thought for second, then his eyes flashed. 'Not "the cleaner". No, someone's misunderstood. It should be "the cleanser", as in ethnic. The Serbian word is *čistač*, and that's how it translates best. It was Tadic's nickname in Yugoslavia.'

Seventy-eight

Aileen de Marco looked at the pile of green folders that still sat in her in-tray, letters drafted for her signature by the Scottish civil service. Parliament had a lengthy summer recess, but the requirements of government were continuous. She was considering the text of a reply to a letter from a Conservative MSP, from Dumfries, seeking special compensation for a constituent, a mounted policeman who had been kicked by his horse, when her phone rang.

'I've finally been able to place your call,' Lena McElhone, her private secretary, advised her. 'He's just got back to his office. I like his new secretary,' she said. 'He sounds like a nice guy.'

'He is,' the First Minister told her. 'And to save you asking, he's straight and he's single. Maybe the two of you should meet to compare notes about your bosses.' She smiled as she waited for the call to be connected.

'What have you been saying to Gerry Crossley?' said Bob when he came on line. 'He sounded more than a wee bit flustered when he put you through.'

'Me? Nothing at all. How's your first full day been? I'd have called you sooner but I've been tied up in meetings, then when I did try, you were out.'

'I've been away. I had to take an unexpected trip with Neil; somebody had information he said was for our ears only.'

'Who was it?'

'Dražen Boras.'

'Jesus!'

'Wrong department, love, wrong name. I'll tell you all about it when I get home. I'll be a while yet, though. I've called a general meeting about our various murder investigations, a brainstorming session.'

'Are you making progress?'

'Seems like it. That's what the meeting's about; I want to pull the threads together.'

'Is that how you plan to run things in CID from now on?'

'I'm going to be hands on, sure, but this was Neil's idea. He reckons I'm still the best detective on the force . . . I'm not going to argue with him either . . . and he wants my input.'

'Good luck, then. I hope it helps. What do you want for supper when you do get home?'

'Nothing much. I ate like a hog last night.'

'OK, I'll do something light, a salad perhaps.'

'That'll be fine. I'll call you when I'm ready to leave.'

'Use the mobile. I might not be home myself by then. I'll see you, whenever.' She made to hang up then stopped. 'Oh,' she exclaimed, 'I almost forgot that I had a reason for calling you. You do remember we're having guests for dinner tomorrow night, at the official residence, don't you? Randy Mosley and Denzel Chandler.'

'Of course,' he replied, but only after a second's delay that suggested he had not.

'It's still all right, isn't it? I realise things have changed a bit since we made the arrangement. I'll postpone it, if you want.'

'No, not at all. We'll all be ready for it by then. Randy's having a hard week too, so it'll be a welcome break for her. Just the four of us, is it?'

'Yes, but I can add to the party. Alex, if you like. It's a private affair, our expense, not on the hospitality budget, so I'll be doing the cooking.'

'Let me think about that. Meantime, my troops should have gathered by now. See you later.'

He hung up. Aileen was about to return to the matter of the unruly police horse, but as an afterthought, she buzzed her outer office. 'Hey, what did you say to get Gerry Crossley flustered?' she asked her private secretary. 'Have you made a move on the guy already?'

Seventy-nine

Bob Skinner sat at his desk and pondered upon the day's discoveries. In his mind he could see a jigsaw, its pieces laid out before him. He was a distance short of seeing the finished picture, but he knew that it was there to be assembled. One more check was needed, he felt, to verify some elements that were still only suspicions.

He picked up his secure telephone and dialled a number. Apart from the access that his rank gave him, Skinner had two important personal contacts within the security and intelligence community. Piers Frame was one, but their relationship was based on leverage that the Scot had gained during an investigation in the past, one that he had been seconded to carry out. The other was a friend, and a trusted colleague, with whom the darkest secrets could be shared.

Until a few days earlier, Amanda Dennis had been acting head of the security service, but with the appointment of one of the new Prime Minister's favourites as the permanent director general, she had reverted to her former deputy status. While Whitehall tended to empty at five like a football ground after the final whistle, he knew that she was usually at her desk for longer than most of her staff, and so he was not surprised when she answered his call.

'Bob,' she said. 'Congratulations. I heard this morning.'

'Thanks. I'm sorry our po-faced leader hadn't the sense to do the same with you.'

'I'm not,' she said. 'The DG's a public figure these days. I'm old school; as deputy I'm under the radar and that suits me far better. You'll be fine at the top of the tree, though; in your service it pays to be highly visible. What are you after today, or whom?'

'Straight to the point, eh, Amanda,' he laughed. 'My people are trying to clean up the mess left by the murders of two authors, and now a third man, an associate of our chief suspect.'

'Glover and Mount? Yes, I've heard about those. I'm a Fred Noble man myself; keep him safe, Bob, please.'

'We're doing that, but I don't really believe he's in danger. Ainsley and Henry were working together on a project; they were keeping it secret, not discussing the subject matter, but I, we, believe it was to be a book about a Serbian war criminal, General Bogdan Tadic, whose story seems never to have been told, although it was one of the bloodiest chapters in the whole Balkan conflict.'

'The Cleanser?' Dennis murmured. 'Yes, I can see why that would be provocative in certain circles. But you're not suggesting, are you, that we're behind their deaths, or even the Americans? There was no need to go to extremes. Even if they'd finished their work, they'd have been prevented from publishing.'

'On what grounds?'

'National interest.'

'Bollocks, Amanda. We've got no interest that I can see in covering up Tadic. The Americans are sensitive about the fact that they tried to assassinate him, that's all. Anyway, I'm not suggesting that. I'm looking for a man named Frankie Coben, one of Tadic's henchmen. He was thought to have been killed in the botched attempt on the Cleanser's life, but that seems to have been an exaggeration. His name's cropped up; in fact I believe that he killed the two authors, and his own sidekick.'

'I see. What do you need?'

'I need to know more about him. Where he came from, who his

parents were, whether they're still alive. I need anything that will lead me to Coben. There are no photographs of him, only a photofit, and you know how reliable they are. I could be in the same room as the man and be none the wiser. But nobody can wipe out his entire past; I need to get into that, to find a way to identify him.'

'I'll see what I can do,' Dennis promised. 'Strictly speaking this isn't our affair, but if he's involved in serious crime within our borders, that gives me grounds for intervention.'

'Thanks. There's something else. Tadic was tried in camera; his crimes were never in the public domain. Yet Glover and Mount were looking for the witnesses against him. I need to know how they got the names. All I can offer you as a starter is that Henry used to be a diplomat.'

'A spook?'

'Possibly, but I don't know. Whether he was or not, he couldn't have come up with those names during his service. He was retired when they were discovered. So there must be a current source.'

'And I want to know who that is,' the intelligence officer said firmly.

'I'm sure. While you're looking for the leak, I'd like to know the status of the witnesses . . . although I'm pretty sure I know where one of them is right now.' He gave Dennis the three names.

'Information required yesterday?' she asked.

'Yes,' he replied, 'but at a pinch tomorrow morning will do.'

The chief constable hung up, rose and walked into his outer office. Crossley was still there.

'On your way, Gerry,' he said. 'This meeting could be a quick one or it could last all night. No need for you to wait on.' He glanced at him. 'What's put the smile on your face?' he asked.

'I've just been asked out,' the PA replied. 'On a date. By a woman. Convention says it should be the other way around. And I've never met her.'

'Ah! Lena McElhone. Careful, young man; they tell me she bites.'

Crossley grinned. 'I don't mind that, as long as her teeth aren't too sharp.'

Skinner was still chuckling as he stepped into the meeting room at the end of the corridor, where Neil McIlhenney waited, seated at the conference table with DIs Sammy Pye and George Regan. Before each of the inspectors lay a folder: the murder books, chronologically ordered records of every step of their investigations. The trio stood as he entered.

'No,' he said firmly. 'I'm not the Prince of Wales . . . whom God preserve, in something clear and preferably eco-friendly . . . and I'm not the President of the United States. I'm a professional colleague, and you're senior officers, so you stay seated when I come into a room.' He took his seat and looked at the superintendent. 'Have you said anything about our trip?'

'No, Chief. I thought it best left till you joined us.'

'Fine.' Skinner turned to Regan. 'Hugo Playfair isn't who he said he was, George. He's an intelligence operative, Lazar Erceg, one of the four names on Glover's list, inserted into Serbia by the Americans, with private assistance, to find witnesses to atrocities by a war criminal, General Bogdan Tadic.' He nodded to Pye. 'His nickname is the Cleanser, Sammy.'

'So that's why Sauce's email respondent crapped herself and hung up on him.'

'From what we've learned, I don't blame her. Now, the witnesses Erceg was sent to unearth, and who he did find, were the other three names on that list, Mirko and Danica Andelić, and Aca Nicolić, Danica's brother. They gave evidence against Tadic in the Hague, and he was convicted, but he's being retried, and Mirko is essential to that process. So you see, guys,' he told the inspectors, 'your investigations cross over.'

'Yes,' said Regan, 'but how do the two authors fit in?'

'They were working together,' Pye replied. 'Trying to trace the witnesses, and Erceg as well. Clearly, they were doing a book on Tadic.'

'That's the background,' said Skinner. 'And in that background is the man called Coben, Frankie Coben, associate of Tadic and doer of some of his dirty work, believed to be dead, but not quite. We believe he killed Glover, Mount and now his hired associate, Ed Collins. Why did he hire Collins, Ainsley Glover's future son-in-law, of all people? Good question, but here's an even better one. When Coben sent him to see Andy Martin, using his name, to warn him off getting involved with Glover, how did he know that Glover had visited Andy? When he sent Collins, again in his name, to buy the cigars that were booby-trapped and used to kill Henry Mount, how did he know that Henry was involved at all?' He looked around the table. 'Ideas?' he asked.

'We keep hearing about the possibility of a third person in the project,' said McIlhenney. 'I'm wondering whether it's possible that Collins was him, and was passing information to Coben.'

'I doubt that, sir,' Pye countered. 'June Connelly told us that Glover couldn't stand him, and only tolerated him because he was his daughter's boyfriend. By the way, remember the references by DCC Martin and the witness McBain to the man they saw having a military bearing? Ray and I asked the *Saltire* editor about his background; he told us that after he left university, Collins did three years in the army, on a short service commission.'

'Another hole filled,' said Skinner. 'For what it's worth,' he grinned, 'and it had better be worth a lot, gentlemen, I believe that Coben was given all that information by Mount and Glover themselves. I believe that Coben was the third man in the project; that like Collins, the two dead authors knew their killer . . . but clearly, they didn't know him as Coben. They knew him as somebody else. Coben is moving among us, guys; some of us have probably met him.' He leaned back in his chair, in a sudden movement. 'OK, that's what I know so far,' he said, addressing the two DIs. 'What do either of you know beyond that?' He frowned as Regan's phone rang.

'Sorry, sir,' he said, checking the caller number on its display. 'It's McDermid. I told her she could call if she got any new relevant information.'

'Answer her then, but put her on speaker, if you can.'

'I can do that.' Regan took the call and laid his phone on the table. 'Lisa,' he warned, 'I'm in a meeting with the chief and others, and we can all hear you. If it's not urgent, call later.'

'It is, sir,' the DS replied, 'or I wouldn't have called.' She sounded offended.

'OK, Lisa,' Skinner called out, 'let's hear it.'

'I've finally had feedback from the translator, sir,' she said.

'What translator?'

'We found letters in Mustafic's van,' she explained. 'They were in the Cyrillic alphabet, in Bulgarian we thought. We sent them for translation, with the label on his jacket. The reason it's taken so long is that we sent them to the wrong translator. It isn't Bulgarian at all, it's Serbian. And the jacket wasn't bought in Bulgaria, but in Zagreb.'

'Now why doesn't that surprise me?' said the chief constable quietly. 'Tell me about the letters.'

'They're love letters, sir, and they're years old. They're from a woman called Danica, to somebody called Mirko Andelić.'

'Yes,' Skinner exclaimed. 'Lisa, you've just tied something up, with a neat bow. Thanks.' He reached out and flipped the phone shut, to end the call. 'So that's it. Asmir was really Mirko Andelić, the key witness in the Tadic trial. I see what happened; after it was over, Lazar Erceg, the man who found him, took him underground, away from the Cleanser's people, who were undoubtedly very keen to kill him. That's why

Coben got involved with the project: Mount and Glover were looking for him, so he joined with them, let them do his work for them, even guarded against outside interference by having Andy Martin warned off, then followed up until he found something to discredit him. Finally, he got his man.'

'That means that Tadic goes free,' McIlhenney pointed out.

'To what fate? Tadic is a pariah; if the Americans don't kill him, his own people probably will, especially after we eliminate Coben.' He frowned. 'But,' he murmured, 'how did he get to know about Playfair and Asmir?'

'There was a report in the *East Lothian Courier*,' said George Regan, 'a few weeks ago, of the council's application for an interdict against Derek Baillie's traveller group. Playfair spoke on their behalf in court and his name was in the paper.'

'OK, but that doesn't help. How did he know who Playfair was?'

'Well,' the DI murmured.

'Spit it out, George.'

'Colin Mount told me that his father made a mystery trip a couple of weeks back, to a prison in England.'

'What? Brankholme?'

'Yes, sir, how did you know that?'

'Because Neil and I have just been there, and the man we saw didn't say anything about having had a visit from Henry Mount.' He gazed at McIlhenney. 'Now why weren't we told that, I wonder?'

'Dražen only contacted us when he saw the photo in the paper,' the superintendent replied. 'Why would he tell us if Mount had visited him? And why would Boras contact him in the first place?'

'Mount contacted Dražen, man. We're sure he has a source in the Foreign Office who's been feeding him information on the Tadic case. Tomorrow Amanda Dennis will put a name to that person, and we'll find out, I'll bet you, that he told Mount about Dražen's involvement.

Clear as day: Henry goes to see Dražen, he's told about Hugo Playfair, and he goes back and tells Coben, the third man in the project. That's what Coben needs and, bingo, they're all fucking dead. Why didn't Dražen mention Mount? Who knows . . .' he frowned, thinking fast '. . . unless he genuinely was doing us a favour but didn't want to attract any more attention to himself than that. And why would that be? Oh no,' he gasped suddenly. 'No, no, no, surely not.' He snatched the phone from the table and called the communications centre. 'Chief Constable,' he barked. 'Get me HMP Brankholme, now.' He sat waiting, his three companions drawing tension from his. Finally the prison switchboard replied. 'Deputy Governor Arnott, please.'

'I'm sorry, sir.' The telephonist sounded rattled; Skinner seized on it.

'Governor, then, now; this is Chief Constable Skinner, Edinburgh. We were in your place today.'

He waited for over a minute, until a man came on the line. 'Garfield Haywood, Governor. I'm sorry, Chief Constable, you find us in crisis. We've lost our star prisoner, the man you visited earlier.'

'And how the fuck did you manage to do that?' Skinner growled.

'It looks as if our security is better on the way in than on the way out. My deputy seems to have taken the man home with her. Her husband called to see her, then they left together, only it wasn't him. It was Dražen Boras wearing his clothes. We found Jake bound and gagged in his underwear, and locked in her office. I'm still not convinced he isn't an accomplice. What the hell would make her do it?'

'Have you any idea how wealthy the man is, Mr Haywood?' He hung up, staring at McIlhenney.

'Gone?'

'Gone, and I am not looking forward to telling Maggie. Fuck it!' He turned to Regan. 'That was a blot from the blue, George. Any more while you're at it?'

The DI twisted in his seat, nervously. 'Maybe, boss,' he said. 'Those cigars: Colin said they were a gift to his dad from the Edinburgh Book Festival.'

'Jesus.' Skinner clenched his fists on the desk. 'And how many people are involved in running that? Dozens, including the board, and maybe more, if you count part-timers. I shouldn't be surprised. This whole thing started there.' He closed his eyes for a second or two; when he reopened them they were staring, at nothing in particular. 'Didn't it, though?' he whispered. He reached out for Pye's bulky folder, his murder book, spun it round and opened it. The first entry was Ian McCall's report, of the discovery of Glover's body. The second was Randall Mosley's statement. The third was the text of the dead author's email, sent in the last moments of his life. He read the words aloud, 'randy yurt dying,' then looked at his colleagues. 'What's that?' he asked.

'A dying man's cry for help,' Pye replied.

'It looks that way,' Skinner agreed. 'But . . .'

Eighty

Next morning, the chief constable was behind his desk at five minutes past eight. He knew that Amanda Dennis, a single, career-driven woman, was an early starter as well as a late finisher, and wanted to be there when she called. As he waited, he scanned the morning's press, left in his outer office by the night staff before they departed.

Ed Collins' death was as widely reported by the Scottish titles as he had expected, given the man's profession. Some newspapers speculated upon possible reasons for the murder, ranging from gambling on football matches to his being silenced to prevent him breaking a story. 'Closest to the truth,' he murmured. But none made a connection to the death of the two authors, other than the *Sun*, which splashed a front page picture of 'Tragic Carol Glover, the woman who lost dad and lover in the same week'. The wording seemed to imply carelessness but stopped just short of hinting at guilt. Only the *Saltire* hazarded no guesses, as only its editor had been told the truth by Skinner, and Aislado had no wish to share it with his rivals or anyone else.

But the main story of the morning was the astonishing disappearance of Dražen Boras from Brankholme Prison. The entire story had leaked. Ngaio Arnott's husband had been held in custody for a while, then released on police bail. He was probably in the clear, but the Secretary of State for Justice was twisting in the wind. Skinner was fairly sure that Garfield Haywood had a very limited future in the prison service.

414

He had broken the news in person to Maggie Steele, barely five minutes before it was confirmed by a police spokesman. She had been less angry than he had feared, and eventually philosophical, after Skinner had told her about Boras's volunteering information to the investigation.

'Do you believe him, Bob, that he feels some sort of contrition?'

'I reckon I do; so does Neil.'

'Will they catch him?'

'If they're very lucky, they'll get him in the next few hours. Longer term, they might find him through her . . . he'll dump her eventually. I spoke to the investigating officers, and they told me that the husband's saying he knew she was having an affair but had no idea that it was with a prisoner. Yes, they might get him.'

'They won't, and we both know it. When you and Mario found him, he was using an alias. A man like him, he's bound to have another ready, for emergencies.'

She had been right, and he had been forced to agree. Boras was gone, and would leave no trail second time around.

His secure phone rang, interrupting his musing. He grabbed it. 'Amanda.'

'Good guess. Good news first?'

'Whatever.'

'OK. We've found Henry Mount's informant; in fact we've found where his interest in Tadic began. Mount was never a spook, just run-of-the mill diplomatic service. He was never stationed in Yugoslavia, but he had a posting to Berlin as I think you know, and to Poland. Eventually he was repatriated, so to speak, and given a job in the FCO, in a section that monitors events in certain countries. His Iron Curtain experience led to him being assigned to the Yugoslav section. That's where he saw the intelligence about Tadic's murders, and that's where he met his eventual source. She's a woman called Dani

Cornwell. She worked for Mount when he was an undersecretary, and they kept in touch after he quit. They were close.'

'How close? Trudy Mount's a friend too.'

'They had a thing when they worked together. It stopped but their friendship didn't. She was as affected by Tadic as he was; when she found out about the secret trial, she was outraged. Then when she learned they were going to have to do it all over again, she boiled over and poured out her soul to Mount. He agreed that the story had to be told, and thus . . .'

'It began.'

'Precisely. Ms Cornwell fed him everything she had and kept on digging. A couple of weeks ago she found out about Dražen Boras and his role in planting the man Ergec, and she told Henry.'

'And a few days later he went to see Boras, and probably made himself, and Glover, dispensable in the process. Once Coben had all the information he was going to get from them, the information he needed, he shut them down, and cut their project off at source, stealing their computers and wiping out every trace of their work.'

'He's that thorough?'

'For sure. We believe that his helper, Glover's daughter's fella, removed his hard disk and passed it on. Coben probably burgled Mount's place himself.'

'He killed the associate? The man Collins?'

'Yes. The man was in it for money, but I don't imagine he signed up to be an accessory to murder. My bet is Coben killed him before he could figure out the truth.'

'But can you prove it?'

'Yes, I can, for at least two of them . . . if I can find him. We've got a partial fingerprint on a pen, and we'll find DNA traces for sure on a cigar box that's on its way back from Australia. Plus we'll get DNA from Collins' flat. But I repeat, we need to find him.'

'There, I'm afraid, I can't help you. All I know is this: everything that relates to Coben, and there is very little of it, is in the papers for the Tadic trial. I can't get anywhere near them, nor can anybody in this country, I reckon. They're UN property, and they're sealed. Sorry, Bob, I think you're in a cul de sac.'

Skinner smiled. 'I don't agree, Amanda,' he said. 'There's a man in Scotland who has automatic access to those papers, and I happen to know him.' He paused. 'Was that the bad news, incidentally?'

'Not all of it. The worst concerns the witnesses Danica Andelić, and her brother. They're dead.'

Skinner's heart sank. 'That's what Glover was afraid of, and me too. When? How?'

'Last year. After the trial, it was decided that Mirko and Danica had to be separated for a while, for their own safety, to make them as difficult to trace as possible. He was relocated with Playfair, she was established in Macedonia, and Aca went to Moldova. The Andelić children were taken in by Danica and Aca's mother, their grandmother. They were all gypsies, so they simply joined travelling groups. I don't know how their whereabouts leaked, but they did. Not through Mount's contact, that's for sure; she didn't know. As for the how, they were both gutted . . . a favourite trick of Tadic's, from what I'm told. Given what we know now, it seems your man Coben got to them, and then went looking for Mirko.'

Eighty-one

'That's it, Stevie,' said George Regan, 'all my stuff, like Neil told me to do.'

'Does it bother you?' Pye asked, looking at the folder that his colleague had laid on his desk.

'Are you having a laugh? Of course it doesn't bother me. I've made DI when I thought I might not. If the bosses say that my investigation has effectively become part of yours and that they're to be rolled in together, I do not give a fish's tit. It's a bonus; it means that Lisa and I can get back to solving the usual in our rural beat, which tends to be along the lines of, Who Shot Roger fucking Rabbit?' He glanced around the suite, and beamed. 'It's a real crappy office you've got here, by the way,' he said, without a trace of sarcasm. 'Nearly as bad as Torphichen Place. Ours is really nice; best I've ever had.'

'I know,' Pye agreed wistfully. 'I used to be stationed out there, remember.'

'Well, don't plan on moving back. I mean to be there for a long time; until I get found out, in fact. Not that you would. You're on the fast track, son; everybody knows that.'

'Kind of you, George, but I'm the jammy bastard that got promoted early into dead men's shoes, when Stevie got himself killed. That's what everybody knows.'

'Shite! You're the lead investigator into one of the highest profile crimes we've ever had, and you're going to get a result that'll make you.' He paused. 'You are going to get a result, aren't you?'

'I don't know what you mean by that,' Pye confessed. 'If you mean that we can close the book on who killed Glover, Mount, Collins and your guy, Mustafic, or Andelić, yes. If you mean that we catch the guy, that's another matter. I'm stymied there; it's over to the big boss now.'

'But when he cracks it, and lets you announce the arrest, like he always does, you will take the media credit, won't you?'

'Oh yes,' Pye chuckled, 'you can be sure of that.'

Eighty-two

It was raining, the weather that did least for the grey sandstone from which Ann Street was built. Lord Elmore stared out of his window, on a scene that matched his mood. The news that Mirko Andelić was dead had hit him hard.

He stared at his computer, at the notes for his memoirs, and wondered, very seriously, whether it was worth carrying on, or whether it should be abandoned. He was still considering the question when he saw the new chief constable walk up his drive, and heard his wife greet him at the door.

'Bob,' he said, gloomily, 'what brings you back to see me? Are you going to tell me I've won the lottery? Don't waste your time; not even that would do the job.'

'Claus,' Skinner asked, as he sat, 'what's second best?'

'To what?'

'To throwing away the key to Tadic's cell?'

'I don't know. Hearing that he's had a fatal heart attack?'

'I don't want anything to do with that, but how about catching Coben, how would that do?'

'It would be consolation, I'll grant you.'

'Then help me. I need access to the Tadic trial papers. Can you fix that?'

'I'm a trial judge, of course I can. What do you need?'

'I'm told that the only things that identify Coben are in there. I need them, sent or faxed to me.'

'Right,' said Lord Elmore, his mood transformed. 'Let me have a number and I'll give the instruction. How soon do you need them?'

Skinner grinned. 'For this evening, at the latest. I'm having a dinner party.'

The judge looked mystified, but made no comment. 'You'll have what you want,' he promised.

'Thanks.' The chief constable handed him a card. 'My secure fax number is on there.'

He was still smiling as he walked back to his car, and as he reached for his mobile. He dialled as he slid behind the wheel.

'Leith CID,' a voice answered.

'Sauce? Chief Constable here. I need you to get hold of your Serbian translator. I have further need of her services.'

Eighty-three

He was waiting at the top of the stone staircase as his guests were shown up from the vestibule at street level. 'Randy, Denzel,' he exclaimed, 'it's good to see you. A bit of bad news, though,' he continued as he shook hands with the Book Festival director and her partner. 'Aileen's been caught up in some unbreakable government business, last-minute stuff, some European crisis, and it happened too late to call you and postpone.'

'Oh, what a disappointment,' said Chandler.

'I've found a substitute, though,' said Skinner as he showed them into the drawing room, with its view of Charlotte Square Gardens, and the tents and pavilions that covered it. 'My friend Neil was in the vicinity, so I've co-opted him to fill the empty chair. You've probably met him: Superintendent McIlhenney.' The big detective stood at the window; he nodded as the newcomers entered. 'You're doubly honoured, you know,' their host laughed. 'Any other Thursday, this guy and I would be running around at North Berwick sports centre, kicking a football with a crowd of like-minded idiots.'

'Really?' Randall Mosley exclaimed. 'When Aileen told me that, I thought she was joking.'

'Hell, no! There is life after forty, I promise.'

'Yes,' the director agreed, 'but you tire more easily.'

'I thought you were still short of the milestone,' McIlhenney remarked as he handed each guest a glass of cava.

'I've got Denzel's word for it,' she replied lightly.

'So,' Skinner continued, 'how's the Bookfest going? Are you getting back to normal after Sunday morning's unfortunate events?'

She frowned. 'There is no normal at the Festival,' she told him. 'That's the big discovery I've made in my first year in the job.'

'First of many, everybody hopes; I hear things around town, you know, all of them good, in your case.'

'We'll see. It's a hell of a job, that is for certain. Poor Ainsley; what happened to him was tragic, but it fits under the unwritten law, that whatever can go wrong, will go wrong. On the same morning that he was found, my Nobel candidate, my prize attraction, cancelled on me. I had to fill that hole, as well as the one left by Ainsley's death. Now Fred Noble's uncertain about participating because with Henry Mount being killed, he fears he may be next.'

'You can relax on that score. He won't be.'

She looked at him, curiosity in her eyes. 'You can say that for certain?'

'Sure.' Skinner leaned against the fireplace set in the westward wall of the classic Georgian room. 'He's under round-the-clock protection, and everything that goes into his house is inspected by our people. Nobody's going to get to him, directly as with Mr Glover, or indirectly as with Henry Mount.' He glanced at Chandler. 'You know their work, Denzel?' he asked, then answered. 'What am I thinking of? Of course you do. Your other half runs the Festival, and we're talking about two of the city's most distinguished writers . . . no, three, adding in Fred Noble.' He paused. 'But you'd know them anyway, without that; you're a student of literature, aren't you?'

The man nodded, his eyes a little disconcerted. 'Actually no, it was post-war European history.'

Skinner winked at him. 'Confession,' he said. 'Aileen makes me read up on our guests when we're having dinner parties, but I was a bit busy before this one so I must have got mixed up. Mind you, I'm sure I'm right about your knowledge of contemporary crime fiction. It's de rigeur these days to be up with that stuff.'

'Yes,' Chandler admitted. 'I confess I am an aficionado.' He glanced at his partner. 'As you said, it comes with the territory.'

'So you'll appreciate the irony in the way those two men died. Killed in ways that were drawn from their own stories.'

'No!' the man exclaimed. 'Was that what happened?'

'Yup. It's a secret from the media, of course, but I can share it with you and Randy. Glover was killed with glucose, and Henry Mount by a bullet, planted in one of his cigars.'

'That's right,' McIlhenney chuckled. 'Now, or so my people tell me, Fred Noble won't set foot outside his front door, not even to the Oxford, just in case he's been hypnotised and told to chuck himself under a lorry, or whatever.'

'You get the irony, Denzel,' said Skinner, 'don't you? Glover and Mount, each . . .' he hesitated as if searching for words. 'Oh, damn it, what's the phrase? Shakespeare.'

'Hoist by his own petard,' said Chandler.

'That's it. *Macbeth.*'

'*Hamlet,* actually.'

'OK. Wrong play, wrong royal, wrong country, but you get the point. It takes a certain type of mind to conceive of something like that, and then to follow it through.'

'Yes, I suppose it does,' the man agreed. 'In your career, you can't have come across too many like this fellow.'

'Too right,' Skinner conceded. 'Bastard nearly got away with it too.' He let the words hang in the air for a second, then turned to Randall Mosley. 'Before you came to Scotland, you two were in Europe, weren't you?' he asked, smiling.

She nodded, as if the exchange had passed her by. 'Yes, that's right,

I worked for the European Commission, in the culture section, on the contemporary literature side. Denzel was living in Brussels at the time; we met at a reception.'

'And found you had a common interest?'

She laughed. 'In sex, mainly. I fancied him from the first.'

'You mean it wasn't his pen that won you over,' McIlhenney murmured, sipping his cava.

'Not at first.' She looked at him, wickedly. 'I admit it; it was his sword.'

'They say the pen is mightier,' Chandler drawled in his lightly transatlantic accent, 'but when you put it to the test . . .'

The two detectives exchanged the briefest of glances. 'What was your field when you were in Brussels?' Skinner asked him. 'Randy told one of our colleagues that you're a ghost writer. Is that what you did then?'

'In a manner of speaking. I did a couple of biographies, one of Tito and one of Karadzic. Didn't make any money, though. That's why I took to ghosting; it pays very well.'

'Will the Lord Elmore book be a money-spinner, do you think?'

Chandler seemed to lean away from him; taken aback, literally, by the question. 'It won't be huge, but even if it doesn't earn out the advance I'll be happy enough.'

'How do you think it would have dovetailed with the one that Glover and Mount were working on?'

The writer looked at him, blankly. 'Not at all. Why should it? They did fiction.'

'But not exclusively, as it turns out. They were planning a factual work on the atrocities committed by a Serbian general, Bogdan Tadic, known as the Cleanser. You must have heard of him, surely. Lord Elmore was one of the judges at his trial.'

'Yes, I've heard of him; that episode won't be in the book, though.

Lord Elmore's bound by confidentiality. Even if he wasn't, he fears for the safety of the witnesses.'

'With some justification. I don't think Ainsley and Henry did though; they were driven by Henry's outrage over what had happened, and the fact that it was being covered up. Tell me,' he asked, 'how did you hear about Claus's book?'

'Initially, through me,' Randall Mosley told him. 'I met Lady Elmore in Brussels, just as her term as an MEP was ending. She was on a literature committee. To tell you the truth, she's the reason I'm in my job. She's on the Book Festival board, and she supported my application.'

'Why did you think of applying in the first place?'

'I can't recall for sure. We both felt it was time we moved on, Leona mentioned the job . . . I suppose it was a joint decision that I go for it.'

'I see. One more question, Denzel . . . I'm sorry if this is beginning to sound like an interrogation . . . do you believe that Frankie Coben is dead?'

'What?' Chandler gasped.

'Come on,' Skinner persisted, 'you know about Tadic, you must know about Coben, the general's associate, almost his alter ego. The Cleanser was an animal, practically a fucking cannibal. Coben was very different, Serbian mother, North American father, had a university education then put it to use killing Muslims and gypsies.'

'No,' Chandler exclaimed, 'I don't. This really is an interrogation. What are you suggesting?'

'I'm suggesting nothing,' said Skinner easily. 'I'm telling you what we know: Frankie Coben was reported killed in a missile strike seven years ago. Only that report was wrong. I've been into your background, Denzel; I can't find anything about you that's more than six years old, before the time you showed up in Brussels.' He turned to Mosley. 'Randy, care to fill in the blanks?' She stared at him, eyes wide open, but said nothing. 'Denzel, where were you before that?' he persisted.

'I was drunk,' he said, his voice a whisper. 'I was alcoholic from the age of twenty-five to thirty-three. I bummed my way around Europe then I straightened out.'

'That's funny; those were the years when Coben was killing people in the Balkans. And now he's killing them again. We know that he's in Edinburgh. We know that he killed Glover, personally. We know that he used an associate to buy a box of cigars, that he altered one, very cleverly, and then had that box sent to Henry Mount, as a gift from the Edinburgh Book Festival. We know that before he came to this city he killed two of the three witnesses in General Tadic's first trial, and that he came here to find out the whereabouts of the third, through the person most likely to know, Lord Elmore. Coben's arrogant, unbelievably so; he devised provocative, boastful ways to kill, ways that said, "Look how clever I am." He even had his associate use his name, as if to proclaim his presence. Interesting, isn't it, Denzel?'

Chandler's eyes were crazed as he backed away from him; he glanced at the door, only to see McIlhenney's massive frame leaning against it.

'But then there was a twist,' Skinner continued. 'Out of the blue, just as it became known that you were doing the Elmore book, Coben learned from Ainsley Glover that he was also interested in the Tadic case, and that he and Henry Mount were as keen as he was to find the witnesses. So what did Coben do? He became the third person in their project, probably feeding them scraps to encourage them to cooperate with him, and he waited until they came up with the information he was after: the whereabouts of the last and vital witness, right on our own doorstep. When he had that,' the chief constable said, slowly, 'Henry and Ainsley had become witnesses too, along with his associate, Ed Collins, Ainsley's daughter's greedy grasping creep of a boyfriend. So they went, in a way designed to make us simple plods think that we had

427

a serial killer preying on crime writers, even down to the clue left beside Collins' body, after he'd killed him.' He snatched a pen from his pocket and tossed it to Chandler; he caught it, in a reflex action. 'Is that yours?' he asked.

The cornered man stared at it. 'Yes,' he whispered.

'Sure it is; I knew that already. You stayed in that hotel two months ago, on a trip to The Hague with Lord Elmore, and like everyone does, you brought the pen from your room home as a souvenir.' He fell silent, staring coldly at Chandler as he stood, dumbly helpless. 'You brought it home,' he repeated, 'and stuck it in a mug on your desk with all the others.' And then he glanced to his side, at Mosley, herself seemingly transfixed. '*Esam li dobro shvatio, Frankie?*' he said.

'*Jesi,*' she replied. And then her mouth dropped open. And then she gasped. And then she launched herself at the door.

She kicked out at McIlhenney, expertly, but he was faster, much faster, than she had expected. He blocked her strike, swept her feet from under her, then followed her down, pinning her to the floor. 'Help me secure her, boss,' he said. 'This lady's dangerous and we don't want to wind up missing any vital parts.'

'Absolutely.' Skinner seized her by both arms, lifted her into the air, then lowered her into a chair. The superintendent fastened her wrists, tightly, to its legs with white plastic restraints. 'I used that language trick on a guy a few months ago,' he told her. 'It worked just as well this time.'

'What did you say to her?' McIlhenney asked.

'*Do I understand it properly? Did I get it right?* And she forgot herself and said, "*Yes.*" Or maybe she knew by then that I had.'

'What, wha . . .' Denzel Chandler gasped, behind them.

As he straightened, the chief constable took three sheets of paper from within his jacket and handed them to him. 'Your client got these for me: Lord Elmore. Faxed copies of the personal file of Francesca

Coben, showing next of kin, and her Serbian military identity card, complete with photograph. She's changed a lot, but her skin tone's still the same; and so is her DNA, which we can compare with that of her father, Garland Mosley, a black American soldier who knocked up her Serbian mother, Mira Coben, on a leave in Germany back in the sixties, and who's still alive, in a retirement home in Dayton, Ohio.'

'I never knew,' the man protested. 'I never knew any of this.'

'You will have to convince us,' Skinner told him. 'We need to question you further, to be sure. But you're part of the way there, because it's pretty clear that she was prepared to let you take the hit, to let us go on believing you were Coben, until you were on your way to the nick, and she was out of here, on her way to being long gone. That's why I gave you that going-over, when I knew it was her. But I confess that I didn't until I saw those papers. I really did think it was you.' He glanced at her. 'Sure, her background is like yours; she goes back seven years, and then there's no trace of Randall Mosley, but the blockers for me were, one, that she found Ainsley's body and, two, that message he sent, that last email.' He took the wireless device from his pocket. 'It said, "randy yurt dying", just those three words, and he sent it to her. So, I had to tell myself, she couldn't have done it, because Glover saw his killer, and he sent her his plea for help. Understand?'

'I understand nothing any more,' Chandler sighed.

'Well, now I do.' He waved the device in the air. 'I had a look at the email directory stored in here. The next entry after "Mosley, Randall" is "Mount, Henry". It wasn't a plea for help, it was a warning to his pal, only the poor sod pressed the wrong button, and he sent it to Randy by mistake. She must have crapped herself when she found it in her mailbox next morning. Her first instinct must have been to delete it, but no, she really is clever. She realised that the original, and its destination, would still be on Glover's machine. If she'd made that one, tiny, understandable mistake, she'd have been blown there and then, but she didn't. Instead, she left it there, she went along to the yurt, with a witness, Richards, and they discovered the body. Ainsley would have appreciated that, professionally, and so would Henry. When was the last time you read a murder mystery, Denzel, where the perpetrator actually discovers the body, right at the start? No wonder it's taken us this long to get to her.' He nodded to McIlhenney, then watched as the superintendent twisted Coben's antique chair around to face him. 'Mr Chandler, you'll need to come with us for further questioning. Francesca Coben, also known as Randall Mosley, I am arresting you for the murders of Ainsley Glover, Henry Mount, Edward Collins, and Mirko Andelić, also known as Asmir Musta—'

'What?' Her half-scream, half-laugh, interrupted him. 'Are you telling me that Mirko is dead?'

'You know I am,' he told her. 'You killed him on Sunday evening, at around about eleven.'

'Oh no, I didn't,' she declared. 'I was in Lord and Lady Elmore's house with Denzel until ten forty-five on Sunday. We went there for drinks after our last event. Ask my poor dupe, he'll confirm it.'

The police officers looked at Chandler; he nodded confirmation.

'See,' she said. 'I didn't kill him, but I bless the man who did. The last witness is dead, Tadic is free, my general is free, my lover is free. Now it's his turn to get me out of jail.'

Eighty-four

Aileen sat upstairs in the study, reading a brief on the escalating costs of the Forth River crossing, wishing that her colleagues had followed her instincts and chosen a tunnel rather than a second bridge. Normally she had a mind like blotting paper, but she found that after only a few minutes her concentration lapsed, as she wondered what was happening downstairs. Eventually, she gave up, put the folder back in her blue box and switched on the radio, listening to the folk music programme on Radio Scotland, but with the volume moderate, to guard against any chance of the sound escaping.

She was almost asleep when her mobile buzzed and vibrated on the table beside her. She shook herself back to full wakefulness and picked it up.

'It's done,' he told her quietly.

'Was there any difficulty?'

'None we couldn't handle.'

'Where are you?'

'Still in the building, waiting for a van. We're taking them out the back way, and up to Fettes. Neil and I are going with them, and the new fiscal's meeting us up there. I can't let this lie overnight. I must have charges laid formally before this breaks in the media. There'll be a court appearance tomorrow morning, ten o'clock as normal. I'll instruct Alan Royston to set up a media briefing half an hour before.'

'Will you take it yourself?'

'No. Sammy Pye will be front and centre; he's senior investigator and that's how it works.'

'Did it play out the way you thought?' she asked, wondering why he was not more elated.

'Not quite, but three out of four ain't bad. It looks like she didn't kill the gypsy after all.'

'What about Denzel? Will he be charged too?'

'I don't anticipate that, although the fiscal might have a different view. Coben says that she's actually married to Tadic, that she was with him when the attempt was made on his life. He made her fake her death, to protect her, when he realised that sooner or later someone was going to get him. Chandler was used, all the way along, the poor dupe.'

'I'm a dupe too; she took me in.'

'Me too. We all were, until this evening, when I saw that fax. Christ, she's clever. She had Collins use her name when he saw Andy and when he bought the cigars, knowing that we'd go looking for a man. Nobody outside their circle in Serbia twigged to the fact that Coben was female. Nobody actually studied those documents in the Tadic file, took a close look at them.' She heard him sigh. 'That's what happens when you do things in secret.'

'I'll remember that,' she told him. 'I've decided to follow your suggestion. I'm not doing any more deals with my coalition partners. I'm going to blow them out, and form a minority government. If it doesn't survive the by-election for Ainsley's vacant seat, then so be it. I'm putting my political integrity first, from now on.'

He chuckled. 'We'd better enjoy this place while we can, then. You stay put, and I'll come back here when we're done up the road. If I'm in time, maybe we'll go across the road and have a drink in the Book Festival bar. I suppose I should find the deputy director, if I can, and tell him he's been promoted.'

Eighty-five

'And that's it,' said Skinner, as Brian Mackie and David Mackenzie looked back at him across his meeting table, 'that's how it went. In about ten minutes Sammy Pye's going to tell the media that a woman's been charged with three murders, but he's not going to name her: standard practice, as we all know. About a minute later they're going to be tear-arsing up to the Sheriff Court to find out who she is, so make sure you don't get knocked over in the rush. I wish I could be there, to see the looks on their faces . . . and the expression on hers, even more so.'

'How do you think she'll react?' asked the ACC.

'I think it'll break her,' the chief replied. 'I sensed last night that she was starting to unravel. She couldn't stop talking, once she started. Until now, she's had a total belief in her own supremacy, her own ability to out-think everybody else. Young Collins, for example, ex-army, not an idiot, gets involved for money, and he thought he was dealing with a man. We've been through her place like a dose of salts. We found Glover's hard disk and Mount's computer, and her own records, some of which she hadn't bothered to delete. She contacted Collins by email; there's no indication that they ever met face to face until the morning he died.'

'If she hadn't been caught?' Mackenzie murmured.

'She'd have gone looking for Mirko Anđelić, and found out very quickly that he was dead. It was a pure accident that she didn't see

Hugo Playfair's picture in the press, or read his name, because yes, Henry Mount had spilled it to her and Glover, after he'd been to see Boras.'

'And Boras, sir, what about him?'

'Forget it.' Skinner stood, ending the meeting. He signalled to McIlhenney to stay behind as the others left.

'Do you want me in court, boss?' the detective superintendent asked.

'No, give young Sammy all the glory.' He paused. 'Once he's had his moment, you'd better have him send the Andelić material back to Regan, and tell him it's his again. That's the bugger, Neil. I've still got a killer in my own village.'

'No chance of Playfair being it?' The detective shook his head almost before he was finished speaking. 'Nah, of course there isn't. He was the guy's minder; once he'd lost him, he had to disappear, before we started asking him awkward questions.'

'Yes, like who the fuck was he,' the chief constable exclaimed as his colleague headed for the door, 'and where had he come from. No, it's a local; I'm sure of that. One of my near neighbours followed a man and killed him out of prejudice, battered his head in with a hammer, or similar blunt metal object.' He froze, and suddenly his eyes were somewhere else. 'Or similar object,' he murmured. 'Neil,' he called out.

In the doorway, McIlhenney turned. 'Sir?'

'When you tell Sammy to send that file back to Regan, have him send two items up to me, assuming that we're efficient enough to have the second of them. I want the post-mortem report on Andelić, complete with pictures, and I want George's list of everyone who was in the Golf Inn on Sunday night, before he died.'

Eighty-six

As the old man turned over the soil in his rose garden, his wife's two pet nuisances, as he insisted on calling them, played around at his feet. The bloody animals have been walked twice today already, he thought. Where do they draw their energy from? His strong wrists twisted, flicking some earth at Jarvis with his hoe, then a second damp clod at Joe, smiling as they dodged out of the way. But he was always careful to miss them.

'Must oil that bloody gate,' he muttered as he heard it creak, twice, once on opening, then on closing. He turned to face his visitor, and saw Bob Skinner walk towards him.

And he knew.

'I need to see your stick, Donald,' he said, then bent to pick it up from where it lay on the path. He tossed it in the air, then caught it, spinning the rough, hickory in his fingers, admiring the steel circlet at its neck and then the heavy steel cap at the end of the hand grip. Peering at it intently.

'It was shame, Bob, rather than prejudice, I promise,' Colonel Rendell said.

'Shame?'

'They made me feel unmanned. When those people, that tribe, parked in front of our houses, I was angry; I admit that. Indeed I expressed it forcefully to you at the time. I blustered to Margot, said something about going out there myself and moving them on. And she

435

told me to do just that. And so I set out, I got halfway there and then I saw them, how rough they looked, and those dogs of theirs, and I discovered to my horror and shame that I was afraid to go through with it.'

He looked at Skinner, as if he was pleading for understanding. 'Bob, I've seen service in some very rough places. I was in the Falklands, I was in Northern Ireland, and I never once felt fear, but suddenly, on Sunday, there I was an old man, too bloody scared to tell some ruffians to be on their way, or even to walk his wife's dogs. When you offered to do it, and I accepted, that was the most shameful moment of my life. Later, as I had my usual evening whisky in the Golf, when I saw that man, half-drunk, loud, being objectionable with his friend, I just lost it. I felt myself exploding inside; it was all I could do not to confront him there and then.'

'Donald,' said Skinner, 'don't tell me this now. Wait till you have a lawyer with you.'

'That won't make my story any different; you're going to hear it. I didn't follow him, you know, not at first. He left before me, maybe a minute or so. I walked up Hopetoun Terrace, for an extra breath of air on my way home. Then I saw him again, in Erskine Road. I made for him then, but he cut down the pathway. I caught him up, and I told him that he and his crowd should clear off, and leave us decent people to live in peace and quiet. He called me a stupid old man in his broken English, and then he pushed me away, and turned his back on me as if I was an irrelevance.' The colonel sighed. 'That's when I hit him; once, then again, and although he put his hand up the second time, he still fell. On the ground I hit him again, once or twice more, that's all. I heard him moan, but I turned and walked away.'

'Did you know he was dying?' asked Skinner.

'Honestly, I did not. When I got home and saw the blood on my stick, I realised that I might have hurt him badly. I could have called an ambulance then; I should have, but I didn't. When I found out that he was dead, I almost came to you then, until I heard that you were looking for his friend. I suppose I reasoned that if you thought he did it, best to keep quiet until you found him, and hope that you didn't. It wouldn't have been the first unsolved murder in this area.'

'But it's solved now, Donald. Come with me, please. One of my inspectors is waiting in the street, in a car.'

'Let me go in and pick up some things. Say goodbye to Margot at least.'

'It won't be goodbye, only farewell for a while. No, I know you, old guy. On Sunday, you confused cowardice with realism. If I let you go in there, likely you'd be in the library with a shotgun in your mouth. No more death, Colonel Rendell. I've had enough for this week.'

Eighty-seven

'So that's it all wrapped up?' Ray Wilding exclaimed. 'Randy Mosley did the authors and some old soldier murdered the gypsy out in Gullane?'

'That last charge may be culpable homicide, not murder,' Sammy Pye pointed out, 'if the fiscal offers him a deal for a guilty plea, but that's about it, yes.'

The sergeant handed him a coffee that he had fetched from the office machine. 'And with Mosley in custody, that ought to mean that Fred Noble's safe as well?'

'Yes. I've pulled his protection team out already.' The DI grinned. 'By the way, remember that hypnosis idea of his? Well, I checked with an expert, just for the sake of it. Clinically impossible; it wouldn't have worked.'

'Come on,' Wilding pointed out, 'it was a work of fiction, and it was credible as far as the readers were concerned, so surely that's fair enough?' And then he raised his eyebrows, as if in a show of triumph. 'But if what your so-called expert says is the case,' he asked, slowly, 'isn't it strange that Noble's just walked in front of a bus?'

Pye's face, ever youthful and positive, seemed to age ten years in as many seconds; the mug trembled in his hands. 'Tell me you're kidding,' he whispered.